A SIGH

Tanya looked up into his dark eyes. She felt a wave of delight when she realized he had not forgotten their childhood vows. And now he was back, and she was no longer a child!

A MOMENT

It was as if a flame had been lit between them. He pulled her forward. She felt herself pressed against the rough wool of his uniform, her face buried in its intoxicating masculinity. She could feel his heart beating against her breast.

FOR NOW . . . AND FOREVER!

He lowered his head until their lips met. Never, in all her dreams, had she expected to be so overwhelmed. Suddenly she knew she couldn't endure having him leave her without fulfilling the promise of his kiss . . .

LOVE'S BURNING FLAME

Iris Bancroft

BANTAM BOOKS · BOMBAY · TORONTO · NEW YORK

LOVE'S BURNING FLAME
A Bantam Book / October 1979

ISBN 0-553-12798-5

Published simultaneously in the United States and Canada

Bantam Books are published by Bantam Books, Inc. Its trade-
mark, consisting of the words "Bantam Books" and the por-
trayal of a bantam, is Registered in U.S. Patent and Trademark
Office and in other countries. Marca Registrada. Bantam
Books, Inc., 666 Fifth Avenue, New York, New York 10019.

PROLOGUE

St. Petersburg
1795

PROLOGUE

Tanya Ivanovich patted the long black curls that hung over her shoulders, and she tried, unsuccessfully, to stifle a yawn. She was slender, small for her sixteen years; her features were delicate and large; luminous black eyes shone in a tantalizing mixture of innocence and petulant pride.

Despite her youth, she was not cowed by the ornate surroundings of the Queen's private chambers, or even by the Empress herself, who had ordered her to attend the intimate gathering. She was aware only of her boredom, and her wish that something—anything—would happen.

Catherine, dubbed by her admirers "The Great," lapsed into German, and Tanya repressed a smile. Everyone associated with the Court of St. Petersburg had learned the language. It would have been inexcusable to fail to understand the Queen even when she reverted to her native tongue.

Tanya, who had been born long after the *coup d'état* that had made the foreign bride of the Tsar Peter III the sole ruler of Russia, had found the task simple, mastering the awkward Nordic tongue along with her native Russian, almost from the cradle.

The Empress tapped her fan against the shoulder of her young escort. She looked ludicrous, flirting with a man younger than her own son, but no one dared show his amusement. She was terribly vain. Everyone knew that, at sixty-six, she still considered herself a *femme fatale*, and that death—or exile—awaited the foolish male who failed to appreciate her charms.

Tanya stared at the young soldier who occupied the Queen's attention, a manly figure, blond, with wavy hair and a wide mouth that seemed perenially turned up in a smile. "Ah, Georg! You're such a tease!" The Empress's voice rang out. Tanya lowered her gaze. She was thankful when his response was too muffled for her to hear.

Casting about for some way to banish her boredom, Tanya glanced up at her father. A tall, military man, he reflected the extent of his displeasure with her forced attendance at the Court. She grimaced and turned away. She knew well enough how he felt. He disapproved of the Queen's morality—or lack of it—and he was staring now, in fixed solemnity, at his daughter.

Tanya looked at the Queen's sharp, almost pointed face. It was hard to believe that the woman had ever been beautiful, though portraits of her showed her to have had considerable charm. All that was left now was her lasciviousness, and her love for erotica.

A carving on a high-backed chair caught Tanya's attention and she moved closer to study it more carefully.

"Tanya!" Her father's whisper did nothing to conceal his irritation. "Let it be. There are many things in this Court that aren't for the eyes of a young lady such as you."

Tanya looked away. She knew better than to disobey a direct order from her father.

"Count Ivanovich!" Catherine's sharp tone was startling. "Is there something in my drawing room you feel is unfit for the eyes of your daughter?"

"Most certainly not, Your Grace." The Count had the attention of everyone in the room. "I simply accept the fact that my daughter is young. There's time enough for her to learn the ways of the world when she's older."

"Aha!" The Queen's exclamation was a shriek. "So now you claim I'm old!"

Tanya detected a flush on her father's face; a shiver of terror went up her spine. The Queen was staring at her father with half-closed eyes that barely concealed their fire.

"Your Grace, you know me too well to think I would ever speak ill of your Highness! It was, I assure you, a little matter of no importance between my daughter and myself that should not take any more of your Majesty's time. My daughter understands my orders, and she is behaving herself as a modest young girl should."

Bone china flew across the room. It shattered behind the Count's head. He didn't flinch. "Fool! How dare you insult the Empress! Now you have the gall to call me immodest! How dare you think the life your Empress chooses for herself isn't good enough for your daughter? How dare you 'protect' her from my 'evil' influence?"

The Queen said much more. Tanya stood against the wall, her head hanging, her eyes fixed on the floor. It was horrible to hear her father berated with such vehemency.

The Queen raved on. Disturbed as she was, the cause of the Queen's irritation, Tanya still couldn't resist the opportunity to look more closely at the forbidden carving. She stared at the straight-backed chair that had started the outburst.

The most perfect oak, the grain added to the beauty of the work, but it was the carving that fascinated Tanya. An exquisitely worked figure of a satyr buried his face between the legs of a slender nymph. The girl was lovely, delicate, and even-featured. Her dress, a thin wisp of cloth that concealed none of her more feminine charms, clung tightly to her full breasts. Her legs were spread wide, and Tanya could see the light curls of hair just above the satyr's nose. Unconsciously, she smiled. It looked as if the goat-like creature had developed a mustache!

The Queen's anger, feeding on itself, increased. Tanya

5

blocked out the voice. She wished she could help her father, but she knew better than to interrupt the Empress. The tantrum would soon be over. Everyone knew Catherine regained her control quickly, as long as no one interrupted her while she raged. Aware as she was of her father's discomfort—and of her own, Tanya still couldn't take her attention from the carvings.

The satyr was part man and part goat—but he was clearly male. Between his legs, pushing forward like a spear that threatened to stab the slender body of the nymph, was a shaft Tanya knew to be the creature's male organ. It was large, demanding! In spite of her embarrassment, Tanya felt a stirring within herself at the sight of that wooden shaft, deftly fashioned to be placed between the spread legs of the delicate wooden nymph.

"Mother!" The high-pitched voice of the Crown Prince cut through Catherine's ranting. Prince Paul, a short man in his mid-forties with a paunch, and features that looked like a madman's copy of his mother's, stepped into the room. Stopped in mid-sentence, the Queen turned from the Count. *"Maman. . . ."* Paul's French was rough. Staring at him, Tanya became suddenly aware of the way his trousers fit snugly to his legs, and of the bulge that ran along one thigh.

His eyes swept the room, settling on Tanya's slender body and, instinctively, she folded her hands across her breasts as if, by doing so, she could hide them from his view. She had met him once before, and then, too, he had given her the feeling he was undressing her with his eyes. "I didn't know you were busy, Mother. I'll return later. Unless you would like me to take the young lady into another room?"

Catherine stared at Prince Paul, her eyes filled with scorn. It was no secret that Catherine hated him, or that Paul wanted nothing more than the death of his mother so that he could assume the throne. Everyone knew he believed she had taken the crown from him illegally at the time of the *coup* that had dethroned his father, Peter.

Just as common was the knowledge that Catherine was doing everything in her power to assure that the throne

6

would pass to Alexander, Paul's young son, when she died. She had been grooming the boy for the task since he was an infant.

The other courtiers stirred uneasily. No matter how often their conflict was repeated, it never became easy to stand quietly by as the Queen and the Prince clashed. But this time they were spared the discomfort. Without a further word, Paul left the room. The heavy door, thick with carvings, closed behind him.

Immediately, Catherine renewed her diatribe against Ivan Ivanovich. The importance of sensuality in life. The meaning of eroticism in balanced living. Her face reddening, her breath short, her voice grew shriller with each word.

The Count remained silent. Tanya, eyes closed, prayed he would restrain himself.

Tanya stared once more at the Queen. Catherine's appearance reflected her royalty as well as her age. Of moderate height, slightly plump, she bore herself nobly. Yet years of indulgence had taken their toll, dissipation had dulled her eyes, and her expression was more sensuous than regal. As usual, she was clothed in the latest Parisian fashion; she often dressed, as rumor had it, more like a courtesan than a Queen. Still, there was no question of her authority. She had ruled Russia too long, and had endured too much, to leave any doubt of her rank.

The Empress paused, pulling air in with a loud gasp that frightened Tanya and caused the silent watchers, who hadn't dared to speak since her anger began, to murmur in concern. The Queen wasn't well; everyone knew that. If she didn't soon control her temper, she might have another attack. Tanya had heard of the terror of the Empress's last convulsion, when she'd fallen to the floor, her face contorted and so flushed with blood that it appeared purple. That attack had almost killed her. God forbid that fury aroused by a disagreement with the Ivanovich family should cause another seizure!

The Queen's ranting subsided.

"If you're through with me, your Highness, I'll take my daughter, Tanya, home."

"Take her and leave! But don't think you've heard the

7

last of this! I don't forget men who dare to criticize the Empress of all the Russias!"

Without looking at his Queen, Count Ivanovich grasped Tanya's arm. "Come, my dear, we're going home."

PART I

Russia

CHAPTER I

The night was one of fear and waiting. Contrary to her expectations, Tanya had not been reprimanded by the Count when they had reached the privacy of their home. The Count had, instead, summarily dismissed her, leaving her to the far more terrible punishment of her own conscience.

How could she have disobeyed her father's wishes? And why had she continued to stare at the carvings even after the argument began? What power lay in the figures that could make a girl who had always been obedient continue to stare at them even when it was clear she was displeasing her father?

Anna, her nurse, helped Tanya undress as if she were a child. Stout, kindly, the woman was aware, without a word

11

from her mistress, that things were not right. Tanya gazed thankfully at her retreating back as Anna went to fetch a cup of hot milk spiced with spirits. It had been Anna's presence that had made the death of her mother, the Countess Marie Ivanovich, endurable for Tanya. Long before the night when her mother had died and her brother had been stillborn, Tanya had been placed in the care of Anna, and the soft-hearted, gentle-voiced peasant woman had been mother, nurse, and teacher for her ever since.

Now Anna sat on the edge of Tanya's bed and drew the girl to her bosom. "Don't worry, little Tanyushka, your papa has dealt with such tantrums before. He'll be able to handle this one, too."

"But the Empress was so furious, Anna, she almost had another seizure!"

"If rumor can be trusted, this isn't the first time that has happened. Go to sleep, child. Everything will be better in the morning."

But Tanya couldn't sleep. When she heard Anna snoring behind the door that separated their chambers, she crept from her bed and tiptoed across the thick Persian rug to the passageway that opened into the great hall. She pulled open the door and stepped onto the wide balcony that connected all the upper rooms in the Ivanovich mansion.

Tanya walked across the thick carpeting to the bannister and gazed down into the lower hall and entranceway where, on state occasions, the major domo called out the names of the guests as they stepped through the great doors into the raised reception room. It was Tanya's father's custom to keep a lamp burning below throughout the night, a habit he had started, she had been told, when, after her mother's death, she had often wakened crying in the night, and he had hurried to comfort her.

Tanya was yet too young to have descended the great curving stairway on her way to a formal ball, but she had slid down its bannister often. Once she had even careened right into the arms of Colonel Alexandrovich, who had just arrived for an evening of cards with her father. They had laughed about it at the time, but she had been aware, even then, of a frightening coldness in the man. Thoroughly chastened by his pretended good humor, she had hurried up the stairs to Anna, and she had been careful from then on to look below before she started to slide.

Under the double doors that led to her father's, the Count's, study, Tanya could see the glow of a lamp, and she hurried toward it, her heart troubled by guilt. She could feel a tension in the air that did not usually follow the Queen's outbursts.

Something had been ominous about the last words the Queen had spoken before Ivan Ivanovich and Tanya left. Catherine, in the past, had not held a grudge against her favorite advisor, but things had changed. There had been no underlying friendliness to mitigate the terror of the Queen's anger. Tanya had a premonition that the scene she had observed was a prelude to her father's, the Count's, destruction.

Half-way down the stairs she hesitated and, abruptly, she turned back to her room. Her father preferred to be left alone at night. But when she lay again in her bed, Tanya found sleep still would not free her from her fears.

Once more she rose from her bed and tiptoed into the hallway, down the steps, and up to her father's study. Only after many attempts to raise the knocker did she at last have the courage to make her presence known. "Papa, are you awake?" The loud retort stirred the ghosts that hovered in the flickering shadows behind her.

She heard the key turn in the lock. The door opened. "Tanya, my dear, you should be asleep." His voice was sad, as if he had been weeping.

"No, papa. I couldn't. I feel so ashamed that I caused the Empress to be upset with you."

He pulled her into the room, his strong arms reassuring. "Don't worry, my darling. It wasn't you who upset her, despite her pretext. She is angry with me because I oppose her treatment of the serfs. Ever since Radishchev was banished to Siberia for writing his *Journey from St. Petersburg to Moscow,* I have known the time would come when I would follow him. But I have prayed I would not be forced to leave you before you were safely married. It appears we will not be so fortunate as that."

13

Tanya stared. Men who went to Siberia seldom, if ever, returned—except in coffins. "Father, we can go away. We can visit England, or take a trip to Austria." She held the lapels of his dressing gown. "We must flee, papa, before you're lost!"

He shook his head. "My dear little Tanya, it is too late. Had I wanted to run away, I should have done so years ago. I knew Catherine's designs, but I felt the tradition of friendliness between the Crown and the Ivanovich lineage would protect me."

"But can't we go now, right now, before Catherine has time to exile you?"

"It isn't easy to escape from St. Petersburg, especially in winter. I don't wish to be caught fleeing like some felon. No, I'm prepared for my fate. But I worry about you. You're so young—so innocent. And innocence is a condition not much appreciated in the court of Catherine the Great!"

Tanya stared into her father's face. She wasn't as untutored as he seemed to believe. Anna had taught her much—more, probably, than most young ladies ever learned. The earthy life of the peasant was natural to Anna. She had taught Tanya the details of mating by taking her to observe animals in the spring. And Anna hadn't avoided the conversations that helped Tanya understand that men and women mated in much the same manner.

The Count pulled his daughter, Tanya, close. "Whatever you know, I most certainly can't leave you with any new knowledge. It's too late. I can't even be sure you'll be left with decent clothes and a place to lay your head!"

"Don't worry about me, papa. I'll get along. And I'll get the Empress to free you."

A smile touched her father's lips. "Don't raise your hopes too high. Her Majesty isn't known to change her mind about a thing such as this one."

"But, surely, she'll realize how valuable you are to the Court, and will call you back! She's depended on your advice for so long!"

"My advice, and that from many others. No, Tanya, I'm not essential to the welfare of Mother Russia, and the

Queen knows it. She'll use me, as she has used many before, to make it clear to others that no one, no matter how favored, can cross her wishes—and survive."

"I'll pray that she reconsider and keep you here. Surely, God won't let such a cruel thing happen!"

The Count reached up and stroked her hair. "May God give you the strength your mother had, little Tanyushka. I fear you'll need it." He stepped back and held her at arm's length. "You have so much of your mother in you. Your eyes are hers, like deep black pools of fire. Your mouth, like hers, so soft and full. Your skin is as white as hers was on the day we were married, more like alabaster than human flesh. You're even as tiny as she was. Why, I can hold you beneath one arm without crushing your dress!"

"I have her spirit, too. You've said so, often."

"Yes, you have more than she ever had, and for that I'm thankful. I've seen it evidenced many times in the past. God knows you'll need it in the days to come!"

The Count insisted that Tanya return to her bed, even though she told him she would not sleep. But she was wrong. Her natural need for rest overcame her desire to keep watch with her troubled father.

Sounds of footsteps and voices in the courtyard interrupted her dreams. "Ivan Ivanovich! Open, in the name of Catherine, Empress of all the Russias!"

Immediately, Tanya was on her feet. She pulled on a robe and hurried to her father's room. She was aware of the servants bustling about, like a herd of frightened cattle.

Her father's chambers had not been slept in. Frederick, her father's lackey, stood alone in the middle of the room.

"They've arrested him, Countess. If you hurry, you might see him before he's taken away."

Tanya rushed from the rooms, down the stairs. As she rounded the last curve, a blast of cold air swirled in through massive doors. There was the sound of footsteps, and then the boom, as the heavy panels slammed shut. With a cry of alarm, she ran into the vestibule—and collided abruptly with Colonel Alexandrovich.

15

"Oh, Colonel! Thank God you're here. They've arrested my father! Please, make them let him go!"

The eyes that met hers were hard and dispassionate. "My dear Countess, surely you do not expect me to disobey my Empress!"

She felt as if she had been slapped in the face. He was no friend! He was in charge of the entire affair! She felt outraged. How could he betray her father? Had her father been ordered to arrest Alexandrovich, he would have found another to attend to that duty. She hurried across the marble floor, her feet chilly in her flannel slippers. Pulling aside the drapery, she gazed out into the frozen courtyard.

Her father was being led to a carriage; it was waiting near the iron gates. Clearly not from his stable: ragged horses; carriage in disrepair. Soldiers sat where coachmen should have been. One of the Empress's infamous carriages, designed for maximum security. Tanya could tell from the heavy furs the soldiers wore that they would go directly East.

"Good-bye, papa," Tanya said. There was no possibility that her father, buffeted by the icy wind and heavy snow, could hear her voice.

The Count, her father, Ivan Ivanovich, was staring toward his house, his long arms hanging loosely at his sides. He looked as noble as ever, his head erect, his jaw firm. The Queen had admired his dark, flashing eyes and finely chiseled features as much as she had resented his independent spirit.

A captain of the guard motioned her father inside the blackened carriage.

"Oh, papa! Dearest papa. How am I going to live without you?" Tanya glared at the soldiers guarding the carriage. Were there too many of them? Gregov, her father's personal coachman, had fled to the Ivanovich holdings as soon as the news of the pending arrest had reached the stables. If the carriage went directly to Siberia, it would have to pass through the Ivanovich estate, and if Gregov arrived in time, he could organize a band of serfs to rescue his master.

Tanya folded her hands. "Please, dear God, let Gregov

succeed." She remained silent for a moment, as if waiting for some word from above, but the voice she heard came from outside her window.

"Sir!" The coachman's voice was muffled by the wind.

"Yes, soldier?" The tone sounded familiar, but Tanya was too troubled to place it immediately.

"Shall we move, sir?"

"Not yet. The Colonel has commanded you to delay until he gives the order."

Tanya pressed against the frosty pane and watched as the men on the coach huddled down into their furs. In sympathy she shivered. At least her father was out of the wind! Holding her hand against the frozen glass, Tanya cleared a small circle, but her breath clouded it immediately. Frustrated, she moved to a clear spot and stood back far enough so as to keep the glass from frosting over. Behind her, she could hear the servants scurrying about, but she didn't bother to turn. Whatever needed her attention in the house would wait until the carriage was out of sight.

Suddenly, she remembered the paper that had been propped on her bedside table, her name inscribed on it in her father's hand. She had stuffed it into her dressing gown as she ran down the stairs. Now she pulled it out and smoothed its creases. It was covered with neat, even writing:

Dearest daughter,

I regret I must leave you before you are safely wed. Please don't blame yourself for what has happened; it has, as I assured you last night, nothing to do with you.

I've done my best to raise you without a mother, since I had no heart to remarry after your sweet mother's death in childbirth so long ago. God forgive me if I've failed in my duty. God forgive me, too, if I have erred in your education. Mayhaps, it was my need for the son who died while coming into this world that made me raise you so much like a boy, but I trust you have had enough instruction in the ways of females in our world so that you will not be ill at ease in the society in which you now are thrust.

I didn't expect my disagreements with the Queen to get

*out of hand, or I would have prepared you for this mo-
ment. However, my darling, I know your strength. You'll
survive because you are brave. Remember you're an Ivanovich, and do nothing that will bring disgrace on your name.
God be with you, my darling.*

Ivan Ivanovich

Tanya once more looked into the frozen courtyard. The
coach hadn't moved, and she could see the snow piled on
the shoulders of the silent coachmen. Even as she watched
they straightened up, and their heads turned toward the
entry gate. Someone was coming.

Through the swirling snow came three horsemen—more
soldiers. Their furs were thick with ice. A long bundle hung
over the back of the saddle of one. When the three reached
the center of the courtyard, they pushed the bundle to the
ground. Gregov!

Colonel Alexandrovich, behind her, cleared his throat.
Startled, for Tanya had not realized anyone was near, she
watched him cross the vestibule and throw open the front
doors. Into the entryway swirled a blast of cold air. Tanya
shivered, held her place, unwilling to lose one moment of
the scene before her. Too soon her father, Count Ivanovich, would be gone, and God only knew if ever she would
see him again.

A soldier closed the door. From her place at the window
she could see the Colonel. He was standing on the steps, a
whip in his hand. "Drive on!" His voice sounded sharp,
cutting deep into her heart.

The horses jerked the carriage into motion. Tanya
watched it out of sight. Then her eyes wandered to the
rooftops of St. Petersburg, settling on the magnificent
golden dome of the palace. So peaceful! The city was
peaceful! Infuriating. How could others rest while her father was being deported! They should be up in arms! In
bitterness, Tanya leaned against the window frame. No,
there would be no revolt. Even the serfs on the Ivanovich
estate would not know of their master's arrest until it was
too late. Gregov had been the only hope—and he had been
dropped like a sack in the courtyard. Dead.

With a rustling behind her, Anna's voice carried across the half-empty room: "Come, Tanya, baby! Come to Anna!" The motherly woman stood at the foot of the stairs, her arms extended. With tears streaming down her face, Tanya fell into her nurse's embrace.

"Oh, Anna, he's gone! What shall I do?"

"Do? Why, child, we'll go about seeking his release! And we'll continue to live as before. Your father gave you a name of which you can be proud. There's no reason for you to give up just because he's gone. He would want you to remain true. . . ."

The front doors flew open and a lieutenant stepped inside. Tanya watched him with mixed emotions. She knew him well. They had grown up in the same society, had attended the same children's parties. As children, they had grown close and had even, at one point, exchanged childish vows of love.

He had entered a military academy when he was twelve and she was ten, and she had lost contact with him, though she sometimes thought back with amusement at her youthful infatuation. It had been his voice she heard in the courtyard, instructing the soldiers to wait for Alexandrovich's signal! Alexius Andreiv had returned!

He was more handsome than he had ever been. His strong forehead and classic Roman nose with flared, sensuous nostrils dominated his face. His jet-black hair was almost as unruly as it had been when he was younger, for it pushed out under his military hat with a most unmilitary independence. His mouth was firm, his jaw tight, as if he were holding back his true emotions.

It was to his eyes that she looked. They were dark and filled with sadness, and they refused to meet her glance. This, his first duty upon returning to St. Petersburg, was clearly not his choice. He looked around him, and stepped to her side. "Tanya! Please forgive me!"

Slipping from Anna's protective arms, she drew herself up. It would not do for an Ivanovich to show fear, even in the presence of—of what used to be a friend.

"You are to come with me," Alexius Andreiv said.

A tingling sensation moved through her body. If only he

19

would reach out—would touch her. Impatiently, she pushed the desire aside. "My maid will accompany me!"

The great doors were thrown open once again. "What's this? Lieutenant, what's going on here?" Colonel Alexandrovich strode into the hallway. His heels clicked harshly on the stone. Stopping beside Alexius, he pointed at Anna. "What's this woman doing?"

Alexius saluted smartly. "She's attending her mistress, sir."

Alexandrovich sneered. "Lieutenant Andreiv, you're dismissed. Return to the barracks immediately. I should have known you lacked the strength to carry out this assignment."

Alexius showed no reaction whatsoever. He saluted smartly, turned on his heels, and moved toward the door. As it opened, he looked back, and his eyes met hers. In that glance he conveyed all the love they had dreamed of as children. Then, lowering his eyes, he strode into the snow. Tanya felt a shiver of fear that lasted after the doors closed. Without him, she felt certain, she would receive no further consideration.

Alexandrovich waved his hand toward Anna. "Woman, step aside. Allow your mistress to obey her Queen's command."

Anna, too, had reacted to the change of officers. Like a vixen defending her cub, she froze to the spot, her arms spread to protect her mistress. The Colonel's voice was sharp. "Move!" He swung his sword at the nurse.

"Leave her alone!" Tanya leaped in front of the stubborn woman. "I'll go with you. I don't need to be dragged, nor do you have to wage war on my servants."

A faint smile touched the corners of the Colonel's mouth, the hawk-like face, the thin, tight lips, and the dark, narrowed eyes that peered out from below bushy eyebrows.

"Tell her to do as she's told," the Colonel said.

"May I at least get properly dressed before we leave?"

Tanya, Anna in tow, vanished from view up the stairs. Downstairs, she was certain, the soldiers would be removing the statues that graced the vestibule. The Empress had admired them more than once. Now they were hers.

"It's a pity the Queen has plans for that one!" The coarse voice came from a man who had stared at Tanya throughout the entire encounter. "I can think of nothing better than to have the task of disciplining that morsel!"

The laughter that followed sent a shiver of fear up Tanya's spine. She hadn't expected to be thankful to see Colonel Alexandrovich, for he had always been a cold man. But he was, at least, a nobleman, and might be trusted to protect her honor even though he took her prisoner.

It took only a moment for Tanya to choose a dress, a modest ruby velvet with a high neck and long, fitting sleeves with lace edging the wrists and the neckline. The garment provided the dignity Tanya felt was essential.

She studied her jewel box carefully, finally deciding on a simple pearl necklace with earrings to match. Though plain in appearance, she knew them to be among the most valuable pieces she owned. If she was condemned to follow her father, the price she could get for them might make the difference between discomfort and ease.

When Colonel Alexandrovich knocked on her door, she no longer felt the fear that had threatened to break through her control. Often, her father had spoken to her of the time when he would join her mother, and she would be alone. The advice he had given her at those moments stood her in good stead now. "Be brave," he had told her. "Remember, all who live must die. It is how the survivors deport themselves that matters." Well, she had to prove herself now.

Taking one last glance at herself in the mirror, she turned to Anna. "Now, remember, do as he tells you. No more foolishness."

Anna nodded, her face disfigured by a sullen frown. "Oh, my little Tanyushka! The Queen has only evil plans for you. If she sends you to Siberia, that's terrible enough. But, God forbid, she may decide to keep you with her. Your father had his reasons for keeping you away from the Court as much as he could. It's a den of sinners!"

"Anna! Stop such nonsense! You've never been at Court. How do you know it's so terrible?"

Before Anna could answer, the Colonel threw open the door and stepped into the room. "Hurry! I've given you more time than I should have. The Queen is expecting you."

Tanya moved forward, but before she reached Alexandrovich's side, Anna's bulk blocked her passage. "No! You mustn't go! Your father would have you choose death over such dishonor!"

The Colonel didn't bother to recognize Anna's presence. Stepping around the rotund woman, he held his hand out to Tanya. Proudly, Tanya rested her hand on his arm and sailed from the room. Behind her, she could hear Anna sobbing her protest.

As she stepped into the hallway, Anna called loudly. "Tanya! Come back! Don't go without me!"

Tanya turned. She'd hardly been aware that the Colonel had brought soldiers with him, but now she saw them, two of them, standing at the doorway, their rifles aimed at Anna's heart. She screamed and reached out to stop them, but the shots resounded through the hall.

"Anna!" With a leap, Tanya was back in the room, her arms out to catch her falling nurse. But the weight of Anna's body was too great. The old woman fell awkwardly to the floor, her hands clutched over her heart. Between her fingers, a crimson stain spread until, at last, blood-red drops fell to the floor.

"Anna! Oh, Anna!" Sobbing, Tanya sank beside her nurse, unmindful of the muskets still aimed in her direction. Gently, she lifted Anna's head onto her lap. "Anna!"

For a moment, the big blue eyes gazed up into her own. There was love in them—the devotion of a lifetime. The lips struggled to form a word, and Tanya bent her head to hear. "Tanyushka, remem. . . ." The lips moved once again, but no sound came.

"Anna!" Tanya clutched the beloved form close. There was no response.

In the doorway, Alexandrovich cleared his throat. "Come, don't waste time on a dead servant! The Queen awaits our arrival!"

"The Queen can wait!" Tanya's voice was filled witth anger and pain. "Why did you kill her? What did she do? She was just an old woman who loved me! She wasn't hurting anyone!"

His face was hard and emotionless. "Tanya Ivanovich! Come now!" When she didn't answer, he gestured toward his men. Lowering their rifles, they stepped to Tanya's side and lifted her to her feet. She held tightly to Anna's still body, but rough hands pulled her fingers loose and pushed the corpse to the ground. Then, struggling violently, Tanya was dragged from the room. When they reached the top of the stairs, she stopped struggling. Below her, the servants huddled in the hallway. She had a responsibility to them. She had to show them the courage expected of an Ivanovich.

Her captors sensed her change; they let go of her arms so she could pull herself erect. They trailed behind her, like an honor guard, as she descended the steps, her head held high. By the time she reached the foot of the stairs, she had regained the confidence she felt essential to her proper behavior.

"Boris." The major-domo stepped forward from the group of servants who huddled in one corner of the vestibule. "Boris, have courage. The battle isn't over yet."

He smiled. That had been their signal through the years when she was fighting her father for some privilege Ivan Ivanovich originally denied her. At five she had wanted a horse of her own. She'd won her way that time, and she'd won often in the succeeding years.

"Boris, they've killed Anna. Please, they won't let me stay. Take care of her . . . body."

"Yes, my Lady." She could not but note his use of address. With her father gone, she was the head of the household. Silently, she thanked God she had recovered her control.

Boris turned and spoke quietly to the other servants. In response to his words, they ceased their weeping, growing suddenly still. Only when she reached the big doors did they stir, giving a muffled cheer in approval of her bravery.

The sound off their voices gave her the courage she had only pretended to before. Turning, she smiled at them and

23

waved, as she knew her father would have. Then, gathering her dignity about her with her cloak, she stepped through the doorway into the swirling snow.

Inside the waiting carriage, she closed her eyes. She realized she wasn't in the same kind of vehicle as was taking her father to Siberia. This carriage was elegant: black on the outside, with gold leaf edging the many bends and corners as well as the frames of the windows. It was upholstered in leather that remained soft even in the cold of February. There were satin pillows strewn about. Tanya propped one behind her.

"Dear Mother of God." Her prayer was silent, but nonetheless utterly sincere. "Take care of Anna as she travels up to Heaven. And watch out for my papa. Siberia is such a terrible place." She paused. Should she pray for herself? It appeared she was to receive better treatment. "Dear Mary, help me to remember my father's teachings. And protect me from the evils of the Court—" she paused "—whatever they may be."

When she opened her eyes, she felt soothed. Surely her prayers would be answered! Maybe. . . . Maybe she would even have a chance to meet Alexius again!

There was a crack of the whip and the carriage began to roll. The crunch of the wheels on the snow kept rhythm with the pulsations of her heart. After so terrible an awakening, she knew she should be depressed. But her heart refused to accept the banishment of her father as an irrevocable act. He could be brought back any time! And if she was to live in the Palace, she could plead with the Queen!

There was more that kept her spirits high. She had a natural curiosity regarding the "evils" that so terrified her nurse, and now she would have an opportunity to learn exactly what they were. And she would not be hindered in her investigation by a protective father or a motherly companion. She could not deny it; she felt more anticipation than terror as the carriage rolled through the streets on its way to the grand court of the Empress of all the Russias.

CHAPTER II

She was led into the same chambers that had witnessed her father's humiliation the night before. The Empress's voice was loud—but not unkind. "Tanyushka! Come to me!" Without moving from the doorway, Tanya curtseyed, her eyes directed to the floor. The voice continued. "Come here, I say!"

Timidly, Tanya approached her Queen. A gentle hand touched her shoulder. "Poor little Tanya! How upset you must be! You've been through such a terrible time! Were the soldiers cruel to you?"

Tanya couldn't conceal her surprise. "Your Majesty, the soldiers. . . ."

"Took your father away. But he had to know he couldn't dispute his Queen! He surely realized the effect of his attitude—even on a monarch who loves him!"

25

Tanya lowered her head. How could she answer such a statement?

The Queen continued. "What is incomprehensible to me is his disregard for your welfare!"

Tanya still stood silent, her mind in a turmoil. Was this the hard-hearted Empress that Anna feared and her father fought with so often?

Catherine patted her arm. "Enough of such unpleasant talk! You mustn't worry about your future. You've been brought to the palace to live. You'll be joining my other ladies in waiting." She smiled condescendingly. "After all, you can't be blamed for your father's foolishness."

There seemed no appropriate answer, so Tanya simply curtseyed. The hand pulled on her arm. "Come closer, dear." Tanya stepped nearer the Queen, her heart pounding. Catherine smiled at her flushed face. "Closer! I wish to embrace you, my dear. After all, you are now one of my charges."

The soft arms pulled her close. Following the French custom, Catherine planted a kiss on each of Tanya's cheeks. Then, with obvious reluctance, she released her hold on the firm, youthful body. As Tanya moved away, one of the Empress's hands brushed against the girl's firm young breasts. It was only a touch—and then it was gone.

Tanya found it difficult to sort out her feelings. Instead of some terrible punishment, she had been offered a kiss. She felt confused and uneasy. Had her father been wrong in his assessment of the Empress? But her father was never wrong! She stood for a moment in silence, recalling Anna.

The Queen took both of Tanya's hands into her own. "What is it, my dear? Surely the thought of life in the Court isn't that terrible!"

"Oh, no, your Majesty." Tanya was beginning to cry. "It's Anna . . . my nurse. Colonel Alexandrovich had her killed!"

The change was galvanic. A moment before, Catherine's face had been placid—even loving. Now it was filled with fire. Turning, she screamed for her servants, for a lackey, for the Colonel himself. When Alexandrovich arrived, his face red from the exertion of his run through the halls, she pointed an accusing finger at him. "Does the child speak the truth? Did you kill her servant?"

"Yes, your Majesty." He paused, staring fixedly into his sovereign's face. "She was making trouble, and, as you ordered. . . ."

"Don't tell me what I ordered! I never would have consented to the murder of this poor child's maid!" Catherine's face was bright red. "Leave my sight! I'll attend to your punishment after I've comforted this little one!"

Tanya watched the Colonel as he stepped smartly from the room. Nothing the Queen did would bring Anna back to life, but it would at least avenge her death. "Is he to be shot?"

Catherine met her eyes without flinching. "Don't worry about his fate. It will be no more than he deserves. You're much too lovely to fill your mind with thoughts of revenge. Let your Queen take care of such matters." Again, the royal face was wreathed in smiles.

"Your Highness. . . ." She paused. Did she dare ask about her father's chances for release?

"Yes, little Tanyushka?"

She could not speak of Ivan Ivanovich yet. First she had to better understand her own emotions. There had been moments in the past when she had been perturbed by her father's strictness, and shocked at his daring to criticize the Queen. She had resented his refusal to permit her some of the pleasures enjoyed by all the other young aristocrats in the city: picnics without chaperones, dances that lasted all night—all the exciting things that seemed to bring fun into living.

Catherine took her hand. "You wanted to look at my chair last night. You must see all the pieces." As she spoke, Catherine led Tanya to a large table and crouched down before one of its legs. Instead of a simple wooden stem ending in a neat foot, the curved wood was shaped like the supple body of a female, its breasts protruding outward and its buttocks facing inward. The table top rested on the girl's head, and her toes served to replace the traditional lion's claw.

When Tanya had studied it, Catherine rose and moved to a nearby bench. Here the figures were more erotic. Naked nymphs frolicked across the backrest, chased by sexually aroused satyrs. Tanya felt a stirring in her groin. Such abandon! Would she ever share in such obvious pleasure?

"Take your time, my dear." Catherine put her arm gently around the girl's waist. "Do the figures please you?"

Tanya nodded. All the sensations her strict upbringing had submerged threatened now to overwhelm her.

"Do you understand about your father?" The Queen's voice was low.

Tanya looked up in amazement. In her present condition she had difficulty focusing her attention on her father's fate.

"Well, my child, you need not worry about him. There are many places in Siberia, not all of them as terrible as rumor suggests. He's a nobleman. Wherever he may be, he will be treated well. But he must learn a lesson—one you seem to know instinctively." Catherine's voice grew confidential. "Life is not all black and white. He condemns the Court life because he has been deprived of such pleasures since your mother's death. But that does not make the sensuous life wrong!"

She led the way to another chair that was carved into the shape of a saddle, with. . . . Tanya blushed at the hard shaft that protruded from the front of the saddle, but Catherine did not move away. At last, too ashamed to reject what the Queen seemed to approve, Tanya looked at the exciting object. A warmth flooded her body, and a strange dizziness threatened to overwhelm her.

"You know your father condemned my treatment of the serfs." Catherine's words seemed to buzz in Tanya's brain, but she dared not appear unattentive. "In the light of the frightful horror that has destroyed France, I have no choice. You do understand, do you not?"

Tanya nodded. She wasn't at all sure what the Empress had said.

"Besides, you need to be freed from your father's oppressive supervision." Catherine squeezed Tanya's hand. "You like my carvings, don't you?"

Tanya nodded, and the Queen continued. "You're obviously too passionate and vital a young woman to be squelched under the austere regimen which he imposed upon you. When you have blossomed into the beauty you promise to be, he will learn to accept you—and he will understand that I am right—both about you, and about my country."

Again, Tanya nodded. Her head was spinning. Logic and emotions were so mixed she could never sort them out, of that she was certain. But she was not troubled. Hadn't the Queen said everything would be all right—in time? Surely, if she couldn't trust the Empress, there was no one upon whom she could rely.

The Queen left her then, assuring her that a room awaited her, and that all of her clothes and jewelry had been transported to the palace. "When you're through looking, ring for the maid. She'll show you to your quarters. And remember, my dear, don't worry! Everything will be just fine—now."

In the days that followed Tanya grew more and more convinced that the Empress was, in truth, a warm, kindly person. There were times when she exploded into wrath and meted out punishments right and left, but Tanya had no difficulty understanding her impatience with the victims of her wrath. With Tanya, the Queen was always patient and sympathetic.

The morning of the third day of Tanya's stay at the Court was typical. One of the maids pulled her hair while preparing her for a conference with the Ambassador from France. The Queen's wrath was immediate. "Bitch! Get away from me! You're killing me!" The maid dropped her comb and shrank back. "Who is this creature?" Catherine's voice rose in pitch. "Who brought her here to torture me?"

Lady Bernice, the woman in charge of the Queen's wardrobe, stepped forward, her face a picture of fear. "Your Highness, I'll send her away immediately. I thought she was. . . ."

"You thought! Have you stopped testing the women who're entrusted with your Empress's toilette?"

Lady Bernice cringed. "No, your Majesty. But this one deceived me. She was most gentle during the tests. She never hurt a hair on my head."

"*Your* head! You have a head of wood, with the sensibility of a dead log! If you can't find someone who has at least half the delicacy of your Queen, how can you expect to judge the care of the servants?" Lady Bernice bowed her head in silence. "You've shown a terrible lack of consideration for my person. Another episode like this. . . ." Without completing her sentence, Catherine turned to the mirror. Another woman, who had been standing on the side, came forward and finished the coiffure.

Tanya stopped Lady Bernice later to learn the fate of the unfortunate girl who had hurt the Queen. Lady Bernice seemed uneasy under Tanya's gaze. "I've sent her away."

"But where?"

"Where she won't bother the Queen again."

Confused by Lady Bernice's reluctance to communicate, Tanya let the subject drop. Evidently Lady Bernice was still upset by her failure to please the Queen. Her curiosity, however, seemed to have upset all of the ladies, not only Bernice. The friendliness with which she had been greeted originally vanished. The new attitude of the other women toward her came to a head shortly before the Queen's pre-Lenten Ball, when Tanya came upon a group of women chattering gaily together.

". . . red, with white flowers all down the front. I can hardly wait to step on the dance floor!"

". . . green, with a blue tint woven in. . . ."

". . . silver, from head to toe. . . ."

They all seemed to be talking at once. Eager to share in the excitement, Tanya approached the chattering women. As they recognized her, the busy talk ceased.

"Elizabeth, what gown are you wearing?" Tanya tried to pretend she didn't notice the awkwardness of their sudden silence.

"Oh, a nice one—you'll see it at the ball."

Again, the silence. Tanya stood for a moment, wondering whether she should try again. Then, with a resigned shake of her head, she turned and headed toward the Queen's chamber.

". . . Her Majesty's spy!" The whisper was loud enough so Tanya knew she was meant to hear it. But she didn't permit herself any change of pace, nor did she turn and look back. She was too proud to let her hurt show.

Catherine, as usual, made Tanya feel welcome—and loved. She required the girl's constant attendance, even supervising the production of Tanya's first ball gown. "It must show your shoulders, my dear, and it should be ruby-colored, like the gown you wore the first day you came here. You look magnificent in deep red." Tanya nodded. Whatever her Majesty decided. "You'll wear these instead of the pearls, however."

Catherine motioned to a servant, who immediately scurried over with a large, flat box. With a grand gesture, Catherine presented it to Tanya. The jewels inside sparkled with brilliant red fire. Proudly, Catherine removed them and locked them around Tanya's neck.

Breathlessly, Tanya gazed in the mirror. A continuous chain of rubies set in soft gold rested heavily on her white throat. The stones were perfectly matched both in size and quality. She gasped in amazement. "Oh, it's beautiful!"

"Put the earrings on, too."

Obediently, Tanya removed her own earrings and replaced them with the rubies. They dangled seductively against her neck.

"They look lovely on you. They're yours, my dear."

Tanya blushed. There were times when she felt as if the Queen were wooing her. But that, she realized, was ridiculous! Everyone knew of Catherine's proclivity for men.

The Queen seemed not the least perturbed by Tanya's silence. "The English Ambassador will be at the ball. You'll dance with him as often as he wishes. We must show him Russian women are more beautiful than any to be found in the Court of King George the Third!"

Tanya curtseyed, her hand resting on the jewels. "How can I ever thank you enough, your Majesty!"

The corners of Catherine's lips turned up ever so slightly. "Don't worry, my darling. When the time comes, you'll know what to do."

The following days were too filled with preparations for Tanya to have time to consider the Queen's strange answer.

When her dress was finally finished, she put it on and, with the jewels in place around her neck, gazed at her image. Nanushka, the maid Catherine had assigned to take charge of Tanya's wardrobe, fussed busily with the wide, flowing skirt. Her eyes were sparkling with admiration. "You look lovely, my lady."

"Thank you, Nanushka. I can hardly wait for the ball!" The girl smiled. "It will come."

"Will all the officers be present?" Immediately, Tanya wished she hadn't asked the question. A sudden gleam in the dark eyes of her maid unsettled her.

Nanushka seemed to beg for her confidence. "Are you looking for anyone special?"

Tanya blushed. "Yes. . . . No! I just wondered. . . ."

But she didn't have to wait for the ball, after all. She was in the Conservatory, enjoying one of the few moments when the Queen didn't require her attention. She loved the warm freshness of the air and the many exotic flowers that grew in the shelter of the round glass dome.

Suddenly, she heard footsteps behind her. She turned, alarmed. She had not realized she was not alone. "Oh. . . ."

"Tanya, forgive me for startling you!" The voice of Alexius Andreiv was deeper than she had remembered it to be, and his eyes were still troubled, as they had been that fateful morning. "I've come to explain—and to beg for your forgiveness."

She felt a fluttering in her breast. "I need no explanation. The Empress has already set my fears to rest."

He seemed not to hear her. "I did not realize it was Ivan Ivanovich who was to be exiled! I had been told nothing! Nothing except that I was on duty. Oh, Tanya, can you ever forgive me?"

She did not listen. She had been so sure he had forgotten her! Six years he had been in training—and on duties away from St. Petersburg, and not once had he written to her!

"Are you being treated well?" Alexius Andreiv asked.

"Her Majesty is wonderful! She's explained my father's exile, and she's promised he'll be allowed to return to the Court in time. And she's assured me he is well—and treated kindly." Alexius's face grew grim, but he did not interrupt her. "She's so kind, Alexius! She's given me two maids—she says to make up for Anna's death!" Tanya's face grew sober. "Colonel Alexandrovich had Anna shot, did you know?" Again her expression brightened. "The Queen is always giving me gifts! I can't understand how anyone can call her cruel!"

"Have you seen all the flowers in the Conservatory?" Alexius Andreiv asked.

Tanya looked into his dark eyes. She felt a wave of delight when she realized he had not forgotten their childhood vows any more than she had. He had not forgotten. And now he was back, and she was no longer a child! A strange excitement began in her breast and spread throughout her body.

His voice was husky. "We knew even when we were children, didn't we? Tanya, you haven't forgotten, have you?"

Blushing, she pulled her gaze from his. The musky fragrance of his manhood threatened to overwhelm her senses. She was aware of nothing but his nearness—of her longing to touch—and to be touched in return.

His hand slid up her arm until it reached her waist. Then it moved across her back, pulling her forward. She felt herself pressed against the rough wool of his uniform, her face buried in its intoxicating masculinity. She tilted her head up toward his. She could feel his heart beating against her breast, matching the rhythm of her own.

"Tanya, oh, Tanya!" Alexius Andriev said. She could hardly hear his voice, but she knew its meaning. Her lips parted slightly, and she closed her eyes.

He lowered his head until their lips met. Never, in all of her dreams, had she expected to be so overwhelmed. Her knees grew weak, and she knew she would fall were he to loosen his hold on her body.

"Oh, Tanya! I've missed you so! I wanted to write, but. . . ." He paused. "I was afraid you would think me foolish. We were just children when we pledged our undying love, and I was sure you had forgotten. And then to be involved in deporting your father!"

She rested her head on his chest. "I understood, my love.

I knew you had to obey your orders. It was not your decision to banish my father. And you tried to let Anna come with me to the palace." She looked up into his strong face. "I know now that I never forgot you, even though I thought I did. You were gone so very long."

The corners of his lips turned up in amusement. "So you did not think of me every day, as I did of you! How fickle a woman can be! Didn't you believe that I wanted to marry you? And did you not mean it when you accepted my offer of love?"

She flushed. "I suppose I just wasn't . . . ready, before."

"Well, never mind. I trust you mean it now, for I most certainly do!"

A new fire possessed her body. Pressing against him, she let her arms encircle his neck. Once more his arm tightened around her and his lips met hers. His voice was a whisper, and his breath was hot against her cheek. "Oh, Tanya, my love, I want you so very much!"

His words seemed to startle her into action. She'd been helpless in his arms as long as he held her close. But suddenly she knew she couldn't endure having him leave her without fulfilling the promise of his kiss. Her fingers grasped his sleeve. "Please! You might vanish, too, as my father has! You can't leave me now. It isn't wrong for me to want . . . this. The Queen says it's good to love. My father was wrong when he taught me to suppress my desires."

"Your father wasn't entirely wrong." Now it was Alexius who was uneasy. "You must remember one thing. I want you for my wife, now—and afterwards! Always! Oh, Tanya, I love you so!" As he spoke, he pulled her close again and then he led her into an alcove hidden from the larger room by heavy vines.

When they reached a stone bench, he stopped and embraced her once more. "I want to hold you closer. Wait." Impatiently, he unbuttoned his jacket and spread it on the cold stone.

As if in a trance, Tanya began to unbutton her dress. Her eyes fixed on Alexius' face, she let her gown slip to the floor, where it draped in soft folds around her feet. She untied the cords that held her slips around her waist, letting each one follow her dress.

Alexius gazed at her nakedness, his eyes filled with wonder. "God! You're so lovely!" With sudden impatience, he stepped from his own clothes and then, naked as she, he approached her, a supplicant drawing near the throne of his goddess.

She felt her cool skin touch his hot body. She caught a brief glimpse of his erect manhood, and then she felt him press against her abdomen. The trembling had started once more, but now she made no attempt to control it. Helplessly, she let herself be lifted and carried to the bench. She had no fear, now, only a great longing to feel the joy of his presence inside her body.

Gently, he lowered her onto the rough wool of his coat. "I'll be careful, my love. If I hurt you, tell me, so I stop."

Her voice shook with her emotion. "Alexius, I want you. I want the hurt." Her lips were trembling so she could hardly speak. "I want *you!*"

His hand brushed the soft curls above her mound, moved slowly up her belly. She sat silently, feeling her awareness move with his fingers. He circled her breast lightly, and they began to tingle. She had touched her own body thus when, fresh with the bloom of her first maturity, she had dreamt of the day when she would be taken by a man.

Tenderly, he guided her down on the bench. He knelt beside her for a moment, kissing her and letting his fingers continue their uninhibited exploration. She tried to speak again, to tell him how much she wanted what he had to give her, but all that issued from between her parted lips was a moan.

He moved then, slowly, placing himself between her open thighs. Holding his lips against hers, he pressed against her, the hardness of his body merging with the softness of her own. She felt a momentary sharp pain, and then he was inside, waiting for her to recognize the pleasure of his nearness.

It began deep inside her body—a rhythmic pulsation that directed her thoughts and controlled her movements.

Straining against the hard stone of the bench, she began to move slowly beneath him, pressing against him and then dropping away, her arms encircling his shoulders, pulling him to her.

Gradually, the rhythm of her motions increased, matched by his own as he moved above her. His lips sought her eyes, her ears, the small of her neck, and each touch was like a burning flame. She was panting now, a small moan the only verbal evidence of her growing passion. She wasn't aware of the sound. Then, with a muffled groan, he pressed her against the bench, pinning her down with the strength of his desire.

It was as if her body exploded. She felt herself float weightlessly through the air, her mind filled only with the joy of his nearness. Then, little by little, she became aware of the pressure of his body on hers. She realized the wonder of holding the weight of her lover.

They kissed once more, deep and long. Then, slowly, reluctantly, he rose and began to dress. She stepped into the circle of her slips. Immediately, he was at her side. "Let me help you. You must return to the Queen before she becomes upset by your absence."

"She's busy. She won't miss me."

He stopped his dressing and pulled her again into his arms. "Oh, my little Tanyushka! I was so afraid you'd be . . . spoiled . . . by the Queen!"

Tanya felt once more the confusion caused by his words. Why was he afraid of the Queen? "She's my friend. What would she do to hurt me?"

"Nothing—if I get you away in time. Be on guard, my darling. I'll come for you soon."

"You're leaving?" Cold panic started her trembling again.

"No. But it will take time to arrange our marriage." He paused. "I probably won't see you until it is all settled. In the meantime, say nothing to anyone. Nothing! Your safety depends on your silence."

A footstep sounded in the room behind them, and Andreiv jerked to attention. "Who's there?"

There was no answer. Only the rustle of skirts told them the sex of the intruder. When Tanya looked up again into

Andreiv's face, he was frowning. "We mustn't stay here like this. I was foolish to risk your safety because of my desire. You must hurry back."

Tanya pulled her slips up and tied them about her waist. Then, still unable to hurry, she slipped her dress over her shoulders. Turning back to Andreiv, she smiled over her shoulder. "Button me, please?"

He fumbled hurriedly until, impatient at last, she took over. Then, once more properly dressed, she turned into his embrace. But he didn't fold her in his arms as she had expected. His face was troubled. "You must hurry! It's dangerous for you to remain with me now. Let us hope whoever it was who saw us can be trusted to be silent—at least until the ball. I'll speak to the Queen as soon as I can. Remember, you must say nothing. She can be most formidable if she feels an attempt is being made to take someone she prizes away from her."

"But she treats me like a daughter! She'll be pleased!"

"Nevertheless, wait. You must promise!" His face was stern.

"Yes, Andreiv. Of course I will."

But it was more difficult than she had expected it to be. More than once, as the day of the ball approached, she almost broke her vow and spoke of her lover. What made it most difficult was that she didn't see him again, even though she returned daily to the Conservatory. His absence worried her until she heard there had been a small uprising of serfs, not far from St. Petersburg. Nanushka, the favorite of her two maids, was her informant.

Tanya couldn't refrain from one question. "Will it be over, do you think, in time for the ball?"

"It sounds as if my lady is looking for some particular soldier. Am I right?" The voice was teasing, friendly. For one moment, Tanya was tempted. Surely, there could be no harm in telling a maid of her plans! But Andreiv's words had been so final—and she had promised.

"Maybe. There are many handsome men in the Russian Army."

"Ah, but you have one—am I not right?"

"You're too bold!" Tanya gazed at her coldly.

Rebuked, but not abashed, Nanushka returned to preparing Tanya's bed. But her smile was disturbing, almost a sneer. Surely, Tanya reasoned, she'd given nothing away! But, then, why was the woman so smug—so prying?

CHAPTER III

The day of the ball was filled with last-minute preparations. Tanya's hair had to be washed and set, her dress steamed, her ribbons pressed. It was all so very exciting. Her father had censured the Queen's entertainment as "shameless orgies," though Tanya could see no reason for his condemnation. With all the fuss and commotion, this ball, at least, more properly resembled a children's party. Everyone was filled with anticipation. No corner of the palace was free of the bustle of preparation.

When, at last, the magic moment arrived, Tanya felt sure there was nothing, except Andreiv's continued absence, that could ruin her pleasure. Dressed in her new gown with the Queen's gold-encased rubies at her neck, she swept grandly into the ballroom, certain that, within moments of her arrival, Andreiv would rush to her side.

But, search as she could, there was no sign of him anywhere. Each time a new group of officers arrived at the door of the grand ballroom, she looked for the one face that meant the world to her. But Alexius failed to appear. Finally she could contain herself no longer. She determined to inquire. Perhaps one of the other soldiers would know if he were still out in the field, quelling the riots of the serfs.

But she didn't have to question anyone. Just at that moment Lady Bernice hurried into the ballroom, and when she saw Tanya rushed to her side. "Ah, Tanya, my dear—" Tanya grimaced. Lady Bernice was not usually so friendly. "Have you heard the news?"

Impatient at being stopped, Tanya debated which would free her most quickly, a yes or a no. But Lady Bernice didn't wait for an answer. "Her Majesty has just banished a young officer. I think his name is Andreovich—or something like that. It seems the fool was seen with one of the ladies of the Court—in a most compromising position—in the Conservatory. And the Queen had such great things planned for him! Of course, she was furious! I'm not certain whether the ungrateful man was sent to Siberia or just assigned to Unalaska Island to guard the fur traders, but he will never see the Court of Catherine again!"

Tanya grasped the chair for support. Surely it couldn't have been her Andreiv! "How long ago did it happen?"

"Not more than a few days ago—maybe a week. What a fool he was, to throw away the Queen's favors for some little snip who can give him nothing."

"But, if he was seen . . . with some woman . . . almost a week ago, why did the Queen wait until today to banish him?"

A sly smile brightened Lady Bernice's face. "Evidently someone saw them and waited until now to speak of it to the Empress. How unfortunate it is for that unknown young lady! She'll never see her lover again." The triumph in her tone was impossible for Tanya to ignore.

The blood rushed to Tanya's head. There was no question as to the reason why she was being told this terrible news. Lady Bernice was speaking of Andreiv. And Lady Bernice was the unknown observer who had startled her and her lover in the Conservatory. She knew that Tanya was the "unknown young lady"!

At the same time came the realization of why Alexius had been so concerned about how the Empress was to be told of his desire to marry. Evidently, he was aware of the Queen's lust, and he knew the danger of rejecting her for another. But why, if Lady Bernice had seen them both, if she knew it was Tanya who had been with Andreiv, was she not punished, also? Surely the Queen would feel she was equally guilty!

Lady Bernice seemed to anticipate her question. "The . . . person . . . who discovered the Lieutenant's perfidity appears to wish to shield the Queen from a double disappointment. Evidently, the woman he was with is also one of Catherine's favorites." She paused dramatically. "But the young woman who has shared in Andreiv's shame need not feel too secure. She, too, will be exposed when the time is right." With a triumphant laugh, Lady Bernice swept her way across the room and halted beside the throne.

Tanya stood immobilized, staring after the retreating figure. She was torn between a need to cry and an anger she feared she could not control. How dare Lady Bernice be so flippant in her treatment of other people's lives? And why, oh why, was she so antagonistic? Search her memory as she could, Tanya was unable to think of any reason for Lady Bernice's animosity. But it was real. It had already ruined Alexius' life—and now it hung, like a sword, over what little security remained to comfort Tanya for her loss.

A small group of musicians—horn players, flautists, two bassoonists, two trumpeters, two drummers, and a quintet of strings straggled slowly into the room and assumed their places on the dais. They tuned discreetly and then, with a sudden burst of music, began the fanfare to accompany the Queen's arrival.

Automatically, Tanya curtseyed, her eyes to the floor. But the excitement with which she had anticipated the dance was gone. Her gown, her beautiful jewels, her elaborate hairdress—all seemed unimportant. Alexius was in

41

trouble. Never before had Tanya felt so helpless. She knew that she had contributed to Alexius Andreiv's banishment.

But the Queen was not aware of Tanya's participation in the affair in the Conservatory. When she saw her favorite genuflecting before her, she reached out her hand and lifted her up. "Come, little Tanyushka, you are much too lovely to grovel! Go, my sweet, dance with the British Ambassador! I want to see how quickly you can charm the rough English Lion."

Obediently, Tanya took the Ambassador's arm and moved onto the floor. As she passed, Lady Bernice fastened a hateful glance upon her. She had no control over Lady Bernice, and she was at the mercy of the woman. She might as well take advantage of what little freedom remained to her before she too was denounced.

The music was lovely, brought from France in 1789, as were the fashions the ladies were wearing. It was called a Quadrille, and it had been introduced to the Russian court at the time of the French Revolution, when many aristocrats fled from that benighted country. Even though Tanya had been a child at the time, she remembered their arrival vividly, for it had been the peasants' revolt in France that had caused Catherine to desert her liberal attitudes and reinstate suppressive laws designed to keep the serfs from copying the French.

That had been the point at which her father had begun to disagree with his sovereign, for he had felt that the way to avoid an uprising of the serfs was to give them more, not less, freedom under the law.

The British Ambassador murmured a compliment, and Tanya smiled. Why was it, she mused, that everything reminded her of her troubles? Even the stately dance made her think of her father's exile. Deliberately, she forced her attention to the pattern of the steps: six forward, curtsey, six more, curtsey again. Then twirl sedately as the men moved forward and she took the hand of a new partner.

Not once, as the evening progressed, did Tanya have a moment to herself. With a heart yearning for more news of her lover, she was forced to act the part of a gay flirt. Her instinct was to flee, but she remembered the words of her father. *An Ivanovich does not run away from trouble.* To be true to her name, she had to remain. But she dreaded what lay ahead—when the Empress was informed of her part in Alexius' disgrace.

Most of all, she feared for her lover. As each partner who took her arm showed his appreciation of her dark beauty and each showed his annoyance when he had to relinquish her to another, her thoughts were far from the dance. She was hardly aware of the men as individuals. They were companions in the ball, each with his own cologne, with soft hands or rough, with a body skilled in the dance or with feet that seemed to stumble over even the smoothest of floors.

The hope came to Tanya that Lady Bernice's story was a lie, told only to hurt and tease. Maybe Alexius would arrive, proving the falseness of that wicked woman's tale. But the hours passed, and each new face was that of another stranger. Alexius Andreiv didn't appear.

Tanya was drifting through her sixth Quadrille when she felt her partner stiffen and salute. "Your Highness!"

Automatically, Tanya curtseyed.

Prince Paul didn't bother to answer. Brushing the young soldier aside, he grasped Tanya's hand and bowed slightly. "Madam, may I have this dance?"

She curtseyed once more, hoping to hide the flush that spread to her face. "You honor me, your Highness!"

How strange, she thought as he whirled her onto the floor, *that I should feel compelled to voice such meaningless drivel. I'm not honored; I'm frightened.* Yet, even as she acknowledged her fear, she felt confused. Why should she be afraid of the Crown Prince?

Fortunately, he was a good dancer, and in this Tanya took comfort. However, as they moved forward, he stared at her with a relentlessness that brought an uncomfortable flush to her cheeks. "What is your name, young lady?"

Her voice was low. "Tanya."

"Surely, you have a family?"

"Tanya Ivanovich."

"Aha! The daughter of my mother's antagonist! It appears he lost the battle I interrupted that night when you

couldn't take your eyes from Maman's . . . shall we say
. . . sophisticated furniture!"

There was the same impudence, the same look that
seemed to strip her of her clothing. She flushed with annoyance.

"You blush." Prince Paul's voice was filled with amusement. "Are you still so innocent you don't recognize the
appreciation a man may have for a woman? Or does it
bother you to be reminded of your father's foolishness? He
took a trip to Siberia the next morning, I recall. But what
did he expect? Surely he was wise enough to know one
doesn't cross my mother and go unscathed."

The last words were spoken in open hatred. Despite her
knowledge of the royal feud, Tanya felt a shock. She
glanced toward the Queen.

Paul's voice was dripping with sarcasm. "Don't look to
the Royal Bitch for a new partner. She's much too busy."

He was right. The Empress was no longer watching the
dancers. She was openly fondling a young man whose uniform indicated he was a lieutenant in the Palace guard. The
youth appeared flushed with an excitement he could no
longer conceal.

Tanya looked away. She hadn't seen the Queen in this
mood before, and the sight made her uneasy. Was this what
she had had in mind for Andreiv? Tanya turned back to
the Prince, her face red.

"My God! The sight of mother's games still shocks you?
Can it be she hasn't yet indoctrinated you into her sports?"
Tanya lowered her head. "And I thought you'd be. . . .
Well, never mind. I wanted to get another glimpse of the fe-
male my mother seemed so enamored of, but I didn't expect
to find her still a virgin."

Tanya flushed deeper. She'd heard the other ladies whispering about the Queen, often realizing the last words were
meant for her ears. So that was what they thought she was!
No wonder they considered her the Queen's spy!

"You aren't very talkative."

"No, your Highness."

"All the better. I find women who use their mouths for
speech are usually bores."

Tanya nodded silently, praying the dance would soon end. When, at last, the music stopped, she began to curtsey. He held tightly to her hand. "Ah, but we'll have the next dance, too, my dear."

She wished she could refuse him, wished she could tell him she already had it booked, but she knew even that wouldn't free her from his attention. No other male on the floor would dare to take a partner away from the Prince.

For the next three dances, he didn't leave her side, nor, when they played a Quadrille, would he allow her to move forward to a new partner. When the man behind in the line moved forward, he gestured that he was to be bypassed. Tanya endured his presence with growing uneasiness. She had considered herself fortunate in avoiding him during her stay in the Court, but this more than balanced that pleasure. His look, his touch—everything about him made her flesh crawl. Rumor had it he was mad, and she understood its origin. His eyes were wild, and his actions seemed to rise from some perverse devil that inhabited his body.

It was almost three in the morning before Catherine rose, took the arm of her young suitor, and headed for her boudoir. That was the signal for the dance to end. Immediately upon her disappearing behind the massive doors of the hall, the musicians began to pack up their instruments and the guests began to slowly straggle away. Tanya gave a sigh of relief when Paul abruptly dropped her arm and, without a word of farewell, led his attendants from the room.

For the first time, Tanya had a chance to think of Alexius' fate. Silently, she prayed he was still alive. The Queen had been known to execute men who preferred other women to her, and her father's fate was witness to the Royal vindictiveness. Somehow, she would have to talk to the Queen and convince her to pardon Alexius. She had to. She couldn't live without him! Deep in thought, she passed through the doors.

She didn't at first notice the Prince standing just outside the doorway, but when she didn't stop, he stepped into her path. His voice was husky. "Don't worry, little Tanyushka. I've thought much about you tonight. I'll rescue you from my

45

mother before she has a chance to achieve her desires. You're far too lovely a woman to be snatched away from mankind."

His words seared through her mind. The thought that the Queen might have carnal interest in her filled her with disgust; but even more frightening was the realization that Paul meant to take her for himself. The thought of his arms around her, of his body close to hers, of being penetrated by him, sent a shiver of fear through her. With a terrified shake of her head, she tore away from his restraining arms and raced down the hall. Yet, even as she fled, she knew that, in the entire kingdom, there was no safe place where she could hide.

CHAPTER IV

In the morning light, Prince Paul's words seemed unreal—and inconsequential. What mattered was Lady Bernice's account. Tanya had to seek her out despite her reluctance. The uncertainty with which she had been left was too terrible.

Lady Bernice was alone, working on a lace to decorate the dress she would wear to the Feast of the Orthodoxy. She greeted Tanya as if nothing had created enmity between them.

Tanya determined to take advantage of any good will she might encounter. "Lady Bernice, I've come to ask a question."

"Of course. But first, have you seen my lace? It's almost finished." She held it up, its soft folds draping over her lap.

"It's beautiful!"

47

A small smile touched Lady Bernice's lips. "Have you prepared anything special for the occasion?"

Tanya frowned. "No, not yet. Lady Bernice, I have to know," she began. She saw a face that had become void of any expression.

"You do?"

"Please. I must know if what you told me last night was only meant to tease me. Is it true?"

"Why don't you ask the Queen? You're such a favorite of hers, she certainly wouldn't deny you a bit of information—especially about a man you love!" As she spoke, Lady Bernice's expression became triumphant. "Or you might beg a little. It's surprising how much information that might produce."

Tanya's hands clenched in anger, but she didn't dare express her feelings. If Bernice truly had seen her with Alexius, she had information that could destroy them both. And if the Queen had really chosen Alexius for her next lover, then she wouldn't take kindly to his choosing to wed a simple countess, especially if he seemed determined to reserve his favors for his bride-to-be. Still, there might be some way she could get information without antagonizing the Empress.

She looked solemnly into Lady Bernice's eyes. "Then you won't tell me anything?"

"Ah, but I already have! What you don't know is when I plan to inform Her Majesty as to the identity of the woman."

The temptation to hit at the sneering face that leered at her so scornfully was, for a moment, overwhelming. Almost blind with fury, Tanya turned and ran down the hallway toward the Queen's chambers. Lady Bernice's cold, humorless laugh followed her down the hall.

Raising her hands to her ears, Tanya turned and headed toward the garden. She wandered about without being aware of where she was going. Her eyes were focused on the ground, her attention completely occupied by her problem. She didn't hear the footsteps that moved across the garden, sometimes on the path, but more often on the softening soil. She was turning once more, frustrated at her inability to reach any satisfactory solution to her dilemma, when she was grabbed from behind.

She tried to scream, but before she could take a breath, a large, rough hand was clamped over her mouth. Struggling furiously, she bit at the fingers, finally catching a fold of skin in her teeth. A man's voice cut through the air. "Ow! The vixen bites!"

"I told you to wear gloves!"

"Grab her legs! She's trying to kick!"

The second man bent and grabbed her legs in a vise-like grip, but he didn't stop her from fighting. Furiously, she struggled to break loose. "Damn!" The voice growled. "She's a rough one!"

Tanya strained to see her captors, but they weren't men she recognized. Their uniforms weren't those of the Russian army, yet they were vaguely familiar. Where had she seen them before?

"*Gott im Himmel*! She bit me again!"

Prussians! There were only a few Prussian troops in St. Petersburg—all in the service of Crown Prince Paul!

Grabbing her, they moved her swiftly toward the gate, maneuvering through it cautiously, evidently still fearful she might escape. Where were they taking her? After another turn, she was staring at a coach. The driver was climbing down, opening the door. Suddenly the hand was removed from her mouth.

"Let me go!"

They paid no more attention to her cry than they had to her struggles. Instead, they pushed her into the carriage and shut the door. Her scream was muffled by another hand, far more delicate. Startled, she looked up. Colonel Alexandrovich was sitting opposite her. His voice was soft. "Have they hurt you? I told them to treat you gently." The carriage lurched forward, throwing her into his lap. Immediately, his arms were around her.

"Let me go!"

"Why, my lovely, don't you appreicate an opportunity to get away from the Court for a brief vacation?" She stared at him in silence. Then, in one frantic attempt to free herself, she reached for the carriage door. He chuckled. "I wouldn't bother, my sweet. The door is locked. I have no wish to lose you."

"Her Majesty will miss me!"

"Maybe she will. But I doubt it. She's still too involved with her young lieutenant. If she follows her usual pattern, she won't rise before noon. Besides, you misplace your loyalty. She is on the decline. You would do well to evaluate your position and seek new attachments, as I have."

Tanya ignored his words. "Let me go!"

Lifting her up with a firm grasp around her waist, he slid her onto the seat beside him. "There. Is that better?"

"You must take me back!"

"Oh, must I? And who, pray tell, has given that order?"

She averted her face, listening to the clumping of the horses' hooves on the cobblestones. It was hopeless to protest. All she could do was try to figure out where they were going.

That—and what Alexandrovich had in mind. Tanya didn't look up as she spoke. "Do you seek revenge because I told the Queen of your savagery?"

"Ah, my innocent little Tanya! Ivan Ivanovich neglected the most important part of your education. You may be a skilled horsewoman and an excellent dancer, but you don't know people. Everything I did was on the orders of the Queen! Do you think she would permit your father to be rescued just because his captors weren't wise enough to intercept a message to his serfs? And do you honestly believe she'd permit you to keep a servant who counselled you to live the life of a nun?" She stared at him in disbelief. "You still don't believe me, do you?"

"Her Majesty has been good to me! Surely you can't expect me to believe she'd be so deceitful!"

"You don't want to learn, do you?" He gazed into her eyes. "Have you enjoyed the services of Nanushka?"

"Oh, yes, and Katrina, too."

"Do you think your precious Anna would have approved the massages Nanushka gives you each night?"

Tanya's skin felt suddenly as if she had touched something evil. "How do you know of such things?"

"My dear, I know everything that's happened to you

50

since your arrival at court. Your personal maid reports to me nightly."

"Where is the Queen having me taken?"

"Why should you believe it's the Empress who wants you here?"

"But you said. . . ."

"I said I served her in destroying your guardian angel and in blocking the attempt by some traitorous serfs to rescue your father from his just punishment."

"Then the Queen doesn't know I'm here?"

"I didn't say that, either. You don't need to know who's ordered your abduction. That you'll learn soon enough."

"Do others in the Court report to you, as does my maid?"

"Oh, little Tanyushka! There's no one who doesn't report to someone! Most of the maids are such busy spies they have little time for the duties assigned to them. Some serve Her Majesty; some give their information to the Prince. Can you honestly say you've been unaware of the intrigue that's surrounded you these last months?"

Tanya blushed. She wasn't accustomed to subterfuge. Her father had impressed upon her the importance of forthrightness in all of her dealings, and she had assumed others lived by the same standards. Now, suddenly, she was aware of having lived in a jungle whose laws she didn't understand.

His hand circled hers. "Don't fret, my dear. You're young yet, and you'll learn. Your father did you no favor when he kept you isolated from the life of the Court. But, fortunately, you're free of his tyranny. Now you can learn to live fully, as those around you do."

Abruptly, the trot of the horses' hooves became quiet. Without looking out, Tanya knew they had left the cobblestones of the city streets and were on some unpaved country road.

The coach rolled on, bouncing over an occasional stone that threw them both forward, and Alexandrovich protected her from falling forward with utmost chivalry. Still, his presence unnerved her. He was so . . . slimy! His explanation for his not being punished by the Queen for her nurse's death upset her, because it hinted—no, it proved—that the Queen was not the kind person she pretended to be. Tanya felt betrayed, outraged—and very frightened.

Straightening her skirt, she nervously folded her hands in her lap. "Where are we going?"

"You'll find out soon enough." Alexandrovich leaned over and lifted the shade. The open window wasn't on the side of the door, so she reached for the curtain that obstructed her view. He stretched out his arm and stopped her hand. When she looked at him, ready to protest, the shade beside him was again closed.

"Is it so dangerous that we must remain concealed?"

"It's best you not know the whereabouts of your rendez-vous." As he spoke, the carriage pulled to a halt. She could hear the whinny of the horses and the voices of men shouting to each other. "This, my dear—" He began to rise. "—is where I leave you."

The carriage door opened and, with a swing of his legs, he was on the ground. He leaned into the carriage. "Don't worry; it's only a small distance more." The carriage door slammed shut.

She heard him mount a horse and then, with a shout, the driver of her carriage cracked his whip. The suddenness of the start threw her off balance.

Now the carriage careened along as if the driver was in need of making up for lost time. Tanya was thrown from one side to another even though she gripped the hand-holds for support. When they reached a smooth section of road, she lifted the blind. The farmer-serfs were already busy with their planting, though from the shallowness of the furrows, she could tell they had begun their plowing when the ground was still frozen. It was, however, a practice common in Russia. Summers weren't long enough for leisurely farming.

In the distance she could see a serf, his body bent under a monstrous bag of seed, trudging slowly across the fields. It surprised her that he was alone, and then, under a tree, she saw others, obviously taking a short rest. As she watched, they rose and lifted their bundles. Soon the entire field was dotted with workers. But serfs were everywhere in

Russia. What she searched for was some landmark that would tell her where she was.

The carriage turned off the road and immediately she heard the clop of hooves on stone. They were entering some large estate. They stopped for a moment, and she heard the creak of iron gates being opened. Then they were moving again. She stared out at the bleak landscape. If only Alexius had sent her a note! Then she would not feel so uneasy!

The coach came to a sudden halt. The handle turned, the door swung open.

The next thing Tanya knew, she was being helped out by a pair of amazingly strong, masculine arms, and a voice whispered in her ear. "My dear, I'm delighted you're here at last!"

She gasped in horror. She was looking up into the pale, demented eyes of Crown Prince Paul!

CHAPTER V

Frantically, Tanya Ivanovich searched the faces around her. There was the Crown Prince and his serfs and, mounted behind the carriage, two Prussian soldiers, the two who had abducted her from the garden.

She felt drained of strength. Bracing her feet, she struggled to break free. "Please, your Highness, let me go!"

Paul released his hold. "You're right. We needn't hurry. You're far too lovely a young lady."

Her hands clasped before her, she dropped to her knees. Immediately, four rough hands grasped her arms and pulled her to her feet.

The Prince's face turned dark. He glared at her angrily, until, at last, she pushed the lackeys aside and stood before him once more. Then a smile returned to his lips. "Ah, my dear, you needn't pray to me! I'm the Prince, it's true, but I'm also very much a human being."

She stared at him in horror. Everyone knew he was mad, but never had Tanya realized the extent of his insanity. She struggled to hide her fear. "Your Highness, please. I'm sure your mother, the Empress, will be searching for me. I must return to the palace at once!"

His expression grew ugly. "Don't speak of the Queen to me! She's robbed me of my throne! She has no cause for complaint if I take one worthless female from her grasping arms!"

Tanya shuddered. The hands that had lifted her down refused to remain still. One moved down and cupped her breast, squeezing it roughly. Involuntarily, she cried out, but the hand only held on more tightly. The voice behind her was coarse. "Ah, your Highness, this one has lovely tits!"

Paul showed no anger at his lackey's impertinence; the extent of his depravity was far too great. With a smile of delight, he grasped her other breast. "True, she is a lovely one. Worthy of my attention!"

Then, unexpectedly, his eyes softened. "Are you determined to live like a nun? Or has my mother already turned you toward women for your pleasure?"

"Your Highness, I'm not. . . ."

"You're not opposed to what I have to offer, is that it? You only fear the unknown? Good! I'll be gentle with you, I assure you. You have nothing to fear from me."

She looked at him in confusion. Nothing to fear? Did he mean, then, to return her unharmed to the palace?

He turned on his heel suddenly, as if bored with their conversation. Immediately, she was lifted from her feet and carried from the carriage. "Stop!" His voice was suddenly loud. The lackey paused. "I'll taste a bit of her now. It will make the hunt more exciting to know she waits eagerly for my return!"

Tanya gazed at him in surprise. What had caused him to change so suddenly? When her eyes met his, she shuddered. They were glazed, as if he had lost all touch with reality. He reached up and tore at her dress, pulling it down from her shoulders. She felt the buttons give way, and she was nude from the waist up. The chill of the early spring air tightened her skin and brought bumps of cold all over her body. Quickly, the lackey released his grip and fastened his hands around her bare waist.

Paul fidgeted impatiently with the cords that held her slips around her. One by one he pulled them away, dropping them in a pile on the ground. When she was naked, he stared at her for a moment and then, with a cold smile, bent forward and bit viciously at her nipple.

Her scream was as much from shock as from pain. Around her, the laughter was loud and derisive. Paul gazed at her flushed face with cold disinterest. "If you want gentleness, you must earn it."

He turned away again, as if he had lost all interest in her. When he turned back, his face was calm, and his eyes met hers with open sympathy. "Oh, my dear! You're cold! Nurev! Give her her dress!"

The lackey picked up her dress and draped it around her body. Sobbing, Tanya cupped her injured breast in one hand. Once more she was carried forward, down a stone path that led through a high stand of evergreens. But before she reached the cover of the trees, the Prince called out. Again, his voice was harsh.

She was carried back to the opening, beside the carriage. This time, she determined, she'd not give the Prince the satisfaction of hearing her scream, no matter what he did.

But he didn't bite her again. Instead, his lips encircled the tender nipple, gently massaging it. She felt his tongue touch the places his teeth had hurt moments before, soothing them with moisture. Then, abruptly, she felt his teeth once more, though not quite as forcefully as before. Her body tensed involuntarily.

He glared at her triumphantly. "That's more like it! You shouldn't know for certain whether I'll bring you pleasure or pain. The gateway to female passion is always through torment."

Despite her fear, she began once more to struggle. Paul reacted swiftly. Stepping back, away from her flailing legs, he slapped her hard on the face. "It isn't wise to anger the heir to the throne of Russia! *Maman* isn't well. You know that as well as I do. What will you do when she's no longer here to protect you? You need me! I'll be your king!"

Tanya stared into his face. There was no sympathy there, no understanding. All she saw was his greed, his desire to possess everything he could, especially if the Queen also found it desirable. It was only to prove his power that he wanted her. "Please, your Highness. I'm no. . . ."

"Silence!" The madness was back in his eyes.

She could hear the heavy breathing of the lackey who held her, and the guttural mutterings of the Prussian soldiers. How long did he intend to humiliate her thus? No man but Alexius had ever seen her body, and now she was held up for public display!

He touched her breasts lightly with his fingers, stroking the nipples to a sharp point. "Your body is wise, my dear. It responds as it should to my touch. You're a lovely woman, and a lusty one, though you may not realize it yet. But you'll learn. My touch will bring out the wanton in you as it has in many others. I know you don't understand what's happening to you, but you will. You'll live to thank me for my labors, believe me."

She stared at him, trying to block out the sounds of the soldiers and the lackey's heavy panting. Paul was of medium height, far shorter than the lackey who held her pinned in his arms, but he wasn't a weak man, physically. His features were those of the Queen's, but with a strange warp that destroyed their delicacy. He had spent most of his forty years in frustrated anger, fighting to take the crown he was convinced should have gone to him when his father was deposed.

The years of struggle had taken their toll. Feeble of mind as a child, Prince Paul was close to insanity. He acted more on whim than logic, hitting back at his mother through pettiness, and dreaming of the day when she would die and leave him the crown.

Staring into his wildly insolent face, Tanya determined to try once more for her freedom. He'd said he was going hunting. She'd have time, then, while she was alone in the cottage, to plan her escape. She let her body relax.

He seemed to sense her temporary resignation. Moving to her side, he brushed his lips against her breast. Then, standing back, he let his hands rove over her body, squeezing her breasts, playing lightly over her belly. They slipped down to her hips, lingering playfully. Then, harshly, they were thrust between her legs.

"Look at you!" Prince Paul leered, the madness in his eyes again. "You can hardly wait for the pleasure you know will come! Be patient, my lovely! We'll come to you in good time. We follow our own desires, not those of a wanton slut!"

She blushed in shame. Never had a woman been so humiliated! And before serfs and lackeys—and foreign soldiers! She was too shamed to think, too horrified to even acknowledge the terror of her situation. It was a nightmare! She would waken in her own bed, and this warped man would vanish!

As abruptly as he had touched her, he withdrew. Turning away once more, he walked toward a small stable where a horse stood saddled and waiting. "Take her to the cottage. I'll attend to her when I return."

She prayed the lackey wouldn't remain with her inside the cottage, but she didn't let her praying interfere with her observations. She had to know where she was—and where she could find cover if she managed to escape. She could see a stand of evergreens in the distance, forming a circle around the cottage. The stables, visible from the road, were now hidden from view. They had been to her left as she faced the cottage, and the road was beyond them. The far side of the road offered no shelter. The land was all plowed; but the trees through which she was being carried were evidently part of a dense forest. Land had been cleared for the house, and these trees had been left as shelter.

They broke out of the woods suddenly, into a clearing of about fifty yards, in the center of which stood the cottage. It was a small building, not at all like the other royal structures. There were no windows in front, only a small door that appeared to be made of heavy carved wood. A chimney on one side belched smoke into the clear blue sky.

The lackey covered the distance to the door swiftly, threw it open, and clomped inside. Leaving it ajar, he strode across the room, dropped her unceremoniously onto a bed, and hurried out, slamming the door behind him. She was alone.

Dim as the firelight was, she could see this bed wasn't designed for sleeping. It was covered with a smooth linen, stretched tightly beneath her. There were two pillows made of down at the head. But there were no blankets or coverlets. She was thankful for the fire. Without it, she would have been cold. Slipping off the bed, she began to search the room, hoping to find either a window or another door.

But there was neither. Excepting for the fireplace and the front door, the walls of the room were entirely covered with heavy drapes. She felt all around it, but the walls were solid. Despairing, she turned her attention to the interior.

Beside the bed, the room contained a small dresser, a table on which rested a candelabra and a flint, and an arm chair. Shivering slightly, she sat down to think.

If she set fire to the drapes, would she be able to make good her escape while the servants fought the flames? She abandoned that thought quickly. Most probably, no one would notice the fire, hidden as it would be inside the brick of the walls. She'd burn to death before they realized anything was wrong.

Was there any other way to freedom?

Only one lackey had carried her to the cottage. The rest had remained near the carriage—or gone to the stable.

What about the stable? She'd seen only a small part of it, but she might rightly assume the huntsmen were gone and that the grooms, thankful for time free from their charges, were either sleeping or off on some pleasure of their own. She would have to go there—if she managed to get out. Hopefully, there'd be one horse left she could mount and ride to safety. But first she had to get out.

Then she remembered. The lackey had left the door open when he carried her to the bed. The darkness of the room was too deep for eyes recently in the sunlight. Smiling grimly, she slipped behind the drape next to the door. It covered her completely. Then, hurrying over to the bed, she placed the pillows lengthwise upon it. Hopefully, in the darkness, the mound would appear to be her body. Then, with a prayer that she wouldn't have to wait too long, she returned to the chair.

She dozed once, waking abruptly when a twig in the fire blazed. Walking to the door, she leaned against it, listening for a sound that would tell her whether the Prince was arriving. She heard nothing but a low snore that told her the lackey, too, was taking a rest.

A thought flashed through her mind, throwing her into a panic. She couldn't look to the stables for help in her bid for freedom. When the Prince returned, so, too, would the other riders. The stables would be swarming with men. She'd have to aim for the woods. Hopefully, she could find her way to a cottage where she could get clothing and assistance. If she could avoid the wolves!

She listened for a cry that would tell her those beasts wandered near, but she heard nothing. They were nocturnal animals, and, she reminded herself, the day wasn't half spent. Dejectedly, she returned to the chair. But this time she didn't have to wait long. The sound of horses' hooves told her someone was approaching. As they came nearer, all but one veered off toward the stables. Boot heels crunched on the gravel of the walk.

Tanya rose and moved swiftly across the room. Slipping behind the drape near the door, she waited.

The Prince's voice was loud—and very close. "Open up!"

"Yes, your Highness." The lackey sounded sleepy.

"She's a tasty one, isn't she? One worthy of the most thorough enjoyment."

"That she is, your Highness." He spoke more alertly.

"You may come in with me. We'll enjoy this one visually first."

The lackey's voice reflected his excitement. "Is she truly virgin? Will she bleed?"

"We're sure of it. Her father was an unnatural man, determined to keep his daughter pure. My mother may have enjoyed her body, I know not, but that matters little. She's been too well guarded to have learned the delights a man can provide. 'Tis a pity a woman can experience her deflowering only once. From that time on, she's used—worthless—except for breeding."

The door flew open and the two men entered, blinking in the half-light. Then, leaving it wide behind them, they moved together toward the bed. Paul whispered loudly. "Here we are, little Tanya. Prepare yourself for the joys of mating!"

With a speed born of desperation, Tanya slipped from behind the drape and dashed through the open door. Turning from the path, she raced toward the forest. If only she could reach its shelter, she'd have a chance.

"Catch her!" The Prince's shrill voice added to her distress.

She stumbled as one of her slippers stuck in the mud, but she pulled her foot free and continued her flight barefoot, kicking the other slipper off as she ran. She was gaining! If she could only keep on for a bit longer. . . .

"Faster, Nurev, faster!" Again, the Prince's cry filled her ears. She glanced back, aware that the panting lackey had closed the distance between them.

Gripped by a driving need for speed, she pushed onward, barely skimming over the ground. The cold of the grass froze her feet, but she wasn't aware of the pain. The icy air burned her lungs, and she began to breath more quickly, straining to take in enough breath to maintain her effort.

Suddenly, she stepped on a sharp stone with such force she cried out in anguish. The next instant she was falling, her ankle twisted beneath her. A pair of arms caught her before she touched the ground, and a voice bellowed in her ear. "Got her!"

The Prince called from the distance. "How far did she go?"

"Much farther than the others, your Highness! She almost reached the woods!"

"Sometime we must let one get all the way. It would be delightful to hunt a more wily prey than a fox—just for once!"

Tanya recoiled, and the arms that held her tightened.

The Prince waited impatiently on the path. "This one is sure to give us a proper fight, Nurev, my friend. Though I hate to compliment *Maman*, she does have good taste in women."

This time there was no opportunity for Tanya to escape. She was carried into the cottage by Nurev, who held her in his arms as he stood by the bed. Paul followed him inside, closing the door behind him. Walking to the candelabra, he lit it with a brand from the fire. Then, watching Tanya intently, he moved toward the bed.

Never in her life had Tanya seen a face more evil than his! She closed her eyes, praying for unconsciousness.

"Look at me!" His words were hissed. She opened her eyes. "You're a fiery woman, little Tanya. Fiery—and beautiful! Right now, you fight only for freedom. You fight because you're afraid of the unknown. But before this day is over, you'll fight even more fiercely for that which only a man can give you!"

She shook her head violently, but he only laughed. "Don't deny it! Your tits tell me more than your lips ever can! Ah, you'll make a lusty partner, my hot little kitten. All you need is to have the gate to your desire opened. Why do you resist such pleasure?"

He gave her no chance to answer. His lips were against hers, pushing her backwards. She felt Nurev's fingers loosen and then, pushed by the Prince's body, she was thrown onto the bed. She lay on her side, her head turned so she could see her captors, one hand unconsciously concealing her breasts while the other rested over the soft down below her belly. She stared at the two men with unconcealed hate.

Paul's voice was silken. "Foolish child! Why do you fear me? It is my greatest joy to be the one who awakens lovely creatures like you to the wonder of life! I live for it! You will receive much delight this day, my dear, but you will give ecstasy in return. I wait impatiently for the feel of your maidenhead, and for the power I enjoy as I open your gates of passion!" He turned suddenly to Nurev. "Get the chair!"

When he was seated, he smiled down into her face. "Put

your arms down and spread your legs. I want to enjoy your beauty." She did not dare disobey. Paul continued, speaking as if he were admiring a work of art. "You're truly a beautiful woman, Tanya Ivanovich! Tell me, my love, do you dare say you want none of what I have to offer you? Shall we leave you alone to wonder when we'll return to give you what you desire more than life?" His voice was kind—gentle. The madness seemed to have left him.

"Please, your Highness. I. . . ."

Once more his expression changed. The wild look returned and he stared at her voraciously. "You want me, don't you?" His voice quivered. "Say it, then! Say you want me!"

She dared not disobey, but her voice was barely audible.

"Louder!"

She cursed each word as it touched her lips. It was a lie, but could anyone expect her to do otherwise? "I want you."

"You hear that, Nurev? My little vixen is begging!" Paul rose and moved closer to the bed. "On your knees, then, wench! You may have the pleasure of removing my clothing."

She did as she was told, loosening his breeches and unbuttoning his shirt. But he allowed no more. Swiftly, he moved to the foot of the bed. She prepared herself, expecting him to enter her quickly, but he didn't do what she expected. Instead, he bent down, blowing lightly on the damp hair that bushed out between her legs. His breath felt cold against her hot body. She twitched involuntarily.

"You want it, don't you? You don't even know what it is, and you still want it! Ah, what a lusty little bitch you are!" He blew once more on her dark curls, laughing when she couldn't control her reaction. "Well, my love, I'll make you wait no longer."

With a sudden move, he opened her thighs and dropped between them. Once more she began to struggle. She forced her body to fight him, to push him away, but he only chuckled and, raising himself on his elbows, began to play with her breasts, pinching them sharply and then caressing them gently, moving her swiftly from pain to pleasure. Leering into her face, he began to talk softly.

"Shall I do it now? Are you ready? Fight, little bitch, for the more violent you are, the greater my pleasure! Fight! Battle me!" He paused and lifted his hips into the air. "Now? Do you want it now? Fight harder, little one! I love when a woman fights!"

The meaning of his words penetrated into her pain-crazed brain. He wanted her to fight! He liked when she protested! Then she would fight no more!

Abruptly, she let her muscles grow limp. Her legs fell to the bed, her arms dropped over her head. She struggled to remove any hint of emotion from her expression. He wanted a fighter? He would get nothing!

Without bothering to look at her, he pushed himself into her body and held her pinned to the bed. Triumphantly, he looked down into her face. She looked back at him coldly, her eyes blank, her lips relaxed. All of her instincts told her to continue the fight, but she held her instincts in check. This was once when her mind had to rule.

He moved tremulously within her, and then, with a scream of rage, he was on his feet, his face distorted with fury. "Bitch!" His hand hit her cheek with such force she thought her jaw was broken. "You deceiving whore!" She was trembling now, in terror for her life. "Leading me on—and all the time you knew you were no virgin!" Livid with anger, he hammered at her body with his fist. "Bitch! No virgin could resist the temptation! How often have you held a man on your belly? Tell me, you whore! You dare to play with your King's emotions! You'll see! I can make you rue the day you let another take what is rightfully mine!"

A sob escaped her lips. "I tried to tell you! I didn't ask you to. . . ."

He wasn't listening to her protests. "Slut!" Tears were streaming down his cheeks, and his jaw was trembling. "I should kill you now! You don't deserve to live!" She couldn't respond. His reaction was far stronger than she had expected. "You're like my mother!" His voice broke.

"Deceitful and cruel! Whore!" His breath had grown labored, his face red with anger and disappointment.

Tanya closed her eyes. If she was to die, she didn't want her last sight to be of Prince Paul. She'd think of Andreiv and pray for his safety. Maybe God would forgive her and let her wait for her lover in Heaven. The blows continued to fall, crushing her to the bed with a force that filled her with terror. Again and again his hand slammed against her head, and she realized that the only thing that saved her was the softness of the mattress beneath her. She lost awareness of what was happening. The room grew darker, yet his blows continued to fall. Her head was spinning, and she prayed for death.

As suddenly as he had started, Paul stopped his beating. She could hear him puffing above her, gasping for breath as if he had been running. He would start again, she felt certain, as soon as he recovered. And there was nothing she could do to protect herself.

"Master!" The voice cut through her pain-riddled brain like a knife.

"What is it, Nurev?" Paul was still breathless.

"Master, may I have her? She's not worthy of a Prince, but she's all right for me."

"No!" Her frantic cry went unheeded.

"You want her?" Prince Paul was still panting heavily.

"Yes, master, please. She doesn't deserve one as great as you."

"Take her, then. Do what you will with her. And when you're through, return what's left to my mother!"

Without looking at her again, Paul pulled up his breeches and buttoned them. She heard his feet scraping across the floor, heard the cottage door open—and close. He was gone without another thought to her welfare. She was alone with Nurev.

The hours that followed were endless. The shame, the horror of the insatiable and clumsy lackey was too much for her to endure. There were times when she lost consciousness, when a kind of stupor overcame her. Then she obeyed his directions without a full awareness of her actions.

66

But he seemed pleased no matter what she did—or didn't do. And, like his master, he beat her at his whim.

It was late in the evening when he finally rose from the bed and lifted her inert form in his arms. Roughly, he carried her to the carriage. He didn't bother to cover her nakedness, though he did toss her dress on top of her as she lay in the carriage.

The chill air brought her back to consciousness. Her entire body ached. Her legs were bloody; her face bruised where both men had hit her. Kneeling, because she was too sore to sit, she pulled the dress over her head. Its warmth comforted her agony. She tried to remain conscious through the long ride, but she couldn't. As the carriage rumbled into the city, she slipped once more into a stupor.

At the palace gates, the carriage was recognized and passed without question. Nurev maneuvered the horses until they were close to the stairs that led to the Queen's quarters. Glancing around to make sure he wasn't seen, he climbed down and opened the carriage door. He grabbed the body that lay crumpled on the floor, carried it halfway up the steps, and dropped it on the stones. Then, without a further glance at his victim, he resumed his place at the reins. The whip cracked, and he was gone.

The cold brought Tanya back to semi-consciousness. Steeling herself against the pain, she strained to pull herself up toward warmth—and safety. But her body wouldn't obey her. Sobbing, she collapsed on the stairs and lay whimpering in pain and exhaustion.

She would die, of that she was sure. Closing her eyes, she prayed that death would come quickly. It was best, of that she was certain. She had no desire to live with this shame on her consciousness. She mumbled a petition to God, her lips barely moving. Then, slowly, the coldness grew within her breast—and she slipped into blessed darkness.

CHAPTER VI

"Good morning, my Lady."

Tanya opened her eyes and stared about her room. "Good morning, Nanushka. I. . . ."

"My Lady. You've been ill for some time, but you're getting better."

Tanya struggled to recall the events that followed her trip back to the palace, but she could remember nothing. "How did I get here?"

"Oh, my Lady, it was terrible. 'Twas I who found you, lying like dead on the steps. It must have been God's own will that sent me out to see my man. . . ." She paused, her face crimson.

"Don't worry, Nanushka, I won't tell about your lover."

"Thank you, ma'am, I don't think you will."

"The Queen . . . ?"

"Unless some other has learned of your misfortune, she knows nothing but that you have not been well. I hope you don't mind, my Lady, but I felt it better not to upset her."

Tanya stared at her maid in disbelief. "You mean no one else at the Court knows what happened?"

"I think not. You're so tiny, I was able to get you in by myself, and I used the servants' passages, so none of the ladies saw me." She lowered her eyes. "I'm truly sorry, my Lady. If I. . . . If I. . . ."

Tanya smiled. The effort made her cheeks ache, and she touched them tenderly.

"You still look a bit bruised, ma'am." Nanushka's face brightened. "But you are better, I checked you carefully. I could find no broken bones, in spite of your injuries." Again she looked down. "I would never have spoken to the Colonel if I had known they were going to do this to you."

This time Tanya took Nanushka's hand without attempting a smile. "I understand. The Colonel told me. But you couldn't have known."

Nanushka flushed and lowered her gaze. "I didn't dare call a doctor. Word would have spread to the Queen immediately."

"How long have I been here?"

"Five days, ma'am."

Five days! And she was still sore all over—especially around her buttocks! How much longer would it be before her body recovered completely? "Please bring me a mirror, Nanushka."

Nanushka hurried to the table and brought back a small hand mirror. Leaning forward, Tanya strained to see what damage had been done by her abductors' blows. To her relief, her face showed only slight bruises. "Bring me my powder."

Obediently, Nanushka put the mirror on the chair and hurried to do her mistress's bidding. Tanya picked up the glass and continued to stare at her reflection. "Is that a bruise on my ear?" Nanushka nodded. "You'll have to do my hair to cover it."

"Yes, ma'am."

Taking the small circle of fur in her hand, Tanya applied

powder to her cheek. When she was finished, she stared intently at her image. "It covers the marks, doesn't it?"

Nanushka nodded. "Yes, ma'am. No one will know."

Tanya met the girl's troubled eyes. "Don't worry, Nanushka, I won't ask you to hide me any longer. I'll speak to the Queen myself. If she chooses to banish me—or even kill me—because of my misfortune and my love, I won't complain. I can't live with deceit."

The following morning Tanya awoke feeling far better than she expected. Even the tenderness in her buttocks was diminished. She dressed in a gold linen dress she had had made before the Lenten season began. It accented her dark hair and deep brown eyes in a way she knew would please the Queen. Then, as a final touch, she put on the rubies she had received from the Queen before the ball.

She didn't attempt to make plans or to decide what she would say to the Empress. Though she dressed with a great show of optimism, she dreaded the interview that lay ahead and wished mightily that she could avoid it. To bolster her courage, she kept her thoughts on the mechanics of dressing.

The Empress was in her bath when Tanya arrived. Her face lit up as the girl entered the room. "Tanya! Little Tanyushka! You're recovered, *Ja*?" Tanya felt a glow of appreciation. Her Majesty only reverted to her native tongue when she was deeply touched.

"Yes, your Majesty."

"You're completely cured?" Tanya nodded. "Then come and kiss me! We have missed your bright smile, *Liebchen*!"

Obediently, Tanya stepped close to the tub and bent down. Her head was clasped between two wet hands, and she was pulled lower so that, without rising from the water, Catherine could plant two damp kisses, one on each of her cheeks.

As she released her hold, Catherine turned Tanya's head to one side. "You have a bruise. What happened? I understood you've been ill. I know of no sickness that leaves bruises on lovely faces."

Tanya stared at the floor. Now was the time to speak.

The Empress, herself, had provided the beginning. "It's nothing, your Majesty. I . . . fell."

Catherine snorted. Reaching up, she wiped her hand over Tanya's cheek, exposing the shadow of another bruise. "You've never worn powder in the daytime before. Why do you need it now, if not to cover this injury? And you say you also received this in that same fall?"

Tanya blushed. She'd come so close to failing in her determination to speak only the truth. "No, your Majesty. I was attacked and beaten."

The face before her became livid. "Was it Paul?" Tanya didn't dare look into the Empress's face. "It was, wasn't it? I recognize his handiwork!" The Queen turned to her other ladies. "Why didn't any of you tell me? He thinks he can take my possessions from under my nose! He must be stopped! Why didn't you tell me?"

Tanya's voice was almost inaudible. "They didn't know. My . . . I felt it best not to upset them."

"Upset them! What about me? You worry about a few females' feelings. Have you thought about my honor? Have you considered my right to keep that which I have chosen for myself?"

Staring at the floor, Tanya let the words flow over her. Somehow, even with her newfound realism, she had expected more. There was no concern in her Queen's voice for the suffering her favorite Lady had experienced. There was no objection voiced that a man should be free to deflower any woman he chose without being punished. Catherine was outraged because her son had taken something— *something*—that belonged to her. Never, since the day of her father's exile and Anna's death, had Tanya felt so alone.

She wasn't aware, immediately, that the Queen was indulging herself more than usual in her tantrum. Such occurrences were common enough, and so most of the ladies, Tanya included, had learned to ignore them. But this time wasn't the same as others in the past. Tanya became aware of the uneasiness of the women who hovered around the raging Queen. Lady Bernice, ever-present, tried vainly to quiet her Monarch's ravings, but to no avail.

Catherine launched into a tirade that increased with each passing minute. Not in all her days at the Court had Tanya heard such vile language. Inwardly, she cursed herself for bringing on this outpouring of fury. She should have kept her secret to herself, after all. All she had succeeded in doing was arousing the Queen to a dangerous rage. Staring at the ruddy face, Tanya wondered if she should run for the physician.

Nothing seemed to stop the tantrum. When Lady Bernice attempted to calm her, Catherine only shouted the louder. When two other ladies began to fan her in an attempt to cool her, the Queen threw her soap at them and almost lost her balance. She started by cursing the women for keeping secrets from her, making it clear that Tanya was as guilty as any of them. Then she cursed heaven for the day she had married Peter, swore at the physicians who had delivered Paul. She damned the Empress Elizabeth, her mother-in-law, for taking the child away from her when he was an infant and raising him to be such a warped man. And with each shriek of displeasure she became more flushed, less able to exert any control over her anger.

"Bring some wine." Tanya heard the muffled command and scurried toward the door. But Lady Bernice was ahead of her. Rushing to the Queen's private wine rack, she poured a glass and carried it across the room.

The glass flew to the floor as the Queen threw out her arms in expanded fury. Turning, Tanya saw Lady Bernice stop before the Empress, her face contorted with fear and true concern.

Then, with a suddenness that caused Tanya to wonder if she'd grown deaf, the screaming stopped. Before her eyes, the Queen's face turned from red to a deep purple. Grasping her throat, the angry monarch began to gasp, struggling to draw air into her lungs. Then, with a gurgling sound that sent a shiver of fear up Tanya's spine, Catherine collapsed, her head over the edge of the tub.

"Caterina!" Lady Bernice dropped to the floor, her head resting on the bare breast. The rest of the ladies stood as if frozen. Lady Bernice turned toward them. "Help me! Help

73

me!" Strange, grating noises were coming from the Queen's open mouth.

Tanya rushed to Lady Bernice's side. "What can I do?"

"Fetch the doctor, damn you!"

As if she had been pushed, Tanya catapulted herself from the room. Forgotten were her aches and pains. She returned with the physician to find Lady Bernice in tears, her hands folded on the breast of the naked Queen.

Quietly, the frightened women opened a passage for the doctor. Lady Bernice rose, her eyes glazed. Overcome with a sudden tenderness, Tanya put her arm around the trembling shoulders of the sobbing Lady Bernice. "Don't cry. She'll be all right. The doctor's here, now." Bernice shook her head.

His face a somber mask, the doctor rose to his feet. "Call His Majesty. The Empress is dead."

It was Lady Bernice who directed the dressing of the body, who carefully closed the staring eyes and folded the delicate hands over the still chest. Tanya watched in stunned silence.

"See!" The voice was close to Tanya's ear. "I knew she was the Queen's lover!"

Shocked, Tanya turned to stare into the smirking face of a woman who had snubbed her many times in the past. "How can you say that? Have you no respect for the dead?"

"The dead, like the living, must earn their own respect!"

"But the Queen was good to you, too!"

"Thank God she wasn't as good to me as she was to Lady Bernice!"

Tanya turned away. When she looked back, the woman was gone. Her ample figure could be seen scurrying down the corridor, surrounded by many other ladies who seemed in a rush to leave. "Where's she going?"

It was Lady Bernice who answered. "Bitch! They're going to pay their respects to Prince Paul!" With a sob, she fell to her knees beside the corpse.

Tanya stood in the center of the room, staring about her. One by one, the women were slipping away, following the first deserters to the side of their new ruler. At last, only Tanya and Lady Bernice remained.

The Queen's lover looked up. "You might as well go, too. My Queen has no further use for you."

The words cut through Tanya like a knife. She had no right to share the Lady's mourning, for she didn't feel the same loss. Silently, she turned and walked from the chamber. She didn't, however, follow the others to the Prince. She had no wish to look in his face again. Silently, her head heavy with guilt, she returned to her own chambers. She was hardly aware of Nanushka undressing her and helping her into bed. All she could think of was her guilt. She had been the cause of her father's exile. It was her love for Alexius that had caused him to be sent to Unalaska. And now she was the one responsible for the Empress's death.

Her lips formed a prayer that she would die, that she would no longer plague the world with her presence. When she felt herself slipping into unconsciousness, she had a fleeting thought that her prayer had been answered.

She recovered consciousness slowly, aware that the door to the corridor opened, spilling sound in as someone entered.

"So! My little dove has carried a dagger instead of an olive branch!" She knew the voice so well. Even in her half-sleep she shuddered. "Had I known you'd be so effective a messenger, I wouldn't have neglected your pleasure! You've accomplished what all my spies and soldiers have failed to achieve. You've made me Emperor of all Russia! I owe you my thanks!"

He was right; she knew it. "I didn't mean. . . ."

"Of course you didn't!" His tone was filled with mock sympathy. "But who'll defend you? It was a most diabolical plot on your part to destroy the Queen! Quite obviously, I can't permit the murderer of my mother to go unpunished."

She stared at him in disbelief. Everyone knew how often he had plotted unsuccessfully for just such a result. "But Your H . . . Your Majesty!"

"You try to plead innocence? We both know, don't we, how guilty you really are!" He wasn't toying with her. There was no sign of humor in his expression. She felt the terror of her danger, and shuddered. "Let me see, what shall I do with you? Shall I send you to Siberia?"

He glanced at her sharply and she cursed herself for her inability to conceal her thought that she might join her father. "No, of course not! Such a fate wouldn't be punishment for this little Ivanovich!" He stared idly about the room. "Shall I establish you in a brothel, where you'll be able to indulge your wantonness?" She closed her eyes in terror.

He shook his head. "Never! You'd take too much pleasure in such a fate." He looked long and hard into her face, and then his eyes wandered down her body, stripping the sheet away as if it were not there at all. "You're too lovely to cast aside without thought. I'll have to take my time in deciding your fate."

She breathed a sigh of relief. For the moment, at least, she was safe.

He turned now to Nanushka. His laugh was hard—mirthless. "Go! Your mistress has no more use for you." Nanushka cringed and ran from the room.

Paul stared for a moment longer at the reclining Tanya and then, abruptly, turned and walked to the door. Throwing it open, he revealed two soldiers. "Throw her in the dungeon!"

The door closed behind him. She was alone with her terror.

CHAPTER VII

"Come along, little lady. The Tsar has a new room prepared for you." The tall, brutish soldier stared down into her face. Tanya winced as he lifted her into his arms. Followed by two other men of equal size, he led the way through empty corridors into the late afternoon sunlight.

Tanya gazed at the golden clouds with frantic longing. There would be no sunshine in the dungeon! Anxiously, she searched the path for some sign of help, but it was as if everyone had been removed from the earth. There was no one to watch her as she struggled to free herself, no one to care that she was being confined for a crime she hadn't committed.

One of the men behind her laughed raucously. "Hey, Igor! Is she worth our time?"

Her captor squeezed her roughly. "I suppose so! When we've nothing else to do! She seems a bit thin for my taste!" He paused as one of the other men opened a heavy door. Then she was inside a bare room.

Igor lumbered across the stone floor to a metal grating. Shifting her in his arms, he opened the door and stepped inside. Immediately, he began to descend. The other two men remained behind.

A chill dampness hit Tanya's skin and she shivered. To her surprise, Igor held her closer, as if to protect her from the prison air. Down they went, past heavy doors with small square openings through which she could see wan faces staring out in hopeless pleading. Some of the doors held no hungry eyes, but instead were the source of pitiful cries of anguish. The terror and pain of the day finally took its toll. She felt a surge of despair. Surely, now, her life was over! No one had ever been known to return alive from the dungeons. She was unconscious when her jailor deposited her in her cell.

She awoke to total darkness. Someone had touched her. Frightened, she sat up and tried to see who was near. But the blackness that surrounded her was complete. "Who's there?" She spoke timidly. "Who are you?"

A scurrying noise startled her. Something was running across the floor nearby. Terrified, she held her arms close to her sides. "Please, say something! Don't frighten me so!"

Four small paws landed on her lap, and she screamed in fright. With a leap she was on her feet. Her cry started a chorus of chattering noises around her. Rats!

Trembling in horror, she backed away from the sound. A squeal behind her brought her to a sudden halt. She had stepped on something soft. Something that scuttled away as it cried out. Slowly, she began to walk forward. Maybe she would find a raised bed that would keep her away from the terrible creatures!

Her extended hands touched something cold—and wet. Suppressing her revulsion, she felt the surface. A rock wall. But she had found no bed.

Turning, she moved in another direction, keeping one

hand against the wall. Suddenly, she stopped. Her hand had encountered a protruding ledge. She listened for the rodents. Somewhere in the darkness, they were gnawing; she refused to consider what it might be they were eating.

Deliberately, she turned her attention to the ledge. It was too small for a bed, but when she reached above it, she found another of about the same size. Steps? Purposefully, she searched the slimy wall and found them, neatly formed by long rocks spiraling up the wall.

Deliberately, she climbed onto the first step and reclined against the damp wall, her body supported by the next two risers. Once more she tried to see across her prison, but the dark was impenetrable. Her hand touched the wet rocks behind her and she shuddered. Folding her arms over her chest, she attempted to wedge herself in place. Her body aching and chilled, she stared into the blackness, determined to remain awake. But her exhaustion was too great.

She awoke when a slender ray of light hit her across the face. Startled, she opened her eyes and stared about her. Where was she? Why was she sleeping in such a strange position? She touched the slime of the wall and pulled her hand away in disgust.

With a rush, the memory returned. It wasn't just a terrible dream. The Empress was, in truth, dead. Paul was Tsar, despite his mother's attempt to pass the crown to his son, Alexander. And she was in prison, somewhere within the royal compound. Painfully, she sat up and looked about her. A sharp agony doubled her over. Her abdomen was sore—and very tender. The memory of her night of horror filled her with caution. Gazing carefully about, she stepped onto the dirt floor of her prison.

She located a narrow window, high up near the ceiling of her cell, which admitted a shaft of sunlight. The cell itself was circular, with no doors and only a square opening, covered by a metal grating, far above her head. The stone steps on which she had slept snaked their way up to the only entrance.

The rats were nowhere to be seen, but a half-gnawed bone in the center of the cell gave evidence of the threat they were to her safety. Silently, she determined always to sleep on the steps, for there was no bed or chair of any sort.

A key rattled in the lock overhead. A voice she didn't recognize sounded above her. "Food!"

She looked up. A plate had been slipped through the grating to a small ledge. She hadn't eaten since before the death of the Queen, and she had no way of knowing how long ago that might have been. She stood for a moment, staring at the place.

"Please come and get your food!" The voice wasn't that of a jailor. It was high-pitched and quite melodious.

Curious, Tanya approached the ledge, trying to peer through the grate and the mystery that lay behind it. When she reached her food, she sat down on one of the steps and stared at the plate in surprise. It held meat! Real meat! And vegetables! The same fare she would have had in Court! It wasn't spoiled, either, as she had expected it to be. She glanced upward again.

She was greeted by a pair of bright blue eyes topped by a shock of blond hair. "Who are you?" She couldn't conceal her surprise.

"I'm Alexander."

She shook her head in disbelief. "Alexander's a grown man. He must be twenty or more."

The boy frowned. "I'm not Prince Alexander! I'm Alex Alexandrovich, Colonel Alexandrovich's son!"

That made no sense at all to Tanya. She squinted up into his face. "What are you doing here, in a prison, feeding me?"

"I'm being chivalrous." When she looked confused, he continued. "I'm tending to a Lady in Distress. Papa told me to. He said the Tsar wanted to keep you healthy, so you'd be of use to him when he decided what to do with you."

Her pleasure at her visit was dampened. "But. . . ."

"Don't you like the food I brought you?" He pouted.

She felt ridiculous. He was playing games with her! "Thank you very much. It's delicious."

"You're welcome, my lady."

"Do you often come to the rescue of women in distress?"

80

"Of course not!" His voice showed his impatience. "Papa says you're too beautiful to be left to rot, and I guess the Tsar thinks so, too. Are you really beautiful?"

Tanya felt her spirits rise. If she was too beautiful to remain in prison, then she would, eventually, be released. But to what?

The boy leaned down. "What did you do to offend the Tsar?"

"I don't think I understand."

"Did you refuse to go to bed with him? Papa says the Tsar likes his women willing."

She stared at the youthful face. He couldn't be more than ten years of age. When she was that young, she was hardly aware of such adult behavior. Was this what the Court did to people: turn children into sophisticated old men and adults into madmen? For the first time in her life she understood why her father had restricted her visits, and she thanked him silently. Her childhood had been light-hearted and gay, not filled with intrigue and sensuality. "What time is it?"

"'Tis well past midday. The sun shines through your window near three by the clock."

She looked down at the spot of light. It had moved from where it had wakened her, and was now only a thin sliver against the wall.

The boy cleared his throat. "Are you warm enough? I can bring you a cloak, if you wish me to."

"Yes, thank you. The floor is very damp."

The child rose. He was leaving, and she would be alone. Desperately, she sought some way to hold him. "Do you know how long the Tsar intends to keep me here?"

He looked down. Already, he seemed far away. "Of course not! But papa says it will be a long, long time." He was gone before she could question him further.

What did he mean? If, in truth, she was to be confined for a long, long time, of what use would his chivalry be? She felt somewhat cheered when she remembered her own childhood. A day to her, then, had seemed a "long time." She'd been foolish to ask a child such a question.

She determined to keep her own record of time. Using

the edge of the metal plate, she scraped a line on the wall below the grating. Hopefully, the child would return daily. But if he didn't, she'd still make the climb, if only to keep up her strength. And to avoid the rats. She would do anything to escape them.

Alex returned once more that day, with a jailor who unlocked the grating and tossed down a heavy cloak. Tanya had no time to climb the stairs, and her shout of "Thank you!" went unheeded.

The cloak was made of tightly woven wool, and she recognized it as being part of a soldier's uniform. At first, she was quite disappointed. She'd hoped to feel the softness of her own fur-lined robe. But she soon realized the gift was ideal. The wool protected her against the dampness, seeming to grow warmer when it got wet.

She tried to balance herself on the narrow steps, but she recognized that she would have to choose between being above the rats and being reasonably comfortable when she slept. Fearfully, she ventured back onto the floor of her prison. She would have to adjust to her confinement—and the rodents.

To her relief, she found that they paid little attention to her. There were scraps enough lying about the cell to keep them from hurting her, and to assure herself of her safety, she piled the bones and unidentified garbage into a pile as far from her bed as she could get it. Halfway between those two she dug a hole in the mud floor. That, she determined, would serve as her cesspool.

Her plan seemed reasonably successful. The rats still approached her bed occasionally, but she was prepared for them now, and with the robe to protect her, she felt less vulnerable. She spent much of her time and strength on an attempt to deepen the pit, but the ground was hard. Even the metal plate Alex had forgotten to remove couldn't penetrate very deeply.

She had, at first, been acutely aware of her increasing body odor. Accustomed as she was to a daily bath, she suffered sorely from her growing filth. But, as the days passed into weeks, she grew accustomed to the stench of the dungeon. Once, when she climbed to the top of the stairs to retrieve her food, she caught a whiff of a strange odor. Repelled, she crawled quickly back to the floor. It wasn't until later that she realized she'd been revolted by the odor of fresh air.

The only way Tanya had of keeping track of time was by counting the times the sliver of sunlight fell on her pallet. The row of scratches below the grating grew, but she learned little about her future, no matter how she prodded her youthful visitor.

One day, Alex arrived with an orange fruit. "The Ambassador from Italy arrived yesterday with gifts for the Tsar. Papa brought some of these to me. You tear off the skin and eat them. Like this!" Sitting above her, he produced a second fruit and began to pull away its skin. Tanya followed his directions. Immediately, she found her hands covered with a sticky liquid. "Lick it off your fingers!" He laughed gaily. "It's very sweet."

He was right. The taste of the orange was delightful. She had seen such fruit before, on the Empress's table, but it hadn't been offered to her. Now she understood its charm. It was like a sweet candy wrapped in a heavy skin. The sharp flavor refreshed her as no water ever could.

As the days passed, Alex often brought her such treats. Tanya found his visits served more than as a source of nourishment. His surprises made her look forward with interest to his arrival, and his conversation kept her aware of the world which, without the news he brought her daily, would have passed her by. Yet, much of what the boy described filled her with horror.

"Papa says there'll be more executions today."

"Executions? Has there been an uprising?"

"Oh, no! Papa says the Tsar has to eliminate his enemies."

She remembered the web of intrigue that filled the Court. "But how does he know who they are?"

"Papa says that's easy. He executes everyone who served the Empress. Papa says that's why he changed his allegiance to Prince Paul when he did. He was sure Catherine wouldn't live much longer. Then he frees any who were opposed to her."

Tanya's heart began to beat faster. Her father was one such. "Has he brought any prisoners back from Siberia?"

"Oh, yes, many."

"Do you know their names?"

"Some of them."

"Ivan Ivanovich?"

He shook his head. "Your father? No. Papa says Paul hates him more than the Empress did."

Her heart sank. But there was one more question. "Alexius Andreiv?"

"I haven't heard of him. What's he?"

"A lieutenant in the Qu . . . Emperor's army."

"I don't think so. Do you like pudding? I got it from the Tsar's own kitchen. I caught one of the Tsar's cooks stealing wine, so now he doesn't dare refuse me anything!"

When she was alone, Tanya spent much of her time trying to think of the plans the Tsar had for her. She quickly abandoned the thought that he might want her for himself. His proclivity for virgins was too well known. Did he plan to install her in a whorehouse, as he had threatened? She shuddered at the thought. But compared to a prison cell, such an abode would certainly be more pleasant.

Often she fought a longing that originated in her sleep with dreams of Alexius and the short time they had spent together. More than once she felt his arms about her and heard his voice whisper her name. But, when she awoke, trying desperately to cling to his fading image, her heart would be torn with pain.

Unalaska Island. That was all she knew. It was a place without reality. When she thought of her father, she visualized him standing on a barren, snow-covered plain, devoid of trees. But she could conjure up no such picture of Alexius. He always came to her surrounded by the warm, damp air of the Conservatory, with strange, exotic flowers over his shoulder, and the scent of spring in his hair.

Each day, when she heard the thumping of the jailors' feet, she prayed one of them would come to release her. At the sound of keys rattling and gruff voices, she would rush to the wall and climb to the grating, ready to leave her prison cell on a moment's notice. But each day only brought disappointment. The bright spot of sun reached its zenith and began to retreat, each day moving a bit farther away from her pallet, each day marking a new ebb in her hope for freedom.

The worst days were those that didn't bring Alex to her cell. Then, more often than not, she received no food at all; the jailors didn't consider her their responsibility. After one period during which Alex didn't visit for several days, she couldn't resist reprimanding him for his negligence. "Where were you? I missed you yesterday."

"Oh," his voice was light, "I went riding. Papa took me on a hunt! It was so exciting! The dogs cornered the fox in an old tree and when they pulled him out, they tore him apart! Papa let me watch the whole thing!" He leaned forward enthusiastically. "Have you ever hunted?"

"Yes, my father took me with him." She didn't tell the lad of her reaction to her first sight of canine violence. She'd tried to run to the small animal's rescue, and her father had had to pull her back and carry her from the field.

Alex wasn't looking at her in his usual manner. "Don't press me. I don't have to visit on any schedule, papa said so. If you make it tiresome to be chivalrous, I'll stop coming."

His words filled her with terror. "Forgive me!" She almost groveled in her fright. "I'll not question you again!"

From that time, however, she forced herself not to anticipate his visits. She concentrated on trying to understand her captor. Was it true that Paul had further use for her? If so, what could it be? She asked Alex. "Has your papa told you what the Tsar plans for me?"

"Of course not!" The young voice was scornful.

"He hasn't said when I'd be released?"

A sly smile. "No." She felt sure he knew, yet she couldn't persuade him to tell her.

She was, she realized, being subjected to a refined torture, worthy of the Tsar. She never knew whether Alex would arrive, nor what he would bring her. Yet she dared not ask for assurances from the fickle boy. His threat to leave her hung heavy over her spirit.

Tanya's anxieties deepened. Alex hadn't appeared for an extraordinarily long period. She awoke from a troubled dream to the sound of a key rattling overhead. Her heart in her throat, she raised herself to espy a hand reaching through the grating. A blurred face appeared above her. "Hurry, slut! The Tsar wishes to see you!"

Abandoning her cloak, Tanya rushed up the stairs, fearful that this was yet one more attempt to break her spirit. She was certain the grate would be slammed in her face, yet she couldn't restrain herself.

"Move! I've more important things to do than wait for you!" She recognized the voice. Igor! It was he who had carried her to her prison. "Hurry! He won't take well to any delay!"

Something in the voice reassured her, an urgency that gave her confidence. He had orders he was expected to obey.

When she reached the top step, a big hand grasped her wrist and pulled her from her knees. She felt herself swing out over the opening, and she felt a moment of terror. He could drop her, and her life would be over.

The next moment she was on her feet, looking up into Igor's face. He didn't return her gaze.

"Follow me!" He turned and led the way up the staircase that dominated the passage. She couldn't look up; the light above was too bright, and she had difficulty keeping up with him. When Igor came to a halt to allow her to catch up, she heard a voice. "Help me! I'm dying!"

"Quiet!" Igor snarled gruffly.

Tanya cringed. Her suffering was nought compared to many others held prisoner in this hell-hole.

"I'll never forget this experience." Her voice was a whisper. "I'll always remember the suffering. Always!"

She followed Igor up a flight of steps. When he reached the top step, he unlocked a heavy door and held it open. "Hurry!"

The stone was cold beneath her bare feet, but Tanya was

hardly aware of any discomfort. She padded through the grating, waiting for him to show her where to go. He led the way through the soldiers' barracks, and she followed, blinking to protect her eyes from the brightness.

When the first breath of clear, fresh air filled her lungs, she felt dizzy with joy. The sky was leaden, the ground hard and frozen. But, to her, it was the most beautiful day of her life.

At the palace door, Igor turned her over to another guard. "I leave you. Go with God!"

She was shocked at his farewell. He cursed others who suffered, yet he treated her now with kindness! There was, however, no time to consider the inconsistencies of her jailor. He turned and hurried away, leaving her with her new guard.

CHAPTER VIII

Her new guard, a palace guard, regarded her appearance with obvious distaste. "Follow me." He preceded her down the corridor. At the door to what had once been her rooms, he paused. "You're to go in."

She stared in disbelief. Surely, her rooms had long ago been appropriated by another!

"Enter!" She shrank from the angry voice, grasped the handle, and turned it. Slowly, the door opened.

Inside, she gazed about in wonder. The bed was smooth, as if it had never been slept in. There was no evidence that she had been absent at all. It was as if she had returned from a normal morning of service to the Empress.

"Good afternoon, my Lady!"

Tanya looked up. Could it be that Nanushka was waiting, too?

The girl before her was heavy, with a broad face lacking in any glimmer of intelligence. Tanya spoke quietly. "Where's Nanushka?"

"I don't know, ma'am. I was told to care for you."

"What's your name?"

"Marie, ma'am."

Had Nanushka paid for her momentary show of friendship? Tanya had no way of knowing. Nanushka was gone, that was all. Like a leaf floating on a swift river, she'd passed from view.

"Nanushka was good to me," Tanya mused aloud.

"I'm a good maid, too, my Lady."

"Yes, I'm sure you are. I was just . . . thinking. And I wish to bathe. And I need clean clothes." Tanya glanced down at her tattered, filthy garments. A tub was waiting in one corner of the room, already filled with steaming water. "You were expecting me?"

"Yes, ma'am. I was told to prepare for your bath early this morning."

"Who told you?"

The girl looked away. "I was told."

Tanya stepped out of her filthy clothes and climbed into the tub. Obviously, she would be getting no information from her maid. But she did get good service. Marie scrubbed her long hair carefully, freeing it of snarls and leaving it, finally, fresh and sweet smelling.

As the dirt fell away, Tanya gazed at the rags on the floor. She'd be wearing new clean clothes again! Her skin tingled with the touch of the hot water—and with anticipation of the touch of crisp linen and fine silk. Standing up, she motioned to Marie. "Dry me. I want to dress."

It surprised her how easy it was to slip back into the role of a lady. During the long days in the prison, she'd cared for her own needs as best she could. Her spirits rose when Marie docilely accepted her commands, leaping to obey with a swiftness even Nanushka had never shown.

When her mistress was dry, Marie moved to the closet.

"Would you care to choose a gown?" She pulled open the door.

They were all still there! The deep maroon dress she had worn to the ball, the bright yellow spring dress she'd been wearing when she met Alexius in the Conservatory. She felt overwhelmed. Which one should she wear? "Were you told where I was to go after you helped me clean up?"

"Yes, ma'am. You'll have an audience with the Tsar."

So he'd finally decided what he wished to do with her. "Then I'll wear my maroon velvet."

The dress, however, hung loosely about her, with room enough for both her hands under the bodice. "Oh, Marie! It hangs like a sack!"

Smoothly, Marie gathered the waist toward the back and stitched it firm. Then, putting the gown aside, she took up a brush. The few snarls that were left after the washing vanished before the skillful hands of the maid, until, once again, ringlets fell about Tanya's shoulders.

She gazed at herself in the mirror. "Can you pile it up?"

"Yes, ma'am."

As Tanya watched in the glass, she was transformed into a proud woman, her hair a crown of black above her slender neck and even features.

"You look lovely, my Lady. Ma'am." Marie's voice was hesitant. "The fashion is to wear a spot of rouge. Would you care to try some?"

She'd avoided all such affectations in the past, accepting her father's word that they spoiled her youthful beauty. But now she realized she would look less wan if she followed the custom. "Just a little. I don't wish the Tsar to see that I've suffered."

A knock sounded on the door and Marie scurried to open it. A youthful page appeared, his face clear of all expression. He, too, was new. "My Lady, the Tsar wishes to see you in his study."

Proudly, Tanya Ivanovich rose to her feet. It was encouraging. She felt less threatened in such an informal meeting-place. Still, she had no way of knowing what might happen. Would there be an accounting of her strange prison experience? Would she learn why Alex had been sent to encourage and care for her?

With her returned pride came a surge of anger. If only she could make Paul pay for the horror to which she'd been subjected! She visualized him pleading for her forgiveness, his face streaked with tears, as hers had so often been. Then, with an impatient gesture, she brushed the foolish thought from her mind. She wasn't free from him yet. He could still destroy her with a flick of his hand, as he would rid himself of a fly.

The boy led the way with a dignity she hadn't expected. That it hadn't been Alex had surprised her. He'd been the go-between for so long. Hurrying her pace, she moved alongside him. "Do you know Alexander Alexandrovich?"

"Yes, my Lady. He left for Italy yesterday afternoon. He's lucky to spend the winter where the sun still shines."

"Will you see him again?"

"If he returns. His father has gone as Ambassador to Italy."

"When he does, tell him Tanya Ivanovich thanks him."

"Yes, my Lady."

At the royal chambers, the boy moved ahead, opened the door, and stepped inside. "Tanya Ivanovich!" Immediately, in proper Court manner, Tanya dropped into a deep curtsey, her eyes half-closed, directed toward the floor.

"Ah, you've come! Enter, my little dove!"

Steeling herself against the memories the voice invoked, Tanya rose and looked at her Emperor. Paul hadn't changed as much as she had expected. His expression was still more that of a small boy caught in the vestry than of a ruling monarch. His features were so hauntingly like those of the Empress they gave Tanya a start. But there was a difference. Paul had a crafty look about him, and a wildness to his expression that told her he was still mad, still prey to senseless whims. There was one addition to his face that did nothing to increase his charm. His cheek twitched nervously. The strain of rule was already taking its toll.

He was dressed as if he were going to a formal ball, in a satin vest and brocade breeches. His fingers were covered with rings, one so large it concealed a knuckle. A thick gold

92

chain around his neck fought for the privilege of framing his face, but couldn't overcome the enormity of the ermine collar upon which it rested. He waved one hand. "Come in! Don't dawdle!" His voice continued. "Captain Adam Czerwenki, this is Tanya Ivanovich."

For the first time, Tanya realized the Tsar wasn't alone. A tall figure detached itself from the shadows and moved into view. "My Lady, I'm honored!"

"I too am honored, Adam Czerwenki." Her tone expressed her curiosity.

"The captain has been of much use to us in the Pacific. He leads in his trade with China." Tanya nodded. She knew little of such things. "He's just returned from a particularly profitable voyage, bringing not only many treasures from the orient, but carrying the fruits of a successful year of trade in furs."

Her eyes brightened. "Have you been to the Aleutians?"

"Oh, yes, my Lady, many times. I've brought supplies to the traders who remain on the islands throughout the year."

Did she dare ask about Alexius? A twisted smile on the Tsar's lips warned her to be cautious. "What are they like?"

"The islands? Barren! There's so little there, the men face starvation every winter. It's impossible to raise grain or even feed for animals. Many of the men have risked fights with the Spanish in order to reach lands more hospitable to humankind."

Her heart sank. Alexius was in a worse location than her father!

Paul waved his hand impatiently. "Enough of this small-talk! You'll have plenty of time to get acquainted."

Tanya looked at Czerwenki in surprise.

"His Majesty has suggested you would travel with me." When he recognized the question in her eyes, he continued. "He hasn't spoken of it to you?"

The Tsar laughed. "She's only today returned from a period of penance. In the past, she's had . . . difficulties."

"Then she may decide not to go with me?"

"Oh, no, she's made her decision. She'll be ready in the

morning. She has no desire to return to her previous accommodations."

Paul laughed lightly. "Treat him well, Tanya Ivanovich.
You'll be traveling with him through Siberia. You might
persuade him to visit your father."

She looked up at the man with whom her lot had been
cast. His rugged face was weatherbeaten and dark from
much sun. His dark hair was fringed with grey, but his
shoulders were broad and strong. His long arms ended in
thick, rough hands. There was little of the gentleman about
him, but, despite his thick brows and firm jaw, he didn't
appear cruel. There was a smile playing about his lips she
interpreted to be friendly, and his eyes, closely examining
her, showed obvious desire, as they had from the moment
of her entry into the room.

There was no doubt in Tanya's mind as to what Paul
meant when he instructed her to "treat him well." She was
being given to this sailor as a reward for his services. He'd
expect to use her whenever he wished. Silently, she vowed
she'd use her body to control him, use every feminine trick
she knew to gain her own goals. Tossing her head, she
smiled up at him. "Are you pleased with your new mistress?"

"More than pleased." A new shade appeared in his eyes.
"You're a very beautiful lady." With an attempt to ape his
betters, he lifted her hand to his lips.

She didn't respond at first. Then, with a smile that promised pleasure to come, she slowly withdrew her hand. He
attempted to hold it, but she would not be stopped. Her
voice was low—and very seductive. "We must reserve
some pleasure for the future, Adam Czerwenki."

A cloud covered his eyes. Then, abruptly, he turned toward the Tsar. "Thank you, your Highness. She's a lovely
wench. And, it appears, a lusty one. You are most kind."

Paul waved his hand absentmindedly. He clearly had
had enough of the affair. "Take her and go. You've a long
trip across Siberia to the port of Okholsk. You've done well
in your trading in the past, and I trust you'll be even more
successful in the future. Who knows what rewards will
await you on your next return to St. Petersburg?"

Bowing deeply, Czerwenki backed through the doorway, Tanya following. There was no use protesting. Paul had made her alternatives very clear: The prison, or this sailor.

Outside, Adam Czerwenki paused at the door that led to the garden. "I'll send for you in the morning, my Lady. We leave at sun-up." Once more he took her hand, and this time she allowed him to kiss it.

"I'll be ready. Will there be room for my baggage?"

"You can take one large trunk. We travel light over the wastelands, and the cabin has limited space. Until tomorrow, then." Turning swiftly, he was gone.

Tanya Ivanovich walked slowly back to her quarters. She paused only once, outside the royal chambers. The Tsar was still inside; she could hear him walking about. Clenching her fists, she stared at the heavy door. "I'll come back, your *royal* Highness! I'll come back! The name of Ivanovich will return to honor the Court of Russia in spite of your venom! Nothing you can do to me will destroy my determination!"

CHAPTER IX

A gust of icy wind swirling across the courtyard picked up a handful of snow and tossed it into Tanya's face. It stung her skin. Shivering, she sank deeper into the heavy warmth of her woolen parka.

Her fingers sought the comfort of the smooth gemstone encrusted with gold that adorned her heavy velvet dress. The magnificent necklace the Queen had given her before the ball, and all the other pieces she had brought with her from her home had been removed from her rooms sometime during her imprisonment. Only the broach had been missed by Paul's minions.

The horses stamped their hooves on the snow-covered pavement, their nostrils steaming.

At last her baggage was secured on the runners of the

sled. Then Adam and the coachman took their places, and she stepped up inside the sled beside Adam.

Adam pulled the fur robe up around them both, carefully tucking it over her shoulders. "Let's go, Ilya! It's a long journey!"

Ilya lifted the whip high above the steaming backs of the horses. The sharp crack cut through the early morning air and, with loud snorts, the horses leaped forward. The gates were opened as they approached and, with shouts of farewell, the travelers emerged into the ice-covered streets of St. Petersburg.

Tanya turned for one final look. To her left loomed the white-painted dome of the Conservatory. She whispered good-bye; she'd never forget the wonderful love she'd shared there with Alexius.

Then moving, free of the palace, facing the wind and the crisp cold air, she felt refreshed and, for the first time since her imprisonment, alive. Alive—and eager to face the future.

Casting a sidelong glance, she studied the stern features of her companion. Her mind had been working furiously since she had learned she'd be traveling with him. This, she knew, wasn't the time to speak of Unalaska and her plans to join her lover. First she had to find her father. And the Tsar had said Adam would help her.

"Adam. . . ." Her breath, billowing before her, was caught by the wind. "Would you have Ilya drive down the main boulevard? Please? My home's only a short distance from here, and I've not seen it in over a year."

"Of course, my dear. Are you comfortable? Warm enough?" He tapped Ilya's back and gestured for him to turn to the left.

"Oh, plenty warm, thank you." She drew her hand from under the robe and pointed ahead. "There! That's where I grew up. When we weren't at the country estates."

"They're in the hands of your brother now?"

"Oh, no. I have no brother. When I marry, they'll go to my husband. Even the Tsar can't strip me of my inheritance."

"Why would he do that?" Adam's voice was edged in suspicion.

She paused before answering. Adam wouldn't have asked such a question had he known of her imprisonment! "No reason at all! I don't know why I said that!" She laughed shyly.

His hand sought hers. "It's important, nevertheless. Your husband stands to become a very wealthy man." He looked into her upturned eyes. "Have you any particular person in mind?"

Coyly, she shook her head. "Why no, Adam. A lady must have her father's consent before she marries. And papa was banished before he made any arrangements for me."

Adam squeezed her hand and stared into the white mist that swirled around their circle of warmth. "When I come to the city, I have to stay at an inn. It would be nice. . . ." He drifted into thought, his fingers beating a rhythm against the back of her hand. Tanya smiled in satisfaction. The groundwork had been laid.

After they left the city, they were alone in a white desert. Snow swirled around them, obscuring the road and coating everything in sight. Through most of the journey, Tanya sat buried in the robes, her parka pulled down over her face. Only when they stopped to change horses and to exercise their legs did she move from her rough woolen cocoon.

When at last they reached the hostel where they were to spend the night, she stirred from the half-sleep into which she had been forced by the cold and prepared herself for her next move. Adam was assisting her from the sleigh when the innkeeper approached. Imperiously, before Adam had a chance to speak, she called out: *"Hôtelier!* We require two rooms for the night——" She leaped to the ground, her limbs stiff from the inactivity. "——and quarters for our horses and servant."

Adam took her by the elbow, his face dark with anger. "Why did you say that? We need only one room!"

She blinked at him in calculated surprise. "One room? Why, Adam! I'm a lady—and you're a gentleman!"

He flushed. "Yes, but the Tsar. . . ."

"The Tsar has put me in your care." She prayed silently that Paul had made no loose promises to Adam. "He'd be outraged were you to mistreat me! Please, Adam! We're talking too loudly! We mustn't display our misunderstandings for the amusement of the rabble!"

To her relief, he accepted her arrangement without further question. After a mediocre meal in the common room, Adam escorted her to her quarters. She heard him stride to the steps and descend impatiently.

She was settling herself into bed when he again thumped up to the landing. A second, lighter step accompanied his, and a flutter of giggling followed the deep rumble of his voice. Then his door opened and closed. Tanya snuggled down under the soft blankets. Adam would be easier to handle than she had hoped.

The Siberian border at last! It had taken almost three weeks to traverse the distance Adam insisted he usually covered in ten days of hard riding. His concern for her comfort occasioned many rest stops not normally scheduled, and the terrible weather slowed the horses, who had to be forced to move so they wouldn't freeze.

Tanya, although snug in her fur robes, had grown increasingly impatient at the slow progress, but she restrained herself until she knew at last that Russia was behind them; then she wasted no time in putting her long-smoldering plan into effect.

Each morning, she made Adam aware how unhappy she was; each evening, as they sat together in the common room of some new inn, she made it clear that her growing depression was affecting her deeply. One evening, when she sat silently at the dinner table, not touching her food, Adam could no longer ignore her suffering.

"Tanya, please, tell me what's bothering you. Have I offended you? If so, I assure you it was unintentional."

She sighed but did not reply.

"Is it that I take other women? You can't deny me that! I'm a man. . . ." His face lit up. "Of course! How stupid you must think I am! We've traveled almost three hundred miles together, and we've come to know each other well. You've been ready. . . . And to think I didn't see it right away!"

Tanya let her hand rest lightly on his arm. "You're right when you say we know each other well. But. . . ." Idly, she picked up her fork and pushed at her food. "I. . . . Oh, Adam, there's one thing we've not mentioned. I was hoping you'd remember."

He stared at her intently, his countenance growing dark. Watching him, she waited until he was ready to explode. "You don't remember what the Tsar said to you when we met? About my father?"

"Your father?"

"Yes. How can I love a man who ignores a pledge he made to the Tsar himself?"

His eyes narrowed. "Pledge?"

"You promised you'd help me find my father! Is your word so worthless. . . ?"

His fist slammed on the table. "Don't say such a thing! Since the day we left St. Petersburg, I've made plans for us to find him!" His voice softened. "Didn't you tell me you needed his consent before you could marry?"

"Oh, Adam!" Impulsively, she kissed his cheek. "How thoughtful of you! But you should have told me. I'd have felt very different toward you!"

His gaze was steady. "Grateful enough to. . . ."

She cut him short. "That's what's so wonderful about you! You have the instincts of a gentleman, even though you insist you're only a sea captain! You know I could never consent to . . . reward . . . you without my father's blessing! And so you never even ask me! Are you sure you haven't some noble blood?"

His frown turned slowly into a smile of pride. Picking up his fork, he struggled to imitate her graceful handling of the dainty utensil as Tanya hid her amusement in a mug of wine.

As soon as the meal was over, Adam excused himself and headed for the barracks. He returned a little later, covered with snow but smiling broadly. "Tanya, good news. The commander knew your father's name as soon as I mentioned it. He's informed me we'll find Ivan Ivanovich in the town of Vologda."

"Vologda?"

"It's near the Sukhona River, not quite a hundred miles from here. We should be there in three days if we push." He paused. "You know I dare not travel at night. The wolves. . . ."

Running her hand over her broach, she gazed into his face. "I understand. Is it possible, do you think, to buy freedom for a prisoner?"

His laugh rang across the tavern, and a number of heads turned toward him. "Oh, my little Tanya! Siberia is a land where anything can be bought—as long as you have the price!" His voice grew quiet. "Have you enough money for such a purchase?"

She nodded, unwilling to say more. Gently, she took his arm and moved toward the steps. "You're so wonderful, Adam! Thank you for helping me this way. When we find my father. . . ." She let her voice trail off seductively. Let him reach his own conclusions. The less definite her promises, the easier they would be to break—or at least bend.

The guard at Vologda thought for a moment and then, flipping over the pages of his record book, found the entry they were looking for. "Ah, yes!" He smiled warmly. "I remember him! A tall man, yes?"

Tanya nodded. "He's here! Oh, we've found him!"

The guard looked up in surprise. "No, my lady, he isn't here. My record shows he was sent east to Velihii Ustiug." He looked at Adam. "Do you know where that is, sir?"

Adam nodded. "I've traveled this route many times. I'm glad we're not passing through in the spring. The streets there can be lakes of mud."

"Aye, they're bad all right. I hear a pig was drowned in the middle of the main street last June!" The soldier snorted in amusement.

Adam forced a laugh. "We'll be on our way. Thank you." He paused. "Is there a good inn in town?"

The soldier directed them to a small inn that was in no way superior to those they had found on their own, but Tanya cared little for her surroundings. Her disappointment at not finding her father was mixed with fear. It was not easy to keep Adam at bay, and the longer the journey was, the greater her problems. Her plan was definite. As soon as she found her father she would buy his release with her gemstone. Then the two of them would flee south, far from Adam—and the soldiers of the Tsar. As she fell asleep in her solitary bed, she prayed for her father's safety—and for that of her lover. Then, with renewed optimism, she dropped into a dreamless sleep.

A blizzard was blowing as their sled pulled away from the inn the next morning. Bundling every available robe around them, they braced themselves against the storm as Ilya kept the horses moving. Tanya could see icicles forming on his nostrils, and she knew the beasts, too, must be suffering from the cold.

The first day of travel was very hard on the horses, and it was dark before they reached the inn. Leaving Tanya to arrange for their rooms, Adam turned to the driver. "I'm a seaman, not a groom, Ilya, but we need to care for the horses if they're to be of any use to us tomorrow."

"Sir—" Ilya loosed the harness and headed toward the stables. "—we might change to reindeer. They're far more capable of. . . ." His voice trailed off as he disappeared from view.

When Adam stamped the snow from his boots and joined Tanya at her table, she had already ordered food and drink. She held up a mug of hot goat's milk fortified with vodka. "Have we much farther to go?"

"Unfortunately, yes. We made very poor time today. The reindeer might prove faster, but we may well spend three more days on the road."

Tanya ate the meal in silence and retired as soon as she dared. She felt discouraged—and lonely. But her dreams brought the cheer denied her during the day.

She dreamt of finding her father, securing his freedom by selling her broach, and, as their sled sped out of town, seeing Adam for the last time, stamping into the road, his fist raised in anger and frustration.

She awoke feeling reassured. It would happen just as

she dreamed it. It had to! Soon she'd be with her father—free from the pressure of Adam's constant expectations.

As they approached Velihii Ustiug, Adam lifted her hand and pressed it against his groin. "It's good your father is here. I grow impatient for your love. Feel my desire!"

Flushing, Tanya tried to draw her fingers from his grasp. "Adam! How can you be so crude? Please, you make it most difficult for me. I'm a woman, as well as a lady. I, too, have emotions to keep under control!"

He released her hand. "Of course, my dear. I forget at times that you've been awakened to the ecstasy of love."

"Thank you. The Tsar was a wonderful teacher; the only one of whom I could never be ashamed." The lie caught in her throat, but she concealed her disgust. It had been clear from the start that Adam had been told nothing except that she wasn't a virgin and that Paul had been instrumental in her deflowering. The realization that the Tsar had been somewhat considerate of her feelings had, at first, made her uneasy, but, as the days passed into weeks and the distance from St. Petersburg increased, she reached the conclusion that the Tsar had felt ashamed of his treatment of her—and pairing her with Adam had been his way of making amends.

Velihii Ustiug brought nothing but disappointment. Even in the middle of winter the snow and ice were black with dirt, and the inn—the only inn—was filthy and small. Winds whipped across the barren streets, shaking the small wooden structures and robbing them of heat. Tanya felt warm only when she lay in bed.

Worst of all, however, was the discovery that Ivan Ivanovich wasn't there. Once more they searched out the barracks and consulted the record books. The Count had been sent from Velihii Ustiug to Obdorsk more than a month before their arrival.

Tanya gazed at Adam in despair. "Where's Obdorsk? Is it on our way to the China Sea?"

He shook his head. "Not really. We'll have to go quite a bit out of our way—to the north."

He hastened to reassure her. "Don't worry, Tanya. We'll

go there! I can buy furs in Obdorsk that will more than pay for the trip."

Putting his arm about her shoulder, he led her back to the inn. At the door to her quarters, he paused. "Are you sure you can't see your way to letting me join you tonight? I assure you, I'll not stop searching until we find your father. I'm as eager to get his approval of our wedding as you."

She leaned against the heavy wooden door, resting her arms against his chest. Slowly, she brought her lips to his. She felt his arms slip around her body and pull her close, and she accepted his embrace passively. Then with a moan she burst into tears. Tenderly, he took her chin in his hand and lifted her tear-stained face toward his.

"Tanya, my dearest, what have I said now? You've let me see your love. Surely I haven't offended you by admitting that I desire you, that I can wait no longer!"

She felt trapped. It had been her hope that he would continue to permit himself to be put off until she reached her father. After her terrible experience with Nurev, the Prince's lackey, she had no wish for sex with any man other than Andreiv.

Frantically, she searched for some way to reject him that would still arouse his sympathy. He watched her closely, and she felt his anger rising.

"Oh, Adam!" She let her head rest briefly on his chest. "Oh, I'm so ashamed!"

Once more he brought her head up and gazed into her eyes. His anger was gone. "If it's anything I've said, please forgive me."

"Oh, no! It isn't you! It's. . . ." She paused dramatically. "I'd hoped I wouldn't have to tell you. I thought I'd recover before . . . before you asked . . . this . . . of me!" A sob caught in her throat. "Oh, Adam, please forgive me!"

"For what?" His voice rose impatiently. "What's this all about?"

"Remember when the Tsar said I'd been doing penance?" She waited until he nodded his assent. "Well, he was right—in a way. You see, I was in mourning—for my lover."

His eyes narrowed. "Your lover?"

"Yes." She inhaled deeply. Now that she had decided on her story, she felt more confident. "The Tsar, as my guardian, chose him, a wonderful man about your age. Oh, Adam, I was so fond of him!" Once more she burst into a fit of weeping.

The urgency of his embrace was gone. He held her gently—comfortingly. Aware of the change, she lowered her voice. "He . . . died . . . as he lay beside me. I didn't know enough to heed him when he begged for rest from our passion. I—" She let another sob tear through her chest. "I thought I'd be able to forget him—but I can't. When I feel stirrings of desire for you, I see—" She searched her head for a name. "—Alexei Vasynovich lying there. . . . Oh!" She grasped his arms and pressed her forehead against his chest. "Oh, Adam, I'm so afraid I'll hurt you—like I hurt Alex! I just don't trust myself any more!"

His expression was solemn. "Don't you think it might be better if you came to me? Maybe you'll overcome your fear."

She drew herself from his embrace. "I can't! I see his body so clearly! Oh, Adam, please be patient with me! I know he's gone, and I know you're different. But I need time!"

Gently, he opened her door. "Don't fret, my sweet. I can wait for a prize as lovely as you. But we must talk about it more. You seem to feel you were to blame." His hand rested on her arm. "My dear, passion isn't always fatal. Alex's heart must have been weak. But I can assure you, I stand up well to passion. I'll not fall victim to the sweet death!"

"Thank you, Adam. I'm sure you're right. Thank you for your patience." Before he could protest, she stepped into her room and closed the door.

Throwing the lock, she sighed in relief. What a narrow escape! Silently, she prayed she'd reach her father before she had to contend with stronger demands from her escort.

It was growing more and more difficult to keep Adam at bay.

When, at Obdorsk, they encountered the same disappointing news, Tanya was devastated. They had been traveling for two months, fighting blindness from the snow and danger of freezing in the bitter cold. The endless wastes of white stretched behind and before them, and even though she had been protected by furs during the short days and warmed in a soft bed throughout the long nights, her strength was failing.

The prisoners, she learned, covered the distance on foot, and they had no shelter from the cold as they slept—except that furnished by the snow itself. In spite of her natural optimism, Tanya began to fear her father had not survived.

They remained in Obdorsk long enough for Adam to accumulate a supply of fur pelts which were loaded on sleds. Each afternoon, when the pale sun dropped from its position just above the horizon, Tanya watched the northern lights. The residents of the town seemed unimpressed by the beauty that surrounded them, but Tanya found it fascinating, even daring the cold to stand and watch the display. Adam paid little heed to the phenomenon. He completed his trading quickly, and they were on their way within the week.

She sought Adam's comfort often during the succeeding days of travel, especially when the howls of wolves filled the air around the sleigh. The beasts had been heard in the distance before, but as the baying grew closer and closer, Tanya pressed herself against Adam in a fit of trembling. Hugging her protectively, he signalled to the driver, who was fumbling with a large bag he had carried with him throughout the journey. When the first grey shape appeared out of the white mist, Ilya untied the bag and pushed it out of the sled.

A young doe struggled out of the bag and began to run wildly about in the snow. Before she could become accustomed to her newfound freedom, a grey ghost lunged at her legs. Down she went with a bleat of terror. Tanya felt a shock go through her entire body. It had all happened so quickly! As the wolf and its pathetic victim disappeared from sight, Tanya felt a wave of nausea overcoming her. Siberia was a terrible, savage place! It would be a miracle if her father had survived his banishment.

During the remaining short hours of daylight, Tanya listened apprehensively each time the lonely howl of a wolf sounded over the whistling of the wind. She felt comforted only when, after a long night's rest in a one-room cottage which she shared with Adam, Ilya, and the reindeer, she saw the familiar bag on the seat once more. Throughout her childhood she had heard tales about families who neglected such protection, and who were themselves victims of the hungry predators.

Travel was slow—and endless. Sixteen hundred miles of white wilderness were slowly put behind them. Wolves attacked more than once, until, at last, Tanya no longer felt upset by the sight of the helpless sacrifice. And each long night was spent in another shepherd's hovel, huddled close to malodorous animals in a search for warmth. It wasn't until they reached Viliuisk, almost two-thirds of the way across Siberia, that they were again able to procure private quarters.

Tanya let Adam hurry to make arrangements for their overnight accommodations while she stretched her cramped legs and tried to locate the barracks. When it was clear they were too far away to find that night, she followed Adam into the common room, where the innkeeper was bowing obsequiously. Adam turned his back on the man, his hand extended to help her over the step that led to the dining area.

They ate in silence. Tanya was hungry—and exhausted. She hadn't slept well in the crowded cottages, and she was eager to spend a night without the snoring of laborers and the smell of sheep and reindeer disturbing her rest.

When the table was finally cleared, Adam took her hand in his. "Tanya, I've been thinking these months since we left Obdorsk. You're wrong to shun what both of us desire. I have arranged for but one room. Tonight I am determined to show you that love is nothing to fear, and that I am man enough to survive pleasure in your arms."

The color drained from her face. Weakly, she allowed herself to be assisted from the table and led up the steps. At the door to their chamber, Adam kissed her gently on the lips. "Prepare yourself, my dear. I'll be back in fifteen minutes."

After completing her toilette without removing her chemise, Tanya slipped between the covers and waited, her body tense with cold and fright. It was only a matter of minutes before Adam lifted the blankets and slipped naked beside her.

His pent-up desires were obvious as his arms slipped around her waist and he pulled her close, his engorged manhood pressing against her soft stomach. Tanya shuddered in disgust. Adam had none of the sweet fragrance that had so charmed her in Alexius; he smelled of old perspiration and stale liquor, and his rough hair chaffed her tender skin.

For one moment she forced herself to lie still in his embrace and then, thrashing wildly, she began to scream. She felt him try to hold her, felt his lips try to cover hers, but she moved too swifly. Struggling fiercely, she pulled herself from his arms and huddled in one corner of the bed.

Adam stretched his hand placatingly. "Tanya, please. Control yourself. It sounds as if I'm killing you!"

Gradually, her sobs diminished. "For . . . give me, Adam." Her body was wracked with uncontrollable trembling. "Please! I'm so sorry!"

He moved closer and she drew back. "Please, Adam! Please wait 'til we find my father. Maybe he can help me overcome my fear." She drew her feet beneath her and pressed her body against the wooden bed frame. "Please?"

He sat for a moment gazing into her face, then suddenly rose to his feet and pulled on his clothes. When he was dressed, he strode to the door. "I'll wait, Tanya, until we find your father. But I'll wait no longer. I'm sure he'll agree with me that you only need to be forced to accept me. Once that's over, like the breaking of a maidenhead, you'll be fine again—and eager for love." Without waiting for her response, he stepped into the hall and closed the door behind him.

She listened as he thumped down the steps and returned, a short time later, with the innkeeper and a whore from the tavern. When she was assured there was another bed provided for Adam and his companion, she fell into a deep sleep.

The man who greeted them at the barracks the next morning looked strangely familiar to Tanya, but when she couldn't place him, she brushed the thought from her mind. Adam spoke briefly to the guard and then turned to Tanya with a smile of delight. "Tanya, my love, we've found him at last! The soldier has promised to bring your father to the inn in a half hour."

Eagerly, she let Adam lead her from the barracks into the spring sunshine. It seemed an endless journey around the edges of the puddles to where the carriage waited—and even longer through the slushy streets to the mud-covered log structure that was the inn.

At the door a soldier waited, his boots thick with fresh dirt and spotted with brown stains. "Aha! Captain Czerwenki! You have to move fast to keep up with the Imperial Army!"

Tanya stared at his face. This was the same man who had greeted them at the barracks! His presence filled her with an uncomfortable bewilderment.

The soldier turned to her and saluted. "Madam, the man you want is in your room. We'll come for him in fifteen minutes."

Without replying, Tanya scurried up the stairs. As she turned the corner at the landing, she noticed Adam put a companionable arm around the soldier's shoulder and lead the way into the tavern. Still haunted by a feeling she had seen the man somewhere before, she walked to the door of her room.

A soldier stood outside. "Tanya Ivanovich?"

"Yes." She caught her breath. "Is my father inside?"

The soldier nodded.

"Thank you." She threw open the door and stepped inside. Blinking, she stared into the shadow behind the bed. There, sitting in a chair, was her father. Her momentary

110

disappointment that he didn't rise to greet her was lost in her exaltation. Rushing across the room, she cried, "Papa!"

Still he made no move to rise. "Tanya!" His voice was a mere whisper. "Come to me, my child. Let me hold you once before I die!"

For the first time she realized his hands were pressed against his abdomen. As she knelt at his feet he reached out to hold her—and blood spurted from an open wound in his stomach. With a scream, she pressed her hands against the flow. "Papa! What's happened? What have they done to you?"

His voice was weaker already. "Nurev. He's killed me. The Tsar. . . . I thought Nurev was coming to bring me my freedom."

Nurev! No wonder the man with Adam had seemed so familiar!

The combination of fear and fury that had overwhelmed her during that terrible day in the Prince's cottage returned, and she felt a faintness that threatened to steal her consciousness. But her awareness of her father's injury drew her back. "Papa! Oh, papa! It's my fault! Nurev killed you because of me!"

She kissed his pale face, her own tense and white, and her warm tears ran down his cold cheeks. The blood that gushed from his wound colored her gown, touching her flesh with a warmth that drained his body, but she hardly noticed its presence. She could see what had happened now, as clearly as if the Tsar had written her a letter explaining his plan.

How stupid she had been to think he was being kind! He'd arranged to have her sent on a wild chase across Siberia in order to give Nurev time to reach Viliuisk. And Nurev had been instructed to administer a death blow to her father—and to her dreams. It was all a bizarre plot of Paul's to get even with her for not being a virgin!

"Don't leave me, papa! Please! I need you now more than I ever have!" A sob interrupted her words. "Oh, papa! My dearest papa! I love you so!"

"I love you, too, little Tanyushka!" His voice was noticeably weaker. "I. . . ." A sigh escaped his lips and he became still.

She looked up into his bloodless face. "Papa." She could see no response. "Papa!" She screamed in terror and pulled at his shoulder, willing him to respond. But he fell lifeless against her breast. Trembling, she screamed again. "Help me! My father's dying!"

The young soldier stepped inside, strode across the room, and lit a kerosene lamp. When the soft golden glow fell on the face of Ivan Ivanovich, Tanya burst into tears. He was dead, drained of his life as he sat in her embrace. He was dead—and she was alone with Adam.

Firm hands lifted her to her feet and led her to the bed. Tenderly, as if he regretted his part in her torment, the young man settled her on the coverlet, his face working nervously.

Tanya felt as if she were in a stupor. Her mind seemed unable to register what had just happened. But she was acutely aware of the young soldier lifting her father's corpse into his arms and moving toward the door. His body was so thin! So emaciated! If he hadn't been killed by Nurev, he would probably have died of starvation!

She reached out of her fog and took the pale hand in hers. "Please, don't take him away! I can't. . . ." A sob shook her, but she held tightly onto the thin fingers.

The soldier shifted uneasily, and suddenly she became sharply aware of his extreme youth. His clear blue eyes met hers and then turned away. "Please, ma'am. I've got to go. Commander Nurev is expecting me."

Clutching her father's hand, she looked up into the flushed face. "Will I be able to bury him? Please, at least let me care for his last rites!"

The youth shifted uneasily, his eyes averted from her face. "I'll do what I can, ma'am. I'll try." He paused. "I'm sorry!" His voice broke, and his eyes met hers briefly. "I didn't know what . . . had been done . . . until you called me. The Commander carried him in by himself."

Tanya forced her voice to grow steady. "Thank you. I'm sure you didn't. You're too considerate." She brought her father's hand to her lips. "Forgive me, papa, for what has been done to you!" A cold hard fury was growing beneath her agony. "The Tsar will pay for this, father! Some day, somehow, he will pay. I promise you."

The soldier stood awkwardly, the limp body hanging in his arms. This time he met her eyes with a new resolve. "Ma'am, I'll tell the Commander I promised you that you could bury your father tomorrow. I'm so sorry! I didn't know. . . ." Suddenly aware that he was repeating himself, he saluted and gently removed her father's hand from hers. Cradling the body, he carried it from the room.

As the door closed, Tanya threw herself on the bed, sobs racking her body. Only after she had wept her eyes dry did she think of her own plight. Now she had no hope of escaping from Adam. She had played a tune all across Siberia, and now, at last, she would have to dance to his music. She would have to give him herself—and she had hoped to escape such a fate.

CHAPTER X

A beam of sunlight touched Tanya's eyelids and she was suddenly awake. Confused, she looked around the room. Her eyes fell on the chair where her father had sat, and reality flooded back. Leaping to her feet, she brushed a strand of hair from her eyes and ran into the hall.

She tapped urgently on Adam's door. When there was no response, she pushed it ajar. The bed was empty. Had Adam left her? Was she stranded in Viliuisk, defenseless against Nurev? More likely he had drunk too much and had slept it off at his table!

Hastening to the common room, she searched its dim shadows. It was with relief that she located Adam sprawled in a corner, his arms over his head, his snores echoing through the half-empty hall. Stale beer never smelled so good! She touched him lightly on the shoulder. "Adam! Wake up, it's morning!"

Grunting in annoyance, he shifted his head onto one arm. "Goway!" His voice was thick with sleep and alcohol. "Slut! Goway!"

She recoiled. Slut? Quietly, she backed away. Nurev! He had been speaking to Nurev. She could no longer expect any sympathy from Adam.

A terrifying feeling of uncertainty overcame her. If she had lost her control over Adam, she was no longer safe. Now—before he recovered his senses, she had to run.

The memory of her father lying unburied brought her to a halt. She couldn't leave his grave unconsecrated. Almost immediately, she realized that he would be the first to urge her to get away. She began to move toward the door, thankful that the common room was empty of all other guests.

There was a shuffling behind her and Adam's hand fell heavily on her shoulder. "What do you think you're doing? Incestuous bitch! No wonder you put me off! No wonder you wanted to find your father! You weren't planning to run, were you?" He spun her around and pressed her against the edge of an empty table with his body. The skin on his face was creased from his sleeve, and she could see the blood vessels along the side of his cheek begin to swell and turn purple. "Do you think you would have gone very far?"

The edge of the table cut into her buttocks, and there was no way she could avoid the hardness that swelled in the front of his trousers. He slid one thick hand beneath the front of her bodice and squeezed the firm swell of her breast. When she cried out in protest, he stepped back, a look of disgust on his face. "Whore! Is there any perversion you haven't experienced? God! And to think I wanted to marry you!" The last sentence was barely a whisper.

"Adam, please. It's all lies! Whatever Nurev told you— it's all lies! The Tsar wanted to get even with me for. . . ."

He stopped her with a blow that sent her reeling toward the next table. "Lies? Who are you to speak of lying?" She could see the veins pounding in his temples. "You learned to love from the Tsar? In what dungeon did you conjure up that dream? You served the Queen? Not the way you claimed!" He sucked in his breath with a groan. "I understand it all. The Tsar sent his personal apologies for involving me in his plan, but it wasn't necessary. I realized all along he needed someone he could trust to keep you in line—and to play along with you so you wouldn't suspect!" His lips had turned white, and there were blotches of red on his cheeks. "You thought I believed your stories? Fool! I knew what you were from the start!" His eyes dared her to contradict him.

Tanya bit her lips to hold back her protestations of innocence. They would fall on deaf ears, that was clear. Adam was too much in need of repairing his damaged self-respect. Lowering her head, she let his fury pour over her unresisting body. He stormed on, one-by-one retracting any kindnesses he had offered her in the past. He had avoided her bed because he wanted nothing to do with such a slut! He had deliberately lengthened their journey to add to her torment! And all the time he raved, his eyes told her of the pain and disappointment that filled his heart.

Abruptly, he grasped her arm. "You want to see your father's funeral? Nurev has made special arrangements so the old man won't be alone on his way to Hell! Come!" But first he scrambled up to her room to fetch her cloak.

She was pushed into the cool spring morning. Heedless of the puddles through which they stumbled, Adam dragged her up the street to the gates of the barracks. There, just inside the heavy iron fence, a hole had been dug. The young soldier who had been so kind to her the night before stood at its edge, her father's body in his arms. His jaw was set proudly, and when his eyes met hers, he held them calmly. Nurev stood across the courtyard, three men armed with rifles at his side.

Adam's voice was hard behind her. "Nurev left a message for you, my sweet. One you had best remember. The next time you ask for help, be sure it's from someone you despise. The penalty for assisting you is death!"

Sobbing, Tanya grasped the cold railing. "No! You can't do that! No!" Tears choked her voice, and she leaned

117

against the fence in hopeless misery. "Punish me, Nurev! Don't hurt any more innocent people!"

With a calculating smile, Nurev raised his arm. "Fire!"

The volley rang through the morning air, sending a flock of birds shrieking into the sky. Tanya screamed. The young soldier, his gory burden still clutched to his breast, toppled forward into the pit. Immediately, a handful of ragged prisoners began to shovel dirt over the still bodies.

Roughly, Adam pulled her hands free of the fence. "So now you beg to be punished! Do you then feel shame for your misdeeds? Or do you cry for the wasted body of a man you had only once, when you found your father was of no more use to you? Bitch! Don't waste your tears on me!" Pushing her ahead, he wove his way through the crowded street toward the inn.

As they approached the courtyard, Tanya saw Ilya perched on the coach, his hands loosely grasping the reins. The horses switched their tails nervously from side to side. Even this early in the morning, the flies were already active.

Her foot slipped in a puddle and Adam jerked her free, throwing her roughly against the side of the carriage. "Get in, slut! Get in, and keep your distance from a gentleman! I'll find a use for you that will satisfy my honor, the Tsar's orders, and your desire for punishment. In the meantime, be warned. I'll listen no more to your tales of sorrow and hurt! I know you now for what you are—an unnatural woman without shame! A woman who falls in bed as easily as she lies, and who lies as easily as she takes a breath!"

She stumbled as he pushed her into the carriage, falling into a corner with a cry of pain. Swiftly, he climbed in beside her. "We go to my ship. *My* ship, where my word is law! Maybe, if you behave, I'll use you when I feel the need for release! But you can rest assured I will give you little pleasure. I know enough about females to recognize the difference between pleasure and pain."

Quivering, Tanya pulled her parka over her head, blotting out his red, angry face. She was thrown back as the carriage began to move, but she held herself tense, refusing to touch Adam as he lounged insolently beside her. She needed desperately to be alone, to think through all that had happened. Because she had displeased the Tsar, two men were dead: her father and an innocent youth whose only fault had been his sympathy for a sorrowing woman. Each move of her body, every breath she took, reminded her that they were gone. Closing her eyes, she prayed she would soon join them, for only by her own death did she feel she could make reparation for the part she had unwittingly played in theirs.

PART II

China

1795

CHAPTER I

The town of Okhotsk was as far from St. Petersburg in architecture as it was in kilometers. The weather-beaten buildings seemed to be losing their fight with the elements, and the dirt streets, wet from a spring rain, threatened to swallow the few carriages that dared to venture forth.

The people seemed totally unaware of their dismal surroundings. Free at last of the ice and cold of winter, they greeted each other with smiles and cheerful calls. As she passed them in the carriage, Tanya wished she could cry out to them for help. But the warning she had received in Viliuisk rang in her ears. Anyone who assisted her would surely die. And so, depressed and fearful, she permitted herself to be transported through the town to the wharf.

The docks, too, were alive with activity. Men were loading ships with an urgency that promised early sailings, and urchins, dirty and ragged, darted about between the laborers, stealing what they dared from unprotected pockets.

All activity on the ship came to a halt as the captain boarded, and all eyes watched as he ushered Tanya like a slave before him. Her flesh crawling, she stumbled onto the deck. It had been a nightmare of a journey.

The ship was a typical merchant vessel, round-bellied and clumsy, but it was clear that Adam considered it a beauty. He walked proudly to the hatch and pushed her ahead of him down the ladder. Even in her discomfort, Tanya noticed the two doors they passed and the copper plate with the words, *ADAM CZERWENKI, CAPTAIN*, on the door he finally opened.

He directed her to a mattress that lay in one corner of the room, and then he ascended to the deck. Left alone, she gazed about her. The cabin was not very large, and it was bare of all ornamentation. In the corner across from her was a bunk, a patchwork quilt folded neatly at one end. Beside it was a narrow shelf on which rested a ceramic pitcher and a large bowl, both held in place by a small railing.

In the center of the room was an enormous desk. Its surface was pitted and chipped as if it had seen many years of rugged use, but its ornamented drawers and legs told her it had once been a magnificent piece of furniture. Behind it was a deep, high-backed chair of brown leather. The entire cabin had a faint odor of tobacco and spice, not altogether unpleasant to her nostrils.

She rose timidly, swaying with the motion of the ship, and stumbled to the row of windows that lined the back of the cabin. Settling herself on the wide window seat, she stared out at the vanishing port. All possibility of escape was gone. Now she was at the mercy of Adam—and the unpredictable sea.

A sound in the passageway sent her scurrying back to her pallet. The door swung open and Adam strode to his desk without glancing in her direction. Behind him, a tray in his hands, trotted a lad of about fourteen. His hair framed his face in golden curls, but there was nothing simple or childlike in his glance. He showed a confidence, a self-control, that outshone the captain's brusque assertiveness.

He immediately began to set a place before the captain, and the aroma of fresh-cooked meat assailed Tanya's nose. Adam picked up a bone and began to chew noisily. With one bowl still on his tray, the lad looked up at the captain.

Adam gestured to Tanya. "Give it to her, Ivar, but—" He paused as the lad stopped in mid-motion and looked back. "—I'll say this but once. You are to feed her, and you'll see to it that the cabin is cleaned. But you are not to speak to her. Do you understand?"

"Yes, Captain!" Ivar glanced at Tanya and looked away. Silently, he handed her a dish of slop she felt certain was composed of leftovers from the crew's dinner.

When the boy left the room, Tanya turned to Adam. "Please, let me clean the cabin myself. I don't want. . . ."

His curse cut her short. "Who gives a damn what you want? The lad has his duties. You're not to interfere!"

Silently, she settled on her pallet and picked at her food. Hunger at last forced her to swallow bits she would have thrown to the dogs in the past. But even as she ate, she wondered why she bothered. What was left for her? Alexius? Adam would make sure she never had a chance to reach him!

Abruptly, Adam slammed his mug on his desk and rose to his feet. She held her breath until she heard the door close behind him. Then she rose and moved back to the windows. Sighing, she leaned her head against the cold glass. If only she could open one, she'd leap into the water. Her hand fumbled with the catch and suddenly the glass swung open.

She leaned forward, staring down into the dark water billowing and foaming below her, and she knew she couldn't go through with her decision. Life held nothing for her now—but hope was not entirely dead. Carefully, she drew back inside.

A hand touched her shoulder. "I'm glad you didn't jump. I was ready to catch you."

Startled, she looked up into Ivar's worried face. "How

did you get in? Go away! You'll only hurt yourself by talking to me!"

The lad's blue eyes glowed warmly. "Don't worry! The captain's on deck. He can't hear me."

"But he'll come back. Please, you don't know what you're doing."

"All right, but you mustn't do that again." He picked Adam's dishes from the desk and headed for the door. "I'll be back tomorrow. Don't give up, please."

When the golden sun had finally dropped below the horizon, Adam returned, a lamp in his hand. In the yellow glow his face appeared demoniac, and Tanya shuddered in apprehension. He stood in the center of the cabin, his eyes searching the shadow in which she huddled. When he found her he stepped forward. "Take off your clothes!" His voice was cold and hard.

She knew better than to hesitate. In the weeks since her father's death, she had come to realize the extent of Adam's resentment. He had made it clear that he would not soon forgive—or forget—how arrogantly she had manipulated him on their trip from St. Petersburg. His pride had been severely injured, and now she was paying for her earlier denial to him of her sexual favors.

When she looked at him again, he was stripped of his trousers, his erect manhood demanding her attention. Dropping to his knees, he pushed her onto her back.

She lay quietly in his grasp, uncertain as to what was expected of her and afraid to make the wrong move. But he seemed hardly aware of her presence. Fumbling clumsily, he pushed himself between her thighs. "No. . . ." Her voice was filled with pleading.

His hand crashed down on her cheek, throwing her head against the mattress. "Shut up, slut! Open your legs for your master!"

Quickly, she did as she was told, steeling herself against the tearing pain of his sudden entry. Grunting like a rutting pig, he increased the speed of his thrusts, pushing her farther and farther into the corner.

Tensing her jaw, she prayed for unconsciousness, but her supplications went unanswered. He began to sweat, and

126

drops of perspiration ran down his body, spreading over her stomach and dropping onto her breasts. She coughed. The sour smell of his unwashed skin was overwhelming.

His coarse hair scratched the soft velvet of her stomach as he ground himself deeper against her and then, with a groan, lowered himself onto her body, pressing her into the mattress. She lay still, waiting for him to leave her, praying it would be over soon.

Suddenly, a spasm shook his body and he lay heavily above her, almost smothering her with the weight of his shoulders. Another spasm, and she felt as if she was being hammered into the floor. Then, unexpectedly, he was still.

She lay quietly, afraid to move, afraid even to take a breath. Her head was reeling from lack of air. Darkness, blessed darkness, closed in.

Abruptly, he rose, and her breath returned. He towered above her, his legs braced against the rolling of the deck. "Tomorrow you will be ready—at sunset. I have no words to waste on a slut like you!" Grabbing her blanket, he rubbed it over his abdomen and then, without glancing at her again, strode across the cabin, fell on his bunk, and was instantly asleep.

Trembling, she rose to her feet and crept to the pitcher which Ivar had filled. Dipping a corner of her skirt into the water, she scrubbed her body, washing away the stench of his sweat and his semen. Then, shivering, she scurried back to her bed.

She lay tense and sleepless, staring at the pattern of light the ocean threw on the ceiling and listening to the movements of the sailors overhead. The creaking of the beams as the ship glided steadily through the waves finally lulled her to sleep.

Her dreams, when they came, were filled with fear for Ivar, who seemed far too willing to risk his life to bring a little comfort into hers.

to the ship, he assured her, unless the sea was high, and, much to her relief, the passage went smoothly.

"We're sailing close to the Continent all the way, though you don't see it all the time." Ivar informed her one morning. "Soon we'll be passing Silla and Japan, though the passage is not as narrow as the last one. And then we'll circle around the belly of China, past Chuanchow, down to the Hsi River. We'll sail right up the river to Kwangchow."

Tanya wished she could ask Adam about the land they were approaching, and she remembered how helpful he had been when they first left St. Petersburg. If she had the journey to take again, she would deport herself differently.

It was too late now. He seldom spoke to her, even on those rare occasions when he took her. It was as if she was living with a stranger—a deaf-mute, who acknowledged her presence only when it suited his interest. Sometimes, she felt as if she was invisible! His silence, and his threat to destroy anyone who spoke to her, left her isolated—and terribly frightened.

One morning, as they finished breakfast, the ship began to pitch violently, throwing Tanya from her seat at the window. The waves were enormous, sometimes covering the porthole entirely. The whole ship was groaning under the strain of the high seas. She looked toward Adam, but he finished his food as if nothing important were happening.

Then he rose and pulled his greatcoat from a hook. The door slammed behind him. She heard him clump up the stairs to the deck, and pause to exchange words with John Sikorski, the first mate, who was just going off duty.

Tanya turned toward the porthole. She'd seen John Sikorski briefly when she boarded the ship. The narrowed eyes in the sharp, compact face had ogled her shamelessly. But what had most attracted her notice was the whip that hung like an extension of his right arm, its length coiled like a snake in his hand. Ivar had told her the first mate always carried the whip, and used it freely to emphasize his orders.

There was nothing remarkable about the exchange that had taken place in the corridor. In the weeks at sea, Tanya had grown accustomed to the ship's routine. She was sure, now, that Adam would not return for at least five hours, and that Sikorski would sleep a full seven.

The door behind her opened. "Tanya, how are you taking the storm?" Ivar hurried to her side. "Are you nauseated?"

"No. I'm fine. Are we going to sink?"

He laughed lightly. "This isn't a bad storm. We've been through many far worse!" Dropping his cleaning rags on the desk, he settled beside her. "Do you know where we are now?"

"No. It looks as if we're at the bottom of the ocean!"

"We're only a week out of Kwanchow. People who don't know the Chinese name call it Canton. It's the only place in China where foreigners are allowed to trade. Captain Czerwenki stops there every voyage to trade his furs for silks and jade which he carries to Russia—or to General Baranov, the Governor of the Russian-American colony in the Aleutians. He gets opium from Canton, too, and brings it to the Sandwich Islands. The natives love it, though their chiefs do not approve."

"Why should they object?"

"Opium's a drug that rots a man's mind. Once I went ashore in Canton and saw an opium house. There were men lying all over the floor, smoking pipes. Some of them hadn't eaten in days."

The motion of the ship stilled and he leaned closer to her. "That's not what I came to talk about. When we get to Canton, I'm going to arrange for you to get aboard another ship. I don't know exactly when it'll happen, but at least one night the captain will be—occupied."

"Ivar, please. I told you to leave me alone! You'll get yourself killed!"

He went on as if she hadn't spoken. "You'll have to be ready. Just don't worry. I'll let you know in time." He rose, bracing his feet against the even roll of the ship. "You see," he continued, "the captain always. . . ."

The door flew open. "Aha!" Adam's voice echoed in the bare room. "I leave you alone for ten minutes—even with a child—and you try to catch him in your web. Can't you keep your filthy hands off anyone?"

Rising, Tanya advanced toward Adam, interposing herself between him and the lad. "It wasn't that at all. Ivar was just . . . cleaning. . . ."

Adam looked past her and fastened the boy with his eyes. "Ivar, have you disobeyed my orders?"

Tanya stretched her arms and pulled at Adam's coat. "Please. . . . He was just. . . ."

"Ivar?" The question rang through the cabin like a shot.

"Yes, sir!" Ivar's voice was calm. "Yes, sir, I have."

"At least you don't lie!" Adam glanced down at Tanya in disgust. He towered above her, his temples throbbing. "Sikorski!" His voice was filled with fury.

There was a scuffling in the passageway. Sikorski's face appeared, blinking; he was running a hand through his rumpled hair. "Yes, sir?"

"It seems Ivar has forgotten his respect for the ship's discipline."

Sikorski was instantly alert. Turning toward the dark passage, he shouted a command. "Take him!"

Immediately, two sailors stepped inside. Tanya tugged at Adam once more. "Please, Adam! It isn't his fault! Please!" Her voice rose to a scream, but he paid no heed.

Ivar had not waited for the sailors to reach his side. Holding his head high, he strode from the room. His two guards followed silently behind.

Adam stood for a moment, staring down into Tanya's face. "It appears you take pleasure in bringing trouble to others. You'll come with me." Pushing her ahead, he moved toward Sikorski. "Lead the way, John. You can let the cat loose this time."

Sikorski's laugh sent a shiver of fear up Tanya's spine as they climbed through the hatch to the deck.

When they arrived topside, Ivar was already tied to the mast, his arms high above his head, his back bare. Tanya slipped on the wet planks and grabbed a rope for support, but Adam ignored her. Taking a post where he could watch both Sikorski and Ivar, he pulled her to his side.

Sikorski approached his newest victim like a panther circling its prey. He prowled around the helpless boy, the whip twisting in his hand as if it were alive. He flicked the feathered tip against the bare wooden deck, where it left lines. Sikorski's eyes, staring at Ivar's back, glowed with sensuous fire.

Slowly, the whip curled through the air and landed on the slender shoulders. Ivar winced, but the cry came from Tanya's lips. "Oh!"

Adam signaled her to be silent.

"One." It was a whisper that rose from the circle, yet she could see no lips move.

Again the whip rose in the air. Slowly it moved up and then, with a flick, crashed down, whistling as it fell. "Two."

Tanya bit her lip to hold back another cry. Her fists were clenched, and she trembled so violently, she feared Adam would notice. But he stared ahead at his first mate.

The next blows came fast, each one cutting slightly below the one that preceded it. "Three." "Four." "Five." With each blow, Ivar's body jerked and the flow of blood grew from a trickle to a stream. Frantic with terror, Tanya turned toward Adam, but she couldn't make him meet her pleading eyes. The whispering count continued. "Six." "Seven."

In the pause that followed, Ivar lifted his head, his eyes searching for her in the crowd. When he caught her attention, he smiled proudly, his steady gaze forcing her to acknowledge his strength. His lips formed one word. "Courage." Then the whip landed again on his tattered back. "Eight!"

Sucking in her breath, Tanya stared transfixed. The cruelty she had seen before had always been directed at men— by men. But to whip a child for her misdeeds! Yet, Ivar's single word burned in her heart. His body was bleeding and torn, but he could still urge her to have courage!

Once more the whip rose in the air. "Nine." She closed her eyes, suddenly aware of the smell of fear that surrounded her. Adam might force her to remain where she was, but he couldn't make her watch. "Ten." The word was like a sigh.

A cry started behind her and spread through the circle of men. Startled, she opened her eyes. The last lash had cut crossways over the torn back, leaving the skin in shreds.

Sikorski let the whip fall to his side. His body was limp, and his face was drained of all its passion.

"Cut him down." Adam's voice was hard in the stillness that followed. As the small victim fell to the deck, he leaned forward. "Is he still alive?"

"Yes, sir!"

"Good! Throw him in the hold!" Adam paused and fastened his eyes on Tanya. "Put the woman with him!" Without meeting her pleading glance, he turned on his heel and disappeared into the darkness of the passageway leading to the officers' quarters.

CHAPTER III

Tanya sat up in alarm. "Ivar!" She watched as the lad yawned and gingerly rose to his feet. "What's happening?" The hold shook with a thundering rumble, and when it stopped the heavy pounding of the waves to which she had grown so accustomed was gone.

"Landfall! We must be in Canton harbor." Ivar moved slowly toward the ladder, dimly lit by the crosswork of the open hatch. "We'll only have a few days, so we'd better be ready."

"Ready? For what?" Tanya wiped the perspiration from her face. She had grown accustomed to the stagnant smell of the hold, but the heat was unbearable.

"To move you to another ship. Don't you remember?"

"But you can't do that! We're prisoners here!"

"We won't be for long. You just wait—and be ready."

Sikorski's voice barked out, and footsteps sounded on the deck. Suddenly there was a dull thud. The whole boat shuddered and groaned—and then settled into a slow, quiet roll.

Ivar grabbed the ladder for support. "We're tied to the dock. They'll start trading as soon as the Governor arrives."

"The Governor?"

"Yes. Chung Kai Chang, the Governor of Guandong Province. He doesn't actually handle the trading. He comes to play *pochem* with the captain, while the trading is going on."

She rose to her feet. Ivar seemed so sure they'd be released—and strong enough already to resume his duties. His back was still raw, but the bleeding had stopped and the scabs appeared healthy.

In the days and nights of nursing the boy in the rat-infested hold, she had come to accept her hatred of Adam, and had vowed to herself that if the opportunity came, she would kill him. Gathering up the blanket she and Ivar had shared, she gazed up toward the sunlight. Release couldn't come too soon.

Suddenly, the hatch was thrown open and a man descended. "Captain wants you. Make it fast!"

Shielding her eyes against the brightness, Tanya stumbled on deck. The air was hot and still—and thick with strange odors and noises. But at least she could see the sky again.

Sikorski sent Ivar to the crew's quarters in the fo'c'sle and Tanya to the captain's cabin. She moved slowly, not the least bit eager to learn what fate Adam had chosen for her.

The cabin was empty, but all of her possessions remained as she had left them. Relieved, she stripped and scrubbed the filth of the hold from her skin. She expected Adam to arrive any moment, demanding her submission, but no one entered, and she finished dressing without interruption.

She chose her loveliest gown, a pale blue silk edged with

white lace. Pinning her broach on the ruffle that bordered the low-cut neck, she studied herself in the small mirror. She was definitely thinner—and very pale. But it felt good to be clean and groomed once more. Unbraiding her hair, she combed it carefully and pinned it up in a huge puff.

Her toilette was interrupted by a gentle knock on the door. "Tanya, it's Ivar. Are you dressed?"

"Yes, but—"

Ivar stepped inside. "Don't worry. Captain sent me. He wants you on deck. The Governor will be here shortly."

The deck was bustling with activity. Sample bales had been carried from the hold and stacked near the railing. In the middle of the poop deck a table had been set out and Adam, dressed in his most elegant uniform, stood beside it.

As they emerged from the hatch, Ivar gestured toward the small boats that scooted about in the harbor. "Those are the junks I told you about. People live on them." He paused. "You'll be standing beside me during the game."

Adam glanced briefly in her direction and then turned his attention to the wharf. Four enormous Chinamen, dressed in red, gold and purple uniforms and carrying large bronze swords were emerging from the shadows. Each wore shoes with lifts that raised his feet above the slime of the street.

Behind the soldiers came an ornate sedan chair, not too different from those used in St. Petersburg by ladies of fashion. And behind that came another line of Chinese men. The first ten looked like a flock of colorful butterflies, their large fans fluttering in steady rhythm. The last twenty were garbed in faded blue, their bare feet as dirty as the mud through which they walked. Each carried a large bale on his head.

The procession pushed its way through a drab crowd that paid little attention to its passage. As it advanced, Tanya realized that every man in sight had a long black braid down the center of his back.

The bo's'n's whistle sounded shrilly and the sailors, all surprisingly clean and neat, stood at attention. Sikorski saluted as Governor Chung Kai Chang climbed over the railing and walked sedately aft to where Adam waited.

The Manchu was dressed in a straight-cut yellow silk gown that all but covered his brightly decorated cloth shoes. Wide bands of deep blue trimmed with embroidered storks and flowers edged the hem and cuffs and followed the braided buttons that cut diagonally across his chest and down under one arm. His hands were crossed over his stomach. The long pockets at his wrists bounced forward as he walked.

Under a bright red-domed head-dress, his black hair was neatly combed into the same long braid she had seen on the men in his retinue. His thick black mustache curled down in a circle over his wide, sensuous lips, and his dark, straight brows accented the narrow high-bridged nose that identified him as a member of the Manchu ruling class. His eyes were not slanted.

"Ah, Captain Czerwenki! This humble person is most honored by your invitation." Chung bowed low from the waist. "I pray you will find something in our unworthy warehouse that will interest you."

Adam bowed awkwardly. "I'm sure we'll both profit by our trading. We always do." His hand strayed to a deck of cards that lay near his elbow. "Shall we begin?"

"Ah, captain, impatient, as usual! First we must share some peach wine, for it is the peach that brings longevity. Then, as we entertain ourselves, our menials can tend to the mundane matter of trade."

Chung clapped his hands and immediately a slender bottle of golden liquid was placed on the table. Glasses were produced and filled. As the two men sat down and lifted their goblets to their lips, another servant placed a small metal dish on the table near Chung's elbow. He stuck a thin stick upright in the center and then, striking a flint, lit its end. A sweet fragrance filled the air.

Ivar nudged Tanya. Following his surreptitious gesture, she glanced across the bow of the ship. There, riding at anchor at the next dock was another vessel, a British flag flying from its mast. "That's the one." Ivar leaned close. "You'll sail with it."

She glanced sharply about, but no one seemed to have noticed their conversation. Everyone was watching Chung, who just then waved his arms authoritatively. Immediately, bales of cloth were carried up onto the deck and placed close to where Sikorski and one of the Manchu attendants waited. The trading had begun.

Chung leaned back in his chair and gazed indolently at the activity on the lower deck. He sipped his wine slowly, savoring every drop, and occasionally leaned toward the incense and inhaled deeply.

Tanya couldn't see Adam's expression, but she could tell by the way he fidgeted in his seat that he took no pleasure in watching Sikorski handle a task he preferred to perform himself. Yet, she realized, he dared not lose face by participating in work his guest avoided.

Tanya shifted nervously from one foot to the other and glanced at Ivar. His face was pale, but he stood patiently, as did all the other observers of this strange ritual. The wind shifted, blowing the incense in their direction. Tanya felt a mild nausea. It had been far too long since she had eaten.

A junk slipped swiftly past. The voices that drifted up were oddly sharp and abrupt, their sing-song lilt strange to Tanya's ears. The odor of fresh-cooked vegetables wafted past, and her stomach growled.

Embarrassed, she glanced nervously at the faces of Chung's retainers. They stood silently behind their master, their yellow skin like wax in the late afternoon light. She found it difficult to acknowledge that they were live men and not a row of statues. Not one of them bothered to meet her glance.

Suddenly Sikorski and the Chinaman bowed to each other and turned toward the poop deck. "The trading is done, captain!" Sikorski's voice had a ring of triumph, but Tanya caught the spark that passed between Chung and his silent representative.

Adam picked up the cards, "Good! Have you time for a game or two?"

Chung nodded gracefully, his face devoid of all expression. "You do me a great honor to play cards with me. I am an unworthy opponent."

Without answering, Adam began to slap the cards down on the table.

Tanya watched the two men with undisguised fascination. There was a marked difference in the way they played. Adam was intense, his entire attention focused on his cards. His back was stiff. He was working his jaw fiercely with each play.

Chung, on the contrary, made his every move a gentle flow, as if he were performing a dance with his fingers. His long nails clicked together in a complex rhythm. His expression was inscrutable. He neither smiled when he won nor frowned when he lost, yet there was a complacency about him that convinced Tanya that he was enjoying himself immensely.

Each time a hand was completed, Chung's eyes swept the crowd of men who stood behind the captain. Once Tanya was certain they had come to rest on her, yet, when she smiled, they strayed.

"My game!" Chung gathered the coins that had been thrown onto the table. Gesturing for Adam to deal once more, he let his hands rest before him.

He won the next two games, but lost the fourth. It seemed clear to Tanya that with a wisdom shown by few good gamblers, Chung was giving just enough to his opponent to keep him playing. But as the afternoon turned into evening, Adam grew more and more impatient and his losses mounted.

When the moon hung low over the mast like a big silver shield, Chung drew a small bag from his sleeve. With a grand gesture, he leaned forward. "One more game, my friend. Then I have a gift for you." Seven large gold disks dropped onto the table.

Adam dug deep into his pocket and drew out a matching handful of coins. Picking up the cards, he began to deal. "I, too, have a gift. But I suspect mine will be more of a surprise."

The game differed little from those preceding it. Chung,

calm and graceful, deliberately allowed Adam to win, and when the captain gathered up the gold pieces, Tanya realized little money had been lost by either man, all due to the skill and design of the Manchu.

The cards were put aside and more wine was poured. Shifting once more to ease her tired feet, Tanya gazed about the deck. She'd been standing for hours, and she was weak from hunger and thirst. She could see that Ivar was feeling the strain, too. His peaked face was drawn and set, and his hands were clenched into tight fists. But the torment would soon be over. An exchange of gifts—and the visitors would depart.

Chung waved his hand, and one of his men stepped forward with a small wooden cabinet covered with intricate carvings which, bowing deeply, he placed on the table before Adam. "A bit of the sweet sleep you find so attractive, my good friend." Chung's voice was like velvet. "Unworthy as I am, I have found it most delightful. You will do me great honor if you accept this worthless present."

Ivar leaned close to Tanya's ear. "Opium. He smokes it one night each time we're in Canton. That's how I'll be able to get you off the ship. Everyone will be ashore—at the brothels."

Adam's chair scraped on the deck.

Tanya felt suddenly uneasy. Something was wrong! Adam had said he had a gift, too—yet no package had been brought to the table. She glanced about the deck and almost missed his next move.

Turning from his guest, Adam waved Tanya forward. Then turning to Chung, he bowed awkwardly. "Now, my friend, for my surprise."

A terror that stopped Tanya's breath clutched at her chest and slowed her steps.

"If you recall, my friend—" Adam's cunning smile was directed at Tanya. "—on my last visit you expressed an interest in an Occidental woman. At the time, I said I couldn't bring you one worthy of your consideration. But fortune has put just the right female into my possession." He took Tanya's limp hand into his and pulled her to his

143

side. "She's nobly born and beautiful by our standards. She isn't a virgin, but she can be obedient when properly handled."

A scream built up in Tanya's throat, but she forced it back. Her brain seemed clouded, as if she were in the middle of a terrible nightmare. Fixing her eyes on Adam's red face, she struggled to understand what was happening.

Chung bowed once more from the waist. "This humble creature thanks you for considering his worthless desires. She is far lovelier than I had ever hoped." He paused, looking at Tanya in silence, his expression showing neither approval nor dissatisfaction. Then his eyes shifted back to Adam. "I will send my men to the docks at sunup to begin the unloading. High tide is at noon. All transactions should be finished in time for you to sail."

For one ecstatic moment, Tanya thought Chung had rejected Adam's offer, and then she saw that two of his men remained. Hardly aware of her actions, she grabbed Adam's sleeve and tugged on it frantically. "Please, Adam! You can't do this!" Her voice rose in terror. "I know I've offended you, but I'll make amends! Please don't send me away! Don't give me to this heathen! I'll do anything you want—anything!"

Shaking his arm, he pushed her toward the waiting Chinese. "You'll do anything I want, will you? Then go with your new master. You'll not escape so easily over the walls of his harem, nor will Ivar find it a simple task to transfer you from there to the deck of another ship!"

The fog vanished from her brain. Once more she had been trapped—and once more she had dragged another down with her! Terrified, she dropped to her knees, clutching at the skirt of Adam's coat. "No! He's just a child! He didn't mean what he said! Please, don't punish him because of me! Not again!"

A bitter smile touched Adam's lips. His eyes flicked quickly over Ivar's slender frame. Then a hard smile touched his lips. "His failure is punishment enough! You have taught me to understand the mind of a nobleman!" Swinging her to her feet, he pulled the broach from her bosom. "This is mine. Chung has wealth enough without it." Clutching the jewel in his fist, he turned his back to her outstretched hands.

She felt herself lifted by four silk-clad arms and carried across the deck. The scream she had suppressed tore through her throat and she kicked wildly, but no one moved to help her. Then her two captors grabbed her legs and carried her spread-eagled down to the dock.

As she approached the sedan chair, she turned for one last glimpse of the *Russian Princess*, rolling heavily in the water, the waves thugging ponderously against her bobbing hull. Ivar was leaning over the railing, his sensitive face wracked with agony. "I'll save you, Tanya!" His youthful voice broke. "I'll come back and rescue you, I promise!"

Behind him, Adam's laughter echoed coldly in the darkness.

CHAPTER IV

"Open the gates!" The cry broke the stillness that had surrounded Tanya from the moment she settled herself beside her new master and the heavy curtains had fallen into place. Now she reached out to part them, but her companion's hand stopped her movement.

"No, little dove. You must learn the ways of your new country. It is not fitting that the eyes of ordinary men should ever again rest on you, for you are the chosen of Chung Kai Chang, the Governor of Guandong Province. I am your master—and the source of all your pleasure. I leave you soon. You will wait until the eunuchs bring you into the walls of the women's compound, where you will live henceforth with my other wives."

There was the sound of heavy gates opening and the

scurrying of many feet. Then the chair was lifted up and propelled forward. When they stopped again, Chung slipped out, closing the curtains behind him. Immediately, the chair swayed forward. It passed through another gate and then, at last, it was lowered to the ground. Delicate hands pulled aside the curtains. Tanya had reached her new home.

The air was sweet with incense and jasmine, and the room, far too large for her to see at a glance, was lit by many tiny lanterns. A circle of women surrounded her. All were dressed in ornate gowns, much like Chung's, but without the large pockets on the sleeves. Their straight black hair was braided and formed into knots just behind their ears, but the severe style did nothing to spoil their beauty; it only served to emphasize the high cheekbones and almond-shaped eyes.

The closest girl, not more than twelve years of age, looked at Tanya with large solemn eyes that held a mixture of curiosity and fright. It was she who first reached out and felt the material of Tanya's gown.

Immediately, many other hands joined hers, pulling and prodding, like graceful doves settling down on some new perch. Tanya gazed about her in dismay. She was an oddity—a novel creature to be tested and played with. But not one face showed any sign of friendliness.

She lowered herself to the floor and stepped from her concealment. The circle retreated, swaying gracefully. Tanya's eyes followed their shuffling feet. Every one was tiny—as if it belonged to a four-year-old. And their shoes, delicately covered with embroidery, looked like fine, dainty gloves!

Suddenly the circle parted and a girl about Tanya's age stepped forward. "*How bu how?*" Her voice was soft and musical, and the smile that accompanied it offered a warm welcome.

Tanya looked puzzled. "How?"

"Aha!" All the women tittered lightly.

Immediately, the girl who had spoken began chattering smoothly, her voice rising and falling in musical cadences. Tanya contented herself with watching the delicate fea-

148

tures and dark, soulful eyes. She was a lovely girl, yet Tanya sensed a firmness beneath the soft exterior.

When at last the greeting was finished, Tanya gestured helplessly. "I'm sorry. I don't speak Chinese."

"Ah! You are Russian!"

"Yes." Tanya felt totally confused. "Where did you learn to speak my language?"

"The master taught me. He feels it can be helpful for a woman to know the language of foreigners. What's your name? I'm called Mei Ling."

"I'm Tanya. Tanya Ivanovich."

"Tan Ya. It is a nice name. Has it a meaning?"

Tanya frowned.

"I forget foreigners aren't called Little Flower or Flying Bird, as we are." Mei Ling smiled ·condescendingly. "Come, you must meet the old one."

Everywhere, beauty vied for Tanya's attention. The doors through which she had passed were thick with carvings, and the wood from which they were made glowed like satin. Small alcoves held figures made of delicate stone, pink, lavender, and green, that shone in the candlelight.

Mei Ling paused before one, a pale green statue of a woman. "This is the Queen of the West, the great Hsi Wang Mu. It is she who confers immortality on those she finds worthy." She moved to another, made of delicate ivory. "And this is Kuan Yin, the goddess of fertility." Her tone and demeanor showed that Kuan Yin was her favorite.

Tanya felt in no mood for a tour. "Is there a place where I can rest—and perhaps eat?"

A ghost of a frown touched the delicate features, but the voice didn't waver. "You'll sleep between me and Sing Fa. And we will have fruit before bedtime. But now you must show yourself to the old one, Chung Mei Yang. Come."

They advanced toward a screen that at first appeared to be made of thin paper cut into intricate designs. It was of clear jade. Mei Ling dropped to her knees. "Tan Ya, crawl as I do. I will touch your shoulder when it is time for you to rise."

Just beyond the screen was a small chamber lit with the faint glow of oil lamps and rich with the fragrance of perfume. On a red-draped bed sat a creature so old, wrinkled, and immobile that Tanya doubted it was alive. But it moved suddenly, waving a hand in her direction. A harsh voice cut through the soft hum of female voices. Mei Ling touched Tanya's shoulder.

Tanya was relieved to stand. But she stumbled as her foot caught on the hem of her long skirt, and she reached out to steady herself.

The wrinkled face dissolved in a toothless grin. From inside a deep blue sleeve a bony hand reached out and pointed at her unsteadily. Tanya felt as if she were looking into the face of a skull from which the skin had not yet fallen. The harsh voice rose in angry cadence.

"Bow your head!" Mei Ling hissed. "Kneel and crawl out the way you came. You have displeased the old one. It isn't seemly for a new concubine to look her in the face."

Nervous and upset, Tanya did as she was told. To her surprise she found crawling backwards easier, since her skirt did not catch under her knees. She waited restlessly until Mei Ling rejoined her. The girl seemed somewhat mollified. "I explained as best I could." She spoke quietly. "The mistress doesn't approve of the master Chung Kai Chang's interest in foreign women. Last year he bought a concubine from India, and she was nothing but trouble. At last, one of the eunuchs poisoned her."

"How terrible!" Tanya felt a wave of apprehension. "What did she do?"

Mei Ling shrugged her shoulders. "She was slow to learn our customs—and she offended the gods."

Tanya's uneasiness increased. How could she avoid arousing the same antagonisms? "But didn't Chung Kai Chang protect her?"

"You will call the Governor of Guandong Province, the Great Chung Kai Chang, *master*!" Mei Ling snapped, her eyes suddenly dark and angry. Then abruptly, her expression calmed. "He has no interest in governing the harem. That is a woman's duty, and has been assumed by his mother. It is she, the old one, Chung Mei Yan, who rules our lives. They are in her hands."

Tanya walked along silently beside her new friend. She

had hardly arrived in the women's compound, but she was already certain that she had to escape. As quickly as she could, she would learn what she had to know to survive—and to gain her freedom. "Are all the men who enter the compound eunuchs?"

"All of them." Mei Ling lowered her voice. "They aren't to be trusted—unless you can bribe them with great wealth." She glanced about, suddenly nervous. "They watch us constantly."

Voices from across the compound called merrily. Immediately, Mei Ling quickened her pace. "We must help prepare Ling Hsu. She has been called to the master's bed tonight."

Tanya and Mei Ling watched as three other women assisted Ling Hsu, the twelve-year-old girl, to strip and bathe. The child showed some nervousness, but she held her head high as special herbs were used to scrub her genitals, her underarms, and her ears. Then a different perfume was applied to each part of her body. All the while, she seemed to be listening intently to the chattering of those about her.

Mei Ling turned to Tanya. "They are telling Ling Hsu of the pleasure that lies ahead and what she must do to please her master. Her maidenhead has already been broken—" She gestured toward a wooden phallus that protruded from a statue in the center of the room. "It brings honor on us all when a new wife is taught well."

Tanya looked at the slender, childish body, and the fine sprinkling of black hairs on its pelvis. "How long has she been here?"

"She arrived last week. Every nobleman is different. Some keep their women separate and take their new wives quickly after they arrive. Our master is wise and kind. He allows us to be together—and he values beauty and pleasure too much to risk unpleasantness through haste."

The great doors that led to Chung's quarters opened and a single eunuch approached. "The master awaits Ling Hsu!"

The attendants draped the young body with a transparent silk embroidered with leaping fish that symbolized felicity and fertility. It floated down around her shoulders like a

151

mist. Then, with her head high, the child followed the eunuch from the room. Only a slight tremor in her lips told of her apprehension. The remaining women settled once more into quiet conversation.

Mei Ling led Tanya to her pallet. "This is where you will sleep. There is fruit beside your bed to still your hunger." She gestured toward a young girl on the other side of Tanya's bed. "That is Sing Fa."

The slender girl glanced up at Tanya with big, liquid eyes. When she met Tanya's gaze, she looked down shyly and resumed her embroidery. Mei Ling settled on her own bed. "Tomorrow I will show you how to insert the *ben wa*." She paused. "I don't know when the old one will decide to beautify your feet."

Tanya bit into a ripe, juicy peach. Her mind was racing. The way Mei Ling had looked as she spoke, the *ben wa* seemed to be something pleasant. But beautifying her feet? She knew she would sooner die than have her feet broken, and she decided to speak to Chung about it as soon as she could. But when would she have a chance to see the master? And if he was accustomed to leave the women in his mother's charge, would he interfere on her behalf?

Tanya realized that only time would bring the answers to most of her questions. When Mei Ling lay back and closed her eyes, Tanya settled herself to sleep. She was far more tired than she had realized.

But her worries upset her rest. Her dreams were filled with visions of tiny feet that surrounded her like a magic ring, denying her any freedom.

Once she awoke to hear Sing Fa moaning quietly. The girl's coverlet had fallen from her body and she was working her fingers swiftly between her legs. The sweet fragrance of feminine juices filled Tanya's nostrils, and stirred her own sensuality. Disturbed, yet fearful of rousing Mei Ling, Tanya lay awake long after Sing Fa dropped into a deep sleep. The few pale lamps that glowed in the corners of the large room seemed overly bright. A nightingale sang in the garden. The unrest that had been stirred by Sing Fa's actions kept her in a turmoil.

Tanya stared at the dimly lit statue of Hsi Wang Mu that

glowed in the alcove at her feet. Folding her hands, she began to pray to the Holy Virgin for the courage to persist in her search for freedom.

"Tan Ya. Get up! The old one has no patience with lazy women!"

Tanya opened her eyes and looked up at Mei Ling. Her dreams had been of home. Home—and Alexius. As the reality of her imprisonment returned, she began to tremble.

Mei Ling touched her lightly. "Don't be afraid. Here, I have brought you a proper dress. The one you came in was too tight. It would destroy your body and make you useless for childbearing. And I've spoken to the old one again. She's decided to let you stay, as long as I teach you. So we must begin right away. Here, take these. This is the *ben wa* I promised you." She put three small ivory balls in Tanya's hand. "You must put these far up in your vagina. They will teach you the joy of an aroused body. Your beauty will increase. Then we will fix your hair."

Uncertainly, Tanya took the balls and did as she was told. They felt strange at first, and then she began to feel a warmth in her genitals that sent waves of pleasure throughout her body. Her cheeks grew bright, and she began to move slowly back and forth in a gentle rhythm. Such pleasure she hadn't felt since, as a child, she had stirred her own responses with her fingers as Sing Fa had done the night before.

The gown Mei Ling provided was made of fine satin covered with ornate embroidery and lined with a thin silk material that caressed Tanya's skin like the feathery touch of a baby's hand. It hung loosely about her hips, pressing ever so lightly on her mound of venus, and brushing against her legs every time she moved. Never had she felt any cloth so deliciously soft and erotic, and she was thankful that she had been given no undergarments to interfere with her enjoyment of her new robe. The entire gown was so light that she felt as if she were naked, and that sensation, too, increased her sensuousness.

Already, she was learning a most important fact of Chinese life. Women were erotic objects, whose duty it was to give pleasure to men. They were expected to keep themselves in readiness for masculine contact even though weeks might pass between visits with the master. Childbearing was the only excuse for refusing the master's call.

Next, Mei Ling began to comb Tanya's long black hair. She combed it into two sections, divided by a part reaching from Tanya's forehead to the nape of her neck. Each section she divided into three parts and braided them. She curled the braids behind Tanya's ears in the style of all the other women, and fastened them with small hairpins decorated with butterflies.

Mei Ling spoke of love and of the special techniques the master preferred. "You must remember that it is the master's pleasure that is important. He must be served. A woman who values her own satisfactions above those of her lord is worthless."

At nightfall, when Mei Ling unbound her feet to clean and perfume them, Tanya saw the misshapen, broken arches and the toes that had been forced back until the smallest touched the heel. "Mei Ling, didn't that hurt?"

"Of course." Mei Ling's tone was smooth. "But to be beautiful, it is necessary that the feet be bound. Mine were first wrapped when I was three. That is why mine are smaller than some of the others."

"Three! But then you couldn't play—or run about!"

"I cried myself to sleep every night. I was such a foolish one! Then at last my grandmother came and explained to me how important it was. I'm not the daughter of a prince, like Ling Hsu, but I come from a good family." She paused, a shy smile lighting her face. "The master has written a poem praising the way I sway when I walk. May I speak it to you?"

Tanya nodded.

Mei Ling stared at the flowering pear tree in the garden outside their window.

> Like a willow swaying in the gentle breeze
> so walks the lady Mei Ling, my bride.
> The branches above her sway in jealous imitation,
> for they know they cannot equal her grace.

She looked once more into Tanya's face. "It is a great honor the master bestowed on me."

Tanya asked, "Were the feet of the woman from India bound?"

"No, of course not! But the old one insisted that we do it. The foolish girl fought the eunuch when he began to bind her up." Mei Ling frowned. "You have not said you liked my poem."

"It is beautiful. I only regret that a Chinese woman must suffer so much before she is considered charming."

Mei Ling smiled condescendingly. "You will learn, Tan Ya. There is much you must learn."

That night Tanya's dreams were filled with the pain of broken bones and tight bandages.

In the morning she was subdued. She took no pleasure in the softness of the silk against her bare skin, nor in the embroidered fish, their fins entwined to symbolize domestic felicity, faithfulness, wealth, and abundance, which decorated the borders.

In the garden, she bowed low to each of the seven gods who guarded the doors. Two small boys tumbled out of the weeping willow tree by the pond, almost knocking her down. She stifled her protest. Mei Ling had warned her against interfering with the children. They ran on.

Pensively, she sat on a bench by the tree and let her gaze follow the graceful branches to the crown that towered high above the walls that enclosed her. Just at the point where a branch touched the top of the wall stood a guard eunuch, a bright sword flashing in the sun. All routes to freedom were well guarded. She would have to bide her time—and pray that some miracle would save her from the ever-present threat of being crippled.

CHAPTER V

———

Many days passed, yet Chung sent no order for her to attend him. Tanya worried. If Chung lost interest in her and the novelty of her foreign blood, the old one might take charge. Then her feet would certainly be broken. She had heard much about the old one's cruelty—much of it too bizarre to believe.

After she had been in the compound for a little over a week, she had a close encounter with the woman's vindictiveness. It started when Tanya was awakened by a moan that sounded close to her ear. She glanced toward Sing Fa's bed.

What she saw wiped the sleep from her eyes. The bed normally occupied by one girl now harbored two bodies, closely entwined and moving together in the unmistakable

157

rhythm of sexual excitement. The quick breath and the moans of pleasure, though stifled, sent a shiver of response through Tanya's body. Gently—quietly—she shifted her hips and felt the *ben wa* move within her. The moistness it created increased, and she dropped her hand between her legs, moving her fingers in time to the pounding of her heart.

The shapeless form beneath the blanket moved, and Tanya saw it was Sing Fa and Chi Guar. The older woman was positioned atop the fourteen-year-old, and was rotating her hips much as a man would have done, pushing and thrusting with grunts of pleasure. The sweet tangy odor of female body juices assailed Tanya's nostrils, adding to her own arousal, and bringing her mind and body to sharp awareness of the passion to which she was privy.

Then the light coverlet fell aside, revealing the nude torsos of the two women. They were writhing together, their genitals joined and their legs intertwined. Pendulous breasts hung down and brushed against Sing Fa's firm young mounds and Tanya, watching, touched her own breasts with one hand, gently rubbing the nipples to hardness.

A tremor of excitement ran through her body, and she felt herself jerk convulsively as she pressed her finger deep into her vagina. Her breathing quickened, and she closed her eyes in the ecstasy of sudden orgasm.

When she opened them again, the two women beside her had quickened their pace, and Tanya could see that Sing Fa was moving convulsively beneath the body of her lover. Suddenly the two stiffened and began to jerk violently. They twisted to one side and lay locked together, their moans interrupted only by the convulsions of their passion.

Once more, Tanya gave herself up to her own pleasure. Running her finger lightly over her stomach, she plunged it deep into her body. At the same time, she rolled her hips, her body tense with the strength of her response. And then she, like the two beside her, began to tremble and convulse. A moan escaped her lips, and she lay back. Her thoughts were no longer on the two women, but on the sweet manliness of her missing lover, Alexius.

"Chung Mei Yan! There is uncleanness in the house!"

Startled, Tanya looked up to see Mei Ling standing on her pallet, glaring at the two bed partners. Her normally gentle face was twisted with malice.

Immediately, the room burst into noise. Sing Fa and Chi Guar leaped up, their faces white with terror. Tanya could see the pleading in their eyes, and she looked at Mei Ling once more.

Her friend was unrecognizable. The vicious set of her jaw and the fire in her eyes showed no sign of softening under the imploring gaze of her wanton companions. Tanya felt a shiver of fear.

Suddenly, the great doors burst open and four husky eunuchs rushed into the room. They surrounded Sing Fa and Chi Guar, roughly pushing Tanya aside.

There was a scraping behind her, and the old one emerged from behind her screen. "Take them!" The high voice cracked, and the bony fingers pointed toward the two miscreants.

The four eunuchs tore the two unresisting girls apart and dragged them across the floor to a small rise in the center of the room. There they tied the slender wrists to the feet of a small stone dragon, suspending their bodies off the floor.

The head eunuch, when he entered, carried no whip, but two wooden rods as long as his arm with convoluted hooks on one end. He settled himself before Sing Fa. Another eunuch assumed a similar position beneath Chi Guar's dangling body.

The old one's voice rang out in command, and the eunuchs inserted the rods between the girls' thighs. Tanya saw Sing Fa convulse at the contact, and for a moment she was not able to understand what was happening. The rod moved slowly inside the delicate body, and a moistness ran down the legs, sending a pungent fragrance that stirred Tanya's own responses. The suspended body shook in a convulsive spasm, and Tanya felt herself grow warm as she unconsciously began to roll her hips, keeping time with the gentle thrusts of the long wooden phallus. The other women, Mei Ling included, moved with the same convulsive excitement.

In and out the rod moved, and Tanya could see that Sing Fa was twisting in a blend of ecstasy and fear. The moisture on the shaft dried in the warm night air, and the growing fright of the young body denied any further lubrication. Still the shaft worked in and out, pulling the tender skin as it moved. Small moans beside her told Tanya that the sight had brought all the women to a state of helpless arousal, and that all eyes were locked onto the drama before them.

Suddenly, a shriek of agony tore through the hall, echoing against the far wall and bouncing back to meet another that tore through the throat of Chi Guar. Tanya dropped to her pallet, her body shaking in horror. With one fierce thrust, the eunuch had forced the rod up through the girl's body until its entire length was buried inside. Blood gushed from between the torn legs and covered the arm of the brutal executioner.

The old one screamed in wild pleasure and the eunuch began to rotate the rod, spinning the body above him in ever-widening circles. The screams of the two victims blended together, ringing in Tanya's ears like the cries of tormented birds, and then blessed darkness wiped the scene—and the tortured voices—from her consciousness.

When she awoke, the hall was quiet. Mei Ling, sprawled on her pallet, was snoring softly. Tanya glanced toward Sing Fa's bed. Maybe it had all been a terrible dream.

The bed was empty. Trembling, Tanya raised herself and looked toward the rise where the girls had been tied. She smothered a cry of horror, but she couldn't control the nausea that left her weak and shaking. The long rods lay on the stone below the bodies of the two women, and rope-like cords stretched from between their legs to the hooked ends of the rods. For one violation of the rules of the compound, both had been disemboweled.

During the days that followed the bodies remained in full view. Unable to bear the sight, Tanya spent most of her waking hours in the garden, as far from Mei Ling as she could get. She felt overwhelmed with the horror she had witnessed—and terribly alone, for she realized that none of the other women showed similar shock. They resumed their lives as if the two unfortunates had never existed.

When the stench grew so bad that even the old one in the privacy of her cubicle was upset, the eunuchs took the bodies down and carried them away. The few belongings of Sing Fa and Chi Guar were quickly taken by the other women.

But Tanya could not wipe the picture of their deaths from her mind. She knew now that she would have only one chance to get away. If she was caught, the old one would see to it that her death was terrible—and slow.

Taking her embroidery into the garden, she settled herself under the sheltering branches of the willow. In its shade she at least felt protected.

A branch was lifted, and Mei Ling sat down beside her. "Tan Ya, you must stop pining. There was nothing we could do!"

"You could have left them alone! You didn't have to call the old one!"

"Had I remained silent, I would have been the one to feel Wong Liu's rod. I would have received no more mercy than they, for I have already been punished once for foolish disobedience." She lifted her robe and stretched out her leg. "This is my shame. When I was young, when I first was brought to the governor's compound, I was ungrateful. I loved another, and I believed he loved me. I tried to escape during the trip from Foochow, where I was born. The eunuchs caught me and—" She turned to let Tanya see the scars. "—cut my leg so I could not walk easily again. I have no strength to bear pain for another, nor the courage to face torture."

"Surely it isn't wrong for a woman to want to be with the man she loves?"

"It is wrong for a woman to love any man other than her husband. We are truly fortunate, even though the old one is sometimes cruel. Our master is a good man. He treats us with affection. He makes our lives as pleasant as that enjoyed by the birds that fly in his garden."

"But we aren't free! Doesn't it matter to you that you are a prisoner—at the mercy of an old woman and a warped eunuch?"

"If I please the master, the old one will not touch me. And what is a prison but a protection from the dangers of liberty? A bird left in the wild is subject to the arrows of hunters. The birds in the master's garden are protected from such a death. If we are obedient, we are surrounded by beauty and peace." She took Tanya's hand. "Do you fear the eunuchs now? Take comfort. The master has not forgotten you. Each time I go to him he inquires about your progress. He has instructed the old one to leave your feet as they are—at least for the present." Her laugh was like the tinkling of a silver bell. "So your fears and worries are groundless! As for the two nameless ones, they chose to disobey the rule against sharing sexual pleasure. They are best forgotten. If the master asks for them, the old one will tell him they have died."

Mei Ling's words proved to be true; no mention was made of her feet, and she heard nothing about the two unfortunate girls. And in the days that followed, she continued Mei Ling's lessons.

When Tanya had mastered the graceful hand movements her teacher advocated, Mei Ling turned to other skills. "The master delights in having his entire body bathed with butterfly kisses." She demonstrated the action. "Many a night I have hovered over him, fluttering my eyelids so that my lashes stroked his skin, and he never forgets that it was I who first provided him with that pleasure."

"Have women no purpose other than to bring delight to their men?"

"Is there any better reason for life? It is so short, and death is all around us. The flowers we gather in spring are buried under the summer grass, and we follow close behind them. What better use is there for our time but to master the art of providing happiness?"

Tanya had no answer except her inner knowledge that her own happiness depended upon liberty. Nevertheless, Mei Ling's instructions filled her with a growing curiosity. Chung had said he had a taste for the juices of a foreign woman, yet the weeks went by and he did not send for her. The *ben wa* shifted in her body, reminding her of the pleasure to come, and each time another woman was called to the master's bedchamber, Tanya wondered what magic he possessed to be capable of keeping so many women eager for his attention.

When she gazed on the contented face of the latest companion of his night-time pleasures, Tanya felt a rush of uncertainty. When her time came, would she be all that Chung expected? Would she give him the satisfaction he desired as she lay in his arms? With each passing day she became more aware that, deep inside, she was looking forward to what appeared to be the ultimate test of her femininity.

CHAPTER VI

———

Tanya stood before the great doors that led to Chung's bedchamber. Her call had come that afternoon. Her body had been washed and scented, her hair freshly combed. In her ears rang the last words of Mei Ling. "The master wants to know that he has all of the woman he possesses. You must hold nothing back."

"Come in little foreign jewel! Let Wong Liu close the door!"

Timidly, she stepped onto the heavy rug.

"Ah, Tan Ya!" Chung rose from his bed. "I have waited long for this night. Let my chambers be yours, my bed your bed, my pleasure your pleasure."

She dropped to her knees, but before her forehead could touch the floor, he lifted her up. Softly, she repeated the words Mei Ling had taught her. "This lowly person has come at your command. Tell me what she can do that will give pleasure to the great one."

The master only gazed at her in silence. All the women had told her there was a ritual he followed before he took them to bed.

The chamber was filled with incense. In a golden cage flitting birds sang lilting songs. A lamp flickered near the bed, catching the gold threads of her garment. She held her breath, awaiting some sign of his interest.

Suddenly, the master laughed. "Tan Ya! Had I wanted Mei Ling I would have asked for her. Come to my side, little foreigner. I watched your soft lips move seductively while I played cards with your captain, and I wondered how it would feel to have them touch my thighs. I caught your dark eyes and dreamed of losing myself in their depths. Beauty such as yours should not be wasted in the arms of a beast like Czerwenki!"

Timidly, she stepped forward. He was stripped of all the silken coverings he had worn on shipboard, and his strong arms rippled in the soft light. He was a beautiful man, with narrow hips and muscular legs. A man who was not ashamed to stand bare before a woman.

He touched her shoulders. "Your body is like ivory, white as the snow flowers of Nanchang." His hands cupped her breasts. "You have breasts that should succor princes. May we have a son by this union that will drink the milk of life from your bosom."

Slowly, his fingers trailed to her abdomen, circling about her navel and brushing the dark hair that covered her mound. He rose and faced her, his erect organ touching her stomach. When he moved, a small drop of fluid remained, burning itself into her consciousness.

His lips touched her nipples, bringing them to firm erection. A glow spread throughout her body. Slowly, she began to rotate her hips, pushing toward him in desire.

He let one hand drop to the small button of her pleasure, holding it firmly as he moved. Her breath grew heavy. Vainly, she pushed toward him, but he held her back with the pressure of his fingers. Suddenly, she felt her body quiver. The force of his finger increased, holding her on the brink of passion until she quivered again and again, moaning with unspeakable ecstasy.

When her body went limp, he pulled her to the bed. "Come, my love, let me taste the juices that are sweeter by far than any nectar drawn from the fruits of the trees."

He lowered her gently, his manhood strong and hard, but he did not enter. Kneeling beside her, he placed his mouth where his fingers had been, sucking the juice that wet her tender parts. When he lifted his head, his eyes were soft and his mouth wet with his passion.

She was aware of the perfume of his desire and her own scent of delight. Timidly, she reached out and touched his swollen member.

"Do you wish to taste the sweet juice of my longing, as I have tasted yours?" As he spoke, Chung lifted up until her lips encircled his penis. He smelled of musk mixed with his own natural scent, and her own body responded to his hardness.

He pulled back and she followed, unwilling to release the treasure she had only begun to enjoy. Then he twisted his body until she felt his tongue touch her thigh. With a moan of pleasure she settled into his embrace. When he began to move quickly in her mouth she did not pull back, for she could not endure the loss of his touch, or of the frantic agitation of his tongue. They shook with a common passion, and then lay resting.

Tanya felt as if she had been caught in a dream from which she had no desire to waken. Her body was fluid, soft, and pulsating in his arms. She tried to think of Alexius, but his image wouldn't come to her mind.

Chung rose from the bed. "Come, my love, the juice of pomegranates waits to revive our strength and renew our passion. Let us sit a moment and listen to the songs of the birds and let the night breezes cool our bodies."

The air was fresh and the juice sweet, but no sweeter than his. She smiled into his eyes as she drank.

When his hands played again on her cheeks, she let her fingers flit over his body, like small butterflies. They came to rest on his groin, encircling his hardness, and she felt him cup her moist, sensitive femaleness in his hand.

Locked together thus, they walked back to the bed. He lifted her from her feet and lowered her onto her back. She pulled him to her until their lips touched and she tasted the pineapple sweetness of her own juice mixed with the pomegranate. He climbed between her thighs, sliding his penis deep into her vagina. She thought of nothing but her passion.

They fell asleep locked together, and awoke during the night to renew their embrace. When morning came, Tanya lay immobile, overcome with a sadness she dared not acknowledge. The eunuch Kui li Liang brought fruit for breakfast. Chung sent him for a tray of succulent shrimp in curry and a jug of sweet wine.

They ate slowly, savoring each new flavor. When Chung noticed her downcast face, he leaned close and teased her ear with his tongue. "Has our night together been so terrible you find tears welling in the limpid pools of your eyes?"

She shook her head, the unwanted tears coursing down her cheeks.

"Ah, then, you feel the same sadness that fills my heart. The night is ended, and we must go about our business." He kissed her eyelids. "When the shadows lengthen, you must return again. I have yet to show you the delight that comes to the body when the tongue caresses the foot, and yours are—" He paused, his eyes studying her ankles. "—so different. I am curious as to whether you will have the same sensations as I do, or whether you will respond as Mei Ling does. I must know. And I wish, also, to present myself to some other gate to your pleasure." He smiled down at her. "You, too, have left much undone. Did not Mei Ling teach you her favorite caress?"

Tanya flushed. She had forgotten the butterfly kiss in the heat of her own passion! And in doing so, she had failed in her duty, for she had not remembered to put the master's pleasure before her own!

When he saw her embarrassment and discomfort, he touched her cheek lightly with his fingers. "See, my little

168

foreigner? We have much that is unfinished. You must return again tonight."

The next night passed much as the first, though Chung, true to his word, explored other entries into delight. Anointing her body with sweet-smelling oils, he entered her as she lay beside him, her back pressed against his stomach. To her surprise, she felt no pain, only a thrill of passion that grew with his own until they lay wet with perspiration, locked in spasms of ecstasy.

He let her wash him in perfumed water before he took her once more in the usual way. But he stopped suddenly and directed her to rise. "Wong Liu! I need your assistance!"

Tanya flushed when Wong Liu entered the room, but he paid no attention to her. He helped Chung release a net-like swing that hung from a single cord attached to a pulley over the bed. When the swing hung free, he released the lock on a crank and lowered the swing to the bed.

Immediately, Chung helped Tanya into the swing, directing her to fold her legs against her stomach so her genitals would be open and exposed. Then he lay face up below her.

In response to a command from Chung, Wong Liu lowered the swing until Tanya felt Chung's organ touch the wet lips of her vagina. Chung's hands guided her down as Wong Liu lowered the swing until they were firmly coupled. Then, locking the cord in the crank, he strode from the room.

Gently, Chung began to turn Tanya's body. Her muscles grasped at his manhood as she rose slowly in a spiral above him. With each turn the cord twisted tighter and she was raised higher until she gasped with desire, fearful that he would let their exotic contact be broken. But just before he withdrew completely, he took his hand from her hip and let the rope above her begin to unwind.

Once more she made the spiral twist above him, the speed of her rotation increasing as she descended. She felt a growing dizziness as she rotated around his organ, a dizziness mixed with a sweet lassitude. There was no drive for consummation in what he did, only a desire to continue the pleasure they both shared for as long as possible. Her ecstasy grew with each movement of his manhood within her, and she let her mind whirl with her body until, unable to bear the extreme of her passion, she cried out in delight. Still he did not stop. When the cord unwound, he spun her back, slowing her movement so each change of contact could be relished to completion. She felt herself melt into nothingness. Her body ceased to be matter. Only the soft movement within her, catching her up and holding her at the peak was real.

When she felt him pulsate beneath her, she cried out again and then, her head spinning, she felt her body join in the rhythm of his driving passion. Spasms of delight shook them both until she was drained of all passion. When he helped her from the swing, she fell beside him, too weak from the force of her emotion to move.

In the morning, they once more shared sweet fruits and wine, and he ordered smoked eel and octopus. The tastes of these were different from any foods she had eaten in the women's compound, pleasant, and adding to the savoriness of the big strawberries and soft passion fruit with which he plied her. When they were finished eating, he rose. "Now you must return to the compound and prepare Mei Ling for my bed tonight. Then, when the sun rises once more out of the great sea of light in the valley of Yang-ku, we must be ready for the journey to the mountains. The summer is upon us, and the evil spirits will soon cover the land with death. Mei Ling will tell you what to do to prepare yourself. We will leave tomorrow. You, Mei Ling, Ling Hsu, and Ching Lien will come with me."

He graciously dismissed her.

They were going to the mountains! How many eunuchs would accompany them? How closely would she be watched? She knew that if ever she was to escape, this would be the time.

She hurried back to the women's compound. Escape brought back the memory of Alexius with renewed strength. How could she have forgotten him even for a moment? When she reached her pallet, she took the *ben wa* from under her hard, round pillow; she understood now why the women used them: They gave comfort when Chung lay in another's arms. But, reluctantly, she dropped them into the small bag that held her few belongings. She dared not think of Chung's love again. Her mind had to be clear so she could plan.

Mei Ling showed smug satisfaction at Chung's call, and throughout the day she made small barbed remarks about his need for a real woman to stir his passions. Tanya let her friend boost her feeling of importance. Soon it wouldn't matter how Mei Ling felt. Escape was all that was important. Tanya moved about, helping wherever she could in the hurried packing.

Ling Hsu was agog with anticipation. She had not been outside the walls since her arrival, and she had been born upriver from Canton. She chattered brightly about gaining permission to visit her mother.

At last Mei Ling cut her childish dreams short. "Enough of such foolishness! We are going to the mountains to avoid the cholera! You belong to the master Chung Kai Chang now. Forget your parents, as they surely have forgotten you!"

The sharpness brought tears to Ling Hsu's eyes. Tanya said to Mei Ling: "Why do you speak so harshly? Would it be difficult for her to have her wish? She's only a child!"

"Ling Hsu is a woman, as we all are. She only shows weakness with her jabbering. If she doesn't learn to overcome her homesickness, she will eat her earrings!" She paused. "Maybe that is well. But she must not do it before the master tires of her." Mei Ling continued her preparations for the night.

Tanya wandered into the garden. She remembered the ecstasy she had felt in Chung's arms, but she dared not dwell on it. Somehow, in the weeks of travel that lay ahead, she was determined to escape. The right moment would come, of that she was certain. The moment would come—and she had to make sure she would be ready.

CHAPTER VII

The river boat was a large version of the junks that had crowded about the *Russian Princess*. A long flat deck ran the length of each side, and a house-like structure stood in the center. The hull was painted red, with a large dragon stretching from fore to aft, its tail descending to the water. One large sail was tied loosely to the mast, and coils of rope lay in the prow. The sailors crouched as the girls boarded, hiding their faces from the forbidden sight of the master's women.

When they were settled in their cabin, Chung turned to Mei Ling. "Come, Sweet Flower, sing for me. Your voice will help pass the time and raise our spirits."

Mei Ling's first song told of a prince who went in search of the *jo* tree, behind which the sun rests at night. It

173

praised him for his courage as he at last reached the lake of fire and plucked a flower from the sacred branches.

When she finished, Chung smiled. "Now sing of the gardens to which we travel. Tan Ya and Ling Hsu have never seen them."

Mei Ling began to speak, her voice rising in musical rhythm.

> High in the mountains, where the sky kisses the land
> And weeps that they must always be separate,
> The gods built a garden, filling it with
> The most beautiful flowers in their kingdoms.

She struck a chord on her lute-like instrument.

> Within the walls of this garden are roses that never fade,
> Lilies of the valley that ring with joyous music,
> And willows that no longer feel the need to weep.

Her fingers moved over the strings, keeping rhythm with her words.

> There the master takes his pleasure,
> There the lord of life seeks rest.
> There, where winds dare not blow,
> And even the lord sun is gentle,
> There the master rests his body,
> There the master seeks the truth.

No one spoke until the master rose. He touched Mei Ling lightly. "I will rest now. Later, you and I will seek what joy we can find together."

When he was gone, Tanya caught Mei Ling's glance. "That was lovely. Why have you not sung it before?"

"I did not know it before. It came to me to make the master forget your reluctance at leaving the city."

"I don't mind leaving. But I wondered that the master would leave his people to the plague. I had to know if he was totally heartless!"

Mei Ling's voice was mocking. "Do you know now?"

Tanya sighed. "No, not really. But at least I believe that

the master is not cruel as the Tsar of Russia is cruel. I believe he does not hurt others for pleasure."

Mei Ling's voice dropped. "The Son of the Sun, the Emperor of the Middle Kingdom, is such a man. But he does not bother the governors of the provinces as long as he receives his tribute regularly. My brother told me this before I became a concubine."

Tanya looked into the delicate face. "Doesn't it distress your brother that you are a concubine? Was there no one you could have married?"

Mei Ling's voice was sharp. "It is an honor to be a concubine of the Governor Chung Kai Chang. Because of my position in the master's household, my brother has been appointed a potentate of great importance in Foochow."

"But does it not matter whether you are happy? Is your brother's fortune more important than your life?"

Mei Ling snorted contemptuously. "You do not understand our ways! I have a master who treats me well and doesn't beat me! But I will have more! I will. . . ." She stopped suddenly, her eyes half closed, and glanced toward Ching Lien and Ling Hsu. Then, nervously, her eyes searched the deck. Without looking again at Tanya, she picked up her embroidery.

Tanya stared out at the distant hills. So far, she had managed to escape the intrigue, but she knew it was all around her. Every woman schemed to advance her power over the master, and the eunuchs were spies for the highest bidder.

CHAPTER VIII

After a week of slow upriver passage they reached Kwei-lin. When the wind was still, long ropes were tossed to the bank and coolies pulled the boat. They bent under the load, and their songs reminded Tanya of the boatmen who pulled the barges on the Volga River in Russia.

They had passed many towns as they moved up the Hsi River and all had looked much alike, surrounded by high walls made of a mixture of mud and wood that gave them the appearance of small fortresses. Kweilin looked like that, too. Tanya half-expected to find a wharf on the river-side of the town, but the wall around Kweilin was unbroken. The boat docked at a wharf outside the walled city. They did not immediately disembark. Only a fool, Mei Ling informed Tanya, would venture out into the countryside at night.

When morning came, the eunuch Wong Liu hired carriers and bought chairs. Within an hour after sunrise, the procession was on its way toward the highlands. Chung Kai Chang occupied the first chair, his two carriers setting the pace for the journey. Behind him came coolies carrying the chests of clothes, jewels, and food.

Each coolie balanced a long pole on his head with a heavy bundle tied on the ends, and as his bare feet padded down the dirt road, the bundles swung wildly over the rice paddies. At the end of the caravan were the two chairs carrying the concubines. Only two men were needed for each chair, and the coolies carried it as if it were featherlight. Tanya and Mei Ling rode in the first; the second held little Ling Hsu and Ching Lien.

The journey was slow, and difficult. Despite the rule that the curtains remain closed, Tanya and Mei Ling pushed the draperies apart far enough to permit them to look forward as well as at the countryside. In the narrow mountain paths, the coolies carrying the bundles turned the poles so their burdens swung before and behind them. Often the chairs hung over deep ravines or bumped roughly against steep rocky walls. After one frightful glance down one such ravine, Tanya kept her eyes elevated to the beauty of the rugged mountains. The vistas were magnificent.

The coolies chattered cheerfully as they trudged along, and even on the narrowest paths with the deepest drop-offs, they did now slow their steady pace. They ate little. When the long procession stopped for food and to give the five passengers an opportunity to relieve themselves, the four concubines and Chung Kai Chang ate a bit of fruit and spiced meat, the coolies bowls of rice with a few half-cooked vegetables.

When they at last approached the empty summer house the sun was low in the sky. Mei Ling pointed to the red roofs and the towering trees. "We reach a small meadow near the gate, and then we'll be there. We're fortunate indeed to be chosen to share this week with the master. The old one will not arrive until the house in Canton is clean and ready for us to return to in the fall. And she is a hard taskmaster." Mei Ling seemed to have overcome her ill temper, and their conversation throughout the journey had been light and pleasant.

Tanya was also leaning out. The coolies were slowing their pace. Suddenly, with screams of terror the coolies dropped the chairs into the bushes at the side of the road and ran precipitously back down the path. Tanya landed on her side. She was shaken and she had to struggle for breath. "What's happening? Mei Ling, why have the coolies run away?"

Mei Ling was pushing her way out of the fallen chair. "Bandits! The caravan has been attacked!"

Galvanized into action, Tanya followed her. The noise and turmoil coming from the bushes ahead filled her with panic. She followed Mei Ling to the shelter of a nearby bush. Together, they settled behind its branches, pushing leaves around them to conceal their bright gowns.

Tanya peered at the caravan. Ling Hsu and Ching Lien had both been thrown to the ground. Ling Hsu lay close to the forward chair; Ching Lien almost directly beside it.

Three fierce-looking men pushed their way through the bushes. They were dressed in bright jackets; long pigtails reached down their backs. Their faces were hard and cruel, and their eyes were like small black beads under heavy eyebrows.

One of the three rushed after the fleeing coolies, his sword high in the air. The other two lunged at the fallen girls. They tore the clothes from Ching Lien and Ling Hsu. Ching Lien shrieked as her attacker pushed her into the carpet of leaves. Ling Hsu, too young to believe her life was in danger, kicked and bit her assailant, even as, laughing wildly, he forced himself between her legs. Tanya, terrified, and torn between a desire to run, an urge to help, and the terrible realization that she was helpless to do either, watched.

Suddenly the two men rose. Ching Lien lay lifeless on the ground. When Ling Hsu kicked again at her attacker, he hacked off her head with one swing of his sword.

The two bandits vanished into the undergrowth uphill.

The third bandit, who had chased the carriers down the path, reemerged now, swinging the four heads of the coolies by their pigtails.

Once more the shouting drew close. The bandits trooped past. Two carried Chung Kai Chang's empty chair; four others, two by two, trotted by with the chairs of the concubines. The other bandits carried bundles of food and jewels. All were shouting in gleeful triumph.

Then there was silence. Tanya and Mei Ling crawled out from their shelter. A bird sang in the brush. The air was soon filled again with the innocent sounds of nature, as though the terrible carnage had never happened.

Mei Ling clutched at Tanya's arm. "We were almost killed! I was afraid, Tan Ya, that they would find us!"

Tanya helped her settle on a rock, averting her face from the slaughter. "Will you be all right alone?" She ran to the side of the road, then up the path, to the clearing where the attack had begun.

The grass was red with blood. Heads without bodies. Chung's body lay askew beside the path, his naked limbs streaked with gore. A cut across his abdomen exposed the circuitous twistings of his intestines. His head, its noble eyes wide, its lips parted to reveal strong white teeth, lay severed from him.

In the sky, vultures were circling, waiting to tear into the carrion. Hysterically, Tanya shook her fist into the air. "Go away! Go away!"

The birds settled. She startled them into momentary flight, lunging at them. Her feet slipped on the red of the grass. The birds settled again, waiting for their grisly feast.

Retreating into the brush, she almost tripped over two poles that had been used to carry baggage but which, miraculously, the robbers had left behind. And a bag of lichi nuts. She picked these up and ran back to the trees. She knew now that it was up to her to save both Mei Ling and herself. Everyone else was dead.

Mei Ling was sitting upright, her eyes glazed. A trickle of saliva ran down the corner of her mouth and formed a fine thread that reached the soiled butterflies embroidered on her gown. Tanya bound the poles she had pulled from the underbrush together with a sash. "Climb on," she said. "I'll pull you. We can't stay here. It's almost dark."

Mei Ling was staring into the shadows, babbling incoherently. Gradually her words formed a question. "The master . . . is he dead?"

"Yes! Hurry! We can't stay here all night!" Behind her a bush rustled. Drawing on strength and courage she had not known she possessed, Tanya lifted Mei Ling from the rock and tied her to the poles. Then, bending under the weight, she began to stagger down the path.

"No!" Mei Ling's voice startled the vultures, sending them soaring into the air. "The master will haunt us if we desert him! We must return and say the prayers that put the dead to rest!"

Mei Ling struggled against her bindings, but when she could not free herself, she continued her lament. Tanya pulled her burden down the hill, fighting the impulse to drop the poles and run. "Stop fighting! We can do nothing now. . . . There are too many for us to help."

They spent the night in a shallow cave. Established in the back of the shelter, Mei Ling announced herself safe from evil spirits. In the morning she would return to the master and help his soul find the gates to his Hades.

They ate the lichi nuts in silence.

As she dropped the last seed onto the ground, Tanya wiped the stickiness from her hands. "I was fortunate to find these in the meadow before we left. Without them, we would go to sleep hungry."

"You found them in the meadow—near the master?" Mei Ling began to wail. "Aiyah! We are doomed!" Her body rocked back and forth in time to her cries.

Tanya stared at her in consternation. "Why? What's wrong?"

Mei Ling shrieked that she had eaten the nuts by accident, that it was not she who had stolen them from the ghosts of the dead. At last, and assuring Chung's spirit that she would return to attend him in the morning, she settled down to sleep.

Tanya lay wide awake beside her. Every noise set her

heart pounding; the branches she had gathered for their beds jabbed mercilessly into her ribs. Yet it was not her fear nor her discomfort that kept her awake. She thought of the many miles that lay between her and Canton, and the great ocean that separated Canton from the Aleutian Islands.

Closing her eyes, she folded her hands in prayer. "Dear Mother of God, help me. I must live to find Alexius! I cannot allow myself to die in this foreign land."

Despite the hardships, she felt strangely stimulated. She was free to once more resume her search for her lover, and though she could not foresee the road she would take, she was determined to reach him. It was a long time before she finally dropped into a deep, dreamless sleep.

CHAPTER IX

The path down the mountain was terrifying. At times Tanya literally crawled along the narrow ledge, slavishly pulling Mei Ling inch by inch behind her, fearful the entire time that they might slip and fall. Mei Ling, when she wasn't moaning that the path was too difficult, was praying to the spirits of the dead whom they had left behind. She was convinced that the spirits were following them, and that only evil would come because she and Tanya had failed to return to the scene of the carnage to say prayers for the departed.

Tanya's greatest fear was that the robbers would return—or that she would encounter them on the path. She hid with Mei Ling at the slightest noise, but the path remained empty. And so, after three days of slow travel, the two women finally saw below them the valley and the walled city of Kweilin.

The sun was sinking behind the distant mountains, and the river glowed like a stream of gold. Even her hunger, which was intense, could not distract Tanya from the beauty of the scene.

Mei Ling was jabbering in Chinese.

"What's the matter? What are you afraid of now?"

"The old one! See? See the boat tied up at the dock? It must have taken less time than was expected to close down the city house, for she is at Kweilin already! Aiyah! She will catch us for certain, and we will die for having abandoned the master!"

"She hasn't caught us yet!"

Mei Ling continued to mumble pathetically. Mei Ling was not the same placid, simple girl who had left Canton, complaining about little annoyances and convinced of her own secure future. She was frightened—terribly frightened. Tanya thought that the bandits' raid had broken her spirit; the fear of death—or rape—had broken it.

Once more Tanya turned her attention to the path that lay before her. A short distance below she could see a fork. One branch led back to Kweilin. The other led south, skirting the town completely. Lifting the poles, she resumed her journey. When she reached the fork, she turned south, around the bustling city—and the possibility of encountering the old one's retinue.

The following afternoon they had reached a dry valley. Mei Ling insisted that they glean food from the fields through which they passed, although she had a few coins in her sleeve, secreted before they left Canton, which she had been saving to bribe a eunuch in an attempt to raise her position in the harem.

It didn't matter, Tanya reminded herself. Eventually they would reach Canton, and then their paths would separate.

On the afternoon of their sixth day of travel, they were offered a lift by a farmer. Tanya was wary, but Mei Ling delightedly struggled from the makeshift litter and settled herself on the straw in the open wagon under the hot sun.

Almost as soon as the farmer whipped his water buffalo into motion, Mei Ling was asleep. Tanya stayed uneasily awake.

For the first few kilometers, the farmer went in the direction of Wuchow, as he had said he would. But then, at a fork in the road, he turned and glanced back at his passengers. Tanya pretended to sleep, but she noted that when he resumed his journey, he left the river road. Fortunately, the hot afternoon sun also beat mercilessly on him, and soon he, like Mei Ling, was sound asleep.

Immediately, Tanya shook Mei Ling. Her voice was a whisper. "Wake up, Mei Ling!"

Mei Ling opened her eyes. "Go to sleep, Tan Ya. It is good for us to rest."

"The farmer isn't taking us to Wuchow! Look!"

Mei Ling braced herself on an elbow and gazed around. There seemed to be none of the childishness that had plagued Mei Ling during the first days of their journey. Her eyes seemed clear, her mind sharp. She was wide awake. "You are right. We must stop him!"

"No. He turned on this road deliberately. He intends to kidnap us. We must get away before he wakes up."

It was not difficult for Tanya to slip from the slow-moving wagon and to help Mei Ling down. But she dared not risk making noise by taking the long poles that had served as Mei Ling's litter. And so, as the wagon moved slowly away, she lifted her friend onto her back.

She rested only when the wagon was out of sight. Then she struggled on, not stopping again until she and Mei Ling, still on her back, had reached the fork in the road where the farmer had turned.

As empty as the back road had been, so the river road was crowded. More than once she felt observed. Unnerved, at last Tanya sought shelter in a clump of trees alongside the busy road.

"Mei Ling, maybe we should try to travel at night. I feel as if everyone we pass is watching us."

Mei Ling shook her head. "It is dangerous to travel at night. The robbers control the roads after sunset."

Tanya thought for a moment. "You have some money

saved, don't you? Maybe we should buy passage on a river boat."

Again, Mei Ling shook her head. "No." Mei Ling's eyes were crafty. "I must have my coins. When we reach Canton, I will buy a place in a good brothel. We can never return to the home of Chung Kai Chang."

Mei Ling pulled the coins from their hiding place and gazed at them tenderly. At last she pulled two small ones from her pile and put the remainder back in her sleeve. "Here. We can buy food with these."

After they had eaten, they remained hidden in the shelter of trees until morning.

When the first light of day awoke them, Mei Ling refused to move. "The bleeding has come upon me. You must give me something to stop the flow."

The eyes that Tanya met were glazed and childlike. Mei Ling had returned to her previous condition, aware to some extent of their troubles, yet unable to deal with any difficulties.

Tanya ripped the lining from her hem and gave it to Mei Ling to stuff between her legs. Then, aware that her bleeding had always started at the same time as Mei Ling's, she ran her hand between her own thighs, seeking some telltale moisture. But she was dry.

They resumed their journey. But when they at last reached the marketplace in Wuchow and Mei Ling had purchased rice bowls and chopsticks, and had provided them both with heaping orders of rice topped with succulent bits of meat, Tanya thought once more of her strange condition.

Swallowing a mouthful of rice, she turned to Mei Ling. "Has your bleeding time come early? Mine has not yet. . . ." She stopped abruptly, overcome with sudden fear. She had lapsed into Russian!

She glanced about, aware that her heart was beating wildly—and she found herself staring into a pair of dark, suspicious eyes that opened wide when they met hers.

"Foreign devil! Foreign devil!" A gnarled finger pointed

accusingly at her, circled her face, then jabbed into her cheeks. "Foreign devil!"

Another voice joined in, and soon she was surrounded by a circle of hate. A stone hit her back. A sharp rock cut into her temple. The voices grew louder, more and more people joining in. "Kill the foreign devil! Kill her! Kill her!"

She tried to escape, the crowd moved with her, holding her in their midst.

The shouts turned into a roar and the rain of stones increased. She knelt on the ground, her arms shielding her head. She thought she was going to die.

At first she didn't notice when the stones ceased to pelt her, for her own screams continued, and her body ached with pain. Then she became aware of the sudden silence.

Huddled close to the ground, she lifted her head and stared at the legs of her tormentors. The legs were still there, but they no longer danced about her in excitement. The bare feet, covered with the stinking dirt of the barnyard, were unmoving, and the voices that had been raised in anger now were mumbling incoherently.

One pair of legs faced away from her, the feet braced apart, the knees slightly bent—and their strength drew her eyes to the lithe body they supported. Standing between her and her assailants, his pigtail flapping wildly as he turned his head to include all of her attackers, was a youngish man, somewhat taller than the others. His hands were stretched out before him, and his stance was one of total readiness.

He threw out a challenge which no one answered: "Does someone wish to fight with me? What? No one? How is it you are so brave when the object of your attack is a helpless female? What harm has she done to you?"

He went on: "A foreign devil? That's what you say she is? Then look again! She has the high nose bridge of a Manchu! And do you claim that no Chinaman can learn the language of foreigners? Don't be such simpletons!"

Once more the challenge went out. "Think before you attack another helpless woman, especially one who belongs to Wen Kui Fong!"

187

Her sudden protector, Tanya realized, was Chinese, not Manchu. His features confirmed her opinion. His face, like those around him, was flat, with black, slanted eyes and a bridgeless nose. But there his resemblance to the others ended. There was an arrogance in his face, and a look of satisfaction. This made her uneasy.

The crowd began to disperse, the rocks falling to the ground.

She owed her protector much. Folding her hands, she said, "Thank you, Wen Kui Fong. You saved my life."

"It belongs to me now," Wen Kui Fong replied.

Chinese custom decreed that she belonged to him—he had saved her life; her life was his.

"Why did they stop? Why are they afraid of you?" Tanya asked. She was still kneeling on the ground.

His laugh was short and hard. "So they were right! You are a foreigner! There is no man or woman in China who does not know of the martial arts—of the hands of stone. They know—and they fear. There is no weapon that can overcome one such as I."

"Not even a musket?"

"I cannot fight a cannonball," Wen Kui Fong replied, "whatever its size may be. But in face-to-face combat, as *real* men battle, I can overcome swords and sticks—and even arrows." He bent and lifted her up. "Come, it is time we moved on. Walk behind me."

They had passed outside the gates of Wuchow, Tanya painfully, when Mei Ling suddenly appeared before them. "What are you doing with my servant?" she asked Wen Kui Fong.

"I saved her from being stoned to death. Her life belongs to me," he replied. "Where is your husband, woman?"

Mei Ling's expression slowly changed. She had been, momentarily, a determined woman. But under the slight assault of Wen's question, she crumpled. "I. . . . He. . . ." Her face grew red, and she began to search about her frantically, as if looking for escape.

Wen turned to Tanya and gestured toward a nearby tree. "Sit there. I wish to have words with your mistress."

188

"She is not my mistress! Can't you see? She has lost her mind! Leave us alone to find our way to Canton!"

"Do you wish to be thrown back to the peasants? Silence! Do as I tell you, or I will call the farmers back and help them end your worthless life!"

Wen and Mei Ling spoke for some time, their faces animated and their words flowing swiftly. At first Wen did most of the talking, and Tanya could hear a few of his words. *Brothel* was repeated often, as was *Canton* and *wealth*. And as he spoke, Mei Ling's expression brightened. Her eyes became alight with enthusiasm. Then they bowed solemnly toward each other.

Wen turned to Tanya. "You will carry your mistress to the river, to where the boat is tied against the bank. I am taking you both to Canton."

Tanya stared into his face, anger fighting with delight. Canton! Freedom! But he—a man—was he not going to carry Mei Ling? She had performed that labor long enough!

"You are truly a foreigner," Wen said. "It is not fit for a man to be a slave to a woman unless she be of high rank— or wealthy. Mei Ling cannot walk by herself. Do as you are told."

The weight of Mei Ling on her bruised back increased the pain. Now that she no longer was responsible for Mei Ling's safety, her resentment of the dependency of the autocratic girl began to grow. Throughout the days of travel down the mountain, Mei Ling had made no attempt to lighten Tanya's burden; she had not protected her from the stoning peasants; and now she had assumed the position of her mistress.

And Wen! Although she was thankful to him for having saved her life, she felt no compulsion to accept him as her master! She had had enough bondage! If she could not have freedom, she would be better off to have died under the rain of rocks.

Then, ahead, she saw the boat. What did it matter how Wen and Mei Ling behaved, or what they planned for her? She had her own plans. When they reached Canton, her misery would be over. She would remain only until she found a ship that would take her to Unalaska. The thought lifted her spirits, and she hurried her steps.

As they approached the riverboat, its arched roof and pointed prow steaming in the hot sun, Wen called loudly. "Make way for the Lady Mei Ling!" The peasants and coolies backed away to provide passage, and some even dropped to their knees. Amused in spite of her earlier anger, Tanya smiled and hurried after Wen onto the crowded deck.

CHAPTER X

The moist tropical air of the Xijiang River basin lay like a blanket over Tanya's bare body. It bathed her in perspiration and weighed down her chest with a pressure that threatened to smother her. She had slept on the floor. Her body was sore from the stones and the hard boards. Wen and Mei Ling had shared the only bed in the small cabin.

From the moment Wen had rescued her, he had treated her as an object he owned—nothing more. She understood at last why he had saved her. He needed women to serve him, and he didn't care how he got them.

A movement on the bed drew her attention. Wen and Mei Ling had resumed their amorous embrace—or maybe, Tanya mused, they had never interrupted it to sleep. The two bodies writhed sensuously and then suddenly lay still.

"Do you think we woke her?" Wen whispered.

Mei Ling rose on one arm and looked down at Tanya. "No, I don't think so. She was too tired."

Wen spoke a bit louder. "It was my good fortune to save the foreign one, for then I met you. Together, we will become very wealthy. You will be the mistress of the biggest, most successful brothel in Canton."

He continued, weaving a picture of opulence and power. "We will enter the wharf in proper style. I will rent a chair and make you beautiful in new clothes. We will go to a brothel I know that has fallen upon hard times, and we will take it from Mio Kang, the old woman who has allowed it to fall into neglect. Then we will build it up again to the place of importance it held in the past. She will not oppose us, that I know. And we will become the most prosperous people in Canton."

"What about her?" Mei Ling gestured toward the floor.

"You must keep her. It gives you great prestige to have a foreign slave." He sat up. "Wake her. I will see whether she is worthy to be one of your women."

Rubbing her eyes to feign sleepiness, Tanya allowed herself to be led to the bed. Wen pushed aside the gown she wore. He signalled her to turn slowly. He smiled at Mei Ling. "She is attractive enough—for a foreigner. It is good to see they differ very little from normal women."

A self-satisfied smile touched Mei Ling's lips. "She is skilled, too—in her own way. I taught her what I could of the art of love while we were concubines of Chung Kai Chang."

"She sounds promising." Wen lay back, stretching his long limbs lazily. "Tan Ya, show me your talents."

Tanya stared at his lean body with distaste. Even the sight of his aroused member and the odor of sex that surrounded her failed to arouse her. But she knew what she had to do. Slowly, she let her eyelids flutter over his abdomen. She could feel him move beneath her, and, gaining hope that he might be content with this form of service, she moved toward his chest.

But Wen showed no patience with such refined pleasures. Abruptly, he threw her onto her back and pushed between her legs, moving with a swiftness that destroyed the faint stirrings that had started a glow of warmth in her breast. He was quick—he seemed satisfied when he pushed himself to her side. Immediately Mei Ling was between them, forcing Tanya back onto the floor. As she crawled back to her corner, filled with anger, Tanya heard Wen speak quietly to Mei Ling. "She must be taught not to give too much to any man. She will last longer that way."

When morning came, Tanya slipped out of the small private cabin onto the deck. The broad flat deck served as bed for most of the ragged passengers, and the odor of unwashed bodies and human excreta was overwhelming. She was grateful to be even on the floor in the cabin.

Her head reeling, she leaned over the railing, abandoning herself to a nausea that had plagued her from the beginning of the river journey. She had attributed it first to her injuries, and when they began to heal, to the heat. But as the flat-bottomed boat drew closer to the bay and the breezes from the ocean cooled the nights, the daily sickness did not abate. Yet it was not until Mei Ling began her bleeding time again that Tanya knew for certain that she carried within her the growing seed of her dead master, Chung Kai Chang.

It was Wen who first spoke of the changes that were taking place within her body. Cupping her breasts, he felt their firmness and crowed delightedly. "The foreign one is fertile. Already she carries my son in her stomach!"

Mei Ling looked up at Wen. "He shall be our son—yours and mine! We will let the slave carry him—and feed him after he is born. But he is ours. I have prayed long to the goddess Kuan Yin, and I have been told this is so. The slave woman carries our child so I will be free to establish our business."

Wen nodded, laughing delightedly. "You are right, Mei Ling! It is fitting that the prostitute Mei Ling have another carry her child." He leaped about her, his hands in martial poses, and his feet thumped loudly each time he landed on the cabin floor. "Ah, we will prosper! The child is a sign! When we reach Canton we will go to the temple and give our thanks to the goddess!"

Tanya listened with growing resentment tinged with fright. She was pregnant, and Mei Ling felt justified in claiming the child for her own! And Wen Kui Fong was taking the credit! Their interest in the child could only interfere with her plans to escape. But if Wen thought the child was his, he would treat her well. If he knew it belonged to Chung, he might decide to kill her. She remained silent.

As the days passed, Tanya could not completely reject Mei Ling's claim to the unborn infant. The child was Chung's—it was Manchu! The offspring of the Governor of Guandong Province should not be taken from its homeland.

Tanya's feelings toward the child that grew within her changed from moment to moment. As they approached the coast and she smelled the salty tang of the ocean breezes, she wished fervently that the child did not exist. She had not wanted it, not even as she lay in Chung's arms! She wanted it even less now that she was close to freedom.

Then the thought of the child within her would fill her with an excitement—and anticipation—which she could not deny. Torn by her emotions, she would burst into tears and weep in frustration, bewailing the fate that held her captive.

The brothel of Mio Kang stood on a hill in a line of houses that faced the wharf, its fenced-in courtyard protecting its entranceway from the street. It was obviously neglected. The walls were streaked with dirt and a number of slats in the wooden siding needed replacement. A starving dog lunged at them as they entered the court and ran yipping down the hill when Wen kicked it.

A beggar crouched in the street at the entranceway, his bony hands stretched out in a plea for alms, but Mei Ling showed no sympathy for his poverty. Screaming wildly, she chased him away, cursing loudly and warning him that he would be beaten if he returned.

The workmen who trudged past on the street paid little attention to the newcomers, but a line of children formed across the road. Tanya looked about her. She had decided, in the days' journeying, to make no immediate attempt to leave Canton. She was still undecided as to what she should do about the child she carried. She watched Mei Ling and Wen with growing curiosity. What could they possibly want with such a run-down establishment?

"We will cover the courtyard and let men who wait for service sit in the shade." Wen gestured grandly at the filthy enclosure. "It is of no use in its present condition, and of course it needs cleaning, but we can get servants to do such dirty work."

Mei Ling smiled craftily. "It is a good location, as you said. But it must be painted a bright color, so it will be noticed from the wharf."

Wen nodded. "There is much we have to do. But it stands above all the others. Sailors will see it as they approach!"

Inside, everything was run-down and useless. But their complaints seemed not at all upsetting to the little old woman who trotted after them, her eyes glazed with opium.

Mei Ling settled a statue of Kuan Yin she had bought that morning in a niche in the largest room, glanced quickly at the five smaller rooms that filled the second level, and descended to inspect the kitchen. Mio Kang shuffled obediently behind her.

"My slave will sleep there." Mei Ling pointed to a shadowy corner behind the stove. "She carries the master's child, and must be fed well. What is behind that door?"

Mio Kang bowed. "It is this humble one's sleeping room."

Mei Ling exploded in fury. "And where shall my man sleep? Has he no right to comfort? Must he be sent from his bed if I entertain a customer?"

Cringing, Mio Kang hurried across the kitchen and threw open the door. "I will sleep behind the stove with the slave woman. It is not fitting that Wen Kui Fong settle for less than the quarters that have traditionally been reserved for the manager of this honorable brothel."

Mei Ling snorted her agreement and then, with Wen beside her, departed to purchase new bedding for her establishment. But before she left she assigned Tanya the job of sweeping all the upstairs rooms and of preparing Mio Kang's old room for Wen's use.

Tanya watched the two depart and then picked up a broom. Though Mei Ling had improved some since the disaster that had wiped out the vacationers on their way to the summer retreat, she had never returned to her old, reasonably friendly self. There was an unevenness in her behavior that gave evidence of her emotional upset, and her insistence that the child Tanya carried was, in fact, hers and Wen's convinced Tanya that her friend was close to madness.

Mio Kang scurried about, picking up the biggest pieces of trash that lay helter-skelter about the room. At the sight of the shriveled shoulders and the patient, empty eyes Tanya was filled with sympathy. "Why do you let Mei Ling and Wen treat you this way? The house is yours!"

Mio Kang shook her head, her hands picking helplessly at her torn garment. "I am an old woman who can no longer deal with the problems of running a good brothel. Wen Kui Fong and Mei Ling will treat me well. They will feed me in my old age and provide me with a place to lie down when I die."

"And for that you give them your home?" Tanya's personal feelings of resentment fed on the injustice. "You must fight them!" She coaxed pieces of rotting food from under the stove and swept them into the courtyard. She felt pity for the old woman, and disgust at the neglect she saw all around her. Yes, Mio Kang was right. She was incapable of caring for the house! Still, it was outrageous that someone could just walk in and take it away from her! "How can you be so certain they will give you even that much, once they feel secure in their claim to your property?"

Mio Kang smiled. "I know, because it was just this way I took possession from the old one who came before me. It is the way of life." She slipped a rag under her mattress. "Don't worry about me, little mother. Plan instead for your own advancement. You bear the master's child in your belly. I can see that the mistress is jealous of you. You must take advantage of your position and you will prosper."

196

Tanya helped her pull the mattress across the floor into the kitchen and then together they lifted a large pot onto the stove. Tanya fetched water while Mio Kang poured in a measure of rice.

As she emptied the last water, Tanya paused. "It is not my wish to bear this child." Panting from the exertion, she leaned against the unpainted wall. Mio Kang watched her with unconcealed concern.

Leaving the rice to cook, they climbed the stairs, brooms in hand. Mio Kang patted Tanya's belly. "Don't be impatient, Tan Ya. The day will come when the master will choose you over Mei Ling because you will be the mother of his sons. Kuan Yin has blessed you."

Tanya made no answer. Despite her sympathy for the old woman, she could not trust her secrets to anyone.

When the food was eaten and all of Mei Ling's purchases had been distributed through the rooms, Tanya helped Mio Kang bank the fire and scrub the pots and dishes with sand. Then, exhausted from the day's work, she dropped gratefully onto her pallet.

A rat ran across the open doorway. Tomorrow, Tanya vowed, she would find a cat to keep the kitchen clear of such pests. Tomorrow. . . . She shuddered. She was beginning to plan as if she intended to stay in the brothel!

Slipping from her bed she stepped into the courtyard. Below her, the water of the harbor glowed in the silver light of the moon. There was still no foreign ship in sight.

Alexius' face drifted into her thoughts, and she wondered, as she often had in the days since she learned she was pregnant, what his reaction would be were she to come to him bearing a Chinese infant in her arms.

She leaned against the stone wall of the courtyard and gazed toward the distant ocean. Somewhere out there, far to the north, she would find him. But she had to make her decision regarding her child long before she could ask for his guidance.

A breeze stirred the surface of the water. "If a ship comes in—when a ship comes in—I will try to board it. If I succeed in convincing the captain to take me, I will consider it a sign that what I do is right. I will have faith then that Alexius will receive my child and accept it as his own." Taking comfort in her acceptance of fate as the solver of her dilemma, she returned to her bed. She would look for a ship every day. She might have to wait until after the child was born. But she would try to leave China as soon as she could. She would have to put up with Mei Ling's growing madness and Wen Kui Fong's unwavering possessiveness for only a short while longer.

CHAPTER XI

In the months that followed, Tanya searched the harbor daily, but she could not find a vessel with a destination that suited her. Each week she grew larger until, at last, she knew she had waited too long. The child was due within a few months, and she dared not risk bearing it on the high seas with no woman to attend her.

There were compensations for the delay. The child growing in Tanya's belly became the center of life in the brothel. When the girls weren't working, they talked to her about proper customs, warning her to exert great caution so the evil spirits that always hovered nearby would not become jealous of her good fortune. Especially if she bore a son, she was to show no happiness, for there were ghosts who would certainly destroy such pleasure.

Tanya listened to most of such advice in silence, but when she realized that her compliance with their wishes was of great importance to everyone in the house, she grudgingly did as she was told. To show their happiness with her proper behavior, the girls showered her with gifts. Yuan Ling brought her amulets to make the birth easier. Wing Fui presented her with a small whip, assuring her that a boy who grew up understanding the power of the lash would become a rich and powerful man. Fuin Guan made certain that the small sand box on which the child would spend most of his infancy was prepared long before it was needed, and Tanya even had a special one built for her in her room so she could watch the child as he grew older. Tanya found the sand box both surprising and amusing, and she asked Fuin Guan to explain its use.

"Everyone knows that a child has no control of himself and needs to be tended. What do women do with children in your country? Do they let them satisfy their body functions wherever they wish?"

Tanya shook her head. "We put cloths around them which are washed out regularly."

Fuin Guan grimaced in disgust. "How filthy! You will see. The sand will absorb moisture. It is easy to care for a baby in China!" And since she could find no cloths both soft and absorbent enough, Tanya decided to follow the Chinese custom.

The other girls in the brothel, less successful than the specialists, still brought Tanya tokens of their affection for the child she soon would bear. And all of the girls watched her daily, ready to help her when it became necessary.

All of this attention somewhat alleviated the unhappiness Tanya felt at her necessary delay, though she continued to search the harbor for the appropriate vessel. And it was during one such search that she realized she was being followed.

She had paused on her way to the market to gaze at a ship just entering the port, its sails still open to catch the ocean breeze. It was so beautiful, outlined against the sky and water!

Suddenly, a movement in the shadow of a warehouse

caught her attention. It was the tall form of the eunuch Wi Sung, Wen Kui Fong's newest employee, and he was watching her intently. His long arms hung loosely at his side and his smooth chin was set.

She scurried from the dock. Evidently, though Mei Ling and Wen made little point of it, they planned to force her to remain in China. Wi Sung was strong and swift. She would never be able to outrun him, not even after the child was born.

It wasn't until she was on the road home that she remembered what Mei Ling had said about eunuchs while they were still concubines in the Governor's household. Handing the vegetables to Mio Kang, she hurried to her pallet. In the semi-darkness, she felt for her cache of coins. When her fingers touched only cotton stuffing, she felt a wave of panic. Lifting the mattress, she dug deeper. Still no money.

Sitting back on her haunches, she stared at Mio Kang, who was deeply involved in her task of stirring the rice. "Mio Kang, has anyone been near my mattress?"

Mio Kang looked up, her face devoid of expression. "Your mattress? No. Only the gluttonous cat you insist on keeping!"

Tanya sucked in her breath. "Mio Kang, have you taken my money?" She tried to keep her voice level, but it rose in pitch as she reached the end of her question.

Mio's expression did not change. Clamping her jaw tightly, Tanya stared at the stubborn old woman, silently damning her for her ability to lie without flinching. "Mio, that money was mine. I need it desperately."

"What use have you for money?" The old voice cracked. "The master buys you clothes when you need them and you eat of Mei Ling's food. You have a roof over your head and a bed to sleep in. And when your son is born, you will grow in the master's favor. You are not old, ready to die, and in need of prayers to help you over the great river into the afterlife!" She gasped for breath. "Who will pray for an old, useless woman if she does not pay the priest in advance? Each night I go to sleep unsure that the sun-god will light my eyes when the darkness is over! Who needs money more than I?"

The infant stirred in Tanya's stomach, but it gave her no pleasure. "Is all the money gone, then?"

Mio Kang nodded.

Tanya sank to her bed. She stared dry-eyed toward the harbor where the brave masts of the newly arrived ship sparkled in the sunlight. Without money with which to bribe Wi Sung, she would never be able to escape! She felt tears run down her cheeks.

A hand touched her shoulder. "Do not weep, Tan Ya." Mio Kang's voice was gentle. "Despair is for the old, not for a young woman like you. Why have you need for money? Surely Wen Kui Fong will give you everything you desire and will spoil your child when it arrives!"

Tanya gazed into the tired eyes, trying to steel herself against the sympathy they inspired. When she didn't speak, Mio Kang settled beside her, a conspiratorial gleam in her eyes. "You have a secret! Do you dream of buying a brothel of your own after your child is born?"

Tanya shook her head. "No. I wish only to be free."

Mio Kang looked puzzled. "What is freedom? Were you not living in the master's house, you would starve! There are many who die every day on the streets!"

Tanya chewed at her lip. "I don't just want to be away from here. I want to go aboard one of the big ships and sail away to my own people. I do not belong in China!"

Mio clucked nervously. "It is true, for Wen Kui Fong has said you are not of this land. But you speak our words and think as we do. Was it not you who hit the pots together to chase the evil spirits away when the master and Mei Ling spoke of the child as they stood at the doorway? And was it not you who cried out that you carried a girl when we feared the ghosts might become jealous? Did you not bargain with the farmers today and bring home more than I could have for the same money? You have become Chinese. You belong here—as does your child. You must cease to dream of other lands."

Mio Kang did not move. "You want to travel on that foreign ship that is now in the port when it leaves Canton?"

Tanya nodded. "I must! I belong. . . ."

Mio Kang shook her head. "You belong here! When next you pass a quiet pool of water, or step before the mirror in Mei Ling's room, look closely at yourself. If you went aboard that ship, they would make you a prisoner, as they do many Chinese—and they would try to sell you as a slave in some foreign land! I have seen them carry victims aboard. Is that what you want? To a Chinaman, you still look foreign—or at best, you appear to be a Manchu come on hard times." She paused and looked down at Tanya's feet. "It is your feet more than your face that gives you away as a foreigner. But the men in the ships are not that wise. They will see your gown and your braided hair, and they will consider you to be one of us. Why do you think they would treat you differently from any other Chinese?"

Mio Kang was right. Unless she could make herself look once more like an occidental woman, she would always be treated like a slave by any sailors she encountered. She would have to save her money again, but she would have to do more. Somehow, she would have to make herself a dress—a gown that would be in the occidental style.

Wiping her tears, Tanya tried not to think of the possibility that even after she was properly dressed she could be victimized; even if she paid for her passage, there was a chance that she could end up trading life in Mei Ling's brothel for slavery in some other land.

CHAPTER XII

"How do I look, Mio Kang? Do I look like a foreign lady?" Tanya twirled clumsily about, her protruding stomach spoiling the even shirring of her skirt.

Mio Kang chuckled. "Do foreign women wear dresses made of patchwork?"

Tanya felt her elation fading. "Please, Mio, you've seen foreign women on the wharf. Do I look like someone who would belong on one of the big ships?"

Mio Kang frowned. "You look Korean! Is that the country to which you wish to return?"

A sob rose in Tanya's throat. "Is it my stomach? If I wait until the baby is born and I'm small again, then. . . . ?" She stopped and fumbled with her hair. Undoing her braid, she pinned her tresses in a crown on top of her head. "Now do I still look Korean?"

"Now you look like a woman from Japan. I saw one once when she came to Canton with her husband. She was very beautiful."

Tanya pulled the wooden pins from her hair and rebraided it down her back. Patting the skirt into long folds, she hid it behind the stove. She would wait until Mio Kang was able to steal enough material for her to make a blouse.

But the blouse, when completed, did little to help change her appearance. When she once more hid the costume, repressing a desire to tear it up in disgust, Mio Kang put an arm around her shoulder. "Come, little mother. It is not good for you to be sad when the child is so close to being born. Come to the temple with me and we will pray for your baby—and for the dream you refuse to abandon. Come. We have time before Mei Ling and Wen return from visiting the place where Governor Chung Kai Chang lost his life."

At the temple, Mio Kang went first to the god of old age. Tanya stood awkwardly at the door and then, timidly, approached the figure of Hsi Wang Mu. As Chang's concubine, she had gazed at the statue and prayed to the Virgin Mary. Kneeling, she did so once more, asking for the courage to leave when her opportunity came and for the confidence to prove herself a Russian if she was treated like a Chinese runaway.

When she raised her head, some of her old poise had returned. Mio was standing beside her. "Now, before we leave, you must rub the belly of Ho Tai and ask for a son! Come, I'll show you where he is."

Tanya felt a tremor of uncertainty at participating in such a pagan practice, but nevertheless she left the temple feeling more optimistic than she had in many months.

On the way home, Mio bought Tanya a small figure of Ho Tai, showing her how to conceal it in her sleeve so she could rub it often throughout the day. She was obviously pleased at Tanya's return to good humor. "See! I told you the god Ho Tai could help you." She looked about and then leaned close to Tanya's ear. "You will have a son, I'm

sure. I have prayed for one each time I visited the temple.
I've even drawn a drop of blood from your stomach while
you were asleep and asked a soothsayer to predict with it,
and he has assured me you carry a boy." She glanced
swiftly about to make sure no evil spirits had overheard
her.

Tanya let herself flow with Mio Kang's good feelings. "I
hope so. Wen Kui Fong has said he would put a girl child
into the brothel as soon as she was old enough—or maybe
even kill her. Oh, Mio, he must not hurt my baby, no matter what it is!"

Mio looked at her reprovingly. "Cheer up! Think of Ho
Tai! Think of the prayers you said to the goddess. You will
have a son, and Wen Kui Fong will be proud."

As soon as they entered the kitchen, Tanya knew something was wrong. Mei Ling stood before the stove, her face
distorted with anger. "Mio Kang! Why have you kept these
scraps and sewn them into this strange gown? You know
they must all be made into pillows!"

Mio Kang cringed, but she remained silent.

Mei Ling raised her voice. "Speak, wretch! What do you
mean by stealing all this cloth?"

When Mio Kang remained silent, Tanya stepped forward, but Mio Kang pushed her back and fell on her knees
before Mei Ling. "Please, mistress, forgive me! I couldn't
resist their beauty! Please, I promise I will not do it again!"

Tanya stared into Mei Ling's face. Surely she knew the
gown did not belong to Mio Kang! When Mei Ling refused
to meet her eyes, she stepped over the prostrate woman. "I
did it! Leave her alone; she's an old woman—and she's
done nothing wrong!"

Wen stepped from behind his door. Roughly, he pulled
Mio Kang to her feet and pushed her toward the courtyard.
"Take her out and beat her. It is time she learned who her
masters are."

Mei Ling walked behind the old woman who half-
crawled, half-ran from the room. The door remained open
and Tanya caught a glimpse of Mei Ling as she lifted a
whip into the air.

Wen gripped Tanya roughly by her wrists. "I will not

touch you now, though you deserve to be whipped to death, for my son is soon to be born. But when he is delivered. . . ." He left the room, Mei Ling following.

Mio Kang's bruises were far less severe than Tanya feared they might be. By the time of the evening meal, she was on her feet and working as if nothing had happened. Nor did she reproach Tanya for her part in the episode, except to speak again of the importance of patience—and resignation to what the gods had to offer.

The following day, Tanya took the money put aside for food and started for the courtyard. Mio Kang rushed to block her way. "Let me go today, Tan Ya! I feel no ill-effects from my treatment yesterday. I've spoken to the soothsayer again, and he tells me this is a most propitious day for the birth of a son. Please! You must stay inside!"

"What foolishness!" Tanya gently brushed her aside. "I feel fine. When the birthing begins, I will know. I have no reason to listen to such superstitions." Before Mio Kang could stop her, she was out on the street.

As always, the fresh sea air revived her spirits, and the sight of a new ship in the harbor quickened her steps. When she reached the wharf, she stared at it in delight. It was Russian! Suddenly light-footed, she scurried ahead, her heart pounding furiously. Her foot was on the gangplank when she felt a hand on her shoulder. She was whirled around and lifted up like a child. "Let me go! Let me go!" Her fists pounded helplessly on Wi Sung's broad chest.

Suddenly, a sharp pain started in the small of her back and raced around to her stomach. Trembling, she pressed her hands on her abdomen. "The baby," she gasped. "My God, the baby's coming!"

Without a word, Wi Sung turned and began to run. He held her cradled in his arms, like a father holding a loved child, and his face was furrowed with concern. As he approached the courtyard he called loudly for Mio Kang, and the old woman was ready when he deposited Tanya on her pallet.

CHAPTER XIII

She was aware of movement about her before the next pain began, and then she was conscious only of its intensity. When next she felt relief, she realized that the room was filled with people. Mei Ling and Mio Kang crouched on either side of her, supporting her in a squatting position. Wen Kui Fong was standing far back in the room, gazing into the courtyard. Tradition dictated that he not be present, but he could not stay away from an event so significant in his life.

Before her was an old man dressed in the robes of a priest, and around him, jabbering noisily, were the young prostitutes. Through the curtain of her pain, she was aware that the priest was reciting well-turned phrases which she recognized to be from the classics. Wen Kui Fong wanted his son to have every possible advantage.

In his hand the priest held a censer into which he carefully dropped twenty pieces of grass and several likenesses of crabs. These he immediately set afire, swinging them over her body. When the smoke began to swirl above her head, he changed his rhythm, and she realized he was praying for the successful delivery of a strong male child.

Another pain gripped her, and she bent over with a moan. Immediately, the priest moved toward the door, swinging his censer and shouting loudly. The prostitutes and Mio Kang took up the cry. They were covering up her moans so any evil spirits who might be lurking nearby would not suspect a child was being born. It was good. The pains were coming quickly.

Yuan Ling crouched before her. "You are brave to be silent when you give birth. You are strong, like a true Chinese woman. My mother gave birth to seven after me, just as you are now. She stopped when she finished one row of plowing, squatted, and gave birth. Then, wrapping the child in her skirt, she continued her work. I have heard that foreign women are weak, crying out at birth, and lying feebly in their beds. You assure your child strong legs by bearing him in this manner."

Of the last, Tanya had her doubts, but it was true the birth was easy. The infant dropped gently into the waiting hands of Mei Ling, who handed it quickly to Mio Kang. There was a moment of silence, and then the child cried out lustily.

As Tanya watched, still convulsed with the pain of the afterbirth, Mei Ling rose and took the child from Mio Kang's hands. Wen had turned at the cry, and he approached Mei Ling, his arms outstretched. "Here is the child I have borne you!" Mei Ling's words were stilted. "Gaze upon him with joy."

Wen lifted the baby awkwardly, counting aloud the number of legs and arms, the toes, the fingers, and the ears. Finally, when he had examined the genitals and determined the infant was a boy, he lowered it to the bed, letting it rest in Mio Kang's hands. "Take care of my child, Mio Kang."

A faint smile touched his lips. "It is good that the foreigner gave me a son."

He turned and faced the doorway. Raising his voice, he spoke to the evil spirits that always hovered near when a child was born. "Fool! After all the care I have given you, you bear me a stinking daughter!"

Mio Kang and the girls all looked satisfied, but their cries, too, were addressed to the dangers that surrounded the new infant. "Aiya! Poor baby girl! A life of sorrow awaits her!"

Once more Wen turned to Mio Kang, but his words were still addressed to the jealous spirits. "Wrap this creature in rags! It is only a girl, and not deserving of fine clothes! I will have to find another woman who can bear me a son!"

Immediately, Mio Kang covered the male genitals of the infant. The priest, who had been standing at the door, nodded approvingly. But Mio Kang had one more ritual to complete. Wrapping the child in a blanket, she placed him on Tanya's stomach. "We will call the girl-child Fong Ya." She shouted the words for the benefit of any ghost that might still hover nearby. "When she grows older, she will be a good addition to the master's brothel." She smiled knowingly, and the onlookers began to straggle from the room. They had done all they could. If their efforts had succeeded in deceiving the evil spirits, the infant boy was safe.

A new sensation filled Tanya's breast as she felt the soft body of her child sink into the hollow between her breasts. She touched his tiny hands with awe and stroked the fine black hair on his head. Never in all of her dreams had she imagined motherhood to be so overpowering. Looking at the helpless infant, she knew she could never leave him, nor could she trust him in anyone else's care.

He opened his eyes and gazed into hers. Enraptured, she studied the trusting, defenseless infant. "I love you, Fong Ya. I love you as I have never loved anyone before."

Shifting him to one side, she gazed into his face. His tiny wrinkled features seemed all Chinese, and she felt a sudden pang of disappointment. But it lasted only for a moment.

His skin was pink and rosy, and there was no slant to his eyes. Gently, she kissed the top of his head. He was perfect—and he was hers—all hers!

His bud-like mouth began a sucking motion, and his tiny fists beat against her breasts. Quickly, Mio Kang bent down to help Tanya unbutton the front of her gown and place the hungry little mouth against her breast.

As she worked, Mio Kang began to speak. "You will not have milk yet, but do not worry. The infant's sucking will hurry its arrival and strengthen your body so you will be ready to bear another when he is grown." She whispered her words so as not to threaten the child's safety. "Move him to your other breast after a while, so you will stimulate them both. You must do all you can to encourage the flow of milk."

When she seemed satisfied that Tanya and the baby were comfortable, she pulled some coins from her mattress. "I go now to the soothsayer. He was right in predicting the day of birth. I have taken a strand of his hair and a drop of blood from the afterbirth. We must know what lies ahead."

When she returned, late in the afternoon, she was bursting with excitement. "What good luck! The child was born exactly at noon, which is a fortunate sign. The sorcerer divined his future, and he will grow to be a wealthy man, with a title of honor and learned above all who surround him!"

Tanya smiled indulgently. Even in her satisfaction at the favorable prediction, Mio Kang did not forget her duty to ward off the dangers that still hovered nearby. She had closed the door to the courtyard, and her voice was little more than a whisper. Settling herself beside Tanya, she stroked the baby's dark hair. "I see now that you went out in order to hasten the birth! You are a wise woman, wiser even than one as old as I."

Mei Ling descended the stairs, ushering out a customer. It was she who had decreed that even the arrival of the child should not be allowed to stop the flow of money into the coffers. The girls—and she—had work to do that was equally as important as Tanya's labor.

When Mio Kang told Mei Ling the soothsayer's prediction, Mei Ling snatched the infant from Tanya's arms. Startled by the sudden removal from his warm shelter, the child shrieked angrily, but Mei Ling made no attempt to comfort him. Turning him bottom up, she studied his thighs, searching for the mark that would prove the old woman's predictions to be true. When she discovered a dark spot on Fong Ya's white hip, she crowed with delight and recited a poem Tanya vaguely remembered hearing back in the compound.

> If on the loins the sign be found,
> Then rank with wealth and years is crowned,
> With honor when life's prime is told,
> And, elderly, blessed with yellow gold,
> Yea, though arisen from low degree
> His fate is true nobility;
> His scions, an illustrious band
> Who make a name within the land.

She cradled the howling infant in her arms and then, with a snort of annoyance, pushed him back onto Tanya's breast. Immediately, the crying ceased and the small mouth once more attached itself to her dark nipple. Mei Ling frowned. "Stupid child! He seems not to know that I am his true mother!"

Tanya saw no need to answer. Impatiently, she waited for Mei Ling to leave. But there was more to be done. Mei Ling pulled one small wrist from where it lay pressed against Tanya's body. She tied a bright red cord around the tiny arm, making certain that it would not slip over his hand. Little Fong Ya made satisfied suckling noises, and Tanya held him close, her heart swelling with joy at his well-being.

Mei Ling seemed unimpressed by his quickness at starting to nurse. She fixed her eyes on Tanya's face. "Do not take this cord off! Do you understand?"

Tanya nodded, her eyes on the round face of the child. She hardly noticed when Mei Ling left the room.

Wen Kui Fong returned much later, as the infant lay resting under Tanya's arm, his rosebud mouth working even in his sleep. There was a pride in his face as he gazed at the small bundle, but when he turned his attention to Tanya, his gentleness vanished. "The child is sleeping. Why do you lie uselessly on your bed?" He waited until she rose to her feet and tucked a blanket around the child to keep him warm. "We must understand each other well. You have borne me a son, and for that I am grateful. But you have also shown yourself to be rebellious and untrustworthy. I have not forgotten the affair of the cloth, nor do I fail to understand that it was you who made Mio Kang steal it! She is too stupid to be deceitful."

Tanya glanced down at the bed. Fong Ya turned in his sleep, his hands waving helplessly in the air.

"Mio Kang!" Wen's shout made Tanya jump with surprise. "Why have you not taught this foreign woman the proper way to carry a child? Do it now! For it is not good that he lie alone on a bed."

Mio Kang scurried over from the stove. Tearing a strip of cloth from one of Tanya's blankets, she tied it around Tanya's neck like a sling. The child was placed in front so that any time he was hungry he needed only move his hand and his food would be available. Wen watched with satisfaction.

"Good! Now you must understand. The child is to be with you wherever you go! You may wrap your big gown around him, for he is no longer in your stomach. Your duty to him is to feed him and keep him warm. But you have other duties as well. The girls need their food. Surely you cannot expect Mio Kang to trot up and down the stairs! Hurry, for they have customers who await their services."

Tanya felt her anger rise. What right had Wen to speak thus to her? But before she could answer, the infant's small lips closed around her breast. He lay snug and warm against her body, the sweet smell of infancy filling her nostrils. What would she gain by fighting with Wen? His love for her child more than compensated for his rude treatment of her.

The days slipped by smoothly. Tanya's duties as nursemaid to her child merged easily with the chores of caring for the brothel and its inhabitants. At first she felt some surprise at her own strength, for she had seen women in Russia lie abed for weeks after giving birth, but after a time she forgot; it seemed so natural for her to be active.

She was thankful for the work, for it kept her busy while she mulled through her new situation. Now, when she sought shelter on board a ship, it would be with a child in her arms. Unless she was willing to leave the boy with Mei Ling. The thought filled her with horror. She could never leave her child!

Little Fong Ya grew plump and rosy. Often, as she went about her duties, Tanya felt his pudgy hand creep toward her breast and his soft lips circle her nipple. His constant nearness filled her with a deep contentment.

Nevertheless, as the days passed into weeks, Tanya grew increasingly restless. Mio Kang did all the shopping, for it was generally agreed that it was dangerous to risk the child's safety in the streets. Spring passed into summer and the heat of the city streets poured into the house through the door, left open to catch the occasional breezes that blew up from the ocean. New ships sailed into the harbor, remained long enough to load cargo, and vanished out to sea, but Tanya had no opportunity to investigate them.

There were a few times when Mei Ling and Wen left her alone, as if tempting her to go, but she caught sight of Wi Sung, lurking near the gate, and she made no move to depart. If she was to get away, she had first to convince Wen that she no longer desired to leave.

When Fong Ya celebrated his third month of life, Wen confronted Tanya once more. "You have behaved well, Tan Ya. Can it be that the child has finally made you content with your life?"

Tanya did not answer, but her hand crept around the small body that lay against her breasts.

Wen caught the movement with his eyes. "I see that you have changed. And I also see that it is hard on the old one to trot each day to the market. You will resume that duty tomorrow."

Tanya nodded. She dared not look up into Wen's face for fear he would see her happiness. When he left the room, she settled onto her mattress, cradling the child in her arms. Her plans were fixed. When she saw a Russian ship she would run to it, and now her speed would not be hampered by the clumsiness of pregnancy. Wi Sung, who followed her at a distance, would not have time to catch her.

A week passed before she had an opportunity to test her scheme. As usual, she left the house with her bag and the shopping money tucked safely in her sleeve. Fong Ya slept fitfully, but she felt no concern, assuming that he only reflected her own uneasiness.

The street was bustling with its usual crowds. Small children raced wildly past struggling farmers who staggered under heavy loads of produce piled on their backs. An occasional sedan chair forced all the common workers from the narrow roadway. Soldiers dressed in bright uniforms pushed their way ahead of ornate horsemen bearing gifts for the new governor. A man stopped and relieved himself in the ditch that followed the thoroughfare, but Tanya felt no shock. Garbage from a shadowy kitchen was thrown on the street before her, and Tanya stepped calmly aside:

Suddenly, a beggar pushed himself before her, blocking her advance. He was coughing noisily, and the spittle from his mouth sprayed the air. Tanya drew back in disgust, and before he could recover himself and clutch at her gown, she was on her way. When she saw a stream of clear water running into the harbor, she stopped and washed her face.

She returned to the brothel with her purchases without further incidents, and in the days that followed, she forgot the affair completely. But twelve days later, little Fong Ya began to sicken. His shivering woke Tanya, and his body was burning with fever.

While Mio Kang was sponging the tiny limbs to lower his temperature, he suddenly went into wild convulsions. Mio Kang dropped to her knees, her eyes wide with alarm, and Tanya clutched the child to her breast, praying that he be relieved of his pain.

CHAPTER XIV

———

Mio's screams had awakened the entire household. One by one they scurried down to see what had caused the commotion, and when they saw the child sleeping fitfully in Tanya's arms, they hurried away, grouping themselves at the foot of the stairs and muttering prayers to their private gods.

Wen, who had preceded the women into the kitchen, stretched his arms above his head in supplication. "Oh Great Hsi Wang Mu, what use have you of my worthless girl-child? I keep her only out of pity for her plight, and she would be of no use to you." His voice broke and he lowered his arms in despair. The gods were busy. They had no time to listen to the pleading of one tortured father.

At last the women straggled back to their rooms and

Wen returned to his chamber. But Tanya spent the remainder of the night sitting propped against the wall, her child clutched in her arms.

Throughout the days that followed, the attention of the entire household was focused on Fong Ya's fever, which remained high no matter what measures Mio Kang suggested to relieve it. On the third day the fever abruptly vanished, but before Tanya could express her relief, she discovered small pustules breaking out all over his body. She recognized the symptoms. She had seen the disease in St. Petersburg, and had, in fact, been one of the few children to survive it. Fong Ya had smallpox.

Because her own bout with the disease had been light, she was not prepared for the severity of her son's illness. While the other women in the household burned incense and shouted their prayers for Fong Ya's recovery, Tanya held him close, doing what little she could to ease his discomfort.

And then, on the eighth day of his sickness, the fever returned. The pustules seemed to explode all over his body, and within an hour of the change, he began to have trouble breathing. Tanya paced the floor frantically. She had hardly slept from the moment his illness began, and she was sick herself from exhaustion, but she struggled to find some position for the baby that would ease his struggle for air.

She paced the floor restlessly, listening to the strained gasps, but there was nothing she could do to help. The small face was red, and he labored each time he tried to inhale, as if he was choking.

Mio Kang looked up in alarm from the food she was cooking, and Wen, who daily assumed a place near the courtyard door, there to shout his prayers and toss small firecrackers into the doorway, turned and gazed at the child. The struggle for breath continued, and then, so suddenly Tanya could not at first understand what had happened, his breathing ceased.

A shout of agony issued from Wen's lips and he charged across the floor, his earlier fear of infection forgotten. Mio Kang dropped the spoon into the pot and fell to her knees.

"Aiyah! Aiyah!" Her voice cracked with emotion. "The son of Wen Kui Fong is dead!"

Tanya clutched her child tighter to her breast. "No! Mio Kang, no! He isn't dead! Please!" But the hollow around her heart belied her cries. He was gone.

Wen moved suddenly to his room and emerged with a silken scarf which he wrapped around Fong Ya's head. Then, pulling the body from Tanya's encompassing arms, he held it up before him. "Why have you taken him from me? He was such a small creature!" He sobbed convulsively. "He would never have harmed you!"

Wen wasn't speaking to her—or to anyone else in the room. His words were for the evil spirits he feared. He had done all he could to protect his son—and he had failed. In her heart she felt a kinship for the weeping man, for they shared the same sorrow.

Every member of the household now returned to the kitchen. Throughout Fong Ya's sickness, they had feared infection. Now they feared something else far more. Dead, his spirit could return and punish them for any neglect they might have unwittingly inflicted upon him. His soul had to be placated. Even an infant, once dead, became a thing of terror, to be worshipped in fear and buried quickly—but with all due ceremony.

As each one of the girls bowed before the corpse, muttering her prayers for forgiveness, Tanya looked at Wen. He had moved to the stairs, and he stood there silently, watching the women offer their final good-byes to the dead child. His face was working, and his shoulders heaved.

When, at last, the girls all finished their prayers, he turned to Mei Ling. "Bury my son. And when that is done, get the foreign woman out of my sight. Sell her or kill her—do anything you wish. I do not want to see her again."

It was Mei Ling who brought order to the chaos he left behind. She sent the girls scurrying upstairs, ordered Wi Sung to find a priest and then, leaving the dead infant in Tanya's arms, hurried off to make preparations for the funeral.

Tanya sat alone in the kitchen, gazing at the face of her dead baby. She had loved him so! He alone had made life good in the squalor and ugliness of Canton. She looked at his small disfigured face and remembered how beautiful he had been. She had been too worried to weep during his illness, and now the tears were, at last, released. When Mei Ling and Mio Kang returned and took the child from her arms, she seemed hardly to notice. She was staring ahead in a stupor of misery.

Mei Ling did not hurry Tanya out into the street, nor did she call Wi Sung back to kill her. Instead, she calmly informed Mio Kang that she was to keep Tanya hidden in the kitchen until she had spoken once more to Wen. "He is too upset now to think sensibly. There is no reason to waste money just because the child is dead. We have fed this creature for months, and we must realize a profit on our investment. I will convince him. We will see to it that we get a good price for the foreign woman." She carried the body of Fong Ya out to the waiting priest. Mio Kang scurried with him down the street. Tanya rose to follow, but a word from Mei Ling brought her to a halt. Lying back on her pallet, she cursed the fear that kept her from following her infant to his grave.

As the house settled into mourning, she moved about in an apathetic haze. Her thoughts were erratic, filled with self-reproach. Had she brought death to her child by carrying him into the streets? Was she being punished for the many times she had resented the baby before it was born? Her heart, sore as it was from loneliness and the agony of separation, rejected such responsibility. She had loved little Fong Ya with her whole heart once he lay in her arms, and she had done nothing not approved by the others—by Wen himself. The city was filled with death. Why did she think her love could protect a child so young?

But her understanding did nothing to allay her sorrow. When Mio Kang returned, assuring her the infant had been properly buried, she joined the old woman in the traditional mourning. Tearing her clothes and pouring ashes over her head, she wailed loudly, beating her chest in agony, but through her lamentations she heard the cooing of her lost child. And when her nails dug into her arms in spasms of grief, she felt only the soft touch of his tiny hands.

But her loneliness was the greatest that night as she lay alone—for the first time since Fong Ya's birth—her breasts throbbing with milk, and knew there was no small mouth nearby to suckle her. Then her tears flowed without ceasing, and she knew at last that he was, in truth, gone forever.

"Mio Kang!" Mei Ling's voice cut through the cries of mourning that pervaded even the morning preparation of food for the girls. "Here is a gown. Put it on the foreigner! She has no right to weep with us, for she has no faith in our gods!"

Tanya turned from the pot of rice and looked into Mei Ling's sharp features. There had been a time when the girl had been lovely, her face calm and smooth. Now, already, it was creased with lines of anger and hate, and her eyes were sharp and resentful. She alone in the household seemed untouched by Fong Ya's death.

Her wrinkled face clearly showing her fright at going against traditional mourning procedures, Mio Kang helped Tanya sponge herself clean. Tanya made no protest. She had heard the conflict that had taken place in the big room upstairs. Back and forth the voices had argued, Wen's crackling in fury and agony, Mei Ling's cool and filled with quiet malice. Whatever had been said, they had reached a decision. As soon as morning came, Wen had hurried out to complete the arrangements. Tanya was to be sold immediately.

Before she buttoned the red dress Mei Ling had provided, Mio Kang pumped the overflow of milk from Tanya's distended breasts. Too overwhelmed by her loss to care what happened to her, Tanya endured the discomfort patiently, aware only of how soft little Fong Ya's lips had been when they pulled at her nipples. She felt empty—only vaguely realizing that she should care what was happening to her, but unable to muster any real concern for her own future.

When she was dressed, Wen appeared at the foot of the stairs. His face was strained, and his eyes had a hollow look, as if he had spent many hours in weeping. Despite her dislike of what Wen had done to her and her resentment for the part he had played in her mistreatment, she felt only pity for him now. Whatever he had done in the past, he had loved Fong Ya, and that love bound them together. Her pain and loss were eased because she shared them with him.

Mio Kang grasped her hand, tears streaming down her cheeks. "May you prosper, Tan Ya!" Her tone told Tanya she did not believe it possible.

Tanya looked into the red eyes. "Dearest Mio! I will pray for your soul, even if the others show no concern. You have been kind to a lonely woman. May Hei Wang Mu reward you!"

When she turned, the girls were huddled once more on the steps. Tanya walked to where they waited. "Thank you all for your friendship. And thank you for the love you gave my son! I will not forget you."

Mei Ling was nowhere in sight. She had said good-bye to the Mei Ling who had been sweet and friendly on the night when Sing Fa and Chi Guar had been exposed for sharing a forbidden love.

Wen stood waiting at the door. When Tanya reached his side, she bowed politely. "I'm ready to go. You may take me wherever you will. I can no longer condemn you, or be angry with you for your treatment of me, for you have loved Fong Ya, and I know his. . . ." Her voice broke and the emptiness in her heart increased. Wen's eyes were wet, and though he had appeared impatient to have her gone, he did not turn away from her grief.

They stood facing each other for a moment, and then he turned and stepped into the late-afternoon sun. As was proper, Tanya walked ten paces behind him, hurrying to keep up when his pace quickened. A beggar pushed between them, tugging at Wen's arm. He cursed and pushed him aside.

As they reached the foot of the hill, a small boy chased after them, taunting Tanya for her large feet, but his shouts of derision served only to remind Tanya that her son would never grow to dance down the streets. With a sob, she turned to watch as the puzzled child ran off to join his friends.

Odors assailed Tanya's nostrils, odors which, now that she was leaving, seemed suddenly sharp—and important. Food vendors straggled by, their fragrances fighting for her interest. The penetrating odor of fresh fish drew her attention, but before she could locate its origin, another odor replaced it.

Ahead of her a small boy squatted to relieve himself, and Tanya remembered how shocked she had been the first time she saw a child make use of the odd-shaped drawers which permitted such easy evacuation. Now there was nothing unusual about the sight—only a bittersweet awareness that her son would never grow up, that in her memory, as in his brief life, he would forever remain an infant.

Wen increased his pace, forcing Tanya to run to keep up with him. He turned toward the dock, and suddenly her heart began to race. There were merchants there, that was true, and he might have sold her to one of those. But there were ships there, as well.

She almost laughed when she realized that in her dress she had the clue to her fate. Mei Ling had given her cast-offs. Her dress was red, the proper color for a wedding, but her head-dress was appropriate only for an already married woman. Mei Ling had dressed her thus because she knew she didn't have to please one who knew the customs of China.

On the dock, Wen waved his hand toward a ship that rode low in the water. "You are to go on that ship. You will move quickly to the cabin the ship's master will show you, but you will not take off your veil. Remember! You must remain covered until the ship is far from the dock."

He stared into the water. "You have always said you wished to leave China." He paused, and when he continued, his voice was wavering. "You must not walk too firmly, for the captain believes you are a Chinese maiden." His voice grew steady once more. "I have told him that it is the custom for Chinese brides to remain covered on their wedding night. It doesn't matter once you are at sea. He will have to take you as you are. And until then, you must hope he will be too busy to look under your veil."

Tanya was overcome by *déjà vu*. She had entered China with only the clothes on her back, and she was leaving in the same manner. Quickly, she climbed the wooden plank, stepped onto the deck, and stood waiting for directions from the mate. She glanced down at the dock, but Wen was already plodding up the hill, his heavy step devoid of the lightness that had been so characteristic of him until little Fong Ya's death. His usually square shoulders drooped. Never, she realized, had she seen a man so alone.

The singsong cries of the sailors and the quickening of the wind told her the ship was beginning to move. Behind her the rattle of the anchor chain stopped. When no one paid any attention to her, she felt suddenly lost—and very alone. Did she belong here, on a strange ship, disguised as a Chinese woman? She had seen the ship's name and heard the calls of the sailors; she knew she was on a Spanish vessel. But where was it going? And how would she be received by the captain?

A lithe man in a neat blue-and-white uniform stepped to her side. *"Buenas dias, senorita. Vamonos."* He waved his arm in the direction of the poop deck. Slowly, her legs not yet accustomed to the rolling waves, she made her way to the captain's cabin.

Just before she stepped inside, she saw the master of the vessel. He was tall and thin, with broad shoulders and a strong-looking body. He was facing away from her, speaking to the man who stood at the wheel, and his long black hair blew behind him in the wind. His face remained hidden from her view.

As she entered the dim interior of the cabin, she smiled grimly. The meeting that lay ahead would be a surprise to her, but at least she knew he was Spanish. Her unknown captain—her new master—knew nothing of her origins. Nothing at all.

224

PART III

California

1800

CHAPTER I

Temporarily blinded by the half-light of the cabin, Tanya leaned against the closed door. As in the *Russian Princess*, a wide row of portholes extended across the stern of the ship, with a series of low cabinets forming a seat before them. But in most other ways, this cabin was different. She stumbled across the room and sat down.

The details of her new surroundings became clear in the light that spilled over her shoulder. The cabin was larger than Adam Czerwenki's—and far more cheerful. A large teakwood bed, carved with dragons and covered with red brocade, filled one corner of the room near the door. Across from it was the cabinet on which a wash basin and water pitcher were anchored. A thick oriental rug filled

227

with the same designs she had seen in Chung Kai Chang's household hid the planks of the deck.

The walls were covered with ornate hangings depicting birds and flowers, either hand-embroidered or painted with a fine brush. The door through which she had entered was heavily carved with a mountain scene. A large desk, similarly ornamented, filled the center of the room, and even the chairs showed an oriental influence. Considering his love of oriental art, Tanya wondered whether the captain of the *Senorita Francesca* might not be angered when the woman he had added to his collection was not what he expected her to be.

Tanya turned and gazed for a last time at Canton. Coolies were trudging along the dock, their backs burdened with heavy bundles. Behind a jumble of brothels and warehouses, the sun was turning red, streaking the sky with color. She searched the silhouettes for a last view of Mei Ling's house and finally identified it in the distance, the flags of mourning hanging from its roof and windows. Folding her arms across her breasts, she sadly cradled the memory of the child she could never hold again.

Slowly, the ship changed course until the portholes were facing the main part of the city. Far in the distance she could glimpse the high walls of the governor's palace. A tremor ran through her body. "Good-bye, Chung Kai Chang. I won't forget the beauty you let me share. I wish you had seen your son, Fong Ya. He was so tiny—so helpless!" Throwing herself on the bed, she gave vent to her grief until, exhausted by her weeping, she fell into a deep sleep.

"*¡Maria, Madre de Dios! ¿Que tener aqui?*"

With a start, Tanya was awake. She lay for a moment, gathering her wits, and then she was on her feet, her hands fumbling awkwardly with her disarrayed headdress.

A long, sinewy hand touched her fluttering fingers. "*Descansa, descansa.*"

The words meant nothing, but the tone was soothing. She looked up into the dark brown eyes of a man who, despite his appearance of youth, was at least as old as her father. The glimpse she had caught of him as she boarded the ship had made her aware of his dark hair, but now she also saw his salt-and-pepper beard, pointed neatly, and his thick mustache that almost hid his sensuous lips.

"*¿Quien tenamos aqui?*"

Still adjusting her headdress, Tanya lowered her head, aware from the look on her new master's face and the tone of his voice that there was no need to pretend she was Chinese. Still she did feel a need to explain that she had not been party to the duplicity.

The calm voice cut through her musings. "*Los oriente es persono de dos caras.*" His strong hand moved toward her face and she braced herself for a blow, but he did not hit her. Lifting her chin, he brought her eyes once more up to his own. With the other hand, he gently removed the head-dress and tossed it carelessly onto the bed. She struggled with uncertainty as to which language she should use and then, with a proud lift of her shoulders, chose Russian. "I am not an oriental."

He nodded, a smile cutting a line through his beard. "*¡Sabe! ¿Esta Ruso?*"

She nodded, still wondering at his surprising good humor. When he burst into laughter, she winced, not sure at first that he was not bellowing in rage.

He laughed uncontrollably, moving to his chair and sinking into it weakly. At last, he lifted his head and called loudly. "*¡Juan!*"

A young sailor soon stepped inside. "*¿Si, Capitan?*"

"*¡Venga aqui!*"

"*Si, Capitan.*"

The young man who stood before them was little more than twenty, with a wiry body and a sharp face that reminded Tanya of a bird. His nose served as a point toward which all his other features aimed, both his chin and forehead receding as if pressed back by some monstrous hand. He was far shorter than the captain, but his shortness did not appear to detract from his strength. His arms rippled with muscles and he balanced himself against the sway of the ship with sturdy legs. As soon as he reached the captain, he saluted smartly.

They spoke for some time, and it was clear to Tanya that she was the focus of their conversation. More than once the captain gestured in her direction and his face filled with mirth. At last he bowed to her. "*Me llamo Capitan Manuel de Vincente, servidor de usted.*"

"I. . . . My name is Tanya. Tanya Ivanovich."

"*¡Bueno!*" He turned to Juan, again launching into swift speech. Then, with another bow to Tanya, he left the cabin. Juan stepped toward her, smiling broadly. "You are not at all what the captain expected!"

His words were sweet to her ears. Russian! Wiping her face with her hand, she attempted to repair the damage her tears had done to her makeup, but she could tell by Juan's laugh that all she succeeded in doing was to smear it more. Shaking her head, she looked into his face. "Thank God you speak Russian. I know no Spanish."

"So I see. I learned your language when I was impressed as a seaman on the *Tsarina.*"

Tanya knew nothing of such a ship. "How long did you serve on her?"

Juan chuckled. "No longer than I had to! I've never been treated to the lash as often as I was on that floating prison! I managed to jump ship at the Sandwich Islands while the *Senorita Francesca* was in port." He frowned. "What put you on the *Princess?* I saw no passengers' quarters."

At first hesitantly, then with an increasing rush of words, Tanya recounted her story, omitting only mention of Alexius. When she reached the death of little Fong Ya she burst into tears. It was not until she acknowledged the offering of a kerchief to dry her eyes that she realized the captain had returned to the cabin.

Juan immediately translated her account to de Vincente, who listened impassively, without interruption. When Juan concluded, the captain said a few words to him, though his gaze was directed toward Tanya.

"The captain says he feels great sympathy for your losses." Juan translated. "He, too, has seen loved ones die. He says he feels a responsibility to show you that all seamen are not as heartless as those you have already met.

For now, he suggests that you might wish to rid yourself of the paint that smears your cheeks. There is water in the pitcher. We will return in a short while."

As the dirt washed away, Tanya found herself smiling. Even the memory of her bereavement could not diminish her joy at finally leaving China. She unbraided her hair and let it fall loosely around her shoulders. At last she felt like a Russian! She vowed she would never braid it again.

But it would be utterly impractical to let her hair hang free. And so she carefully rebraided it, but into one thick plait that she threw over one shoulder. Then she stared at her gown. There was nothing much she could do to alter it and so she let it be. But she could not repress the wish that she could dress again in decent, occidental clothing. She took one final look at herself in the mirror and hurried to the door.

She smiled when Juan and Captain de Vincente entered. "The captain says he is happy you feel better," Juan said in Russian. "He is prepared to offer you the best accommodations the *Francesca* can provide, but he regrets that we have no guest cabins. You will sleep most comfortably if you share his quarters. Do not worry. He will give you a separate bed—and privacy."

She looked about the room, carefully avoiding de Vincente's eyes.

"May I suggest, Tanya Ivanovich, that you partake of the captain's kindness," Juan added. "There is no other place for you—unless you stay in the hold."

"Please thank the captain for me. I will stay here, as he suggests."

She could tell by the expression on the captain's face that he needed no translation of her words. A friendly smile lit his face, and the openness with which he met her eyes reassured her. When he turned to speak to Juan, she continued to study his face, and what she saw pleased her.

He was a man of at least fifty, with black hair that was greying around the temples. His face was rugged, revealing a strength of character that had been missing in Adam Czerwenki. Manuel de Vincente was secure in his position of authority, and his confidence permitted him to show consideration for his crew that had never existed on the *Russian Princess*.

His features were long, and he had a small salt-and-pepper beard that tipped his chin, separating itself from his thick sideburns by an expanse of carefully shaved cheek. It was a noble face, one that, Tanya decided, could be trusted.

De Vincente bowed to Tanya and left the cabin. She could hear him issuing orders. Had the fact that the captain made her think of her father, Ivan Ivanovich, swayed her?

There was a shuffling at the door and two sailors entered with a thick mattress. "I suggest you put your bed in the corner farthest from the portholes. The sea can often be violent," Juan said. The sailors positioned her bed and put a screen around it. "I regret we have no dresses suitable for a lady. If you wish, I can bring you some of the cabin boy's clothing. Trousers and a shirt will be more appropriate on the voyage that lies ahead."

"Thank you. This robe seems strange already. I'm tired of looking like a Chinese woman."

While Juan supervised the men, Tanya returned to the one question still nagging her. Why had de Vincente been so calm in his acceptance of what she knew had to be a total surprise to him? He had obviously expected a woman who would share his bed, and she could not believe he would give up such a plan without a struggle. She reluctantly acknowledged to herself that she even felt piqued at his seeming lack of interest.

"Juan, will you help me learn Spanish? I feel most awkward when I cannot converse with the captain, and you can't remain as translator all the time."

He smiled mischievously. "But of course! The captain has already made it one of my duties."

He started by teaching her the words for "thank you" and "for your kindness." Then, as the sailors left, their work finished, he, too, turned to leave.

"One more thing, Juan. Where is the *Francesca* heading?"

Juan pulled a map from a basket that stood near de Vincente's desk and unrolled it. Tanya quickly located Okhotsk in the far upper left corner. Below it was the bulge of land Ivar had called Silla, but which was named Korea, and beneath that was the great belly of China.

Juan's finger pointed to a spot in the middle of the water. "We're right here now, just off the coast of China, near the island of Formosa. The captain will go outside the island this way, past Japan. We came from Sumatra, where we picked up a hold full of teakwood. Now we take the northern route so the captain can see what the Russians are up to before we return to Monterey." He caught her puzzled glance. "Pardon me, ma'am, but the Russians are causing us a great deal of trouble. They're poaching on our trapping and rousing the Indians. We never know when they might try to start a full-scale war." His finger completed its circle, sweeping up past a chain of islands far to the northeast.

Tanya's heart leapt. "Will we be going to Unalaska?"

"Probably not. The Russians have moved their base to Kodiak, and they've just recently built a fort on Sitka Island. Fort Archangel Gabriel, I think it's called. If we don't stop them, they'll build another on the mainland, right on our territory!"

He promised to return with the cabin boy's clothing, and departed. She gazed at the map, wondering if she would be able to persuade the captain to put her ashore at one of the Russian colonies, or if the antagonism that existed between the two countries would make such a move impossible.

De Vincente entered, nodded at her briefly, and studied the same map. Taking instruments from a drawer in the desk, he began to measure off segments from the island of Formosa up past Japan. When a knock sounded on the door, he looked up in surprise. "Come in!"

Juan entered, a roll of clothing in his hands. "I've brought some of Francisco's trousers for the lady, sir."

De Vincente nodded without answering, and watched until Juan left the room. Then he returned to his maps.

Taking courage, Tanya circled the desk. When his eyes met hers, she curtseyed, aware that she might appear ridiculous performing such an act in her Chinese gown. "*Gracias, Capitan de Vincente. Gracias.*"

His eyes twinkled. "*Por nada, senorita. Por nada.*" Once more he looked down at his map.

Tanya gathered up the shirt and trousers Juan had provided and retreated behind her screen. When she stepped out again, de Vincente raised his head. "*Aha! La senorita esta un muchacho.*"

She felt disappointed. She had heard that word used to refer to the cabin boy.

"*Pero, una buena Muchacha.*" His eyes were smiling, and he rose from his seat. She stood awkwardly, waiting for him to move, but he remained still, looking at her pensively. At last he resumed his seat.

"May I go on deck?"

He looked puzzled, so she pointed to the door. Immediately, he nodded. As Tanya left the cabin, he seemed lost in concentration.

Juan was working on some ropes nearby. "You make a pretty boy!" When she did not respond, his expression sobered. "Shall we tour the ship?" She nodded absentmindedly. She felt disquieted and annoyed at herself. She should be pleased that de Vincente was such a gentleman. Why, then, was she mainly upset and angry?

She forgot her perturbation under Juan's tutelage. He took her over the deck, naming each part first in Russian and then in Spanish. The *Senorita Francesca* was a typical cargo vessel, broad of beam and riding low in the water. To Tanya she was beautiful. The large white sails billowing in the wind seemed like mighty wings, reflecting the sun proudly. The deck was spotlessly clean and in perfect order. When Juan reached the central mast, he paused and pointed to the helm.

"There is where the navigator steers. We're taking a northern route." A sailor hurried by, stopping to smile at her as he passed. Juan plucked her sleeve. "The captain doesn't want you to become familiar with the crew."

"Am I his prisoner, then?"

Juan looked surprised. "He bought you from Wen Kui Fong. You are whatever he wishes you to be."

They moved toward the railing. The ship was moving

234

smoothly, raising a wake in the unruffled water. China was no longer in sight.

Juan followed her gaze. "It is sad to leave a land where one has lived," he said.

"I feel no sadness at leaving China." She knew she spoke only a half-truth. Much in China had been terrible, but there had been beauty there, too—and love. "Will we trade with the Russians?"

Juan's face darkened. "Never! The Russians confiscate foreign ships that approach their harbors."

"Tell me about your country. I didn't know the Spanish traded in the Pacific."

"Everyone thinks we do nothing, just because we prefer to keep the wealth of the New World to ourselves! Mexico is a land of wonders, filled with gold and precious jewels. I was born in Culiacan, where the long arm of the Baja California shelters the land from strong surf and the sun shines all the time! Someday, I will return there and take a wife."

"Do the Spanish own this Baja California?"

"The Spanish own all the lands along the west coast of America. We own lands no man has yet explored, and they are all rich with gold! And beautiful, too! There is nothing as lovely as the bay of Cortez, with its slow tides and clear blue waters—unless it be the bays of Sur California. Our journey will take us to the harbor of Monterey."

"Have the Russians any harbors?"

"Not like those of San Francisco or Monterey! Or Santa Barbara, or San Diego. There are so many that belong to us. Still, I hope the captain takes you with us when we return to Culiacan. I will enjoy showing you my home."

It was dark when she returned to the cabin. The lamp's soft glow filled the cabin. De Vincente didn't look up when she entered, and so, after a time, she moved to the corner that now was reserved for her.

Slipping out of her still unfamiliar shoes and trousers, she lay down, her mind dwelling on Juan's statement that to the captain "You are whatever he wishes you to be." Did he mean to imply that de Vincente would treat her as a chattel—as so many men had done before? What she wanted was the chance to direct her own affairs. Was there any hope that her days of being a victim of men's lust and greed were past? De Vincente's considerateness gave her cause to hope.

Then her thoughts turned to Juan. He had shown such pride in his home. Where was home for her? Was it in Russia, where she had duty but no family? Was it, after all, in China, where her infant son lay buried? Her heart told her she would never see either country again. Her home was with Andreiv, where it had been from the moment she lay in his arms in the Conservatory.

She heard de Vincente stir, and extinguish the lamp. She froze, expecting him to appear behind her screen, but though he moved about for some time, he did not approach her corner. At last she heard a rustling on his bunk as he settled down. He began to snore lightly.

She lay for a long time wide awake. Manuel de Vincente was, after all, a gentleman. Maybe, if she spoke to him about Andreiv, he would understand. He might even be willing to help her search for her lover.

The vision of Andreiv, tall, handsome, wonderful Andreiv, pushed itself into her consciousness, and she knew that her hopes for the future were overshadowing her memories of the past for the first time since her life had fallen apart in Prince Paul's cottage.

CHAPTER II

Each day Tanya's knowledge of Spanish grew until she could name all the parts of the ship. Juan had mentioned the animosity between the Russian colony and Spain only once again, and his dislike for all things Russian had upset her. But the following day Juan said, "I'm glad to see you are happy again! I truly am sorry that I spoke of fighting. Loving Russia as you do, I should have known it would offend you."

"It's not that I love Russia so very much. She—or rather the Tsar—has been very cruel to me. It's just that I know someone in Unalaska, and when you mentioned that they were starving. . . ."

"I truly regret having distressed you."

Captain de Vincente called them both to his cabin.

He spoke to Juan first, and when the sailor left, threw himself into his great chair, his narrowed eyes on Tanya's face.

"*¿Por que?*" she asked, haltingly.

Slowly he explained that he wished her contact with Juan to be limited to instruction, and when she seemed to understand, he forced a smile. "*No tengo enojado.*"

He stepped closer and held her chin in his hand, gently stroking her cheek. "*¡Buena! ¡Muy buena!*"

Almost immediately, his expression changed again. Gesturing helplessly, he began to stride about the cabin. "*¿Comprende? ¡Muy buena senorita!*"

She nodded. She was finally beginning to understand. He was frustrated at her inability to understand him. He wanted her to learn more quickly—and he thought she was beautiful! She looked down at the trousers that hung loosely over her legs. Then, holding an imaginary skirt in her hands, she curtseyed deeply. "*¡Gracias, senor!*"

He pulled a chart from the basket beside his desk and began to study it, as was his custom when he wished to be alone. She stood watching and then, aware that he felt the best solution to his inability to communicate was to say nothing, she moved to the portholes.

But his behavior disturbed her. Until he had summoned Juan and her from the deck, he had always behaved toward her as would a perfect gentleman. Was this the beginning of an unpleasant change? Would she learn now that he was no better than any of the other men who had had power over her life?

Francesco, the cabin boy, entered carrying a tray of food. De Vincente, at the desk, stood and pulled her chair back. Gratified, she sat down and waited for him to resume his place. With a flourish, he lifted the cover on the shiny silver bowl. "*Comas, por favor.*"

With a spark of inspiration, Tanya began to name each item of food as well as the utensils. De Vincente was delighted. When she stumbled on a word, he helped her, until what had started as an uneasy evening became a friendly and happy one.

When he poured the wine, he smiled. "*Vino tinto.*"

238

"*Sí, vino tinto.*"

"*¡Maravilloso!*" He picked up his glass and touched it to hers in salute.

He did not, as was usual, take up his charts when the table was cleared. Instead, sitting down beside her on the seat by the bulkhead, he taught her some of the words Juan might have missed. Once more he hammered his hand on the cushion, repeating the word for "angry."

He smiled, frowned, laughed, pretended to cry, each time telling her the Spanish word for the emotion. Then, putting an arm around her shoulders, he softly kissed her lips, barely making contact. Immediately, he pulled back. "*¡Amor!*"

Smiling tremulously, she repeated. "*¡Amor!*"

He returned to his desk.

Confused by his sudden change of behavior, Tanya remained by the portholes, deliberately avoiding looking at de Vincente until it became evident he had no intention of speaking to her again. Then, with a murmured "goodnight" to which he did not respond, she retired behind her screen.

That night Tanya was terribly aware of the presence on the other side of the room. Each time he shifted, as he did often, she awoke and lay stiff and silent, staring at the reflection of the water on the ceiling.

When she slept, her dreams were of Alexius. She was walking toward him, her arms extended, but he showed no pleasure at her approach. More than was usual in her dreams, she was aware of his body. It was tall, strong, muscular. Then it was not his body at all. Suddenly, as if a veil had dropped, she found herself looking at the image of Manuel de Vincente.

She awoke in a sweat. Did she really want this man whom she knew so slightly, this man who fluctuated between extreme preoccupation and total politeness? She heard him shift in his bed, moaning lightly. Her flesh tingled.

The next week Tanya spoke only Spanish with Juan. At last she felt she could do something about the silence that had persisted between de Vincente and herself since the lesson which had ended in a kiss. When Juan mentioned that the ship's stores contained excellent linen as well as fine silver and crystal, she was immediately intrigued.

"Where did it come from? Why is it aboard?"

"It belongs to the captain. He purchased it in China, and he is taking it back with him to Monterey, to furnish the home he is building there."

"Do you think he would object to using it now?"

Juan was silent for a moment. "I don't think he would object to anything you wished to do, *senorita*."

"Are there also any lengths of Chinese silk aboard? Some not intended for trade?"

Juan smiled conspiratorially. *"Si, senorita."*

In a moment, he returned.

Tanya spread the soft silks Juan had brought on the bed, picking two that matched. "Has Francesco had a chance to clean the dishes and silver?"

Juan nodded. *"Si.* Will you need my help any more?"

"No, thank you, Juan. You've made me very happy."

Francesco arrived as Juan left, and together they set the table. Juan had not only provided silver and fine bone china, he had also found a fine cloth of white Irish linen. When the table was finally ready, Tanya stepped back and viewed it with satisfaction. "Francesco, call Juan. He must see how beautiful it is!"

Juan was properly appreciative, though it was clear he did not fully understand why she put such value on the table setting. Then he and Francesco left the cabin.

Removing her shirt, Tanya draped a pale blue cloth embroidered with golden peacocks over her front and pulled a darker one behind, overlapping the two lengths at one shoulder. The overlap she tied with a ribbon that fell from the bundle. Another ribbon went around her waist. Then, spreading the improvised skirt, she concealed her baggy trousers. Taking one more ribbon, she tied it under her breasts, making their rounded rise more marked.

De Vincente, entering the cabin for the evening meal, found her standing behind the table, facing the door as if

240

she were a hostess awaiting her guest. "I felt we should have more formal dinners. I hope you aren't angry."

He moved slowly toward the table. "Where did you get that gown?" he asked, as he pulled out her chair, and then seated himself.

"Juan brought me some scraps from the silk you have sold." She blushed. "Don't be angry at him. He only did as I asked."

"You speak very well now," he said. "I think we can stop the lessons."

"I have much more to learn. Please allow me to continue!"

De Vincente stared at Tanya solemnly, his eyes moving from her head down to her rounded breasts. He looked at her exposed shoulder, and she felt a warmth spread across her.

His voice was low, but she heard it distinctly. "You expect me to permit you to choose a man from the crew?"

She looked into his eyes. "I do not expect to choose a man at all! I thought you gave me my freedom!"

"I also waited until I could speak to you in a tongue we both understood."

"You do not object to—" Tanya gestured at the table and her dress. "—all this?"

"No, it is lovely. But it is not for the eyes of the men."

"I will wear my other clothes when I am on deck."

"I cannot permit you to fraternize with the men. They have a difficult enough time, without having a beautiful woman parade before them daily, a woman they dare not touch. Were we on land, you would remain at home, where other men would not be tempted." He paused. "I particularly worry for my first mate. He is a passionate young man, and I have seen him look at you."

They finished the meal and the wine that Francesco had brought in, and de Vincente hurried from the cabin. When he returned, Tanya was already in her bed.

She heard him move about, pacing between the door and the portholes. More than once she heard him approach the screen. Then he would turn and take up his pacing again.

Lulled by the slapping of the waves, she fell into a dreamless sleep.

She awoke suddenly, aware that she was being watched.

De Vincente was standing at the foot of her bed, his eyes glazing, his hands knotted into fists.

De Vincente extended his hand. "Come with me," he ordered gruffly.

De Vincente's eyes were aglow. "*¡Dios!* You are beautiful!" Stepping back, he ripped off his shirt and dropped his breeches to the floor. His desire was evident, but he showed no shame. Instead, he drew her into his arms.

She had expected violence; but she received tenderness. His lips burned her breast and his body pressed against hers. Then he swept her into his arms and carried her to his bunk.

Placing her gently on the coverlet, he sat beside her. His fingers touched her dark hair, letting it fall loosely to the pillow. They moved to her face, caressing her cheek so lightly she shook with a sudden desire. When his hands reached her neck they paused, and then moved on, making small circles on her flat belly.

They ran lightly through the hair on her mound of venus, the touch stirring long dormant sexual juices. Then, as if he was totally unaware of the effect of his exploratory probing, he moved his fingers to her legs, running smoothly down them and up once more to her thighs which were clamped rigidly together.

Slowly, imperceptibly, he forced her legs apart, until, in a spasm of determination, she pressed them together again.

"You intend to withhold your services from me? I have been a gentleman, and maybe you have forgotten that I am a man, too. You may be willing or you may resist, but I can have you whenever I desire."

Tanya moaned and rolled from the bed to the floor, kneeling before him, fear warring with passion. She looked up at him in supplication as he watched her impassively, his manhood still erect. Then, gently but firmly, he placed both his hands behind her head and pulled her to him. When she felt him shudder at the contact, she experienced a long-lost sense of power. Under the stimulus of this new emotion, she found herself pursuing a more aggressive role, using her tongue and her lips to manifest her aroused eroticism.

He grunted with pleasure and leaned back, his hands following her head, catching it, ever so often, and pressing it toward his surging desire. Each time, lightly, she slipped away, only to return again, even more fervently.

With a groan that almost sounded like agony, he pulled her to her feet, held her close for a moment, and then lifted her up and lowered her to the bed. He was upon her immediately, pressing himself between her thighs. She echoed his cry, clasping herself to him with a strength that lifted her hips from the bed. Then she was once more pinned down, as he penetrated and began to move within her.

Tanya felt herself grow faint from the intensity of her response. She was aware of a voice crying and she realized it was her own. Her arms reached up as if powered by some unseen force and moved up and down his back, increasing their speed as he increased the rhythm of his thrusts.

Suddenly, she felt his body grow stiff, and he began to shake convulsively. Clutching him desperately, she felt herself slip into a strange state of semi-consciousness. She heard him cry, and his cry was echoed by a voice she knew to be her own.

When at last he lay still she felt herself too weak to move. She waited, expecting him to withdraw, but instead he rolled slightly to one side, remaining firm within her. A new sensation grew in the warm moistness between her legs. Slowly, ever so slowly, he rolled until she lay above him, her body pressed down on his, connected by their desire. Gently he placed his hands on her hips and began to rotate them.

She closed her eyes. In her half-consciousness she was aware of his voice, whispering, cajoling. "*Buena*, Tanya. Tanya *Linda*. Oh, I have wanted you from the moment I saw you asleep on my bed! My dearest!"

She felt herself melt once more with pleasure, and then he held her quietly, keeping their contact as they fell asleep.

When she awoke, she lay as she had slept, cradled on his

firm body, his manhood now soft between her legs. She felt no desire to lift herself from his chest. Then he moved and pulled a blanket over her nakedness.

He whispered softly into her ear. "I must beg forgiveness for my behavior last night. I. . . ."

Her hand touched his lips. "You bought me. Please, Captain de Vincente, do not embarrass me with apologies for what is your due."

A tiny line of a frown cut across his forehead. Taking her hand from his lips, he kissed it and lowered it to his breast. "You must call me Manuel when we are alone. And you must let me speak. I am no longer a young man, though you made me feel last night as if I were filled with the fire of youth. This is my last journey, for I plan to retire when I reach the Bay of Monterey. You will perhaps understand when I tell you I have led a solitary life. What women I have known have been trash, picked up on the docks. But you . . . you are not the same. You are a lady. I had determined to wait until I could tell you of my desire, but . . ." he groped for words, ". . . you strained my control beyond all human endurance when you greeted me in your new gown."

He paused, then with a deep breath, resumed. "I must say now what I wished to say before this evening. I wish to have you as my wife when I settle in Monterey." She opened her mouth, but he quickly touched it with his hand. "No, please don't answer immediately, for I am certain your answer will be 'no.' Take your time. I will try not to disturb you until I get your answer."

"It is foolish for me to continue to sleep on the cot," she said. "It is not comfortable, and it is chilly. Please, whatever my answer, let me remain here with you."

He smiled. "If that is your wish, you know it is mine. I will not press you for an answer. You need not make up your mind until we come to rest in the harbor of Monterey."

When he was ready to go on duty, he held her in his arms. "I will send Juan to you with more of the cloth, and with a needle and thread. It would please me greatly if you

244

dressed thus for dinner every night, for it would be like a celebration."

He looked pensively at her face. "One more thing. I would prefer that you did not leave the cabin again. It is not easy for me, and I am responsible for my ship and the conduct of my crew." He hurried on deck.

Scrupulously, during the first weeks afterward, she followed his wishes. She spent most of her time sewing and preparing for the evening meal, which always was the highlight of her day. But as the weeks passed, her confinement began to wear on her and she was overcome by a feeling of listlessness.

Manuel was gentlemanly to her at all times. It was only when she occasionally repeated her request to walk on deck that he seemed not to listen.

The ship had passed the islands of Japan and was moving north when the seas turned rough, demanding Manuel's constant presence on deck. That night Tanya spent alone, trembling each time the ship dipped into the hollow between waves, and shuddering in her aloneness when a crest slapped against the hull.

Toward the middle of the following day, when Tanya could tell by the gentle movement of the ship that the struggle with the sea was past, Manuel stumbled into the cabin. Francesco appeared immediately with food and, tired and hungry, Manuel ate, and then, throwing himself across the satin patchwork she had spread over the bed, fell into an immediate and deep sleep.

When Tanya finished eating lunch, she changed into the cast-off clothes Juan had provided her when she first arrived on shipboard. Then, quietly, she crept up the stairs onto the deck. When she felt the fresh air hit her, she filled her lungs, and let it out with a sigh of pleasure. Mindful of the importance of staying out of the way of the men, she moved to the railing behind the longboat.

A voice at her elbow startled her. "*¡Buenas dias Senorita!*" It was the first mate, Martinez. Unnerved, she turned and ran for the hatch. Halfway there, she paused. Why was she acting to foolishly? He had done her no harm! But when she looked back, she saw his eyes fastened upon her with an intensity that sent a shiver of fear down her back. Even after she turned away she could feel his gaze piercing her, penetrating her clothes to her bare flesh.

She was trembling when she reentered the cabin. Manuel had not stirred. Gratefully, she closed the door and hurried to the bank of seats. She vowed she would not disobey Manuel again, and she prayed that Martinez would not speak of their encounter. But it took most of the day for the memory of his piercing eyes to fade from her memory.

CHAPTER III

————

"Captain, the sea is rising!" The cry was accompanied by a heavy knock on the cabin door.

Manuel sat up. Tanya watched him sleepily as he pulled on his boots and greatcoat. "Go back to sleep, my love." His voice was gentle. "I'll return shortly."

She was asleep before he left the room, her body tossed around in the bed by the force of the waves. She awoke when the door opened again, but she did not bother to open her eyes. Manuel would soon be back in bed to comfort her.

"So he has left you alone—at last!"

She recognized the voice though she had not heard it very often. Martinez, the first mate! She sat up, holding the blanket before her naked body. "What's the matter? Has something happened to the captain?"

Martinez shook his head. He was far from a prepossessing man. His pudgy body reminded Tanya of a stuffed child's toy, and his hair stood out like rough wool under his cap. Only his eyes were out of keeping with the rest of his appearance. They glowed like hot steel, and they burned with desire and lust.

"Go away!" Despite her fright, her voice was steady. "The captain would not approve of your presence here!"

"I'm sure he wouldn't." The natural soft lines of his face became hard and cruel. "But I must speak to you, and he seems determined to keep us apart."

"What have you to say that cannot be spoken before your captain?"

He flushed. "I beg of you, madam, take pity on my plight! Each night I lie in my bed on the other side of this wall and listen to your passion. And I go mad! I cannot endure having you so close and yet being kept so distant! Surely you have room in your heart for one who loves you! I will be good to you, I promise! I will make you happy!"

Inexorably, he pulled her to him.

"Please, *Senor* Martinez. I belong to the captain! Surely you understand!"

Martinez suddenly sprawled at her over the mattress. In that same instant, Tanya slipped to the floor. Unmindful of the icy cold, she reached for the basin that stood nearby, the water inside it frozen solid. Lifting the heavy bowl above her head, she braced herself for his assault.

Martinez pulled himself up and staggered toward her. She could see now that he was drunk. "Please. . . ." His hands extended pleadingly. "*Senorita!* I . . . ."

"Stay back—or I'll. . . ." Tanya's strength was multiplied by her fear and anger. She was holding the bowl in the air over her head.

A huge wave hit the side of the ship, and at that same moment, Martinez grabbed his chest, a strange guttural sound forcing its way out of his constricted throat. The impact of the wave caused Tanya to lose her balance and control of the bowl, which fell forward. Tanya grabbed for support, felt her fingers slip; then her head crashed against the decking and she lost consciousness.

Strong arms lifted her and placed her on the bed. Faint as she was, she moaned in protest.

"Tanya, dearest! What happened? I left you safe in bed and return to find you naked on the floor and Martinez lying dead at your feet. You're frozen!" Manuel was tucking blankets about her shoulders. "Can you speak?"

She nodded weakly, but she was shaking too hard to control her voice. "He. . . . He . . . tried . . . to . . . attack me!" The warmth that surrounded her seeped slowly into her icy limbs. "He wanted me to. . . ." Overcome by hysteria, she began to shake again, sobbing helplessly.

There was a noise near the door and she looked up to see two sailors lift the body of Martinez from the floor. "Prepare him for burial." De Vincente added: "If you are asked, he died in the line of duty. This shame should not be allowed to ruin his reputation." He waved his hand and the men departed.

Immediately, he turned back to Tanya, his warm breath comforting her frozen cheeks. "It's all right now. It's all over. I should have been more aware of Carlos' problems." He covered her pale face with kisses, pressing his body over hers. His heat gradually brought her back to normalcy, and she dropped into a restless sleep.

When she awakened, her body was burning with fever. Vaguely, she recognized Manuel approach with a cool cloth for her brow—and then she lost consciousness once more.

The next time she opened her eyes, the sea was calm and sunlight reflected on the ceiling of the cabin. Francesco entered the room. "Are you feeling better?" He approached her timidly. "You've been sick for over a week."

She took the cup of soup he handed her and brought it to her lips, her hand trembling at the effort. "What happened to Mar . . . Martinez?"

Francesco looked surprised. "Didn't the captain tell you he was dead? He hit his head on a beam and broke his neck. We buried him right away." The lad's thick features brightened. "There were no sad faces when he cut water and sank. Mr. Gonzales is first mate now, and we couldn't be happier. He treats us so much better. Of course. . . ." He lowered his eyes.

"Of course what?"

"I guess I shouldn't say it but . . . Mr. Gonzales isn't the seaman Martinez was." He smiled suddenly. "But he'll learn, I'm sure."

Tanya grew stronger with each passing day—and more aware of the truth of Francesco's words. Manuel spent little time in the cabin. He rose at sunup and ate alone. Often Francesco was sent with broth at noontime, and Manuel did not return to her until well after sunset. If she awoke at night, he was not beside her.

He grew increasingly exhausted until she felt compelled to speak. "Manuel, please. I've recovered completely, and I want to help, not hinder you. You're wearing yourself out! Please, promise me that tonight you will not return to the deck. Surely Mr. Gonzales can handle the ship alone by now!"

His glance was sharp. "What have you heard of Gonzales?"

"Only that he is the new mate—and that the men like him. But you have been on deck day and night, as if he were not there at all! Is he incapable of handling the ship?"

Manuel was silent. Then he sent for Juan and directed him to tell the cook and the cabin boy that Tanya and he would eat together. He helped her wash and dress, and when her hair was combed loosely around her shoulders, he settled her in his great chair.

When she protested, he shook his head. "You must humor me to this extent. You are still weak, even though you don't think you are. I can use a stool until you are stronger."

The cook outdid himself in the preparation of Tanya's first solid meal. Each dish had a fragrance of its own, and the wine was dry and rich. The cabin was chilly in spite of the bright fire Juan had lit in the pot-bellied stove, and Manuel insisted that she put on his greatcoat. But it fit her so poorly that he excused himself and fetched one from Martinez' empty cabin. The pudgy first mate had been much shorter than Manuel, and his jacket fit Tanya's small body a bit better.

As he tucked it around her shoulders, she looked up into his haggard face. "Manuel, you must sleep. Please. I'll watch and call you if the sea grows high again."

He pulled a bottle of brandy from his drawer. "You're right. I must learn to trust Gonzales . . . , though. . . ." He poured them both a drink.

She lifted her glass and touched his lightly. "To a safe end to our journey."

"To my ranch, and to the lovely lady who will make it my home."

They drank in silence, and Tanya knew Manuel's thoughts were not on her but on the sea that glowed ominously through the darkened windows.

"Come, Manuel. It's been a long time since you slept without worrying about my welfare. Tonight is my night to care for you." Taking his hand, she led him to the bed. Though he was reluctant to follow, he lay back thankfully and fell into a deep sleep.

Fearful lest she disturb him, Tanya pulled the great chair to the side of the bed and settled in it. The oversized jacket was warm, protecting her from the chill of the air.

Manuel snorted in his sleep and turned onto his back. She gazed into the calm face with unconcealed affection. It was obvious that he loved her, and that he wanted her for his wife. But in spite of her appreciation of his kindness and her true fondness for him, she knew she did not return his passion. In her heart only one man reigned supreme. Alexius. "I'll tell him when the storm is over. I'm cruel to let him dream of a future with me when I cannot—will not—stay in Monterey."

He stirred in his sleep and murmured her name. She felt a soreness in her heart at the thought of disappointing so kind a man. But if she didn't tell him. . . .

The ship lurched, almost throwing her from her seat. The sea was rising again. When no further swells threatened to rock the ship, she settled back, her head against the large wings of the chair, lulled to sleep by the movement of the vessel.

A loud boom brought her immediately alert. Manuel was on his feet beside her. "Damn!" His voice was angry. The door to the cabin had been blown open by the force of a wave that had almost capsized the ship. "Gonzales. . . ." He was pulling on his greatcoat and running toward the flooded passageway. "Tanya, dear, stay where you are! I must go immediately to the deck." The water washed over his boots as he vanished from her sight.

Tanya watched the wetness spread over the cabin floor, licking at the softness of the heavy carpet. Above her she could hear the men running about and shouting loudly over the roar of the wind and the pounding of the sea. Manuel had gone out in the maelstrom without hesitating, but she had no wish to leave her chair even to move to the bed. Her mouth dry with fear, she listened to the fury that surrounded her.

When it stopped, she was stunned. A moment before the noise had been so intense she feared the ship would crack up. Now it rode on still water. Shivering, she rose and pulled the chair close to the portholes. She was hardly aware that she tucked a blanket around her, or that she dozed in spite of her determination to remain awake until Manuel returned. She assumed that the storm was over. She was not knowledgeable enough to realize that Gonzales had unwittingly brought the ship into the very eye of the tempest.

The storm hit again with such suddenness that she was taken completely by surprise. The ship groaned and creaked under the lashing of the sea, and the wind howled through the bare masts as if determined to break them asunder.

Then a new silence wiped away all the raging sounds that had, moments before, caused her to panic. She sat immobile, her eyes fastened on the windows. The ship was falling into a deep trough. Tanya could see nothing but the wave as it hung high over the vessel.

It hit with an overwhelming impact. Crushed between the monstrous wave and the rising pressure of the undulating sea, the vessel exploded like a walnut squeezed in a giant nutcracker. Deck and masts shot upward; the cabin walls splintered and broke. The portholes through which Tanya had watched the storm shot out before her and she was pulled through one into the raging sea.

She gasped with shock as the water hit her, and it was that intake of air that saved her life. When she surfaced, she was alone in the water. "Manuel!" Her voice was smothered by the rain that concealed the very sky above her. "Help!"

A large wave tossed her against something hard, and she grasped frantically in the darkness. Her fingers slid over something rough and slimy. And then she was once more bobbing helplessly in the water.

The wind howled over her head, tossing bits of the wreckage at her like powerful missiles. Her life was over. She knew it. Yet she continued to fight the storm.

Suddenly, a large, dark object thrust itself into her view. Propelled by the force of the storm, it towered over her. She screamed and began to paddle away from what she felt sure was certain death. And then the water stilled for a moment, and she found herself clutching onto the wide girth of a shattered portion of the mainmast.

Her heart pounding furiously, she climbed onto the bobbing float. It rested steady in the waves, a crossbeam keeping it from spinning. Another large wave hit, and she wrapped her arms around the heavy support, digging her fingernails into the wood with such force that sharp pains shot up her arms.

The wave subsided. She had not been thrown back into the sea. Again and again the ocean tore at her make-shift raft, as if it was determined to take her to that nether region where it stored the bodies of those who were lost at sea. And each time she fought to maintain her feeble hold on the floating refuge.

When first she felt the slap of the rope against her arm, she recoiled. Were the monsters of the deep rising to drag her under?

Once more the slap, and this time the rope coiled around her wrist. She pulled away—and saw that there was no threat in the touch. Trembling with cold and terror, she pulled the rope to her and secured herself to her haven. Her fingers shook as she fastened the knot. Then, secure for the first time since her sudden exodus from the cabin, she lay back and let the water toss her where it would.

Each time the waves hit, she tensed her body and held tightly to the ends of the rope. Her shoulders ached, her throat was raw from screaming against the howling wind, and her skin felt as if it had been scraped raw by some mighty claws. Would the storm never end?

Her eyes fastened in terror on each new wave, she began to pray. God had supported her through others horrors. If it was his will, she would survive this one, too.

A swell picked up the shattered mast and moved it on its crest. Water from the sky and from the deep washed over her tortured body, and she screamed in agony.

With an abruptness that tore at her raw flesh, the movement stopped. Another wave hit her, but her resting-place remained steady.

When next the water washed over her, her feet were dislodged and they trailed into the surf. Caught by the undertow, they dug into the sand. She drew them up with a start. Had some new monster come to attack her? Clutching her legs to hold them safe from danger, she waited for the next assault.

When the force of the next wave barely shifted her on the mast, she opened her eyes. The sky above her was glowing in the first faint rays of dawn. And her temporary raft had lodged in a shallow stretch of water, safe from the worst of the tempest.

She tore at the rope with her bleeding fingers and slid into the undulating water. The salt stung her skin, washing her mind clear. But her arms gave way as she fell, and for one moment she submerged.

She came up sputtering. Staggering blindly, she lunged toward the distant shore. She fell once, landing on a sharp stone that cut her hand. Pressing the wound to slow the bleeding, she hurried on. And when she at last reached the beach, she fell exhausted onto the dry sand.

When she regained consciousness, the sky above her was clear and the sun reflected brightly on the quiet ocean. A high cliff cast a shadow that extended far into the water. She shivered convulsively. The storm was over—and she was safe. But she had no shelter—and no food.

After standing for a time in silent appraisal of her circumstances, she began to walk toward the cliffs. There had to be some way up. But where had she landed? Manuel had spoken often of Monterey. Had she reached that coast?

Again she studied the beach. Far to her right the rocks seemed to turn inland. If she could find no exit from the beach, she might at least discover more substantial shelter. With a sense of purpose at last, she turned her steps toward this new goal.

The distance was far greater than she had expected it to be. At noon the sun peaked over the cliffs, and suddenly the sand grew hot, and Tanya's wet garments dried quickly, steaming slightly. As she walked, Tanya forced herself to recall everything Manuel had said about his homeland. Monterey Harbor had high cliffs to the south. Did it also have them to the north? She could not recall. Were there other harbors along the rocky coast? Yes. He had said something about San Francisco Bay, some distance to the north.

The storm had driven the *Francesca* north, that Manuel had told her. So maybe she was close to. . . . She quickened her pace. Ahead, the rocky wall seemed to vanish. Moving down to the water line, she began to run. The sun was moving quickly. She had little time left in which to find shelter.

When she came upon the entrance to the bay, she stopped in surprise. It appeared to be an inland sea, so large it was, stretching far into the distance. Had Manuel led her to believe that Monterey Bay was so enormous? No. Her heart began to beat wildly. Could she have been so fortunate as to have landed close to San Francisco Harbor?

Following the curve of the sand, she ran along the edge of the bay. And then, suddenly, she stopped, a gasp of surprise on her lips. From the far shore, just inside the entrance to the bay, a boat was moving out from the beach. Most of the men who plied the oars were soldiers; she could see the uniforms gleaming in the sunlight. But at the head of the boat sat a man garbed in a dark brown robe. And it was he who waved at her, and whose voice called out some greeting. Even from the distance, she could tell that he spoke Spanish.

She recoiled when the men reached her side of the water and leaped from the boat, muskets in hand, but the man in a brown robe held up one arm and they stopped in their tracks. "Stop! Can't you see that it is a woman?" He advanced toward her, his arms extended. "Welcome to the Mission Dolores! We saw a ship go down in the storm. Is it possible that the Good God has saved your life?"

Tanya felt her knees grow weak and, as he reached her side, she fell forward. She was not aware of strong arms catching her. nor of being carried over the sand to the waiting boat.

CHAPTER IV

The room was dark—and very still. Was the storm over at last? And if it was, where was Manuel?

"Ah, *senorita!* You are awake. I will call the *padre!*"

Tanya stared in the direction of the voice. Who was in her cabin? And who was the *padre?*

Slowly, her awareness returned. She had awakened as if from some terrible nightmare. But now she remembered. It had not been a dream! The ship was destroyed, and she was. . . .

"Where am I? What is this place?"

"You are in the Mission Dolores. Please, I will call the *padre*. He told me to let him know as soon as you awoke."

The woman who stood before her was garbed in a long straight dress that gave no indication of her femininity. Her long black hair hung in a braid behind her, and her dark eyes seemed filled with honest concern. Her skin was dark, more of a brown than a yellow, but her eyes were strangely reminiscent of Mei Ling's. Tanya stared at her with growing alarm. "Am I still in China?"

The eyes narrowed, and a frown creased the forehead. "China? What is that?"

Tanya inhaled. "Where am I, then? Where is this Mission Dolores?"

"Why, here, of course." The woman smiled nervously and backed toward the door. "I will call the *padre*."

He entered the room like a breath of comfort. Somehow, when Tanya saw his face, she ceased to care where she was. As long as the *padre* was nearby, all was well.

He approached her bed and stood at its foot, gazing at her with kindly eyes. "Thank God you are safe. I feared you might have survived the wreck only to die in bed. But God has other duties for you to perform. He is not yet ready to accept you into heaven."

Tanya stared at him, her eyes wide. "*Padre*, please, where am I?"

A smile lit his face. "Why, you are in California, on the Bay of San Francisco. The ship you were on, was it the *Senorita Francesca*?"

"Yes, *padre*. Manuel de Vincente. . . ."

"Was the captain. Poor man! He planned to settle in Monterey when this journey was over. The Heavenly Father had other plans for him." He crossed himself and, for a moment, closed his eyes. "You are not Spanish, are you? What were you doing in the *Francesca*? I did not believe Manuel to be a sinful man."

Tanya blushed. "I. . . . He planned to marry me when we reached California. He wanted me to share his retirement with him."

The *padre*'s eyes sparkled. "And did he say that Father Dominic would perform the ceremony?"

"Well, no. . . . But I'm sure he meant what he said. He was a very sincere man."

The smile had returned. "Yes, of course, you are right.

But we will say some prayers for his soul, nevertheless. Are you able to get up?"

Tanya dangled her feet over the edge of the bed. The dizziness did not return. She stood, and still she felt steady. "*Padre* Dominic. I must leave here. Is it possible to get a ship that will take me to the Russian settlement?"

He frowned. "You mean Fort Archangel Gabriel? There is no use attempting to go there. We received news just recently that the Tlingit Indians raided the island of Sitka and burned the fort to the ground. So far as we know, the settlement is destroyed. The Russians have no foothold in America any more." His expression sharpened. "It will be best that you not mention Sitka to any of the others, particularly the soldiers who come here to mass. The Russians have been a thorn in our side for many years. Few of our men regret their misfortune. Come, the matin bell is ringing." Folding his hands inside his wide sleeves, he slowly led the way from the room.

The mission stood gracefully among the scrub brush that seemed to cover all the hills as far as Tanya could see. The garden which she immediately entered as she left her room was the only green area in sight, except for a small plot of ground slightly below the structures, where a number of laborers worked with hoes and rakes between neat rows of new sprouts.

Tanya gazed in amazement at the plants that surrounded her. Father Dominic paused. "They come from Mexico. They seem to take well to this climate, though they grow better near Monterey, and even better in San Diego. Come, the congregation is waiting."

The congregation was composed entirely of Indians, until a few soldiers entered after the service began and lined up at the front of the chapel. None of them paid the slightest attention to the native converts—nor did they seem to notice Tanya. When the mass was over, they filed noisily out, without a word to the *padre*, and climbed up the hill to the Presidio. Father Dominic led Tanya back to the garden. "You may come here later to pray. Though your Church differs from ours, your God is the same. Come, I will show you the rest of the mission."

The buildings that surrounded the garden were built of adobe covered with a white paint made from clay. The roofs, composed of bright red tile, shone in the late-afternoon sun. It was a beautiful, though oddly barren place. Even the exotic plants she had noticed on her way to the chapel seemed uncomfortable in their spartan surroundings.

A door opened out from one of the rooms, and a man appeared. Slender and quite tall, with dark, curly hair that threatened to burst from the braid in which it was confined, he was garbed in fine silk trousers with a jacket of Chinese silk brocade, with full ruffles at the wrists. His expression was gentle, and his deep brown eyes rested on Tanya with open curiosity. He sauntered into the garden. "Ah, *padre*, so you got my word! I knew you would find the right servant for me—though I had somewhat hoped it would be a woman."

Father Dominic smiled gently. "God's blessing on you, my son. What is this you say about a servant? I received no message."

"I sent a messenger asking that you choose an Indian who might tend my household. My mother is ill, and the Indians around San Carlos are either working for the *padres* or are too lazy. You did not receive my letter?" His eyes fastened on Tanya's face.

"No, my son." The *padre* stepped in front of his new charge. "Maybe, however, this young woman will serve you and the Senora del Norte. I will ask her." He turned to Tanya. "My daughter, this is Sebastino del Norte, one of the few, but important, settlers at the Mission of San Carlos Borremeo de Carmelo. I know his mother well, and she is a good woman. She will take pity on your plight, and not blame you for the accident of your birth. If you have no other plans, you could do far worse than accept employment in the del Norte household."

Tanya looked from priest to landowner with a growing confusion. "I don't know. . . . I. . . ."

"Never mind, child. Take your time. I will speak to Sebastino further and you may listen. What is said may affect

260

your decision." He pointed toward a nearby bench and turned his attention to del Norte.

"This child is the sole survivor of the wreck of the *Senorita Francesca*." The *padre* paused and met Sebastino's eyes squarely. "She is Russian, though she speaks our language most fluently. I have learned nothing else, as yet." He turned back to Tanya. "What is your name, my dear child?"

"Tanya Ivanovich." The full meaning of the *padre*'s earlier words suddenly crashed into her consciousness. If the Russian settlement on Sitka was destroyed and all the residents massacred, Alexius was dead! That was what the *padre* had told her—and she had hardly listened! Alexius was dead!

She felt Father Doninic take her arm and guide her to the bench. "What is it, my child? Are you feeling ill?"

It spilled out, half in Russian, but Father Dominic seemed to understand her bereavement. Gently, he helped her to her feet and led her back to the chapel. "Stay here, my daughter, until you regain your composure. God has a purpose in keeping you alive, though now you speak of death as if it were your friend. Pray to Christ, and he will comfort you."

She sat where he left her. Alexius was dead! Her heart felt leaden within her breast. Alexius was dead! Now, truly, she was all alone!

She was unaware of the passage of time. At first she stared without thinking at the crucifix that dominated the nave of the church. When she slipped into prayer, it was without conscious motivation. Her first prayers were fragments of agony, spilled out before her God. But gradually, her supplications took form. She prayed for her father— and for the lad who had died because he tried to help her. She prayed for Mio Kang and for the infant son who had succumbed to smallpox without ever truly knowing life.

Last of all, she prayed for Alexius. At first her prayers were filled with self-pity. But gradually they changed to sincere petitions for his welfare in Heaven.

It was dark when she emerged from the chapel, but the

padre and the young Spaniard still sat together on the bench just inside the garden. They rose as she approached.

She stood silently before the *padre*, and the peace that filled his soul spilled over to comfort her. "All is well with you again." His voice was gentle. "The pain and loneliness will pass. Think now that those you love are with their God."

She nodded, her heart too full for speech.

The young Spaniard stepped to her side. "Tell me, child, how old are you?"

She looked at him in surprise. "I . . . I'm not certain. I was born in the year seventeen eighty-two."

He closed his eyes in thought. "Then you're twenty-one. A woman, not a child at all. Are you recovered from your faint?"

She nodded. "The *padre* told me of the Indian raid on the Russian settlement of Fort Archangel Gabriel. I. . . . I had a friend there."

The young face remained filled with compassion. "I regret your loss. Did you come from there?" He paused. "No, that's right. The *padre* told me you were a passenger on the *Senorita Francesca*. You are fortunate to be alive."

Father Dominic held up one hand in a benediction. "We will let the dead rest. Her bereavement is too recent. Tell me, would you consider taking her as a maid? I feel a responsibility for her future, and you know how difficult it is to control the soldiers here. I have enough trouble keeping them away from the converts."

Sebastino met the *padre*'s gaze. "I don't know. I had hoped for . . . more of a woman. I have no need for a girl who fancies herself a boy. Tell me, father, have you facilities for a bath—and clothes that are more appropriate for a woman? I feel we both might think more clearly were she to resemble a boy a bit less. And let us delay any decision until after we have eaten, for I am hungry, and if she has been without a protector for the time you say, she is probably close to starvation."

The *padre* called, and two female neophytes appeared. They were dressed in loose garments that reached their ankles, but the unattractive gowns did not succeed in concealing the basic strength of their bodies. Their features were clean and strong, and their skin was a golden bronze, like the color of the adobe, as if they, too, had been fashioned from the earth.

They led her into a small room, filled a tub with water, and placed a gown like their own over a nearby chair. Tanya slipped out of her clothes and settled into the tepid water.

As she scrubbed the dirt from her body, she gazed about. The room was bare of all but essential furniture. A bed stood against one wall. A chair on which her new dress hung was placed beside it. And on the wall at the foot of the bed was an enormous crucifix. A small window and a door both opened onto the garden. There was no other entry.

When her bath was completed and her hair freed of dirt and snarls, Tanya stepped from the tub. Immediately, one of the neophytes hurried her into her gown, as if she were ashamed to view another's nakedness.

The soft cloth of the gown rubbed her unprotected breasts and scratched her stomach, but that mild unpleasantness could not detract from the pleasure she derived from the feel of the skirt against her legs. She took a step, and it folded around her thighs like a caress. But she could move no farther. The hem trailed onto the ground and caught under her feet.

One of the neophytes provided her with a sash which she tied around her waist. Now her dress clung loosely to her breasts and hips, and she could walk. With a final pat to her hair which she had left unbraided, she stepped into the garden. Silently, the neophytes led her to another building and pushed open the door.

Del Norte rose as she entered, his eyes alight with a new respect. "*Madre Dios!* What has happened?"

Confused, she backed toward the garden.

"*Padre!* Look at her! She is beautiful!"

The father's face darkened. "Is she too beautiful for you to remember your honor—and hers?"

Del Norte laughed. "Father! For a man of God, you have a most deliciously wicked mind! Rest assured I am not like the soldiers, taking any woman I see. Nor am I a simple neophyte who can be hurried into a union just to save you from the fear of mortal sin! I am a Spanish gentleman, and I behave in a manner befitting my rank."

The father's face lit up. "I accept the rebuke. Still, there is a decision to be made. Tanya? What is your wish?"

She accepted the seat del Norte drew out for her and smiled her appreciation for the glass of wine he offered.

He lifted his glass toward her. "A toast to Tanya Ivanovich, my new housekeeper. May our relationship be a happy one."

She put her glass to her lips. "To my new employer. May I please your mother as I seem to please you."

"But not in the same way, I am certain!" Del Norte's voice was playful.

Father Dominic looked at her glowing face and then turned quickly back to Sebastino. And Tanya was certain she detected a concern in his eyes that increased when Sebastino rose and gallantly refilled her glass.

CHAPTER V

Sebastino del Norte leaned from the carriage and signaled a halt. He pointed to a pile of loosely stacked rocks, like a pillar, beside the road. "That is the northern boundary of the del Norte ranch."

The journey continued. But two hours later, when they had not yet reached the residence, Tanya understood the reason for his vanity. "What do you raise on all this land?"

"Blessed little! Maize, grain for the cattle—and cattle. Not much. But there will come a time when the valley of Carmelo will be one of the most fruitful in the world."

It was difficult for Tanya to visualize this land any other way than it was. Yet there were signs of activity. At some distance from the road, Indians were harvesting grain and loading it onto a wagon. The men were dressed like the converts in Father Dominic's mission, their chests bare but with long trousers. The women wore dresses much like her own. They moved slowly under the direction of an overseer who appeared to be Indian but who, Sebastino informed her, was a half-breed.

The main buildings of the ranch came into view shortly thereafter. All the structures, even the barns, were made of adobe with red-tiled roofs. Neat, well-tended fences enclosed the stable and the barnyard. The main house stood apart from the other buildings, surrounded by a planting of trees and shrubbery. A red flagstone walk led to a gate beyond which was an enclosed garden much like the one at the Mission Dolores. Two women hurried out to greet the carriage.

Donna Maria Carlotta del Norte stood slightly ahead of her daughter by the ironwork of the gate. Matronly, hatless, her greying hair was done up in a bun near the center of her neck. Her long black dress, brightened only by white lace at the neck and wrists, was of a fine taffeta that reflected the glow of the setting sun. Her face revealed the peace of her soul as well as her obvious delight at the return of her only son.

Angelina Francesca del Norte pushed ahead of her mother. She was slender—almost fragile, with delicate but plain features and shining black hair that hung down to her waist. Her youth was, by far, her most charming attribute, at least from a distance. When Sebastino stepped from the carriage, she dashed into his arms with a cry of delight.

Sebastino turned from his sister to his mother. With his sister still hanging on his arm, he took his mother's hand and brought it to his lips, and then, with some embarrassment, submitted to her embrace.

When the familial greetings were completed, Senora del Norte gestured toward Tanya. "This is the woman the *padre* gave you? Has she knowledge of housework?"

Sebastino cleared his throat. "Mother, I did not bring back what I went to find. This is Tanya Ivanovich, a Russian—" He held up his hand to silence his mother's protest. "—who was a resident at the Mission Dolores when I arrived. Please, mother, I will explain more about her later.

Suffice it now that she will take over the chore of managing the house, and I have consented to let her train some of the young women from the fields to help her. It is settled, mother. If she proves to be a disappointment, I will send her back."

Tanya had curtsied when Sebastino introduced her, but now she was standing erect and gazing into Donna Maria's eyes. Angelina dropped her brother's arm and stepped in front of Tanya. "Have you ever been in the royal court? I understand the Russian Tsar has naked women attend him instead of lackeys!"

Donna Maria snorted her disapproval. "'Gelina! Enough! Will you never learn to exercise discretion?"

Tanya met the girl's sparkling eyes. The girl was beautiful after all! Her eyes were large and dark—and full of life. And they more than compensated for whatever plainness affected her other features. "Yes, Angelina, I attended her Majesty, the Tsarina Catherine for a time. But as for the Tsar's personal idiosyncrasies, I have no knowledge, though I doubt the rumor. There is a limit even to what a Tsar may do."

Angelina bounced enthusiastically. "Oh, 'Tino, how exciting! Did you know she had lived in the court?"

Sebastino looked sharply into Tanya's face, a new respect in his glance. "No, she had not had time to so inform me." He turned back to his mother. "Please, mama, will you take charge? I need to visit the stables. Melino should be foaling soon."

Donna Maria nodded. "You're too late, my son. But you can thank God that the mare survived. I swear she gave birth to a demon. He was kicking as he was born, and he's already dashing about the corral like a yearling!"

With a quick bow to his mother, Sebastino departed. Donna Maria regarded Tanya with a warmth that settled Tanya's discomfort. "Come along, Tanya Ivanovich. You must tell me how you came to be in the Mission Dolores—and what persuaded you to dress like a native. And, for 'Gelina's sake, you will have to speak more about the Russian court." She opened the gate, and turned again toward

Tanya. "It seems inappropriate for you to remain in that garment. I will see if I have a more appropriate dress."

True to her word, the Senora del Norte produced not one but a dozen dresses which no longer fit her and gave them to Tanya. Because both she and Angelina were much taller than she, Tanya spent hours hemming the garments, but when she was finished she felt more like a member of civilized society.

Her chores were simple—and fascinating. The house had been neglected for some time and so Tanya set about the task of cleaning every room. She brought two women in from the fields, choosing them carefully so as to find those best suited for such careful work, and within a month she had the hacienda in immaculate condition.

Angelina was her constant companion. When work was being done, she watched with fascination, especially when Tanya was teaching the Indian women their duties. Tanya was at first embarrassed by the attention, but soon she realized she had nothing to be ashamed of. Under her tutelage the two natives became quite acceptable servants, even developing the skill needed to serve the food and clean the delicate fabrics that were used in the ladies' clothing.

Tanya was careful to edit her stories of her past life so as not to shock the sensibilities of the delicate Angelina, but when she spoke of her experiences in China, she could not hold back the tears. She dabbed her eyes with a kerchief and was suddenly aware that Angelina was not her only companion.

"You have had a son, then?" It was the Donna Maria.

"Yes, *senora*. He died of the smallpox."

"You have led a most exciting life, my dear. How is it that you are content to live in such solitude as a servant in a provincial *rancho*?"

Tanya met the older woman's eyes. "*Senora*, I have had enough of the sort of excitement that has filled my life to date. I want nothing more than to be allowed to spend the rest of my days in peace."

"You have no plans to remarry?"

"Whom would I find?" Tanya gazed pensively toward

the stables. "Besides, when there are lovely, fresh girls such as your daughter, who would choose a woman such as myself?"

Donna Maria took Angelina's hand and gazed at it thoughtfully. "My little 'Gelina will probably wed one of the Rancheros from Santa Barbara. Tino has spoken to me of two possible choices. But in answer to your question, don't be too sure you will never find a man who wants you. On a frontier as rugged as this, there is much value placed in a woman who has courage and strength—and who has already proven herself to be fertile."

CHAPTER VI

"Look at him Tanya! Isn't he handsome?" Angelina had perched herself on the fence next to Tanya and her mother and gazed adoringly at her brother. Sebastino had little time to watch the women, though he was clearly aware of their presence. Little Diablo, the foal that had been dropped the day before Tanya's arrival, was a year old, and it had been decided to begin his training.

Tanya watched the spirited colt with open delight. "Yes, 'Gelina, he is. Look how he struggles to maintain his freedom! What a stout heart the little fellow has!"

Angelina turned a pouting face toward Tanya. "I wasn't speaking of the colt, Tanya Ivanovich! I was looking at my brother. Don't you admire him, as well?"

"Of course, 'Gelina! He's a good brother, I'm sure. But it isn't my place to analyze his qualities."

It was the Donna Maria who responded. "What is your place, Tanya? Have you considered that question at all?"

Tanya gazed at her mistress in surprise. In the year that had passed since her arrival, and in the long hours of conversation with the del Norte females, she had come to feel that the hacienda was her home. Her duties, though in some ways demanding, did not include physical labor; that was relegated to the two women she had trained.

"Why, *senora*, my place is housekeeper to the del Norte family."

"You discount, then, the education you have given my daughter?" The *senora*'s voice was gentle.

Tanya blushed. "No, of course not. But she would have learned proper Russian court behavior swiftly on her own, had she found it necessary."

Angelina slipped from her perch. "Tanya, you're too modest. I don't think I ever would have learned how to dance—or anything—without you!"

Donna Maria gestured to her daughter to be quiet. "Tanya, I think it is time I enlarged your responsibilities." She glanced at Sebastino who was leading the colt in a circle in the corral. " 'Gelina is not the only child I have who needs instruction in manners."

"Senor del Norte? You want me to teach him manners?" Tanya could not repress the incredulity in her voice. "*Senora*, he has manners to spare already!"

"Ah, but the wrong kind! He is well qualified to lead a female astray—" Donna Maria gestured Tanya to contain her protest. "—I know that very well. But I want grandchildren. My late husband, the Don del Norte, died without ever seeing his son settle down. I know it gave him pain to see such a waste of all the training he had given 'Tino." She watched as Sebastino led Diablo into the barn. "You would not be aware of it, but he has settled down considerably since your arrival. Never before in his life has he devoted so much time to the ranch."

Tanya watched Sebastino vanish into the barn. "Just what am I to do?"

"Oh, please, ignore my words. You have no need for more assignments. What I do intend is to suggest that you put Elmira in charge of the preparation of dinner. I know you have been working toward that goal, and I believe she has learned enough. You should have time to exercise a bit more." She headed toward the corral gate. "Come, we'll speak to 'Tino about getting you a horse."

Sebastino led the women into the stables without a question, but he looked from her to his mother with obvious amusement.

"I would give you Diablo, but he is still quite untamed, and I am sure you would prefer a gentler horse."

Tanya looked at the yearling. "Is he ready for the saddle?"

Sebastino was close to laughter. "Yes, mistress Ivanovich! Do you think you can handle him?"

Tanya stepped toward the beast, her hand extended. He reached out and pushed his muzzle under her fingers. She stepped closer and stroked the black nose. "When I was 'Gelina's age I had already broken my own horse. But, of course, I have only ridden once since then."

"You are willing, then, to acknowledge that he might need to be saddle-trained by another?"

"No. But I realize how fond you are of the beast. He is a noble animal. I wouldn't be impertinent enough to suggest that I handle his training. I will be content with any horse you choose to supply me."

"Well, whether you want him or not, he's yours. I can't give you Melino; she's 'Gelina's horse. And the stallion is mine. He'd throw anyone who tried to mount him—other than me. But Diablo seems appropriate. You both arrived at the same time."

Tanya rested her head against the colt's nose and stroked the silken muzzle with growing tenderness. "Thank you, *Senor.* I never. . . ."

Sebastino turned to Eduardo, the groom. "Break Diablo to a side saddle. And when he is ready, he will belong to Senora Ivanovich."

Tanya spurred Diablo and raced up the rise. At the top,

she halted, startled by the beauty that lay before her. She had been climbing most of the morning, and now the bay glistened below her, surrounded by the deep green of the woods. This was the view Manuel de Vincente had described so often.

Dismounting, she tethered her horse to a nearby tree. It was good to be alone for a time. Angelina, charming as she was, sometimes demanded too much of Tanya's attention.

Manuel. . . . Tanya recalled the gentleness of the big man, and his devotion to his dream. She wondered when it was that he had trampled up this hill to view the bay, and, suddenly, she regretted that she had not followed his footsteps long ago. Settling on a log, she leaned against a nearby tree.

A noise in the underbrush brought her to immediate alert. She rose and moved close to her horse, prepared to flee if flight were necessary. The noise continued.

Then Diablo nickered, and his call was echoed by another horse nearby. Someone was coming. With a regret for her lost solitude, she turned to greet the newcomer.

"Tanya!" Sebastino's voice was rich and melodious. "I have not seen you here before."

"I have not gone this far before." She paused. "I have had this spot described to me by a friend—long ago. It is as beautiful as he claimed. The bay is like a jewel!"

"This is my favorite lookout. I remember an old sailor used to visit here, years ago, when I was young. I talked to him once, and he claimed he was going to build a home on this hilltop."

"Yes. Manuel de Vincente! Remember, I spoke of him. He was drowned at sea."

Sebastino touched her cheek with his hand. "Tears? For an old sailor? You have a big heart, Tanya Ivanovich."

"Manuel described this spot so well! Poor man! He never lived to see his dream come true." Sorrow for Manuel—and for Alexius—both of whom died unfulfilled, flooded her eyes with tears.

Sebastino leaned forward, his arm around her shoulder. "You mustn't cry, Tanya. A man's life is filled with dreams and disappointments. But any man who had the joy of knowing you has known God's most wonderful gift. You are so gentle—so filled with love and trust. You are a rarity in a world of disillusionment and hate. Father Dominic has spoken often of such innocence, but until now I had not believed it existed."

Tanya was aware of his arm tightening around her waist. And suddenly, all the longing, the unfulfilled desire she had felt since learning of Alexius' death spilled out. With a sob, she pressed against the warmth of Sebastino's arms.

His lips were on hers now, gentle at first, then strong and demanding. And she had no thought to resist. Her arms tingled as his hands slipped over her shoulders and reached her waist. Then, with a sigh, she was pushing against his body, her kiss as hungry as his.

He held her for a moment in his arms, his passion growing, and when his lips sought the small of her neck she felt a tremor. "Sebastino! Oh, Sebastino!"

"Tanya! My dearest Tanya!"

Gently, he lowered her to the ground, and they lay for a time side-by-side, locked in an embrace. Then, tenderly, he began to unbutton her gown.

When she lay before him, exposed to his view, he gasped, and bent to kiss her breasts. Then, deliberately, he rose and removed his clothing. He stood for a moment above her, his erect manhood demanding her attention, and then he stretched beside her, his legs touching hers. Her skin tingled at his touch, and the moistness between her legs increased. They kissed again, and when he drew back his head, she gasped for breath.

Her thighs parted as he rose above her, and then she felt the gentle demand of his desire. She gasped his name as he pushed himself into her body, and then, with a sigh of delight, she savored his wonderful closeness.

She was not aware which of them began the movement. As the rhythm grew, she lost what little awareness she still had of her surroundings. " 'Tino, oh, 'Tino!" As her passion grew, her body grew light, unreal. She was aware of nothing but their contact, nothing but the wonder of their union.

When, at last, he lay still above her, she shuddered beneath the fullness of his weight, straining to hold him, to keep him in her arms. But he did not pull away. He pressed above her, his frame shaking, his lips seeking hers. And her own body trembled in response. She felt the explosion of her passion as it met with his—and then she was quiet.

The next day, Sebastino was gone. He left no message. Tanya rode every morning, often returning to the hilltop where she had shared his love. But as the days passed with no word from him, she abandoned the hill and took Diablo across the fields and beyond the borders of the ranch.

She had reached the crest of a rise overlooking the road one morning when she saw a carriage moving swiftly along. Spurring Diablo, she raced toward the road.

But when she reached the carriage, she reined in surprise. It was not Sebastino's carriage, as she had expected it to be. Inside the ornate interior of the black carriage was a young woman and her duenna. Tanya was ready to speed off when the duenna leaned out through the window. "Senorita! Is this the road to the del Norte ranch?"

Tanya paused. "Yes, Senora. It's ahead only a few miles."

The duenna leaned out all the farther. "Senorita! Will you ride ahead and tell the Donna Maria that Senorita Ines is on her way, at the request of Senor del Norte, and that the Senor will be along later?"

Tanya felt stunned. Sebastino bringing a woman to the hacienda? It could mean only one thing. Before she galloped off, she caught a glimpse of the Senorita Ines. She had never seen a more lovely woman.

The guests arrived before Donna Maria was able to prepare a room for them, but she took their sudden arrival in good grace. Tanya found it far more difficult to adjust to the presence of another young woman in the house. She immersed herself in supervising the preparation of the dinner, much to the dismay of Elmira, who had grown accustomed to her power in the kitchen.

Nor could Tanya face conversation with the lovely guest. Long before Sebastino's return, she excused herself. She slept not at all. She heard, later, the sound of Sebastino's deep voice and Senorita Ines' bell-like laughter.

The days that followed she spent in loneliness and soul-searching. When she wasn't working with the maids, she was riding Diablo. She returned one afternoon, however, to find the house back to normal. Handing the reins to Eduardo, she hurried into the kitchen. "Elmira, where has she gone?"

Elmira shrugged her shoulders. "Back home, I suppose, *Senorita*. I thought you didn't care about seeing her."

Tanya flushed. It was embarrassing to think that the native woman also could guess her emotions. She hurried out of the kitchen.

The sun was low on the horizon, and the smell of roast beef cooking filtered its way from the kitchen, fighting with the fragrance of the jasmine. Tanya wandered disconsolately along the path of the garden, stopping occasionally to gaze at the petals of a bloom that did not seem to know the sun was setting. She did not hear the footsteps behind her.

"So you have decided to come out of your hiding!"

She turned in alarm. "Sebastino! I. . . . I have not been well."

"Yet you are well enough to ride Diablo when you are certain I am not around."

"I think the time has come for me to leave."

"Leave? Leave the Rancho del Norte? Leave Diablo?"

"Please." She gazed at the ever-changing ocean. "I clearly am no longer needed here."

"Have you thought to consult those of us you will leave behind? It is possible we do not share your sentiments."

"I have made up my mind. I wish to travel around the Cape to the United States." She paused, hardly aware that she was speaking aloud. "Or perhaps to the Sandwich Islands."

"You must have important things to do, that you will leave us on such short notice. And without even a destination in mind!" He stepped before her. "I had anticipated quite another reception—or have you forgotten already."

She could not forget, but neither could she ignore his more recent behavior.

277

"I am asking you to be my bride."

Tanya reached for support. "You are asking me to marry you? But what of Senorita Ines?"

Sebastino's laugh was startling. "Oh, my dearest Tanya! You reach conclusions without facts! Senorita Ines is my cousin; we do not marry cousins here. My mother had asked that I invite her to bring news of her mother, my aunt, who is ill. Why, I've known her all my life!"

His arms circled her waist. His lips pressed against hers. She met him without reservation. She was home—at last.

They sat together in the garden until the red glow of sunset faded into darkness.

CHAPTER VII

"Oh hurry, Tanya, hurry! The horses are saddled and mama is already in the carriage." Angelina was almost bouncing in her eagerness. " 'Tino is growing impatient!"

"Don't worry, 'Gelina. I'm sure 'Tino won't leave without us. And if he did, we'd just race him to the post—and get there before him."

Tanya rose from her dressing table and patted her riding skirt smooth. Twirling about, she took one last glance at herself in the mirror. Then she hurried toward the kitchen.

Despite her new status as mistress of the hacienda, Tanya, in the three months that she had been married, had refused to abandon her duties as supervisor of the house servants, though she had given more authority to Elmira.

Angelina scurried beside her. "Tanya, that's a marvelous

thought! I'll run and tell 'Tino and mama to go ahead! We'll catch them long before they reach San Francisco." She hurried off.

With one final glance around the kitchen, Tanya hurried after her sister-in-law.

Diablo and Melino were waiting on the road beyond the gate. The carriage, with Sebastino mounted on Demonio riding alongside, had almost reached the crest of the first hill. Taking the reins from Eduardo, Tanya leaped into the saddle. But she did not immediately spur her horse toward the vanishing carriage.

Angelina shifted restlessly in her saddle. "Tanya, let's ride toward the sea first. At the speed the carriage is going, we could reach San Francisco before it left the boundary of the ranch!"

"No, 'Gelina. I don't think we should. The rains have washed loose many rocks and mud. It isn't safe. . . ."

Angelina was off, her hair flying behind her. And she was headed down toward the unstable ground close to the cliffs. With a cry of "'Gelina, stop!" Tanya raced after her.

More than either Tino or Donna Maria, Tanya was aware that Angelina had not given up her dream to see Spain. For a time after the wedding, 'Gelina had shied away from Tanya, convinced that her loyalties were now wholeheartedly with her husband. But, finally, on a long ride across the ranch, Tanya had convinced the girl that she understood the restlessness that made the thought of settling down so distasteful.

"I want to make my own decisions, Tanya!" Angelina's face had set in anger. "I know it is ill-mannered of me, but I can't help it! I don't want to be sold to the highest bidder, like a prize heifer! What I truly want is to travel to Spain! I don't want to spend my life here in the wilderness."

Tanya had laughed at the comparison. But she had taken the statement to heart. When she was able to inform Angelina that she would be permitted to make the final choice between her suitors, she did so with pride. But Angelina had shown little thankfulness. "What difference does it make? With either one, I'll be stuck in a hacienda! I'll have a baby every year—and I won't even be able to visit with you when I wish!"

"Maybe. But it might not be quite so bad. Have you thought that one of the young men might share your wish to see the King? You will have an opportunity to speak with them both, even though a duenna will chaperone you. Why don't you ask them?"

Tanya had assumed that Angelina was encouraged by the advice, for she had not raised the subject again. But now this wild ride on dangerous ground! Spurring Diablo with her crop, Tanya leaned over his neck. "Careful, boy! Careful!"

Diablo stumbled, and she went flying over his head, landing with a jolt. The next thing she knew, she was staring up at the sky, gasping for breath, and Angelina was looking down at her.

"Oh, Tanya!"

Her breathing grew easier. Her body felt sore, but she could find no broken bones. She looked into Angelina's contrite face. "It's all right, 'Gelina. Thank God, I'm all right. Now, please, let us follow the road."

Yet something had happened in the fall, Tanya knew. She had kept one secret in her heart, knowing that soon she could tell Sebastino she was with child. Now there was a stickiness between her legs. Her bleeding time had started, after all! And she had been so sure. "Wait, 'Gelina!" When her horse came to a stop, she tucked one of her petticoats beneath her legs. She would not be certain until she could examine her stained garments.

Just before sunset the travelers arrived at the new palace of the *Gobernador*. Tanya hurried to the room that had been assigned to her and Sebastino and returned, having changed her clothes and done what she could to cover her paleness. Her fears had been well-founded. She took her place beside 'Tino, and among the revelers. Thank God, she had not told him of her expectations! He, at least, had nothing to mourn. Her spirits rose.

Yet Donna Maria would know or guess. In the year and a half of living in the same house with Donna Maria, she had not yet grown accustomed to the sensitivity of the older woman. They had spoken together often, and many times Tanya had been aware that Donna Maria knew her feelings before she, herself, was fully aware of them. Yes, she would sense the loss. But surely she would also be aware that the opportunity would come again!

As soon as the greetings were over, Sebastino retired to the stables with the other men. It had been a glorious summer for the entire string of settlements. Harvests had been double that of previous years. They had food enough—and to spare. And to celebrate, everyone who could had made the trip, a new residence having been built for the *Gobernador*.

Angelina, her face aglow with her sudden importance (she was, after all, the only one of her friends to be so close to matrimony), hurried off to be with the other girls who sat chattering about the last fiesta, when they had all become lost in the woods and had had to be rescued by a general search. Their duennas, somber women whose lives were dedicated to protecting the honor of other people's children, sat nearby.

Senora Maria Carlotta joined the older women, and though Tanya realized her place was with the matrons, she was uncomfortably aware that she did not quite belong. She could not share her experiences with them. And, in spite of her honorable position as Sebastino's wife, she was still a stranger—a Russian in Spanish territory.

Slipping from the room, she strolled toward the harbor. Far to her left, the roof of the Presidio caught the afternoon sun. Below her, the mission bells rang out the call to vespers. She looked north across the glimmering bay. Father Dominic was expected down from San Francisco, probably some time tomorrow. It would be good to see the *padre* again, and to show him that she had found the happiness he had wished her.

Angelina joined her. "I worried about you, Tanya. I'm sorry if you aren't enjoying the fiesta."

"Oh," Tanya settled back on a rock. "I'm not unhappy. How could I be? I was just thinking of my past—and of how happy I am with Sebastino. I am a fortunate woman. May you, too, have equal happiness."

"Well, if you're not lonesome." Angelina rose and turned toward the bay. "What do you look for out there?"

"Nothing." Tanya felt light-hearted again. "I just like to watch the ocean—and dream." She let her gaze sweep over the blue horizon. Then, startled, she stared at a particular point. Had she seen a ship?

But when she tried to point it out to Angelina, she could not succeed. At last, convinced that she had been imagining things, she rose and followed her sister-in-law back to the *Gobernador*'s mansion. The sun was close to the bank of fog that hung over the water. Soon the fiesta would begin.

The Indians, always ready for holiday, had already begun to dance and sing in the courtyard.

At dinner Tanya studied the face of her host.

The Gobernador Neve's mien was noble, his features rugged, and his eyes sharp. They explained, Tanya thought, the ease with which he governed the military. Something about him reminded her of Manuel de Vincente.

He was also tall. His wife was petite, and she succeeded in making herself invisible in even the most auspicious situations. Angelina whispered to her that the Donna Concepcion was a princess. Their twelve children bubbled about like a flock of geese, into everything, and always shouting noisily wherever they landed.

When the formal music began, led by a band of musicians who seemed to materialize out of nowhere, the guests left the tables and hurried to the patio. Dancing continued until the moon was high in the sky. For Tanya, it was a delightful evening. Every man in the assemblage danced with her at least once, and the *Gobernador*, who seemed charmed by her foreign beauty, insisted upon guiding her around the floor on three different occasions.

When the musicians took a rest, she wandered down to the courtyard and the field where the Indians were entertaining themselves with drums and rattles made of gourds. It was then she noticed the soldiers. They were also together. They were drinking.

She looked up at Sebastino, who had followed her out. "Is there no one to watch the harbor?"

He smiled indulgently. "Ah, my Tanya! No other female would even think of that! No, there is no one, at least not tonight. There is no need. The Indians are friendly, there are no ships in sight, and this is a fiesta. There will be time enough for duty when the celebration is over."

Taking her husband's arm, she let him lead her back to the dance. "How long will the fiesta last?"

He tucked her hand possessively under his arm. "Oh, for at least a week. We get together far too seldom to rush."

The dance had resumed, and the sky was light the next time the music stopped. Tanya was so exhausted by the revelry that she fell asleep as soon as she lay down in her bed.

She was awakened by the shouting of a child under her window. "Ship in the harbor! Ship in the harbor!"

Sebastino struggled into his trousers. "Is it Spanish?"

The boy was sputtering with excitement. "No! The soldiers say it's Russian! We're being invaded!"

CHAPTER VIII

By the time Angelina and Tanya reached the shore, a long-boat had put out from the ship and was slowly pulling toward shore. The soldiers from the Presidio, most in some state of disarray, were struggling to overcome the effects of the night's celebration. In spite of their lack of organization, they were successfully putting down a barrage of cannonballs that threatened to scuttle the craft.

Tanya looked about her in alarm. If they were not stopped, the Russians would be killed. Sebastino had hurried ahead of her and he stood now beside the *Gobernador*. Next to Senor Neve stood Father Dominic.

Tanya ran to his side, a cry of delight on her lips. "*Padre!* Thank God you have arrived. Please, you must stop them! They're going to kill everyone in the longboat!"

"But that is our intent, *Senora!*" Gobernador Neve seemed amused at her agitation.

She turned to the *Gobernador*. "Please, Senor Neve. They are my countrymen! Please let them live! I will take full responsibility for their behavior!"

The *Gobernador* burst into laughter. "You, *Senora?* Can you control the actions of twenty men?"

Tanya nodded frantically. The soldiers were readying for another sally. Senor Neve called to one of the officers. The preparation came to a halt. With a curt bow, he strode ahead to the beach to greet the landing party.

Father Dominic held out his hands. "Thank you for your assistance. I had just finished speaking to the *Gobernador* regarding the sin of unnecessary killing, but I believe your appeal was more to his satisfaction. He is not overly fond of religious lectures." He offered her his arm. "Come, let us descend and see who it is you have rescued from drowning."

Halfway down the slope, Tanya pulled away from the *padre*'s restraining arm and ran toward the craft. A shaft of light from the morning sun had lit the faces of the two officers. "Ivar! Little Ivar. Ivar Alexseevich! Is it really you?"

The young man turned in surprise. "Tanya Ivanovich?" His mouth fell open. "Tanya! I thought you were killed in China!"

She danced in delight. "No, Ivar! Oh, how wonderful! How absolutely wonderful!" She took Ivar's hand and led him to where Sebastino stood beside the *Gobernador*.

She explained as best she could the reason for her delight. "Sebastino, it was Ivar who tried to save me from being sold in China! Oh, to think he would appear here, in Monterey! Isn't it wonderful?"

Sebastino seemed mollified by her explanation, but he still eyed Ivar with suspicion. "Does he speak Spanish?"

Tanya translated the question. Ivar's response was short. "*Nyet!*"

"Does anyone in his party?"

Tanya again repeated the question. Ivar smiled. "*Ya.* My

companion, Lieutenant Carl Feodor. But, Tanya, he is not half as capable of translating as you."

It was finally arranged that for the length of their stay, Tanya would serve as interpreter. Reassured by her recognition of one of the officers, the Spanish settlers, led by the *Gobernador* and Sebastino, returned to the *Gobernador*'s new residence, where breakfast waited. And, of course, the Russians were asked to share the repast.

Tanya settled herself beside Ivar. "What has happened with you? When did you move from the merchant ship to the Imperial Navy?"

"When we returned to China and found that Chung Kai Chang had been murdered, I thought you were dead, too. I. . . ." He scowled. "I could stand no more of Czerwenki. So I wrote my father, and he got me transferred to the navy."

"Stand up and let me look at you! Oh, Ivar, you're a man!"

Ivar flushed. He was taller than he had been, and the peaked look that had distinguished him when he was a boy was gone. But his eyes were just as steady, and his face had a calm dignity that filled her with pride.

"You must be very brave, to have reached the rank of lieutenant so quickly!"

"My fortune came at another's expense. On my first cruise, one of the superior officers died and everyone below him was advanced." He sat down and resumed his meal. "Tanya, I come with a serious problem. The colony in Sitka is close to starvation, and a delegation has been sent to trade with the Spanish for food to see us through the coming winter. Captain Boris Ilianski, of the *Balalaika*, has a hold full of the finest Chinese silk and porcelain, as well as some exquisite furniture. Do you think your friends will consent to an exchange of goods?"

She hesitated. "I don't know. Why not?"

"Oh, Tanya, how thoughtless of me! Before we talk business, I must know how you came from China and what your position is in this Spanish colony."

She explained quickly, leaving out large sections of her story. When she had spoken of her marriage to Sebastino, she paused. "Ivar, I was told that the Fort Archangel Gabriel was burned to the ground. Can you tell me what happened? I knew some of the soldiers."

His face grew solemn. "It was a terrible massacre, I am told. But one of the officers, Alexei Andreiv, had been injured on a reconnaissance expedition and had been transported to Kodiak. He has informed me that. . . ." He looked at Tanya in alarm. "Tanya! Are you ill? What is the matter?"

Sebastino hurried to her side. "Come my love, you are overwrought! Too much excitement and not enough sleep! I promise you, the men will be treated well, and we will do with their Carl Feodor's services as a translator until you are better."

With a reproachful look at Ivar, he ushered her to her room and remained until she was settled in bed.

When at last he left to return to the festivities, she lay staring out of the window, her mind in a turmoil. Alexius was alive!

She rose impatiently and hurried toward the door. She had to learn more! To know that he was alive and yet not know his whereabouts—that was torture, indeed.

She was stopped by the sound of Feodor and Ivar speaking with the *Gobernador* just below her window.

". . . if the Captain would be allowed to land and present our case." Ivar's diplomacy was impeccable.

She waited while Feodor translated and the *Gobernador* replied. Yes, it would be permissible, since the young man was a friend of the Senora del Norte.

Ivar expressed his appreciation. "With your permission, *Senor*, I will return to the ship and notify them of your willingness to discuss the question of trade. Captain Alexius Andreiv will be most gratified at your generosity!"

Tanya sank into a chair. Until she had regained her composure, she dared not show herself to her husband.

CHAPTER IX

On the patio, chattering women surrounded her, Donna Concepcion at their head. The *Gobernador*'s wife took charge and ordered that she be led to a bench, and then, by a glance, limited the size of the circle that formed. Donna Concepcion and Donna Maria were looking at her with sharp, piercing glances.

The questions came too quickly to answer. "What happened?" "Are you all right, now?" "What are the Russians doing?" "Is it an invasion?"

Through them all, the voice of Donna Concepcion sounded clear and strong. "Tanya, what have the Russians to give us in trade?"

Relieved, Tanya enumerated the many items Ivar had named. "There is silk brocade from China, hand-woven in

Fuchow. There is porcelain. Ivar also told me that they have crates filled with delicate, hand-carved furniture!"

In the general excitement that followed, she excused herself, and, still aware of the watchful eyes of her mother-in-law, she sought shelter in a grape arbor. She did not, however, remain alone for long. Angelina settled beside her. "Oh, Tanya, what *really* happened? Why did you almost faint? Was that young man once your lover?"

Impatiently, Tanya shook her head. " 'Gelina, you let your imagination run wild!" But when it was clear that her protests did nothing to allay Angelina's suspicions, she quickly told of Ivar's role in her past.

Angelina looked at her sharply. "Then it's someone else! You mustn't try to deceive me! I'm not 'Tino, who sees only what men are willing to admit exists!" She pressed close. "You can trust me! You're the best friend I have!"

Tanya chewed nervously on her lip. "Ivar isn't the only officer on the ship whom I know. There is another. . . ."

"And *he* was your lover! Oh, Tanya, how exciting! What are you going to do? Will you speak to him?"

Tanya frowned in annoyance. " 'Gelina! Stop acting so foolishly! I have no idea whether he knows I'm here, nor do I intend to make an issue of the past. I am happy as I am, and I intend to remain that way. What will I gain by resurrecting what is over—and dead?" She hoped Angelina did not notice the catch in her voice.

Angelina hugged Tanya. "Oh, how thrilling! You must see him! How wonderful to have a lover who longs for you but cannot approach you! Tanya! It's so romantic!"

Tanya rose. "Angelina Francesca, if you do not calm down, I will speak to your mother! You're acting like a child!" She stamped her foot. "Stop it! I will never confide in you again unless you control yourself!"

Suddenly subdued, Angelina composed her face. "I'm sorry, Tanya. I can't understand why you are not excited, as well! Please tell me, are you going to see him?"

"I see no way to avoid it. The *Gobernador* has asked the officers on the *Balalaika* to join the fiesta. The trading will not begin until tomorrow."

"Tanya! Angelina! Come here! I wish to speak to you!"
It was the Donna Maria.

They hurried to her.

Donna Maria began, "You seemed strongly affected by
the young man's words, my daughter. What is he to you?
Angelina, go away. I wish to speak to Tanya."

Angelina left, giggling.

"'His name is Ivar Alexseevich," Tanya said, "and he
was cabin boy on a ship that took me from Russia to
China, many years ago. He was good to me then, and I
owe him much. Naturally, I was delighted to see him
again—and to learn how he has prospered."

"That is good. It was not delight, but dismay I saw in
your face, however. Is there someone on board the ship
whom you fear? If so, I will speak to the *Gobernador* and
have his freedom restricted." She touched Tanya's hand.
"My dear, I have grown to love you. I know a little about
your past, and I can understand your desire to put it behind you. I will not stand by now and let it rise to destroy
your happiness—and my son's new contentment."

"He brought news that a settlement in Alaska had been
wiped out by the Tlingits. I knew many people there."

The hand closed comfortingly around hers. "Ah, so that
was it! I think I would have fainted at such sudden knowledge. Were there many women and children who were . . .
slaughtered?"

Tanya sat silent for a moment. There probably had been
some women, but hardly the sort to arouse sympathy in the
breast of a respectable matron. "No, not many."

Suddenly, one of the Neve daughters ran across the patio
and curtseyed awkwardly. "Senora del Norte. My mama
wishes to speak with you."

Both women rose and hurried after the child. Donna
Maria patted Tanya's hand. "We will speak more of this
later."

Senora Neve's boudoir was elegantly furnished with the
best that could be brought from Mexico City. The chairs
were of dark wood, with ornate carvings on the armrests
and the backs, and the padding on the seats was a thick

velvet. The Empress Catherine's furniture had been carved, too, but with quite different designs.

"My husband tells me we are having guests for the remainder of the fiesta and that they are your friends." Senora Neve's voice was melodious.

Tanya curtseyed. "Yes, *Senora*."

"Do you know the captain?"

"No, *Senora*. I know only two men. One a lieutenant who served as cabin boy on the *Russian Princess* many years ago, and the other the officer who is to be in charge of the trading."

Donna Concepcion looked at her sharply. "I will see to it that you have an opportunity to speak to your friends, but I must have your assurance that you will behave with discretion. Men are so sensitive about their women, and I detected the green devil of jealousy in Sebastino's eyes when he hurried to rescue you this morning." She turned to Donna Maria. "Maria Carlotta, I think you may wish to speak for a time with your daughter-in-law. Have you visited our garden?"

In the garden, it seemed to Tanya that Donna Concepcion's word had preceded them. The garden was empty. The smallest children were being herded down to the beach to play in the sand, and all the women, including Angelina and her friends, were busy decorating the patio for the evening's dance.

Donna Maria took Tanya's hand as they sat down. "My dear, I would be comforted to know your relationship with these two men."

Tanya inhaled and gazed out over the rows of flowers. "Ivar is only a friend. A very dear friend."

"And the other?"

"I. . . . I loved him once. But I thought he had been killed when the Tlingits razed Fort Archangel Gabriel."

"Do you love him still?"

Tanya met her mother-in-law's solemn gaze.

"I love 'Tino. I would do nothing to hurt him."

Donna Maria's eyes sparkled. "I will serve as your duenna if he wishes to speak to you alone. Take courage, my child. You are among people who love you. We will

give you strength to resist temptation. Now it is past time
for your ride. You went to some trouble to bring Diablo up
with you, and he must have his exercise."

Tanya patted the curls her maid had just finished fash-
ioning. "Thank you, Rebecca. It looks lovely."

"My dear—" Sebastino's voice came from across the
room. "You would look lovely in rags, with your hair in a
braid down your back! Don't ever forget it! I have the most
beautiful wife in the whole of Califa!"

Tanya smiled warmly at her husband. "Thank you 'Tino.
You spoil me!" She twirled and looked again in the mirror.
Her dress was green, her favorite color, with deep maroon
piping in all the seams. Long sleeves and a high neck concealed her delicate shoulders and slender arms, but they
could not hide her perfect figure. The bodice fit snugly,
molding itself over her high breasts and hugging her waist.

In honor of the occasion, Sebastino dressed in the identi-
cal colors, only reversed. His dark maroon velvet suit was
designed in the latest style. His cravat was ivory white, and
his dark hair hung in loose curls that stopped at his shoulders. He held out his arm. "Come, my dear. The Russians
have arrived, and their Feodor has no talent for the fine
points in our language."

Tanya took Sebastino's arm and approached the patio.
But for all her preparation, she still was not ready for that
first sight of Alexius.

He was changed from the youth who had loved her in
the Conservatory so long ago. His shoulders were broader,
his head held with greater pride. And where his upper lip
had been shaven before, he now wore a small mustache.

He was standing beside Senor Neve, with Feodor acting
as his interpreter. All three men stopped speaking as she
advanced, but she was aware only of Alexius' eyes—of
Alexius' magnetic presence.

Alexius did not move. But the look he returned was the
same. She felt the embrace of his gaze, and her pulse quickened. He loved her still—and wanted her with the same
passion.

Resolutely, she turned toward the *Gobernador*. "Good

morning, Senor Neve; gentlemen—I am most happy to be of help."

Gobernador Neve explained that he had been giving the Russians advice on farming in cold countries. "I spent some time in Patagonia, where the weather is fiercely cold throughout the winter. The natives there do some small farming, and I suspect that Senor Andreiv might find knowledge of the technique they use of some help in Alaska."

Tanya translated the *Gobernador*'s words. Alexius also seemed to have recovered his poise. He nodded to Feodor, who immediately excused himself and joined another group nearby. Then, his eyes still on Tanya, he responded to the *Gobernador*'s advice.

"Please thank the governor for his consideration," he said in Russian. "I am amazed to find you at last—and here, of all places! Ivar was right. You are more beautiful than you ever were. I love you. I must see you alone." His voice never changed. "Tell the governor that I appreciate his interest in the welfare of the Russian colony."

She turned to the *Gobernador*. "He thanks you and asks for further details. He also says he is pleased to see that I live among such kindly people."

Senor Neve launched into a detailed description of Patagonian farming. Thankfully, Tanya accepted the demands put upon her as interpreter. But her skin tingled at the nearness of her lover, and when she met his eyes, she had to force herself to break the hold.

Sebastino remained beside her, a frown disfiguring his usually placid expression. When he showed suspicion at the length of Alexius' replies and the shortness of her translations, Alexius ceased to add words of affection to his replies, but this did not succeed in relaxing Sebastino's alertness.

Tanya was relieved when a bell sounded to call them to dinner. The food was placed, as breakfast had been, on a long table from which the guests served themselves. The young people sat on the grass in groups of giggling excitement, and the matrons and gentlemen spread themselves out on the various benches that edged the patio. The *Gobernador*, Alexius, Sebastino, and Tanya sat together facing the bay.

Despite her resolve, Tanya grew more agitated by the minute. More than once she had to ask the *Gobernador* to repeat his words, and she carefully avoided Alexius' face when she spoke to him, until Sebastino said, "What's the matter with you, Tanya? Are you angry with our guest? What is bothering you? Why do you refuse to look at him?"

He continued swiftly. "Has he changed from when you last met? You have not spoken of his relationship to you. Was it in St. Petersburg where you knew him?"

Tanya had hardly heard his words. Her eyes had locked with Alexius' and suddenly, her nervousness was gone. His look was warm—but devoid of any demand. He would do nothing to risk the success of his mission.

She turned to her husband. "Yes, 'Tino, it was in St. Petersburg. He knew my father well, and seeing him reminds me of my father's suffering in Siberia. I'm sorry if I have seemed rude to him."

Immediately, Sebastino was solicitous. Tanya bore his apologies with growing discomfort. To lie to her husband was bad enough. To make him feel guilty was unforgivable!

The musicians began to play light music as the servants gathered the dishes and cleared away the table. Then, with a burst of riotous laughter, the dancing began. Tanya's first dance was, as was proper, with her husband. Then she circled the floor with the *Gobernador*, and then with the Russians. When Alexius took her in his arms, his actions were totally impersonal. Although she knew how important it was to them both that their relationship not be exposed, she could not repress her disappointment. She felt relieved when he passed her on to the next partner.

She was dancing with Ivar when she noticed that Senora Maria Carlotta had taken Alexius' arm and was standing near the entrance to the garden. The next time she circled the floor, they were gone. She gazed into the darkness with growing trepidation. When the allemande was finished, she would excuse herself and follow. Somewhere in the shadows, Alexius would be waiting. And nearby Maria Carlotta would be watching the meeting, sympathetic, but ready to protect her son's honor if she felt it was being threatened.

CHAPTER X

The dance ended. On the patio Sebastino, who had been dancing with Isabel, one of Angelina's friends, was in what appeared to be deep conversation. The *Gobernador* was sitting on a bench with Donna Concepcion and Feodor. Angelina, her attention flitting from one of her suitors to the other, was standing beside Ivar.

Donna Maria had discretely arranged the tryst. No one had noticed her leaving. The ground below Tanya's feet dipped slightly, and she found herself in a small culvert. The chattering of the merrymakers was well-nigh overwhelmed by the loud fiddling of the crickets, and the song of a nightingale. Suddenly, Donna Maria was beside her. "Tanya." Her voice was low. "He is just ahead, waiting on a bench. Remember, I will be nearby if you need me."

"Thank you, Donna Maria. I will." She searched the kindly face. "Mama, I. . . ."

"I do not wish to know more than I do. Go. The time is short."

Impulsively, Tanya threw her arms around her mother-in-law's shoulders and kissed her on the cheek. Then she was on her way to where her lover waited.

When she saw him, her impulse was to run into his arms, to bury herself in the silken ruffles of his shirt, to feel again his wonderful closeness. But her pace did not increase. She stopped close enough to touch him, her arms pressed tightly against her body. She saw his arms move upward and then fall helplessly to his sides. He had spoken to Maria Carlotta. He knew the rules that governed their meeting.

They sat side-by-side on the bench, his hand enclosing hers. Tanya's entire awareness was in her fingertips. His voice broke into her reverie. "Tanya, oh, my dearest! I have missed you so!"

She told him briefly of her travels, passing quickly over her time in China and dwelling on the shipwreck that had tossed her onto the coast of New Spain where, miraculously, she had been discovered by the *padre* Dominic.

When she finished, he commented briefly about her father, and then he said, "The child? Tanya, it hurts me to think of your bearing any child but mine."

"Stop, Alexius! Please. You must not speak that way!"

His fingers tightened around hers. "You know I have never stopped loving you."

"Yes." It was barely a whisper.

"You must come with me. When the trading is over. You don't belong here, among strangers!"

Her fingers tensed. More than anything, she longed to agree—to know that she would be his. "Alexius, I can't. I have a responsibility here."

"Do you love this Spaniard?"

She did not answer for a time. When she did, her voice was thoughtful. "In some ways, yes. He has been good to me, Alexius; he has never asked more than I could give."

His voice was harsh. "Is that all you want—for the rest of your life? Can you send me away—now?"

Tears came to her eyes. "Please. I must do what is right. I cannot dishonor a man who has done nothing to hurt me."

"Does our love count for nothing?" There was anger in his tone. Anger—and terrible agony.

"Alexius! Please! I cannot stand it!"

The broad figure of Maria Carlotta loomed in the darkness before them. Tanya rose. Her hands were her own once more. She whispered, "I love you, Alexius. I always will."

He towered above her, and for one moment she feared he would take her in his arms. Then he was gone. But she knew she would never forget the pain and anger in his troubled voice.

Tanya spurred Diablo up the golden hillside away from the glimmering bay, glad to be free at last from Donna Maria Carlotta's worried gaze. The remainder of the dance had been a nightmare in which she struggled to resist the longing to run into Alexius' arms. At last, exhausted and troubled, she had retired, only to lie staring at the ceiling.

'Tino had been particularly loving when he joined her, and she had not dared to put him off, though for the first time in their marriage, she closed her eyes when he kissed her and pretended, deep in her heart, that the lips that touched hers belonged to another. But his love had finally overcome her hesitancy, and she gave herself to him with wholehearted acceptance.

She had awakened early and hurried to the stable, determined to ride all day. The actual trading was finished. All that was left was to load the cargo—and she was not needed. She was determined to remain away until the ship sailed—or at least until the crew went aboard. She dared risk no further meetings with Alexius.

At the top of the hill she drew Diablo to a halt. The settlement below was beginning to stir. Smoke billowed from the kitchen chimney. Children rolled on the grassy mound near the patio, and their laughter sounded faintly.

Donna Maria Carlotta, who had greeted her as she emerged from the kitchen, was sitting at the edge of the patio, gazing down at the bay. Sebastino stood beside his mother. He had risen as she left their room, and he had announced that he was returning to the del Norte estate for a day or two to supervise the foaling expected any day.

The *Balalaika* floated in the harbor. A longboat was beached close to the dock. The sand was empty, and so was the slope above it.

Tanya turned Diablo's head toward a culvert of live oak. Spurring him to a gallop, she leaned low against his back. The wind rushing through her hair seemed to clear her mind, and when she drew rein under the shade, she felt refreshed. She dismounted and led her horse to a brook where he drank deeply. Then she tethered him to a nearby bush to graze.

Tanya had found this cove on her first ride from the Neve hacienda, and she was charmed by the secret beauty of the spot. The dark leaves etched themselves against the deep blue of the sky, and the gentle whispering of the stream seemed to comfort her. She settled on a rock and leaned back, letting the peace of her surroundings flow over her troubled spirit.

A branch crackled behind her and she sat up in alarm.

"Tanya! I hoped I would find you here!"

"Alexius!" She was on her feet and in his arms. His lips pressed against hers with a wild hunger.

Suddenly, she drew back. "I cannot. Alexius, please!"

"Will you deny me—and yourself—one hour of love? Tanya, you know I love you. And you know how long we have been apart. We will be separated for the rest of our lives."

His arms tightened around her, and this time she could not resist. They drew apart impulsively, and when she faced him again, he, like her, stood bare of clothing. She gazed at him with growing desire. And then she was in his arms, her breasts against his bare chest.

He lifted her in his arms and carried her to a moss-covered alcove. She felt the soft ground beneath her back, and then she felt only his nearness. He touched her body lightly, his eyes filled with love—and admiration. "Tanya, my love. You are so beautiful!"

She stilled his lips with a kiss, drawing him to her. The weight of his body on hers filled her with a new feeling of completeness. She breathed his name; she opened her thighs to welcome him.

He moved gently at first, the memory of the girl she had been tempering his passion. But her response was that of a woman—a woman who knew love and who could give ecstasy. She moved with him, her thoughts drowned in her passion. Was she still in the woods? She was not aware of the trees around her—or of the moss under her back.

The years of separation faded into unreality as she twisted beneath his thrusts. Nothing had changed—and everything had changed. She knew him, knew his wants and his desires—knew his passion. And her responses were directed by her own desire and her own longing. She felt light currents as her fingers caressed his back, and then the explosions began in her brain. She knew nothing but his presence—his love.

They lay, arms intertwined, her legs resting on his. A ray of sunlight touched the dark of his hair and lit it with golden shine. Rising on one arm, she bent and kissed his damp stomach. "Alexius! I must go. Now, before I lose all power to leave you."

"I am resigned. I know you are right. But I will be waiting, if ever you leave here. I will love no one. . . ."

A loud retort cut him off. Somewhere nearby, a gun had been fired. Tanya leaped up in alarm and began to dress. But Alexius caught her shoulders and held her still. "Quiet, my love! It's all right! Ivar and Feodor rode with me. They have been standing guard, to protect us from wild animals."

She felt her tremors quiet, and she slowed her dressing. "If they are nearby, we must be ready." The guilt she knew would come was filling her consciousness. "Alexius, we mustn't stay here!"

Alexius pulled on his breeches and settled down to put

on his boots. When he rose, he turned toward the source of the noise. "Holla! Ivar! Feodor! Come ahead!"

He took her in his arms and kissed her. "Remember. I will love you always!" Then, a small smile on his lips, he turned to greet his friends.

They approached noisily, trampling through the brush and calling out as they came. Ivar broke into the clearing first. "I'm sorry if our shot disturbed you. Feodor thought he saw a mountain lion."

"Did he kill it?" Alexius did not release his hold on Tanya's shoulders.

Feodor shook his head. "I don't know. You called before we could begin searching. Are we ready to go?"

"Yes. We must leave." Alexius pulled away slowly, letting his fingers trail down her arm until only their hands touched. With a sudden motion, he swept her once more in his arms. His hungry lips sought hers, pressed against her.

She stood helplessly, watching as he mounted his horse. But he did not ride away immediately. "Tanya. If there is a mountain lion nearby, you must leave, too. It isn't safe for you to be alone."

She took Diablo's reins and leaped into her saddle. When they reached the edge of the woods, he paused, Ivar and Feodor close behind him. Their eyes met once more. "Good-bye, my love."

She held Diablo's reins loosely, unwilling to leave. Alexius bent over and flicked Diablo's rump with his riding crop. With a whinny, the spirited horse leaped forward. And by the time Tanya reined him in, Alexius was gone.

Carlos, the stableboy, drew his horse to a halt and leaped to the ground. "Senora Maria Carlotta! The mare has foaled! I have been sent to inform Senor Sebastino that he has a new Diablino!"

Donna Maria Carlotta touched her arm. They had been sitting together on the patio, watching the children play. The ship had sailed early that morning, and Tanya, her heart sore, had been thankful that Sebastino was not beside her to see her sadness.

Donna Maria Carlotta had understood her distress. "You will recover, my dear. When 'Tino comes back and you are beside him again, all this will fade."

"Carlos! What are you saying? Senore del Norte left here yesterday to be with the mare when she foaled!"

The boy looked suddenly confused. "Oh, no, *senora*! He has not been back at the ranch! We had to handle the foaling alone!"

Tanya felt a sudden fear clutch at her heart. "Did you pass him on the road?" Her voice rose. "Maybe he was waylaid!" She grabbed the boy's arm. "You must have seen him!"

A look of terror filled his face. "No, *senora*! As God is my witness, I saw no one!"

She was trembling now. If 'Tino had not gone home, as he had said he would, where was he? She knew with a certainty that drew strength from her limbs. Tottering, she sank to the bench. Maria Carlotta gazed into her troubled eyes. "Tanya! What is it? What is the matter?"

"'Tino. I think I know where he is!" She forced herself to rise then. With her mother-in-law trailing behind her, she ran to the stable and waited impatiently as Eduardo saddled Diablo. Just before she mounted, she turned to her companion. "Mama. I think 'Tino knew. I think he followed me. And I am afraid. . . ." She could not continue. Leaping onto her saddle, she spurred Diablo to a gallop. She was only vaguely aware of men on horseback following her as she sped up the hill.

She skirted the woods, crossing the creek at one end of the growth of oaks. Feodor had come from inland. And he had fired his gun when he was close to. . . . She refused to think of what else had transpired that day. Feodor had thought he was hunting a mountain lion.

Ahead, the underbrush obscured her vision. She was galloping when she came upon him, and she drew rein just in time. Demonio lay where he had fallen, a bullet hole through his head. And on the ground where he had been thrown when the big horse fell, lay Sebastino.

303

CHAPTER XI

The chapel glowed brightly in the late afternoon sun, throwing a halo of light over the shrouded body that lay before the altar. Tanya crossed herself and moved slowly down the aisle. Soon the chapel would be filled with worshipers, and Father Dominic would say the words that would guide 'Tino's spirit into Heaven. Now, for the last time, he belonged to her.

She knelt beside his bare wooden coffin and rested her folded hands on the sharp chiseled frame. He lay as if he were sleeping. Only the strange waxiness of his skin and the transparent delicateness of his eyelids were silent proof that what lay before her was an empty shell.

"Dear God—" She lifted her eyes to the painted face of the Christ that gazed down in agony from the cross. "Forgive me for my sins, and take the soul of 'Tino into your heart. You have known pain and suffering. I thank you for sparing 'Tino any suffering."

She gazed into the silent face. She had never until just before his death given 'Tino reason for jealousy. Nor had she denied him her love. Had 'Tino known? Had he seen her with Alexius? She had slipped from grace once—and for that one sin, he was punished!

Donna Maria Carlotta knelt at her side. Her hands enclosed Tanya's, and her eyes were steady. "My daughter, you must not blame yourself."

Tanya gazed into the loving face. "But I . . . your son is dead, and all because I. . . ."

"Because he was not above the mortal sin of jealousy. Tanya, you are not to blame. I am sure of that. But there is little we women can do to change the way our men feel about us. They love us—but they own us, too. And jealousy is the evil fruit of such possessiveness."

Tanya lowered her eyes. She could never tell Maria what had happened. Feodor had warned one of the grooms that he had shot a mountain lion in the woods, and it was accepted now that 'Tino's death had been a tragic accident. But the guilt lay heavy on Tanya's heart when Padre Dominic arrived to begin the service.

CHAPTER XII

Tanya shifted in the saddle and turned toward her companion. "Father, have we far to go before we reach San Francisco?"

This was the road she had traveled with 'Tino when she had first gone with him to his ranch.

"No, my child. Do you not remember the road?"

"Not much of it. I was in a carriage—and 'Tino and I were talking—some of the time."

"Ah, yes." The *padre* pointed ahead. "There! See? We have reached the south end of the bay."

The remainder of the journey was filled with memories. As they reached one rise, Tanya remembered that it had been there that Sebastino had spoken to her of the ocean, far to the west. Repressing a sigh, she spurred her horse.

Diablo whinnied and shook his head. When he caught up with the *padre*'s mount, he slowed again to a trot. Tanya patted his neck. "Good boy! No reason for rushing!"

Father Dominic glanced up as she joined him. "It is too bad you must relive the past on this journey, but we must not question God's will."

"I do not, *padre*. Not any more. But I can't help but remember how much 'Tino loved life. He was very young to die."

"He had much while he lived, my dear. You gave him pleasure few men ever know. He told me so himself."

She shook her head. "I also gave him cause to mistrust me. And it was that which killed him."

"Jealousy is a sin, my child."

They rode for a time in silence. Tanya thought of her last conversation with her mother-in-law. Donna Maria did not want her to leave. "There is money enough from 'Tino's estate to care for all three of us. Please, I will miss you if you go."

Tanya had insisted, though she did accept the portion of the estate 'Tino had allocated to her. The task of selling the land had been taken over by Senor Neve himself, and he planned to purchase the greatest mass of it. The price was eminently fair. In her saddle bags, Tanya had more gold than she had ever seen before. Still, even when the question of money had been settled, Tanya had found it difficult to leave her family. "Oh, Tanya, my daughter!" Donna Maria Carlotta had pulled her into her arms. "I wish you would stay. I have come to love you dearly!"

It was Father Dominic who had replied. "She must do what God tells her to do—and what your son commanded. He wanted her to return to her own people if he died."

Tanya took Donna Maria's hands. "Mama, the *padre* is right. Your hacienda was home to me because of my love for 'Tino—" Her voice broke. "—and his for me. It is best that I go my own way—and find my own peace."

The farewell had, nevertheless, been difficult. Donna Maria's kindness had made Tanya love her as if she were

308

in truth her mother. And Angelina had become like a real sister.

"There! If you look, you can see the roof of the Presidio!" Father Dominic pointed across the hilltops to where, in the distance, a red roof caught the setting sun.

Far over the hills, she could see the bay gleaming brightly. 'Tino had been so happy when first they met. And Manuel. He had dreamed of happiness he never found.

"Padre, will I always lose those I love? Have I sinned so badly?"

"My child, you must not question God's will in your life. Maybe, when you find the purpose he has for you, you will understand."

She let her body roll with the sway of Diablo's descent. "Is it possible that I should not go at all? Perhaps I should stay here—with you—as a nun."

"Oh, my daughter! I have thought of that, but I cannot find agreement in my soul. No, there is something else for you. Were you to remain at the Mission with me, you would be plagued by the soldiers in the Presidio. They are, I fear, weak in their Christian consciences." He paused. "Tanya, my child. You must renounce the pride that now controls your life. Do you believe that it is you, and not God, who rules the fate of mankind?"

"Oh, Father, of course not!"

"You can have it only one way. Either God rules all, or he has given you special powers not bestowed upon most of us. Which is it?"

He touched her shoulder. "Consider, my daughter. You say you are to blame for Sebastino's death because he was jealous of you. But did he in any way differ from his friends? Are not they all possessive of their women in a way that seems unnatural to you?"

He continued. "The *Santa Susana* is due soon from San Diego. You will have time to wait for your luggage to arrive from Monterey. Within a fortnight, you will be on the high seas."

The sun was overhead when, after a long night's sleep, she climbed up the hill above the Presidio to gaze down at the ocean. Somewhere, slightly to the north and far out to sea, Manuel's ship, the *Senorita Francesca*, had broken up under the pounding of tempestuous waves. A fog hovered far out to sea, and she remembered how it closed down over the shore each night. Soon she would be leaving this land. Soon she would begin her search again. But now, at least, she knew that Alexius was alive! And she knew that the *Balalaika* was headed for the Sandwich Islands. She sat alone most of the day, staring out at the ever-moving water. And when she returned to the mission, she felt that the worst of her remorse was washed away.

Her luggage arrived the next day. As the Indians carried her trunks from the waiting carriage, she glanced wryly at the *padre*. "I leave with far more than I had when I arrived. It did not seem right that I take all my clothes with me, but Mama insisted."

"You do not think that you will need them?"

She shrugged her shoulders. "I don't know. I hardly know where I am going. I suppose at least at the start of my journey it does no harm for me to carry luggage. I can always leave it behind later, if it is necessary."

"You must stay for a time with a friend of mine. Father Timeteo has a mission on the largest of the Sandwich Islands. From what he has written, ships from every country dock there to trade. Surely, if ever there is a place where you will find your Alexius, that is it—in a land where all nations are welcome."

The last trunk was placed on the floor and the Indians scurried away. Father Dominic spoke to the last one, who returned with an armful of bags.

When they were alone again, the *padre* put the bags on the table. "You must break up your gold into these bags and then fill them with grain. It will keep the coins from rattling when you move. Keep no more than twenty gold pieces in your purse and tie all the others under your slips. The captain of the *Santa Susana* is as honest as any man— and his men come to confession when they are in the harbor. But your wealth could tempt them greatly. Do not reveal the other bags to anyone. And until you sail, bury your money in your trunks."

Tanya spread the gold on her bed and stacked it into piles. "Father, I cannot take all of this gold with me. Some of it belongs here—for the mission."

"Are you sure, my child? You face an unknown future. You will need money whatever you do."

Carefully, she counted out a stack of gold pieces and put them in his hand. "Father, pray for Sebastino. And sometimes, if you can spare a thought, for me—I will need your intervention in Heaven."

Father Dominic dropped the coins into his pocket. "They will fill the poor box, and many will thank you for your generosity. As for prayers, I have never stopped praying for your happiness—nor will I. And I will remember Sebastino, for he is responsible for this beneficence." He paused. "I will send a man with a bag of grain. When you are finished, join us for matins."

The *Santa Susana* arrived a day earlier than the Father had expected, and the men began immediately to scrape and paint the battered hull. For a week the Indians moved back and forth from the ship, unloading the cargo of weapons for the Presidio, and the sacred objects, including a large bell, that had been sent from Mexico City at the *padre*'s request.

Tanya stood each morning at the gate to the Mission garden and watched the activity. When the cargo was unloaded, the loading began. The *Santa Susana* was a merchant ship much like the *Senorita Francesca,* with a round belly and a deep hold. They filled her with grain and lumber—and with hides from slaughtered cattle as well as with pelts from sea otters, many of which had been confiscated from ships that had strayed unwelcome into the harbor.

When the loading was completed, the *padre* had her trunks brought to the shore and loaded into a long boat. "I have spoken to the captain, Tanya. He is going first to the Sandwich Islands, and he has promised to deliver you there. Your passage will cost you two of your gold pieces."

He helped her enter the longboat. "I have told him that my friend is expecting you, and that you are traveling to the Islands to visit a sister who is a nun. He can be trusted, but remember my warnings. And when you land, go directly to the Mission. Father Timeteo will help you get settled."

Captain Jose Rodolfo was a short man with a round belly and a pudgy face. His hair, a yellow grey, stood out against the tan of his face like a shock of ripe grain. He bowed slightly as she reached the deck, and led the way down to a cabin which had been set aside for her.

Father Dominic stood beside her as her trunks were placed against the wall in her cabin, and before he turned to go, he studied the door. "Good! You must keep your door locked. Captain Rodolfo has requested it, and I, too, feel it is important."

"For a man of the cloth, you are surprisingly suspicious, Father."

"I am a realist, for all of my calling. I pray for my fellow men, but I know their weaknesses."

The captain had the crew lined on the deck when Tanya and Father Dominic returned. "*Padre,* you have blessed the lady, and you have listened to all of our confessions. But I beg of you, bless the ship, too. Some of my men consider it bad luck to have a woman aboard. A small prayer will help them allay their fears."

Father Dominic chanted loudly, and then, with a final benediction, climbed down into the boat and was rowed ashore. When the sailors were back on deck, Tanya returned to her cabin and locked the door. Above her, she could hear the rattle of the anchor chain and the trampling of feet as the men jumped to the orders of their captain.

She ventured on deck once—as the ship reached the mouth of the bay. The roof of the mission gleamed in the late-afternoon sun, and far above it the walls of the Presidio glowed a deep pink. The island, which on her first view of the bay had seemed like a ship, floated in the middle of the water, and as she watched, a flock of birds circled over it and settled in the trees.

Manuel de Vincente had been right. California was a

very beautiful land. And the people who lived in it were, for the most part, good—and friendly.

A voice behind her barked an order and she turned to watch the first mate direct the unfurling of the sails. He was a tall slender man with unusually wide shoulders and hands that seemed out of keeping with the thickness of his arms. But his face drew her attention. His enormous nose protruded before him like the bill of a parrot, and behind it, his eyes gleamed like small black lights.

Carefully, so she would not interfere with the work of the crew, Tanya crossed the deck and descended to her cabin.

PART IV

The Sandwich Islands
1805

CHAPTER I

___

Tanya felt again the nausea that had troubled her periodically throughout the journey. It had been a terrible crossing. Shortly after leaving the bay of San Francisco, she had developed a swelling in her neck, and her body had burned with a high fever. She had kept to her room, not because of any danger from the crew, but because she felt far too ill to dare the deck.

Her food had been brought to her by Olivero, a young lad who reminded her of Ivar, but whose delicate features and soft voice seemed more fitting for a woman. By the time the *Santa Susana* reached the largest island in the Sandwich grouping, she had recovered from her illness. But she was weak and very pale.

To celebrate their arrival at Kona, Captain Rodolfo had

had her carried up and placed on a cot on the poop deck.

The air was warm and moist, a breeze kept it from becoming oppressive, and the sweet smell of flowers and fresh wet soil was a delightful change from the eternal winds and cabin-smell, and wet of the passage.

From the shore came a stream of long canoes filled with half-naked natives, their songs of welcome filling the air. They swarmed over the railing of the ship, their arms laden with necklaces of brilliant flowers. She could hear the words of their song. *Aloha! Aloha!*

Captain Rodolfo stepped back from the railing. "They're greeting us in friendship. Their word, *aloha*, means both hello and good-bye."

Golden-skinned men and women, dressed in little more than a few feathers or flowers, were draping their *leis* around the necks of the laughing sailors. The women, unlike the Indian natives of California, wore skirts without blouses, and their bare breasts were decked with flowers. The men wore loincloths, though many new arrivals, both male and female, who swam out from the shore, wore nothing at all. Yet they showed no shame at their nudity.

"Beg pardon, *Senora*. I hope the savages don't offend you." Captain Rodolfo obviously was not himself disturbed by the display of bare flesh.

"No, *Capitan*, thank you. I find them most beautiful— and totally innocent—like children."

"Good! You are an unusual woman to take such an attitude. I regret that you were ill most of the journey and I did not have the opportunity to speak with you more often." He turned again toward the lower deck. "Do you feel up to joining the celebration?"

Tanya began to rise and then, suddenly dizzy, settled back on her cot. "Thank you, no. I will watch, if you don't mind. I find myself surprisingly weak."

"Olivero tells me you ate blessed little during the journey. You might be suffering from a touch of scurvy as well as from your illness. I will have him bring you some of the fruit the natives have carried on board." He bowed formally. "Now, if you will pardon me, I see that I am expected below."

There was a scuffling at the ladder and two native officials stepped aboard. Their bodies were a golden color, like those of the lesser greeters, and they were fully as tall and well-built. Tanya had never seen so many beautiful people. These two, however, wore straight patterned skirts that reached from their waists to their bare feet, and, over their shoulders, capes that tied under their chins and floated out behind them. Bare-chested, they also wore *leis*. But their faces were solemn, and their expressions did not change, even when they greeted the captain.

They made no move to leave the railing. Captain Rodolfo stood before them, a sudden look of sobriety on his face.

The taller of the two spoke for some time. Captain Rodolfo responded with a speech of equal length. Then the second visitor began, gesturing occasionally in the direction of Tanya's pallet. When he finished, Captain Rodolfo was frowning.

This time he spoke with more animation, and Tanya realized he was arguing with the two officials. But they showed no willingness to be persuaded. When he finished, they grunted, and the taller one stepped up on a pile of ropes. His voice carried over the laughter of the swarming natives and the smiling sailors, and immediately the celebration stopped. One by one the natives hurried over the railing. Many climbed back into the canoes in which they had arrived, but some dove into the water to swim back to shore. The sailors seemed ready to protest, but at a gesture from Rodolfo they settled down, gathering in small knots as far from the two officials as they could.

The two officials climbed solemnly into their official canoe and were paddled back to land. Captain Rodolfo hurried to Tanya's side. "*Senora*, pardon, but it seems we are in trouble."

She braced herself and waited for him to continue.

"Those two officials were Kanalio and Nuiaui, second and third in command under King Kamehameha and in charge of all shipping into the harbor of Kealakekua Bay. Since last we visited the islands, much has happened here. King Kamehameha launched an offensive against the king of Kauai, gathering the largest number of boats he has ever commanded. But when they reached Oahu the warriors grew sick and died, wasting away before his eyes. The only thing that kept his offensive from turning into a total rout was that his enemies, too, suffered the same sickness.

"He has decided that his people have been weakened by contact with white visitors who are, themselves, not well, and so he has arbitrarily ruled that all who land on the islands must be strong—by his standards. You were seen to need help climbing onto the poop deck, and so you are *kapu*."

"*Kapu*? That is why the natives were sent away?"

"Yes. *Kapu* means forbidden, prohibited. It makes no sense, for we know that you are recovered, and that your weakness is due to your need for food. But if I expect to trade again with Kanalio and Nuiaui I cannot disobey them." He stared at the distant shore. "At least not openly."

"Not openly? What do you mean?"

He smiled at her alarm. "You are *kapu* now. But if we can get you ashore and you can help Father Timeteo in the mission, as I understand you intend to, they will, in time, forget their prohibition against you—I believe." He pointed to a tall building that towered above the trees a short distance down the beach. Its thatched roof was wet with dew.

"*Senora*, do you see that structure?" He waited until she nodded. "It is in a special enclosure where natives go to rid themselves of *kapu*. If they have displeased the gods—or Kamehameha—and they do not wish to be executed, they hurry there where they are safe from all forms of retribution. Then they go through some ceremonies that cleanse them. When they leave the Refuge, they are accepted again into the native society."

"You are suggesting that I might go there?"

"Maybe. If we can get you ashore." He bowed. "If you will excuse me I will go ashore and speak to Father Timeteo. He might have some suggestion. He has had much experience with the natives."

The bay in some ways reminded her of Monterey, though there was more foliage and the rocks were black instead of white. The natives, too, seemed more independent and proud than were the quiet, submissive savages who populated the missions in California. Father Timeteo, she felt certain, had a much more difficult time finding converts than did Father Dominic and the others who populated the missions along the coast of California. And who was Kamehameha? Captain Rodolfo had spoken of him twice, and both times his voice had shown respect—almost fear.

Olivero climbed to the poop deck. "*Senora*, here is an orange—and some strawberries. They will make you feel much better."

Tanya nibbled first at the succulent red berries, relishing their flavor. But when she began to peel the orange, she was overcome with a memory of the young lad Alex, and the orange he had brought her as she lay in prison in St. Petersburg. She ate it slowly.

She was sitting up when Captain Rodolfo returned. "*Senora*—" He did not succeed in concealing his disappointment. "—I have spoken to the *padre* and he is willing to hide you in the mission for a time. He opposes the thought of your entering the Refuge, but I feel that you must not take his advice on that matter. There are converts with whom you can speak who will help you more than he. However, none of them had any suggestions as to how you might leave the ship without being observed."

He gazed at the main deck where Arnaldo, the first mate, was directing the stacking of the cargo in preparation for unloading. "We'll remain here all day, stowing our new cargo. Since the natives are now afraid to consort with us, we will sail at dawn tomorrow. Maybe you should continue with us to China."

"No, thank you, *Capitan*. I have spent enough time there, and I have no wish to be stranded in Canton. At least the town of Keei is new to me." She smiled. "I find the challenge here exciting." When he frowned, she continued. "If I do not succeed in making myself acceptable to the islanders, I can go elsewhere in some other ship. If I understand correctly, this harbor is used by all the ships that trade with the islanders." She rose and stood beside him. "Captain, what is it you are unloading?"

He pointed to the grain that was stacked in barrels at one end of the deck. "You saw us load the wheat. It is for the *padre*, who is determined to teach the natives to grow something more than fruit. You did not see us load the cattle which have caused Arnaldo considerable trouble throughout the journey. They are a gift from Father Dominic's mission to Father Timeteo. The otter furs are a gift from me to the King Kamehameha, and I will give the two delegates who boarded us earlier the hides from the steers. I have free access to the port because I don't forget to pay tribute to the savage rulers. Not every ship receives the welcome we usually get."

"I hope my malaise has not destroyed your relationship with Kanalio and Nuiaui."

"Don't worry. No damage has been done that will not be repaired when they receive their gifts. For all of their pretense at diplomacy, they are savages at heart."

She was staring at the large barrels when she had a sudden spark of inspiration. "Captain, have you any barrels that have already been emptied?"

He looked at her in surprise. "A few. You have a plan?"

"If the natives have no idea how many barrels you should be delivering to the *padre*, maybe you could arrange to take one more. I could easily fit inside one as large as those are."

"You feel well enough for so rough a passage?"

"Even if I still felt sick, I have no desire to be kept on board. Please, do you think it is possible?"

Captain Rodolfo nodded and hurried down to the main deck. Tanya went below to her cabin. There was little that she had to do to pack her trunks. Despite her sickness, the passage had been pleasant compared to the terror of her previous experiences. The captain had been a gentleman from the start, and though he had maintained a distance between them, she did not resent his aloofness.

Olivero appeared in the passageway. "*Senora*, the captain is ready for you on deck."

But as she reached the doorway at the head of the steps,

she was met by Arnaldo. *"Senora,* you are to come with me. It is better if you enter the cask where you cannot be seen by the natives."

She paused for only a moment. "My trunks? Will you have a problem with them?"

He shook his head. "With your permission, we will transfer your possessions into other barrels. They will be less suspect."

She thought of the gold she had buried among her skirts. She had considered packing it in one of her chests. "No, that will be fine." She paused. "I trust the barrels will be clean."

"As clean as we can make them. I regret the inconvenience this foolishness on the part of Kamehameha is causing you."

She was just ready to ask about this king who had such power over the natives and who could cause sea captains such difficulty, when they reached the ladder that led to the hold. Arnaldo went ahead, and when he stood in the dark below her, she followed.

The barrel, smelling strongly of fresh grain, stood before her. One of the sailors turned a small keg upside down to provide Tanya with a step and Arnaldo held out his hand to support her.

She sat for a moment on the rim of the barrel, and then she let herself down into its darkness. She swayed slightly, and there was a dull thud against the side of her hiding place. Jose Arnaldo looked at her with a sudden sharpness. But before she had an opportunity to determine the meaning of his glance, she was directed into a crouching position by one of the sailors, and the lid of the barrel was closed above her.

CHAPTER II

Tanya closed her eyes as she felt the barrel swing free. "Dear God—" Her thoughts blocked out the terror. "—make it work!"

It seemed like ages before she again felt the deck of the ship below her, and the swaying that had almost brought on a fit of nausea was over. There had been a thump as she reached the wooden planks, and there were many more around her as the remainder of the cargo was brought up from the hold.

She settled in as comfortable a position as possible and closed her eyes. Until she reached the mission, she was dependent upon the care of the sailors.

She was jolted anew as the crane lifted her once more and she was again swinging loosely. Her tiny prison was thrown against the side of the ship and her head hit the slats. Dizzy and increasingly uncomfortable, she attempted to brace herself. When she thudded to rest in the longboat, she breathed a sigh of relief.

But her respite was short. No longer shielded from the sun by the superstructure of the ship, her barrel grew hot. Her head swimming, she leaned toward a crack between two slats and sucked in the cool air. Then, somewhat revived, she shifted to remain close to this bit of comfort. If she pressed her eye against it she could see a bright line of blue.

The longboat began to move. Tanya could hear the creaking of the oars and the cursing of the men as they bent their backs to the load. And above all the other sounds was the voice of Arnaldo issuing orders.

By the time her barrel was removed from the longboat and placed on the sandy shore, Tanya was close to fainting. Never had she experienced such heat—or such closeness. Yet she dared not move or complain for fear her hiding-place would be discovered.

". . . only grain and supplies for the *padre*." It was Arnaldo, and he was standing close by.

The voice that responded was Kanalio's, questioning again the contents of the barrels.

"If you wish, we can open them to show you." Arnaldo leaned in front of the narrow crack that gave Tanya her only glimpse of the beach. "Here, Luis, bring your knife!"

There was the sound of tearing wood and then a murmur of voices.

When Arnaldo spoke again, he sounded brusque. "Tell the honorable gentleman that this is what all the barrels contain. Grain. Nothing else."

The translator jabbered for a time, and then Kanalio replied. Tanya heard Arnaldo curse under his breath and the sound of tearing wood resumed.

There was a silence when the tearing stopped, and then the crunching sound of footsteps in the sand. Even in her hiding-place, Tanya was aware of the release of tension. Kanalio had pointed out the next barrel to be opened, and fate had guided him to bypass the one that contained her clothes—and the one in which she hid.

Once more the barrel was lifted, this time between two sturdy men who, with no attempt to keep it level, trundled it up the beach and into the coolness of the woods.

The journey into the mission was accomplished without further risk. She was dropped unceremoniously to the ground and the top of her cask was pulled away. Gasping in the refreshing air, she rose and looked about.

She was inside the living quarters of the mission, in a dimly lit chamber that contained a bed, a small stool, and a sea chest. On the wall was the ubiquitous crucifix, with a gaunt figure of an agonized Christ hanging from it. But the face of the Savior was not like the one she had seen in Father Dominic's mission. This one resembled the natives who had swarmed over the deck earlier in the day.

Jose Arnaldo reached out to help her from the container. In spite of her care, one of the bags of gold bumped against the side of the barrel as she reached the floor, and she heard a sigh come from the corner where two sailors stood.

Of all the men on the *Santa Susana*, they appeared the least savory, but one in particular caught her attention. His arms bulged beneath a short-sleeved shirt, and he stood with his legs braced as if he had not yet grown accustomed to the stillness of land.

His bulbous nose seemed to meet the point of his chin, and his lips appeared compressed between these. Sharp blue eyes stared at her from under pale, bushy brows. He was gazing, not at her face, but at the folds of her skirt.

She felt a chill. The friendliness with which she had been treated by Captain Rodolfo, by Arnaldo, the first mate, and by the cabin boy, Olivero, was not present in the eyes of these two men.

"Ah! Senora del Norte! I am delighted to see you! I am Father Timeteo."

The priest stood just within the doorway. He was taller than Father Dominic, and far more robust. Yet his skin was a strange pale white with many dark freckles over his nose and forehead. His hair was a brilliant red, and his ears stood out under the glowing halo as if to support its weight. His bald pate was ivory white.

His features were broad, and filled with warmth. His lips were turned up in what appeared to be a perpetual smile. A faint tint of red at the end of his wide nose suggested that he shared more than company with the sailors who passed through the mission doors. In his hand he held a piece of paper.

"I have just been reading Father Dominic's letter. He tells me you hope to stay for some time on the island—until you can take a Russian ship to Sitka. He also mentions that you have not paid your full fare for the crossing." He turned to Arnaldo. "If it is all right with you, I will reimburse you now, and you can settle things with the captain."

Arnaldo nodded, and signaled the sailors to take the barrel in which Tanya had traveled into the courtyard. Then he followed Father Timeteo from the room. Before he left, the *padre* paused. *"Senora*, we will await you in the library. I am sure you will want to change."

When the door closed, Tanya pulled open the chest that stood in one corner of the room. When she saw it was empty, she transferred all of her clothing into it from the two small barrels that had been brought from the ship. Then she removed a green linen gown from the chest and spread it out on the bed. She unbuttoned her damp heavy dress and tossed it into a corner. She would have to find some facilities for washing it later.

There was no mirror in the room, so she was unable to see how she looked in the light summer gown, nor did she find it easy to comb out her damp hair. When she decided she was presentable, she headed for the hallway.

Midway across the room she paused. She had kept the money bags tied under her petticoats throughout the trip, but now she feared her hiding place was no longer safe. The linen in her skirt was not heavy enough to cover their bulges, nor could she discount the manner in which the one sailor had eyed her. In all probability he suspected that she carried some form of valuables hidden in the folds of her skirts.

Returning to the bed, she removed the four bags and lay them on the mattress. One she pushed under the pillow. A second she hid behind the chest. The last two she put inside, under some of her clothing. Then, with a new lightness to her step, she hurried from the room.

Arnaldo rose as she entered the study. "*Senora*, I hope you are more comfortable now. I regret that you were forced to endure such an unorthodox method of entry, but you are safe as long as you stay in the mission."

"I am much better, thank you. I'm sure part of my weakness was simply from lack of food. I could not digest anything during most of the journey."

Father Timeteo chuckled. "Well, you should have no difficulty here. My cook does wonderful things with the simple foods the natives have been taught to cultivate, and I have set some of them to grinding flour so we can enjoy fresh bread." He turned to Arnaldo. "My thanks to you again. Is there anything I can do to help you or Captain Rodolfo before you depart?"

"Yes, *padre*. If possible, I would like to speak to King Kamehameha. And then, in the morning, the *captain* has requested that I ask you to bless the ship."

Father Timeteo nodded. "As for the blessing, I will do so with pleasure. King Kamehameha, however, is another problem. I am told that he is preparing himself for a *heiau*, a purification, and will not be available to anyone for something over a month. What business you have must be conducted with Kanalio and Nuiaui."

Arnaldo turned back to Tanya. "I am pleased that you are where you wish to be and that your plan was successful. But I assure you, you would be far safer on board ship." He lifted her hand to his lips and was gone, Father Timeteo following, closing the door behind him.

The room was small. The walls were made of rough timbers covered with a thick white paint that resembled the adobe of the missions in California. But there the similarity ended. The ceiling consisted of woven mats resting on straight, narrow logs, and the same kind of mats served as carpets underfoot. The windows were wide and high, looking out on a garden that was bursting with color and rich with a thousand fragrances. On the walls were shelves of books and scrolls. At one end of the room was a desk, and it was there Father Timeteo headed when he returned.

The *padre* paused before resuming his seat. "Do you know Jose Arnaldo?"

"No, Father."

"He is a strange man, but an honest one. He warned me that you might be in danger, not only from the natives, but from some of his own men."

Tanya rose and moved closer to the desk. "Father, I have a confession. I brought more than enough money to pay for my passage, but Father Dominic insisted that we handle the cost in the way we did. I will, of course, repay you. Did he mention that I would reimburse you in his letter?"

Father Timeteo shook his head. "Correspondence between us is written for other eyes than our own. It would not have been safe for him to mention your reserves. These days, you cannot tell who might be able to read what we write." He rose. "Come, you will want to give thanks for your safe passage. When you have finished your prayers, come back here and I will introduce you to the converts. I have taught one of the women to speak Spanish, and I'm sure she can be of great help to you."

'Ohi'a'Lehua was as beautiful as her name. Her black hair hung loosely over her shoulders, and even though she wore the *mu'mum'u* that the *padre* required as covering for all females, Tanya could see that she had a firm, well-shaped body. Most noticeable of all were her eyes. Large and deep, they glowed with friendship—and sharp intelligence. She appointed herself Tanya's assistant—and companion.

When they were alone, Tanya mentioned the Refuge and Captain Rodolfo's suggestion that she might go there to overcome her stigma of *kapu*.

"The *padre* would not approve." 'Ohi'a'Lehua's eyes were big with surprise.

"Would Kamehameha, Kanalio, and Nuiaui consider it

an outrage for a foreign female to make use of their rituals?"

'Ohi'a'Lehua shook her head. "I do not believe they would, though one cannot speak for the King. But it takes two weeks to complete the ceremony. Father Timeteo will have to be told."

"Then I will tell him."

But in the study, Father Timeteo, Captain Rodolfo, and Jose Arnaldo were sipping liqueur and conversing quietly. She determined to speak with the *padre* in the morning.

It was well past midnight when she heard the two officers take their leave. She lay for a time in her room, listening to the cries of the night birds and inhaling the sweet fragrance of the night-blooming jasmine. Far in the distance she could hear a drum beating a steady rhythm. She was committed to stay on this strange island, and despite the inhospitable behavior of the two native leaders, she felt pleased and excited. Had she been foolish to come so far alone? She fell asleep with her question still unanswered.

CHAPTER III

Tanya opened her eyes and stared into the darkness. Something had awakened her—a sound different from the forest noises that had lulled her to sleep. Tense with fear, she gazed about the room.

She heard it again—a scraping near the window. A shadow appeared, blocking the moonlight that had cast a square of light on the mats that covered the floor. The shadow moved and a man climbed into her room. She recognized him instantly. Enrique, the sailor who had looked so pointedly at her skirt after she emerged from the barrel.

He paused, outlined against the window, and looked around. It was then she saw his knife. He held it clutched in his right hand, its blade pointed down, but he raised it when she stirred, and he moved slowly toward her.

He paused when he reached the bed, but she feigned sleep. When he shuffled on, she risked a peek. His back was to her, and he was heading toward the chest. She held her breath. Heeding the *padre*'s words the night before, she had locked the chest, and the key hung around her neck.

Enrique cursed when the lid refused to move under his fingers, and then he turned again toward the bed.

Suddenly her arms were grasped in strong hands and she was dragged into a sitting position. She tried to pull free, but she could not escape the hands that shook her violently back and forth, snapping her head forward and backward as if she were a cloth doll.

"Where is it? Where have you hidden the key?" Enrique's face was dark and twisted in anger. "Give it to me!"

He put one hand over her mouth and bent her back against the bed. She could feel the cord that held the key move under her high-necked gown, and she prayed he would not notice it.

His voice was a hiss in her ears. "Don't try to scream. If you do, the natives will know you are here, and the *padre* will not be able to save you."

She bit at his fingers, and he pulled his hand away with a curse. But she made no attempt to cry out.

He stood above her, his massive shoulders blocking some faint light. "Tell me where the key is—and where you hid your gold." He snarled when she shook her head. "Don't pretend you don't know what I'm talking about. You had it hidden under your skirt when I carried you here."

"I gave it to the *padre*!" She spit out the words.

With one movement he jerked the blanket from the bed and pulled her nightgown up over her hips. His lips were turned up in a leer. "There are other treasures to be had in your room, *Senora*. You have guarded your honor closely all the way from California. But you have no one now who can keep me from you." He pushed his hand up under her gown and leaned over. "The gold can wait. You're too passionate a woman to be without a man."

For a moment she was too shocked by his actions to move, and then she was filled with anger—and disgust.

He seemed unaware of her response. His hands were on

her thighs, and he was pushing them slowly apart. She moved then, reaching under her pillow for the small bag of gold. At the same moment that she pulled away from his grasp, she swung the bag over her shoulder. There was a dull thud as it crashed onto his head. He fell forward over the bed and then slid to the floor.

Immediately, she was beside him. Tearing strips from the hem of her gown, she bound his ankles and his wrists, pulling his arms behind his back. And then, fearful that he might summon the natives when he came to, she gagged him with another strip of cloth. She was panting from exertion and fright, and her heart was pounding furiously.

She padded down the hall to the *padre*'s chamber.

"What is it, daughter?"

"*Padre,* I need your help. I'm sorry if I woke you."

"It's all right. I was not sleeping." He appeared at the door still dressed in his robes. "What is the matter?"

She led him back to where Enrique lay on the floor, and explained briefly what had happened. He was frowning by the time she finished. "Arnaldo was right. I will speak to *Capitan* Rodolfo in the morning. In the meantime, I think I should return your assailant to the ship."

He untied Enrique's legs and prodded him onto his feet. "Lock your door, *Senora.*"

Sleep would not come. She could not calm the excitement brought on by the attack—and the success of her defense. Through the window she gazed out over the bay that sparkled through the trees. The fear and uncertainty that had clouded her thoughts of the future were gone. Her mind was made up. Tomorrow she would seek shelter in the Refuge, and she would not speak to Father Timeteo. The time for cowering in fright at what might face her was past.

"Explain what you can, 'Ohi'a'Lehua, and blame me for going, if the *padre* is angry. I'll make my position clear when he can no longer stop me." 'Ohi'a'Lehua had guided her through the woods to the Refuge.

Tanya stood in its gateway and gazed into the early morning darkness. She could see nothing but the large building whose roof had been visible from the ship and a circle of huts sprinkled in the woods around it.

She embraced 'Ohi'a'Lehua and stepped into the clearing. The gate closed. Whatever was to happen would begin soon.

She had received some assurances from 'Ohi'a'Lehua that increased her confidence. Her time would be spent in solitude inside one of the empty huts. She would eat only the food provided by the priests, and she would cleanse herself with water drawn from the hole far below Mokuaweoweo Crater. At the end of fourteen days she would be allowed to return to the mission. Not even the great Kamehameha would discount the importance of the cleansing that freed her from the *kapu*.

A priest stopped her as she approached the first hut. Obeying 'Ohi'a'Lehua's advice, she crouched low and followed him as he led the way to an empty hut. She crawled inside and settled herself on the mats that were spread over the floor. She stared out through the small arched opening. It would be her only view of the island for the next two weeks. The mats recalled to her Mio Kang and the thin pallet on which she had slept in Mei Ling's brothel.

The days passed slowly, filled with reminiscences and many prayers. Her food was delivered by a priest who left it just outside her door. The water was provided in a similar manner, contained in large dry gourds that had been painted with the faces of demons. No one spoke.

Each morning, noon, and evening, drums beat a rhythm at the great door to the massive building. Once a priest walked by leading a penitent. On another occasion, a priest was followed by two men who showed signs of recovering from injuries. 'Ohi'a'Lehua had told her that many soldiers went to the Refuge after a battle to rid themselves of evil spirits, for they believed that without such a cleansing, they would surely die in the next fighting.

One other woman entered the Refuge while she was there: a golden-skinned native who appeared to be recovering from some debilitating illness. When Tanya returned to the mission, she learned that the woman had grown ill in Father Timeteo's mission and had decided to renounce the

Christian doctrine and return to her native gods. She had tried to resume her place in the village without going through the cleansing process, and had been completely ostracized. At last she had submitted to all of the old rituals.

Most of her time Tanya spent in reverie. She recalled in detail her tryst with Alexius in California, and felt certain that wherever he now might be, he still loved her dearly. She dreamed often of finding him, and considered, one by one, the places where such a wonderful encounter might take place.

He had told her he loved her—and surely he had shown the depth of his emotion. Yet, she could not continue her search, like some helpless female running after her one protector. If he loved her. . . .

If he loved her, he would come to her! She had only to make her presence known in Keei, and he would seek her out! As the days passed, her feeling solidified. She vowed that she would find some way to make her presence on this island known to every ship that dropped anchor in the harbor. News would travel—and eventually he would come to her!

On the day of her release, Tanya was weak from hunger and pale from the days spent in the hut, but she walked back to the mission with a firm step.

An angry Father Timeteo greeted her. "You have made your peace with the pagan gods of the islanders. Now you must show your faith in the One True God!"

Father Timeteo asked that she take confession and do penance at the altar. Then he led her into his study. "My child, do you realize the risk you have taken? Do you understand what you have said to the natives regarding our attitude toward their customs?" He settled himself behind his desk and stared into her face.

"Yes, *padre*. I have said that I respect their customs and will not knowingly violate them. But surely that has no affect on the mission."

"I have no idea what effect it may have. That only time will tell. But you must understand that by placing yourself under their rituals you have made yourself subject to them now and in the future. They will expect you to live accord-

337

ing to their traditions. You must be prepared to be accepted as one of their own. How much do you know of their rules and taboos?"

"Nothing, except that I was *kapu* because I was ill."

"Do you know that it has been due to my influence that the custom of murdering women who violated the *kapu* has ceased? No, I thought not. Well, maybe now you understand why I would not have approved of your act."

He rose and stepped around the desk. "However, it is done, and we have no way of knowing whether you will be adversely affected or not. Go to your room now. 'Ohi'a'Lehua awaits you there. She has worried about you as much as I, and will be pleased to see that you have survived."

She sought him out a few days later. "*Padre*, I have been thinking. Father Dominic told you in his letter that I hoped to find a Russian ship which I could take to Sitka, but he said nothing of my reasons."

Father Timeteo nodded.

She continued. "I hope to find a way to be reunited with a man I knew long ago. The last time I saw him was in Monterey—before my husband, Don Sebastino del Norte, died. Now I wish to find this man, Alexius Andreiv, and discover what my feelings are toward him." She looked at her folded hands. "I do not wish to be dependent upon him when he arrives—if he arrives. Nor do I desire to chase across the ocean in search of him. I have spent too many years of my life looking forward to happiness. I wish to settle here, at least for the time. Eventually a Russian ship will arrive, perhaps his, or I can get news to him through the captains of other Russian ships." She paused. "Father, I cannot be certain as to what I should do."

"Are you seeking my advice?"

"In a way, father. Is there any way I can draw ships to this island and avoid the dangers of searching from one port to another? 'Ohi'a'Lehua has told me that many of the foreign ships that come to the islands do all of their trading with the kings of Kauai and Niihau."

"There is little to draw travelers here, to Keei," Father Timeteo replied, "other than my mission. If you truly in-

338

tend to remain for a time, you might be able to help us—
and King Kamehameha as well. An inn close to the mission would attract ships and provide the men with a place
to do their trading. You could use the gold you brought to
purchase materials and food from and for traders."

"I have never operated such an establishment."

"Ah, but you have told me you were willing to accept
advice. Listen, then, to what I know, and then speak to
'Ohi'a'Lehua. You must create an atmosphere that will be
comfortable to both the seamen and to Kamehameha's delegates. I can think of nothing that will serve your purpose
better—anything that will be more welcome on this island."

She discussed her project with the *padre* on many other
occasions, and equally often with her native friend.

CHAPTER IV

———

Tanya awoke to the sound of natives singing *Aloha!*, and she knew another ship had entered the harbor. She quickly pulled on a gown made of Chinese silk and, with a glance at the houseboys and the cooks, she hurried into the garden that surrounded her inn.

The months since her cleansing from the *kapu* had been busy ones. After further consideration, she had decided to follow Father Timeteo's advice and build an inn and meeting house for traders, close to the mission. 'Ohi'a'Lehua taught her what she needed to know about the *kapus* that would limit native participation in her project, but after discussions with the *padre*, she elected to ignore some of the requirements.

Kamehameha was a strict supporter of all the *kapus*. No

woman in his household ate with the men, nor did she dare to set foot in the men's eating houses. When Tanya decided to build one dining hall to be used by the traders, she was catering to the preferences of the foreigners—and running afoul of the *kapus*, but she had been given to understand that the natives did not expect the newcomers to be affected by the traditions.

She followed native architecture in the construction of her inn, building a large circular structure with the main room in the center and a series of small rooms circling the outside. Each room was created by mats hanging from large beams which formed the ceiling. And each room opened to the garden that surrounded the building.

But there the resemblance to native buildings ended. She enclosed each private room with netting to keep insects away, and the large meeting room was lit by oil lamps. The furniture was the sturdiest she could find.

Because of the *kapu* that kept all Hawaiian women out of men's eating houses, Tanya had difficulty finding helpers. Male converts at Father Timeteo's mission worked in the building she constructed for the common sailors, and though it was clear that the seamen would have preferred female barmaids to the waiters, the men were needed to handle the rough crowds that sometimes assembled.

Their biggest problems developed when two ships from different countries were in the harbor, for many of the sailors seemed to take their countries' battles personally. Only when she made it clear that she would refuse to serve any man who started a fight, did things get under control.

'Ohi'a'Lehua was the first woman to dare to violate the prohibition against females that had kept Tanya dependent upon males for her servants. At first, the girl only worked in the private rooms, cleaning, making beds, and bringing fresh water. But at last, encouraged by Tanya's habit of sharing food with the captains of each ship that arrived, the native girl consented to serve the food. Still, out of consideration for the dark-eyed, serious girl, Tanya never asked her to serve when Kanalio and Nuiaui were in the hall.

Once her inn was built, Tanya found her problems decreased considerably. Each ship that dropped anchor brought with it some supplies she needed. She bought chairs and tables and her Limoges dishes and eating utensils from *Le Jeune Fille*, a ship out of New Orleans, that had traveled around the Horn. Cotton for stuffing mattresses came from the port of Norfolk, Virginia, in a sprightly ship named the *Virgin Queen*, and from another ship, from Boston, she purchased a cast-iron stove. This had occasioned a minor celebration, for the natives had never seen so strange a contraption. The cook named the dark metal monster *Imu Pele*, oven of the Goddess, Pele.

Her inn became an instant success among the seamen. When they were anchored in the bay, officers came to spend the night on softer beds than they had in their cabins, and she served them food from the islands and food purchased from every part of the world. She traded with many of the captains herself, and the meeting house became a center of exchange for the seamen and the island.

Shortly after the building was completed, Kanalio and Nuiaui visited. 'Ohi'a'Lehua served as translator, for Tanya had not yet mastered the exotic language. Because of the presence of the native girl, the meeting took place in the garden of the inn.

The men greeted Tanya as she had often seen them approach the *padre*; they held their hands together before them, and they bowed very slightly. When they spoke to her, they used the title *sir*.

It was Kanalio who did the talking. "Sir Tanya, we have been aware of your consideration for the customs of our people—and of the time you spent in the Refuge. The Great King Kamehameha has empowered us to deal with all traders on this island during his absence."

Kamehameha, after the disastrous plague that had wiped out many of his warriors, had remained on the island of Oahu to cleanse himself in a *heiau* and to plan his future strategy to unite the islands. He was convinced that he must shield his people from the growing foreign influence, but he was not inclined to push the traders out; in fact, he was growing wealthy on shipping. When Kanalio and Nuiaui had informed him of Tanya's inn he had welcomed it, for it served to encourage the merchantmen to visit the island of Hawaii as well as Oahu, where most of them were accustomed to trade.

The new arrival was riding gently in the harbor. A long-boat crept slowly toward the shore, surrounded, as all visitors were, by a flotilla of singing natives. Father Timeteo awaited them. The *Elizabeth* had returned from England.

The sailors pulled the longboat up onto the sand, carefully avoiding the dark protrusions of lava that edged the beach, and the three officers joined the *padre*. Captain Harold Farnsworth was a massive man with a shock of blond hair, deep blue eyes, and a body as firm and muscular as a native's. Ronald Evars, his first mate, was black, with large eyes and teeth that shone white against his lips. Roger Greenwood, his second mate, had brown hair and eyes to match, and after this sea voyage, his skin blended with his hair; he looked as if he had been carved from teakwood. They were all youthful.

Tanya held out her hands in greeting as the three men approached. As long as the *padre* was watching, she would make her greeting properly formal.

"Ah! Senora del Norte!" Harold Farnsworth brought her hand to his lips. "It is good to see you again!"

"I am delighted that your journey has been a safe one, captain." She let her eyes rest on his golden hair. "I trust it has been profitable, as well." She turned to the other officers. "Gentlemen, I am pleased to see you again."

Farnsworth took her arm and they began to walk toward the inn. "We have had a most profitable trip," Farnsworth said "—for us, and for you. And for the great Kamehameha! I come with new orders for sandalwood. It was a brilliant suggestion of yours that the Chinese might use the wood to carve furniture for export. And worthwhile for everyone concerned. We profit from carrying the wood to Canton, and when it is made into tables and chairs, we profit again from carrying it to England—and to the United States of America."

Captain Farnsworth paused at the entrance to the meeting room. "And my dear *Senora*, I bring you other news. While I was anchored in Canton, I met a Russian officer, Vladimir Nikolaiovich. He was intrigued that a Spanish senora should call her inn on Keei The *Balalaika*. He seemed most interested in learning more about the mysterious woman." His eyes sparkled. "I am sure the next time they trade in the Sandwich Islands, curiosity will pull him and his captain here!"

"What was the name of the ship? It was not the same as my inn, was it?" They entered the main room of the inn.

"No, my dear *Senora*, it was not! The ship was the *Russian Princess*, Captain Adam Czerwenki commanding. I met Vladimir at a brothel uphill from the wharf. The captain was lost in opium dreams." He frowned. " 'Tis a foul habit. One that will destroy him unless he keeps it under control."

Tanya stiffened at the name.

"My dear *Senora*, is something the matter? Are you ill?"

"No, Captain—no. I know this captain—and his ship. I was surprised. Is he planning to visit Hawaii soon?"

"That I cannot say, since I spoke only to his first mate. But from what he said, Czerwenki is looking for a new contact on the islands. His old one, the first mate informed me, is dead."

"Was his native contact a man named Hanahelio?"

"Please, *Senora*, don't ask me to remember those names; they all sound alike to me—almost as bad as your Russian names that end in 'vitch!' I do know that the *Russian Princess* used to put in to harbor at Oahu. Do you know something of their reasons for seeking a new port?"

"It is my understanding that Hanahelio was executed only a year ago for trading in opium, and that the ship from which he received the poison was banned from the island. I'm sure that King Kamehameha would not be pleased if I provided Czerwenki with a new port of entry."

Captain Farnsworth frowned. " 'Tis a dangerous thing to anger Kamehameha, even if you are a foreigner. I regret that I spoke of you to Nikolaiovich, and I advise you to send him and his captain away quickly when they arrive." He took her hand in his. "My dear *Senora*, I know of your desire to meet your Russian friend, and I was only trying to help."

Tanya forced a smile. "It's all right, Captain. Please,

don't let us spoil your visit with such problems." She met his eyes, and her expression relaxed. "Oh, Captain! It's good to see you again!"

In the years since her arrival on Hawaii, she had come to terms with her emotions—and with the men who stayed at her inn. Most were simply good friends with whom she shared an occasional draft of ale. But Harold Farnsworth had become more than a friend. His ebullience was contagious, and his quiet wooing had finally broken through her reserve.

When he put into port, her solitary bed became a place of warmth and, if not love, at least strong passion. She pulled him toward the table where his two officers waited.

The two officers had taken seats in the empty dining hall. 'Ohi'a'Lehua crossed the room langorously, four glasses of ale in her hands. Tanya sat down between the first and second mate. The voices of the sailors were ringing up from the beach on the way to their own building. It was good to have the inn occupied again. The last ship had pulled anchor a month before. "To trading! May we all continue to be successful!" She touched glasses with the men.

"You earn your share far more than Kamehameha does, that's a sure thing!" Captain Farnsworth grinned. "I would not have thought to use your buildings as storehouses for the exchange of goods between countries that would not trade with each other. We now have a market for grain which we could not deliver to Sitka ourselves, and a way of selling silks and many sundries to the Spanish, who won't accept us in their harbors. You have made us all wealthy."

"It is you who have been kind to me." Tanya sipped her drink and smiled at her friends. "You assist me in helping my friends—and you share the profits when you succeed." She signaled to 'Ohi'a'Lehua, who, in a moment, was followed by a trusted convert from the mission carrying a large, heavy metal chest in his arms. He placed it on the table.

"Let's finish our ale and have a bite to eat while we wait for Kanalio to arrive."

At her mention of the name, 'Ohi'a'Lehua's eyes widened

346

in alarm and she scurried from the room. The converts knew she entered the eating place reserved for men and foreigners, but she still dared not let the leaders of the natives know how far she had strayed from tradition.

The man who had carried in the chest vanished into the kitchen and returned shortly with a tray of cheese and fruit.

"Did you get all the foodstuffs I requested?" Tanya looked eagerly into Farnsworth's blue eyes. "Father Timeteo has worked miracles with his converts, but he still cannot raise enough grain to feed all my guests and still have enough for his mission—and his care of the poor."

All three men chuckled. The first mate's voice was deep and melodious. "Aye, that we did. And more, to boot. The captain has a gift for you that should ease your burden."

Kanalio and Nuiaui arrived. They had long ago learned to ignore Tanya's presence in a room where food was served to men, though they continued to ease the shock of such a violation of the *kapu* by addressing her as a man. Nuiaui bowed as he entered. "Ah, Sir Tanya. And Captain Farnsworth! I trust the trade has gone well!"

The Captain nodded. "Very well, indeed, gentlemen. Your King will be pleased with the revenue we have brought him."

They took their places at the table, their eyes on the metal chest. They resented the fact that she, Tanya, a woman, was conversant with the problems of finance, and more than once they had hinted that they ought to get a larger share of the money that was made by the trading.

But Tanya received more because she stored the grain—and the other cargo—and because she took the risk by advancing the gold needed to buy space on ships. She made the payment to Kamehameha through the two officials as a necessary tax, no more, though she made it gladly. The officials did nothing to contribute to the success of the ventures.

The division of profits from the metal chest went smoothly, the two natives watching closely. When each division left her with the largest pile, they grunted. She pushed her coins from the table into the emptied chest.

At the end of the accounting, Kanalio and Nuiaui placed the share allocated to Kamehameha onto a large cloth, tied the four corners together, and left. Their farewells were as formal as their greetings. As usual, Tanya could see that they were not fully satisfied. And she wondered, also as usual, just how much of the coins the two men carried off actually found their way into Kamehameha's coffers.

She turned to Farnsworth and his smiling officers. "Please, Captain, what is the gift Evars spoke of? It isn't fair to make me wait so long!"

"Nothing personal, I'm afraid. I know your fondness for perfumes and jewels, but I also know you buy what you want from traders who transport only quality goods. And I'm sure you strike a far better bargain than I ever could! I have a small gift, however, that I feel certain you will value—and one I am certain Evars will be glad to bring ashore. He has played shepherd to six heifers and a magnificent bull. If the bellowing that kept us awake can be believed, you will have a full herd as soon as you release them and let the lecherous beast take his fill of his harem. Maybe that will free you of your dependence on the *padre*'s cattle."

Tanya threw her arms around Farnsworth's shoulders with a cry of delight. It was so like him to give her just what she needed—or wanted—the most, and then to deprecate the importance of his offering.

The first mate, Evars, and Greenwood, the second mate, their share of the profits tucked securely in their pockets, took their leave to supervise the unloading of the ship, promising to take the greatest care with the stock. Kekua carried Tanya's chest back to her rooms, followed by Tanya and Captain Farnsworth. When they were at last alone, Farnsworth pulled her into his arms. "Ah, lassie, I have missed you! Time was when I could only look forward to my return to England. Now I count the days until I see your lovely face, and can hold you close once more!"

He carried her across the expanse of her rooms into the shaded privacy of her sleeping quarters.

348

CHAPTER V

The *Russian Princess* dropped anchor one week to the day after Harold Farnsworth set sail for Malaysia. Tanya had spent the week torn with worry. Her first impulse had been to speak immediately to Kanalio and Nuiaui and to let them quash the opium trading before it was revived. But a fearful doubt held her back. The trader Hanahelio had not been alone in his dealing in the drug. There had been others who smoothed his path, who directed the unloading and storage of the material, and who sold it to the natives. Yet there had been no exposure of co-conspirators. That meant only one thing to her: Hanahelio had been a scapegoat, thrown to Kamehameha to appease him. Others, higher in power, had gone free.

At last she had brought the problem to Father Timeteo.

349

"My daughter. Why are you so quick to condemn your own countrymen? Maybe you are wrong in your assumption of their guilt. What evidence have you? Deal with the newcomers—if they arrive—as you would with any ship. You can always refuse to accept contraband if it is offered you."

At the time the *padre*'s words had soothed Tanya's worries. But now, watching the *Russian Princess* drop anchor, her anxiety returned. The natives were swarming over the sides of the ship, and Father Timeteo was waiting on the beach. As she watched Adam Czerwenki climb over the side of the ship into a longboat, she knew it was not only the problem of dealing with his wish to trade in opium that bothered her. She had no desire to revive old memories.

She had been such a child when she had tried to manipulate him! And when she had failed, she had become so helpless, been so humiliated. For one moment she gave in to her repressed fears, and then, once more, she tried to master them.

In control of her emotions, Tanya swept down to the beach. "Welcome to Hawaii," she said.

Adam Czerwenki had watched her approach, the expression on his face changing from surprise to anger—and then to cunning. By the time she reached the place where the *padre* and he stood, he had assumed a cloak of gentility that she recognized from her first weeks in his presence.

The years had not changed him for the better. The leer that had become a permanent fixture on his face during their journey from Okhotsk to Canton had etched itself deeply into his features, and his mouth was dourly turned down.

Yet he held out his hand with a smooth courtliness. "Senora del Norte! Your fame has spread over the whole Pacific! It is an honor to meet you at last!"

The first mate also bowed. "Vladimir Nikolaiovich at your service, ma'am. We heard of you from the captain of a ship that flew the English flag—while we were anchored in Canton. We were delighted to learn that a Russian woman had become friendly with the great King Kamehameha."

"Have you come straight from China?"

"Yes, *Senora*. We have a hold full of cargo that might be of great interest to you."

The new first mate was, in his own way, no better than John Sikorski, the man who had beaten Ivar so unmercifully. Vladimir Nikolaiovich stood no more than five feet four inches. His dark hair hung raggedly around his warped face, and his nose was bent to one side, as if it had failed to heal properly after a fight. A purple scar stretched from his temple down his left cheek, turning his mouth up in a perpetual sneer.

Adam glared at the *padre*. "Do you do all of your dealing on the beach, where anyone who comes along can listen?"

"The *padre* is interested in trade, too, *Senor*. However, if you wish, we can speak in private. *Padre*, will you excuse us?"

Father Timeteo nodded. "If you need me, Tanya. . . ."

Tanya did not immediately lead the way to her inn. She held her hand out to the second mate. "Sir, I do not believe we have been introduced."

Adam's face grew red. "This is Sergei Antonovich, *Senora*. I see you have not lost your interest in men."

The young man who took her hand was little better than his superiors, but she detected a ghost of breeding behind the beard that covered most of his face. He bent low over her fingers and touched them lightly with his lips. "Senora del Norte, I am honored."

"I find it important to at least know the names of the people with whom I trade, Sergei Antonovich." She turned to Adam. "Gentlemen, shall we go?"

She sat with them at the same table where she had shared food with Harold. Antonovich helped her with her chair; he was the only one to wait until she was settled before seating himself.

'Ohi'a'Lehua brought a bottle of vodka and four glasses. Adam Czerwenki snatched the container from her hand and filled his glass. The second mate filled his own glass and hers, and then handed the bottle to Vladimir Mikolaiovich. Adam no longer attempted to conceal the malevolence in his eyes. "Tanya Ivanovich! I had not expected to see you again. It seems you have a great talent for survival."

"Captain Czerwenki, we are not here to discuss my life. I believe you have some merchandise to exchange."

He was greyer than he had been when last she saw him—and far less prosperous-looking. Obviously, he had not benefitted from the coup that had resulted in the Tsar Paul's assassination and the ascendancy of his son, Alexander, to the throne. The new Tsar had begun to reinstate many of the reforms his grandmother had established before the French Revolution had driven her to reject all forms of freedom. He clearly was not interested in dealing with Czerwenki.

His jaw clamped tightly, Adam leaned back in his chair. Tanya turned to Nikolaiovich. "Sir, what is the nature of your cargo?"

"Silk and jade from China."

"Is that all?" Tanya looked into Czerwenki's dark, angry eyes. "Silk and jade I can always use, but my greatest need is for spices from Malacca."

Adam growled his answer. "We did not visit Malaysia this trip."

She smiled. "I assume your interest is in the grain for Sitka?"

"Tanya Ivanovich!" Adam rose to his feet. "We have one other product that is much in demand here on the Sandwich Islands. A drug most valuable in the treatment of the disease that I understand decimated the forces of Kamehameha two years ago. From what I hear, he failed in his attempt to conquer the last two islands in the chain only because his men contracted the dread cholera."

Tanya folded her hands on the table. "So I have been told. But what medicine have you that will overcome that dread disease?"

"Opium! It has proven itself most valuable in Canton. In all the time there has been trading in that city, not one user of the substance has been struck with the plague."

Tanya shook her head. "Why do you try to pass a poison off as a useful medicine? King Kamehameha is strongly opposed to the importation of opium into his lands. No, captain, I have no wish to anger the king."

Adam leaned over the table, his face close to hers. "Listen to me, Tanya Ivanovich! I have heard of your murder of the son of Wen Kui Fong, and of your escape to a Spanish ship when the bereaved man attempted to punish you! If you show an unwillingness to trade with me, I will return you to China, where justice still awaits you!"

"Whatever you have heard from Wen Kui Fong is a lie. The child of whom he speaks was mine—and he died of the smallpox. As for your returning me to China, you will not find it easy to get me aboard your ship. I have many friends here on Hawaii."

His laugh was filled with malice. "Think on it, Madam. I have need of a contact here on the island, as far from Kamehameha as possible. You are in a perfect position to assist me. If you refuse. . . ." He did not bother to finish his sentence. He rose and his men followed him out.

Tanya found Father Timeteo in his study. He did not share her distress. "He can do nothing, Tanya. If he accused you of asking for opium—or even of importing it— he would be risking his own life as well as yours. And, besides, Kanalio and Nuiaui know you well enough to believe your word over that of a man like Czerwenki."

Tanya sighed. "You're probably right, father." She moved toward the door. "Still, I will be happy when he leaves."

She returned to the inn at a leisurely pace, her thoughts slowly growing calm. She had been foolish to let his threats upset her.

'Ohi'a'Lehua greeted her at the garden gate. The girl was trembling, and her eyes were wide with terror.

"'Ohi'a'Lehua, little Flower, what has happened?" Tanya drew the girl close. "Why are you so frightened? What has happened?" she repeated.

'Ohi'a'Lehua tried to speak, but her lips would not obey her wishes. When, at last, she spoke, her voice was faint and tremulous. "Kanalio—Nuiaui. They're in the eating room!"

Tanya stared at the girl in confusion. And then, slowly, she understood. "Did they see you?" 'Ohi'a'Lehua nodded, her lips white. "But that shouldn't worry you, little Flower! You are a Christian. You have left the *kapus* behind. They have no power over you any more."

'Ohi'a'Lehua's shaking body told Tanya that her words were not true. She drew into the shadows of a nearby bush. "Do you fear that they will try to carry out the punishment in spite of your change in belief?"

"Oh, *Senora*! No islander is free of the *kapus*. I should have known! They will come. The *Kahunas* will come—and they will punish me." She began to sob quietly. "I am lost! There is no hope for me!" She dropped to her knees.

Tanya pulled the girl up. "Nonsense! You're a Christian! You believe in one God, not in hundreds of little mean gods who are served by *Kahunas*. Come, I will take you to the *padre*. He will tell you what to do."

She led 'Ohi'a'Lehua into the chapel and to the altar. As soon as she let go of the frail shoulders, the girl fell into a crouch, her head buried in her hands. Tanya hurried off to Father Timeteo.

His calmness reassured Tanya. Together they returned to the chapel where 'Ohi'a'Lehua had remained just as Tanya had left her.

Tanya spoke in a whisper. "If only I had not allowed her to serve food! I should have known she would be in danger!"

Father Timeteo took her hand. "Tanya del Norte, stop and think. It was not you who suggested that Flower serve in the eating room. She asked to be permitted the privilege. You cannot blame yourself because she thought she had, but hasn't, overcome her superstitions." Automatically, he made the sign of the cross. "Now go, my child. 'Ohi-'a'Lehua needs me."

'Ohi'a'Lehua did not return to the inn, and the other girls, when they heard of her plight, disappeared, frightened, even though they had never set foot in the forbidden area of the inn. They did not return to the mission the

354

next day, and Tanya realized they were afraid to associate with 'Ohi'a'Lehua.

'Ohi'a'Lehua bore little resemblance to the cheerful, bright girl who had helped Tanya so often in the meeting room. Except in the company of the priest she refused to leave the chapel, and when he insisted that she spend some time out-of-doors, she remained in the mission garden. Her face was drawn and pale, and her eyes stood out like dark coals, burning with fear.

Hiku, the native boy who shared 'Ohi'a'Lehua's serving duties, informed her that while she had been at the mission speaking to the *padre*, Adam Czerwenki had returned to the inn accompanied by the two native officials, and that the three men had spoken together at length.

It was then that 'Ohi'a'Lehua had stepped for a moment into the dining area, and had seen Kanalio and Nuiaui. No, they had not seen her. Hiku had observed that all three men seemed most satisfied with the direction of their talk.

As Tanya reached the door to her rooms, a figure detached itself from the shadows. It was a native lad, and he was alone. He bowed slightly. "*Senora*, I am Kekua, 'Ohi'a'Lehua's brother. I must speak with you."

A large stone bench circled a lobelias tree, and he sat awkwardly beside her. "*Senora*, I must know. How did my sister. . . ."

"I am told she ventured into the meeting room when she thought it was empty, and that the captain of the *Russian Princess* had brought Kanalio and Nuiaui there without my knowledge. She thinks that they saw her, but Hiku thinks that they did not. However, it is all the same. You know how careful we have been. She has never been asked to serve when Kamehameha's representatives were present."

"Yes, *Senora*, I know. 'Ohi'a'Lehua was always a brave one—daring to go where women should not. It is not your fault she thought she could break the *kapus*." He gazed out over the water toward the ship. "Now she has learned. The god of the *padre* is not strong enough to overcome the *Kahunas*. There are others who wish to rid the land of the *kapus*, and maybe they can help her. But I will pray that Hiku is right, though to her it is all the same. Kanalio and Nuiaui will show far less charity than she would receive from the fiercest of gods."

CHAPTER VI

The dugouts of the natives began to drift back toward the shore, and even from her place just within the garden, Tanya could hear their songs of *Aloha* floating over the water. She smiled at Father Timeteo, who stood beside her. "I'm thankful that they are gone. Somehow, when I sent out word that I wished to trade with Russian ships, I did not think of Adam Czerwenki. Now I know it was my wish to be rid of bad memories that made me think he was dead."

Father Timeteo's fingers fondled his crucifix. "My child, it is good you have freed yourself of such a wish even though it lay hidden in your heart, for such evil thoughts poison the soul." He waved a greeting to Kekua, Flower's brother, who came bounding up the beach, hurrying toward the mission. "I have been able to do far too little with poor little 'Ohi'a'Lehua. And I find myself losing heart when I realize how little my teaching has meant to these innocent children. They recite the rosary at my bidding, but they still fear the *Kahunas*, and they dare not violate the *kapus*. The forgiving power of Christ has not touched their souls."

"Maybe you ask too much in too short a time, father. I have overheard many of the more daring natives question the wisdom of the *kapus*, especially those against women eating with men. You must not forget that Kamehameha is very strict in his observance of all the laws. The people cannot advance ahead of their king."

Father Timeteo let his fingers glide up his rosary beads to brush an insect from his cheek. "I fear I show the same human weakness which I reproach in you. I grow impatient." Again he held the crucifix. "Thank you for reminding me that all will come about—in God's time, if not in mine."

They turned toward the mission. "You were worried about Captain Czerwenki's threats and over his insistence that you deal in opium. You have not spoken of it to me again. Tell me, child, have you something to confess?"

"No, father." For the first time since the arrival of the *Russian Princess*, Tanya felt lighthearted. "No. He made no mention of it again. And I watched the unloading of his cargo, including the coolies he had brought for sale, very carefully. There were no extra parcels smuggled ashore in my shipment." She paused. "I hope you can put the coolies to use on the mission grounds—or maybe in the fields. I could not leave them in Adam's power. Yet, I fear they are too weak to do much work."

"They haven't recovered from finding someone so far from their home who speaks their language!" Father Timeteo smiled. "But you will have to keep them, though I appreciate your offer. I must have work for my converts. They should do well at your inn. Kekua tells me that Hiku has fled, along with most of your workers. Fear of the pagan gods is stripping you of your help."

The Chinese were crouching at the door to the mission.

Except for one they were a sorry lot. Ten scrawny China-men with long pigtails, gaunt faces, and eyes filled with suspicion. The eleventh man seemed different. He was taller, with more flesh on his bones, and with some courage in his eye. It was to him that Tanya spoke.

He had been waylaid in a narrow alley near the gover-nor's palace in Canton, where he served as cook, and had awakened to find himself in the hold of a moving ship, surrounded by these frightened, jabbering coolies. "I am not like these animals who huddle so helplessly together." He held his chin up and brushed at his gown. "I am the governor's second cook."

"Do you wish, then, to return to Canton? I am sure I can book passage for you."

"Aiyah, no! There will be another already taking my place. You have put me in your debt by rescuing me from the Russian thieves. Now I must help you, to show my appreciation." He put his hands together and bowed his head. "I am Sung, the cook. Is there any work I can do for you?"

Tanya pointed at her inn, and he brightened perceptibly. "Ah, madam, I can do all of your cooking, as I did for the Governor. And—" He glanced toward the other men who were hovering together, staring at Tanya in wide-eyed si-lence. "—I can manage that herd of worthless flesh for you as well, if you wish." He smiled ingratiatingly. "It is not fitting that a princess handle such menial tasks."

Sung, too proud to work for a commoner, had promoted her to royalty. Tanya was amused. She was, however, after all, a Countess born.

"Very well. Lead the others to the inn. I shall be there shortly."

She stopped in to speak to 'Ohi'a'Lehua, and to pray, as she did each day, for a more welcome visit than she had just experienced. She still dreamed of the *Balalaika*, and hoped it would arrive.

When she reached the kitchen of the inn, Sung had al-ready set the coolies to work. She spoke to him long enough to establish a rate of pay for each man and a con-siderably higher one for him, and then she went to her

359

rooms. Adam Czerwenki's visit had put a strain on her emotions, and she was in need of a rest.

In the days that followed, Tanya grew to appreciate the luxury of acting the lady. She was free of some responsibilities. She was able to spend more time in barter with the next ships, and Sung, she could see, approved of her skill in trade.

He started immediately to renovate the kitchen. He organized his ten-man team so that all the chores that needed doing were cared for. Tanya's rooms were put in order as soon as she left them. She found her bath drawn at night. The rooms that she let to visiting officers, and the building for common seamen were kept in immaculate condition. Even insects that had been a scourge to the native workers were cleared away from the inn. They also built a wide, solid enclosure for the bull. The heifers were allowed to roam free on the verdant glens.

She spent an increasing amount of time at the mission with 'Ohi'a'Lehua, who showed no improvement, no matter what she said—that she had been seen, as she thought, or hadn't been seen, according to Hiku—or what measures the *padre* tried. Tanya expressed the fear that the girl might simply die, but Kekua assured her that would not happen. "The *Kahunas* want to keep her alive—at least for the present. She is a special case, for she dared to violate a *kapu* deliberately. I think they wish to use her as an example. They are not pleased that some of the people have listened to the words of the *padre*."

"Kekua, how can you speak so dispassionately of your own sister? Is there nothing we can do to save her from her fears?"

"It is more than her fears, Madam del Norte. She has no power to resist the *Kahunas*. If they will it, she will live. If they choose, she will die. It is the way."

Kekua acted as her guide in walks she now took along the shore and into the villages. She delighted in the beauty of the native children, all of whom seemed to be perfect in body and in face with their golden skin and dark, flashing eyes. She was reminded of her Fong Ya.

Often the children would decorate their hair with colorful flowers and dance together. At a stream that ran through a lava bed and tumbled over a small cliff into a sparkling, clear pool, children from the village gathered, and frolicked in the water like river otter at play. One by one they slid down a lava tube and flew out over the pool, landing with a splash in the water.

Taking up a pad and pencil, Tanya settled herself under a tree to sketch. Beside her she placed a handful of food she knew was not *kapu* to attract the children to her. It had been years since she had done any sketching.

She worked longest on the picture of a lad of about twelve, who informed her that his name was Kamakau. He showed particular bravery in his acrobatics on the slide. After many attempts, she put her pad aside and rewarded the boy with a piece of dried beef, which he took eagerly, darting away to eat it in private. Yet, when she looked at her work, she knew she had not succeeded in getting down the joyful liveliness and bright intelligence that shone in his face.

Tanya returned from these outings much refreshed. For days thereafter, she attempted to convince 'Ohi'a'Lehua that she should brave a trip to the falls and slide, but the girl was unresponsive. Kekua finally put a stop to Tanya's efforts. "You must not worry so. She knows what the *Kahunas* will allow, for her pain will increase if she disobeys them. Let her be. It is as it has to be."

Tanya spoke again to the *padre*. "Father, is there nothing we can do? 'Ohi'a'Lehua used to be such a happy girl!"

"Daughter, you continue to fret as if you considered you were responsible for her dilemma. You must free your mind of such fears. 'Ohi'a'Lehua must overcome her trust in the *Kahunas* and accept the True God. Until then, she will suffer. Her prayers—and mine—are for a strengthening of her faith. And they will be rewarded. I can see now a power she did not possess when first she came to the mission for shelter. Be patient, my daughter. 'Ohi'a'Lehua will triumph over her terror, and her victory will serve as an inspiration to every other convert—and to the many natives who do not yet dare to step forward and partake of God's grace."

He led the way from the chapel into the garden. "Come, sit beside me and tell me of your excursions. I sometimes regret that I am so occupied with the duties here." He held up his hand in anticipation of her protest. "No, my child, you should not have left the Chinese to help me. You brought them ashore and paid for their freedom. You deserve their thanks. Now, tell me what you saw."

She described the playful children and the beauty of the pond. "Kekua says the natives believe that the goddess Pele made pipes through which she could roar when she was angry, and they are, in truth, strange formations. It was so lovely! And as the children played, many adults came by and watched. Some even joined their children in their games." She gazed at the bright red blossoms of the 'Ohi'a'ai tree. "Are we right, *padre*, to try to change this paradise? The natives seem so free—like happy children."

He frowned. "Is 'Ohi'a'Lehua a happy child?"

"Oh, no! But she is torn between the customs of her people and those of foreigners who know nothing—or very little—about her traditions."

He smiled sadly. "I understand how you feel, Tanya. But you are wrong. In the first years of my stay here, I saw ten women cruelly murdered because they broke the *kapus*. And have you ridden north past Kamehameha's *heiau* at Puukohola?" Tanya shook her head. "Well, you must, for it is a monument to savagery you should not ignore. It was built the year I arrived, and according to native tradition, it was significant in establishing Kamehameha's power."

He began to pace under the bright red blossoms, his hands running up and down over his beads. "Ritual demanded that men be sacrificed periodically throughout the construction, and that their bodies be buried in the foundation. But most shameful of all was its dedication."

He paused and gazed up at the small cross that topped the structure of the mission. "When Kamehameha was ready to dedicate his *heiau*, he invited his chief rival here on Hawaii to attend—ostensibly to make peace with him. But when the man and his entourage arrived, every one of them was murdered. Keoua Kuahuula was the principal sacrifice made that day to Kamehameha's war god, Ku-ka'ili-moku."

Tanya shuddered. "How terrible! It is hard to believe! All the captains speak of Kamehameha with respect!"

"Yes. He can act the civilized ruler. But he is a savage at heart. I spoke of his chief rival, Keoua Kuahuula. It is important that you understand that they were cousins. In all probability, when they were children, they played together on the slide you saw and were just as merry as the boys and girls you watched yesterday. Tanya, a pagan religion is destructive, not only because it denies its followers knowledge of the True God, but because it encourages murder and human sacrifice."

Two days later, Kekua appeared at Tanya's garden gate. "Senora del Norte, I bring news. The great king Kamehameha is returning to the island for a visit! I have spoken to the *padre*, and he is taking precautions so no attempt to steal 'Ohi'a'Lehua will be successful. But I am sure the great king will come to visit you. Through your inn, you have brought much money into his hands."

In spite of all the *padre* had said about the king, Tanya was aware of a feeling of excitement. A savage he might be—especially by Father Timeteo's standards—but there was no denying his power. And the thought that he might show some appreciation for her service on the island delighted her.

Throughout the village the preparations began. Natives who customarily spent most of their days in indolence suddenly became industrious workers, building platforms and dwelling-places for the king and his many wives. A special area was set aside, dedicated to the *Kahunas*, and purified for the use of the monarch. And food was gathered from the many fruit trees. Sugar cane was stacked in preparation for the feast, and ten wild boars were captured and fenced in—to be killed and roasted on the night of Kamehameha's arrival.

In her own preparations, Kekua served as a special consultant, advising Sung on what to cook and how to prepare the dining area for the great king's presence. And Tanya was informed that since she was a foreigner, she would be permitted to sit with the king while he ate, but she would not be allowed to share the feast. That honor would be reserved for the *padre*, who would not break *kapu* with his presence, since he was male.

The exhilaration increased with each passing week. Special sacred songs were sung throughout the days, and garlands were gathered for leis that would be worn by the warriors who accompanied the king on his journey. Women were appointed to make new feather leis for the king's wives. They used only the yellow-gold feathers from the 'O'O birds, and they chanted rituals as they labored.

Only 'Ohi'a'Lehua did not share in the general excitement. She isolated herself even further from the other women in the mission and spent hours on her knees in prayer to her Christian God. Tanya dreamed of the possibility that on the day of the great feast she might persuade Kamehameha to give her friend a special pardon, in celebration of the day.

One morning, two weeks after the preparations began, Father Timeteo called her to his study. She dressed carefully, as was her habit when she went to see him, and hurried to the mission. The *padre* was sitting quietly in his study. "Tanya, there is something you must see."

He led the way into his infirmary, where he kept those converts who showed signs of malnutrition or illness.

"Oh, *padre*, is it cholera? God preserve us from such an outbreak at this time—or ever!"

"No, my child, it is not cholera. Look."

A man huddled in the shadows in one corner of the room. The normal golden color of his skin was lost. He was gaunt and greyish. His cheek bones stood out on his face, and through the skin of his mouth she could see the outline of his teeth. His eyes were glazed. He stared at the ceiling with unseeing steadiness.

"Father! Surely it is cholera. I know of nothing else that wastes the body in that manner."

"No, my child. He suffers from no disease. He came to me carried by his brother, who had found him lying in the forest. He has been smoking opium—probably every day since the *Russian Princess* entered the harbor."

"Opium? But, father, that's impossible! I even searched the Chinese workers before I allowed them off the ship! I am certain that no opium was smuggled in."

"Are you, my child? Did you watch the ship each day—and night? And did you hear all that passed between Kanalio, Nuiaui, and Adam Czerwenki?"

It was true that the three men had been together in the inn. And Hiku had told her that they left with obvious signs of satisfaction. "Kanalio and Nuiaui? But they are the officials chosen by Kamehameha himself! Do you suggest that they might have. . . ? Father, we must report this to Kamehameha as soon as he arrives! He will want to depose men who work to destroy his people with poisons like this!"

Father Timeteo held up his hand. "No, daughter, not yet. I believe there is more. First we must learn the extent of the problem."

Together they walked into the village of Leei. There, a man lay stretched out beside his hut, unaffected by the excitement that surrounded him. Another huddled near a fire, seeking warmth, despite the heat of the sun that bore down on his bony shoulders. A young lad sat under a tree. Despite a general thinness and the beginning of a pasty blanching of his skin, she recognized him as Kamakau, the twelve-year-old boy who had so charmed her at the lava slide. He had the same glazed eyes that had so startled her in the wasted man at the infirmary. "Oh, father, this is terrible!"

"Do you know this boy?"

"Yes. He was the child who was so skilled in his play at the slide. I sketched him—or, rather, I tried to sketch him."

"And did you give him a treat for posing for you?"

"Yes, I did! But. . . ."

"And did others see you?"

"Of course. I had nothing to hide. I have no desire to break the food *kapus* and get the children in trouble."

"Would you recognize the others who were at the falls that day?"

"No. How could I? I only noticed Kamakau because of his skill and daring." Again she looked down at the child. "Father! Is it possible? Who would do such a thing?"

"You have told me that Kanalio and Nuiaui showed jealousy during the trading. They have great power on the island, and they might not like sharing with you what they think should be their trade. My child, you are in grave danger. Many people saw you take cargo from the *Russian Princess*, and many saw you move about the villages in the past months. It was with the Russians that Hanahelio traded, and I suspect that Kanalio and Nuiaui knew that Czerwenki carried opium in his hold. We must be prepared to save you from Kamehameha's wrath, for I fear no one will believe that you are not responsible for the devastation that has been wreaked on his island."

She could think of no way to stop the plans that Kanalio, Nuiaui, and Adam Czerwenki had set into motion. They retraced their steps to the mission and the inn.

CHAPTER VII

Tanya watched the *Spanish Star* maneuver the shoals and burst into open sea. It had been a good visit—and a profitable one. Once more she had grain in her storehouse to send north to Sitka. Captain Joaquin Ernando signaled his farewell with a dip of his mainsail and was gone. Slowly, Tanya returned to the inn. If her calculations were correct, the next Russian ship would not arrive for three weeks.

"Sung? What is the next Russian ship we can expect?"

Sung appeared in the doorway to the kitchen. "The *Tsarina*, great lady. Already I am preparing cabbage for *shchi*, and sour cream for *borshch*. Captain Vassili is particularly fond of *taidetud vasikarind*, and I plan to surprise him with a tender rolled shoulder of veal. I have chosen the calf already, and the coolie Fantzu has the task of fattening it up for slaughter."

"And when is the *Elizabeth* returning?" She could not quite hide the anticipation in her voice.

Sung met her glance. "It, great lady, should be in the harbor within the week. If I have not yet conveyed the thanks of myself and the lowly beggars who work beside me, please accept them now. You are most generous!"

Tanya gazed toward the open kitchen door. "Are the quarters we have built adequate? If not, feel free to add what you need."

Sung bowed once more. "You are too kind. We already have more here than any of us would have had at home. Even I, who lived in the palace of the Governor, never had the luxury you feel I deserve here. We will be spoiled if we receive any more."

He returned to his work. She had grown accustomed to the formality with which he treated her, and she knew his sentiments were honest. So, also, was his bookkeeping. Often he dealt with the merchantmen to procure supplies for the inn, and Tanya was aware that he was as expert at striking a good bargain as he was at roasting a side of pork.

Tanya wandered slowly toward the mission. Captain Ernando had offered to take 'Ohi'a'Lehua away with him to California—or Mexico, but the unhappy girl had refused.

"No. I must stay here. It is forbidden for islanders to leave their home."

Kekua had assured her there was no such ruling, but had shown no willingness to force his sister to leave. "She will do what she has to do. It is better to die here, among friends, than to travel to a strange land and die alone."

Once more she and Father Timeteo went over the plan they had devised to subvert Kanalio and Nuiaui's scheme. The father would speak to Kamehameha during the feast. He would tell about the attempt Adam Czerwenki had made to sell opium through Tanya and how she had refused to cooperate. He would speak of the conversation that had taken place between the two officials and the Russian captain. "They will be planning some dramatic way of presenting the problem to their king. We will simply broach the subject before they have a chance. Don't be concerned, Tanya. Everything will be fine."

Reassured anew, Tanya once again entered into the spirit of celebration. In the village, she was met with smiling faces and children who draped her shoulders with flowers. At the inn, the Chinese workmen were eager to show both their gratitude and their efficiency. At last, exhausted from all the activity, she went to lie down.

"Great Lady! Come quickly! There is a ship coming into the harbor!"

The afternoon sun had just touched the top of her blinds, and above the great 'ohi'a'ai tree she could see the clouds beginning to gather. Soon it would be time for the afternoon rain.

Throwing on a shawl, she joined Sung at the gate, his long glass balanced against the post. "Great Lady, it is a ship, but not one I know."

She also looked out through the glass. Far out to sea, a ship bounced through the ocean swell, its bow pointed directly toward Kealakekua Bay.

"I can't read its name, Sung. Did you get a look at it?"

"Yes, Great Lady. It was the same as the name you have painted over the door to the inn. The *Balalaika*."

"You are certain? The *Balalaika*?" The wind turned the ship to one side. The letters read clear. Sung had not been mistaken. The *Balalaika* was, at last, pulling into her bay!

When she emerged from her rooms where she had gone to prepare herself for Alexei Andreiv, the shower had abated, and drops of water were formed on the edges of the leaves and hanging from the petals of all the flowers. The sun had returned, lighting each watery gem until it shone like a diamond.

The natives who were not busy with preparations for the king's arrival had scurried to the beach and were already paddling out toward the sea. Their voices carried up to the inn. "*Aloha! Aloha!*"

Tanya straightened the folds of her skirt and patted the curls that hung softly over one shoulder. She had checked the mirror more than once while she dressed. She touched her cheeks. Maybe she should have put on some color? But the warmth of her skin told her such artificialities were not necessary. Excitement provided a charm that no paint could ever duplicate.

The sun was low on the horizon when the ship finally sailed into the Bay, towing the empty canoes of the native greeters behind it, and dropped anchor. A longboat was being lowered and eight sailors scrambled aboard. Then, with lovely golden-skinned girls draped over their arms, three officers climbed into place. The flotilla was on its way toward shore.

It seemed an age before the boat scraped against the sand and the men leaped onto the beach, greeted by Father Timeteo, his hands extended in blessing and welcome. For Tanya one face stood out. Ivar Alexseevich!

Ivar rushed to her side. "Tanya! I knew it had to be you! How many Russian women with Spanish surnames can there be?" He embraced her and kissed her hand. "I have been eaten alive with curiosity. What happened to bring you from California?"

The captain at his side cleared his throat, "This is Captain Boris Ilianski. I believe you met him in Monterey."

Captain Ilianski took Tanya's hand and brought it to his lips. "Madam, I am delighted! Yet I must repeat my second mate's question. What has brought you so far from home? You seemed quite content in California when last we met." He turned to the third man. "*Senora,* this is my first officer, Leonid Pavelska. So you still use a Spanish name? And where is your husband?"

When Tanya hesitated, uncertain as to how much to tell how soon, the captain continued. "Ivar tells me you knew the captain of the *Russian Princess.*"

"Yes. Ivar and I . . . suffered under him some years ago."

"Well, no one will suffer again—at least not from his cruelty. He surrendered without a fight, and is on his way to prison in Siberia. The Tsar learned that he was trading in opium, a commodity made contraband by agreement between all the naval powers. We were sent to question him, and when he learned of our mission, he slipped from the harbor in Canton during the night and made for these islands. We only caught him on his return, as he sought shelter near Malaysia. Did he drop anchor here?"

"He was here—not more than eight months ago. And I fear he succeeded. There have been many natives who purchased the drug. Two officials appear to have cooperated with Captain Czerwenki to bring it ashore."

Sung had vodka and small Russian cakes waiting when they reached the dining area. "Captain, tell me about your trip. How does the colony of Sitka fare now?"

"Far better than ever before, since they have been receiving shipments of supplies from a kind trader here on the islands. Ivar was certain you had something to do with the new prosperity when he heard of the trades that were being made. I must admit I had difficulty believing him. I was certain he had let his imagination run amok."

Tanya took a sip of vodka, smooth and rich, the best to be had from Okhotsk.

Ivar leaned toward her. "Tanya, what happened in California, to your husband? I saw the shadow on your face a moment ago, when we asked you."

She spoke of Sebastino's death and of her decision to come here, and gazed into her friend's eyes. They never wavered—and they were filled with surprise and sympathy.

"We concluded that 'Tino had been killed by accident, since Feodor reported seeing a mountain lion before you boarded the *Balalaika*." Her eyes showed her inner fears. "You saw nothing when he fired?"

"Nothing! As God is my witness! Oh, Tanya, had we known! We had no thought that you might be followed!"

She sat silently, letting the sweet calm of relief fill her breast. "And Alexius?"

"He has returned to Russia, where he serves the Tsar Alexander. I hear rumors that he keeps much to himself, appearing only when the Tsar commands him."

"Oh, Ivar! How wonderful that he is restored to his position in Court! He is well?"

"As far as I know, though I do not think he will ever

371

recover from losing you. Why have you not gone to him? You surely know that he would welcome you with open arms!" He rested his hand on hers. "Now that we have found you, you must come with us. We can take you as far as Okhotsk."

She lifted her small glass and touched it to his. "Perhaps. I was not ready before. And I did not know where to go." She turned to include the others. "Come, Captain Ilianski, gentlemen! One more toast to the future! It is all that matters for any of us."

They were enjoying the beauty of the tropical sunset in the garden, when Kanalio and Nuiaui appeared at the gate. "These two men," she explained, "are representatives of the king Kamehameha on the island of Hawaii. Tomorrow, when we begin to trade, they will join us."

Kanalio, unceremoniously, came straight to the point. "Sir Tanya, it is not permitted to trade during a time of celebration. The ship will have to leave the harbor until after Kamehameha's visit is over."

"But I thought the king wanted trade! Why would he object to an exchange of goods in his presence? Surely there will be some time during the festivities when business can be transacted!"

"Sir Tanya, you are a foreigner and you do not understand. The ship cannot remain in the harbor. You must tell the captain. He must leave at high tide this morning. It will be bad if he is even within sight of land when the king arrives!"

"He will be permitted to return when the visit is over?"

There was no change in the expressions on the two faces. "Of course." Kanalio's voice was gruff. "Trade is the life of the island."

"And how long will the king stay? I must know. The ship cannot remain offshore without some idea of how long they must wait!"

"He will stay for two days. Then he will return to Oahu." As abruptly as they had appeared, they left.

Captain Ilianski said, "Is this the way they treat all ships?"

"Oh, no! This is the first time Kamehameha has been on Hawaii since my arrival. I don't know how things are done when he is in residence. But please, humor them. I know they want to trade—and I have more grain that can go to Sitka. Surely you can wait two days!"

The captain cleared his throat. "We will do it. But only because you are Ivar's friend. I am not accustomed to being brushed aside by natives."

"Thank you. And if you will, you can do me a favor. We are expecting the *Elizabeth*, a British ship. With such regulations in effect, I do not want them to anchor and unwittingly violate some *kapu*. Will you keep a lookout and stop Captain Farnsworth for me?"

Ivar said, "Don't worry, Tanya. We will stop him. And we will do nothing to destroy the good relationship you have with the native chief. We will leave at high tide. But we will count the days. Expect us three days hence. There is still much we must talk about."

The sky was barely light when the officers reached their ship. It lifted anchor and began to move out of the harbor.

Tanya was filled with a strange apprehension, and she hurried toward the mission.

Father Timeteo scowled. He also looked after the vanishing sails. Finally he said, "Something is amiss. Kamehameha has never objected to trade—even when it interrupted the most abandoned celebration. Only worship in the *heiua*—or its construction—is cause for such interruptions. You must be very careful. I fear that Kanalio and Nuiaui are fabricating a trap—and you are their intended prey."

At the inn, Tanya forced herself to attend to what duties had to be done. Sung would have to know that there was no need for special food. They would be having no guests for breakfast.

CHAPTER VIII

Tanya listened for the sounds of the awakening village, but this morning, over the eternal pounding of the ocean, only the cries of birds could be heard. Then she remembered that Kamehameha was expected at any time. The villagers would be down by the shore awaiting him.

Uneasy, she attended to her toilet and pulled on a dress, struggling with the buttons.

In the garden, a brillantly red 'T'iwi' bird flitted by, toward the forest, setting the leaves of the young lobelias tree into wild motion.

"Sung!" she called. The Chinaman appeared at the door to his room, looking as neat as if he had never been to bed. "Come—and bring your glass!"

From the crest of a small hill just outside the garden gate

the gently curving shore was visible for miles to the north, and far away, close to the great Puukohola Heiaui, a line of war canoes was drawn up to the edge of the forest.

Together they scanned the countryside. It was Sung who first saw the procession, about half-way between the empty war canoes and the village.

Warriors led the parade. Behind them, carried on the shoulders of six husky men, came Kamehameha. He was followed by his wives, each on her own chair. Circling around the line of marchers danced the villagers, tossing flowers into the path of the spectacle.

Tanya handed the glass to Sung and strolled down the hill toward the village. The opium users, who had been much in evidence on her earlier visit, were nowhere to be seen. She searched under the trees and even stepped inside some of huts. But no one was about.

With each passing minute the chanting of the approaching procession grew louder. Perturbed, Tanya strolled back toward the inn. Suddenly there was a movement in the woods beside her, and Father Timeteo stepped to her side.

Father Timeteo said, "It wasn't wise for you to wander through the village alone."

"But surely the people who received the opium know it was not I who sold it to them. They could speak on my behalf if I am accused by Kanalio and Kuiaui."

"You are right. But it will not help. They will be silent, even though they may like you. They fear their superiors—and the *Kahunas*."

From the chapel they watched the triumphant king enter the village. The villagers scurried about in frenzied activity.

The seven large boars who had been slaughtered two days earlier and had been buried in ovens made of clay and stones, now were removed and placed on heavy wooden spits over beds of glowing coals. The fragrance of the juicy, well-cooked meat filled the air. Children poked at the roasts with long sticks and sucked the juice from the end when it cooled.

Tanya sought out 'Ohi'a'Lehua who was laying on her

pallet, staring ahead with eyes that seemed to have lost the ability to see. " 'Ohi'a'Lehua," she said, "you must not allow yourself to be so unhappy. Everything will be all right! The father will speak to Kamehameha and make everything fine again. Please, little Flower, you have many friends who love you. Don't abandon yourself to despair."

"Kamehameha has arrived at the village?" 'Ohi'a'Lehua's voice was husky and weak.

"Yes. Just now."

"They will come for me soon! I will be glad when my torment is ended."

Father Timeteo brought her food. But she refused to eat. She was listening to the excited sounds that came from the village.

Tanya, her arms crossed over her stomach, watched as Kamehameha finished tearing the meat from a bone, tossing the stripped white shaft into the woods behind him. Father Timeteo, sitting beside her, was also eating, but she, a woman, had not received any food.

Suddenly the noise of the drums ceased. In the unnatural silence a thin figure emerged from the forest. Kamakau! Some others followed.

The once-strong boy could hardly walk. His legs were bare sticks, and his shoulder blades stuck out from his body. His head resembled a skull that had dried in the sun.

Kamehameha was standing up in his place, his finger pointed at the hapless child. "Bring him to me!"

His men took the boy's shoulders and pushed him forward. He fell weakly to the ground and lay, his face buried in the dirt, at the ruler's feet.

"Kanalio!" Nuiaui!" Kamehameha's shout brought the two officials to his side. "What is this? How did the boy come to be in this state?"

Kanalio bowed. "Great one. It is the drug, opium. There is no doubt. We have found others who suffered more—and two who have already died."

A howl of rage emanated from the great jowls of Kamehameha. He was a frightening figure when he was at ease.

Angry, his massive shoulders flexed, his arms swung wildly about. His eyes were pinpoints of black. And his brows hung like dark clouds over his face.

When his raging at last ended, the villagers had rounded up all the victims of the drug from the forest; they huddled together before the king.

Kamehameha stared at the culprits in silence. Then, with a loud roar, he turned to his aides. "Kill them! And let it be known that anyone who is found using the poison will suffer a like fate!"

The feasting resumed. Strong hands carried the condemned into the woods. When the king's men returned, their weapons were red with fresh blood.

Kanalio and Nuiaui had settled themselves beside their king, and they were whispering to him furiously.

Father Timeteo turned to Tanya. "Kanalio and Nuiaui are filling Kamehameha's head with falsehoods. You must remain to show that you have nothing to fear—to prove your innocence."

It was not easy for Tanya to remain. The abandon of the celebrants, some of whom had had relatives who were victims of the slaughter, filled her with horror. And the king and his two advisors cast angry glances in her direction.

At last Kamehameha rose again to his feet. "Hear me!" A deathly silence fell over the crowd. "I speak the truth!" His voice rang through the village. "From this day onward, no Russian ships will be allowed in the harbors of the islands! Any man, woman, or child seen speaking to a Russian or boarding a Russian ship to bring welcome to the sailors will be put to death!"

"*Padre!*" Tanya whispered, "how can he? It was only one ship that caused this trouble! And that ship has been stopped. Ivar told me that Czerwenki has been caught and condemned to Siberia for his crimes."

"Are you sure of this?"

"Yes, *padre*. Ivar would not lie to me."

"Good!" Abruptly, Father Timeteo rose to his feet. "Great King Kamehameha!" All eyes turned to watch him as he approached the ruler. "Our friendship goes far back to when you were building the great *heiau* at Puulohola, before you became the favorite of the great god of war and came to rule all the islands. Hear me now, for I have knowledge that is important to the safety of you—and your people!

"The Senora del Norte has informed me that she was told the captain who brought the opium to your shores has been punished. He will not return to the islands. Why should others suffer for his crimes?"

Again Kanalio and Nuiaui whispered to Kamehameha. Kamehameha pointed a long finger toward Tanya. "Father Timeteo, we can understand why you seek to defend this woman—and her countrymen. She has poisoned your mind and heart as she has poisoned the bodies of our people. When she is gone, you will be cleansed again. And the drug will not return to our shore. Take her back to her inn. We will decide her fate before we leave the island."

He sat down. The audience was over.

Sung met them at the gate. "Take care of her," Father Timeteo said. "Do not let her out of your sight! She is in grave danger."

Sung bowed slightly. "We will do as you say. I will appoint men to watch her all the time, and we will arm ourselves. Our lives are worthless if she is hurt."

Father Timeteo hesitated for a moment and then, shaking his head, he hurried toward the mission.

She lay for a long time, staring out at the 'Ohi'a'ii tree. The banquet had ended, and the sound of drums filled the air. Shouts of pleasure informed her that the dancing had begun in earnest.

Rising, she stepped into the twilight and gazed out toward the sea. If only she had not complied with Kanalio and Nuiaui's demand that she send the *Balalaika* away! They had deliberately misled her to cut off any chance that she might escape.

A sudden light flashed far out beyond the reefs. She picked up Sung's glass, but the trees that surrounded the inn blocked her view. She hurried out of the garden and up onto the rise which served as her lookout, two coolies, who had been appointed her guardians, following her. The light flashed again.

Balancing the glass against a tree, she focused on the distant glimmer. A ship! It was coming toward land, its bow pointed directly toward her lens. She leaned forward and tried to read the letters that ran back along its side. She could not read its name, but she could see, even at the great distance, that it was speeding toward the island. It would reach the harbor some time during the darkest part of the night.

Behind her she heard a movement. She turned to see the two coolies fall beneath the blows of heavy clubs.

"Sung! Help!"

A heavy net fell around her shoulders and she was lifted up into the air.

"Help! *Padre!* Sung!"

Sung's startled face appeared at the kitchen door. With a shout of anger he charged across the garden. But he was not fast enough. She was dragged into the woods. The net that held her was lifted. She was hanging over the massive shoulder of a tall native who began to run through the forest.

Behind her, the cries of her would-be rescuers grew faint. Finally, she heard them no longer.

CHAPTER IX

She knew only one thing for certain. She was being carried upward. Tanya continued to scream for help until a hand was clamped over her mouth and a voice close to her ear ordered her to be silent. In the dim light of the forest she could not immediately make out his features, but when she did see them, she could not recognize him. But she was reasonably certain he was one of Kanalio's private guard, a secret band of men dedicated to defend the two officials.

She gazed about her. There was no need for further cries. If she had been heard, someone would follow her. If her shouts were thought to be part of the celebration, it was too late to enlist help. She wondered if the two coolies had lived after the attack. If so, they would surely sound the alarm.

In the meantime, she felt an urgent need to be aware of where she was being taken. She searched the woods for some landmarks—but all the trees looked alike in the half-light. Her captor moved with a steady pace, exerting no more effort than if he had been strolling along the beach, but when she looked back, the ground dropped away precipitously.

They emerged from the woods suddenly, and Tanya found herself gazing up into a bright orange sky with purple specks of clouds floating slowly across it. An 'Io hawk hovered. Behind her in the woods, an 'Elepaio bird called to its mate.

The ground appeared black and very rough. Her captor was traveling over an enormous volcanic flow that had hardened into long furrows, like a plowed field that would never nourish seed. She vaguely recalled that Father Time-teo had spoken of a volcanic eruption that had occurred in 1801 which had buried one village and turned large stretches of woodland into fiery, barren wasteland.

They entered another grove of trees that had miraculously escaped the killing heat of the volcanic flow, and she was again plunged into darkness. Her captor trudged on, silently and steadily. If he was being followed, it was clear that the pursuit did not worry him.

He stopped when he reached the next clearing. She estimated that she had been traveling for the greater part of an hour. A thousand stars glittered above her. She could see the rim of the crater. She was placed on her feet.

The net was pulled away with one swift motion. She took one step. A massive hand circled her wrist, propelled her upward toward a line of small huts, pushed her into one.

Tanya fell, and lay for several moments recovering her breath. Then she crawled to the opening and gazed at the bizarre scene spread out before her.

There were nine huts like her own, dimly visible, little more than straw cages made of lauhala mats. Hers was the farthest from the crater, and since she had not seen any others as she was pulled up the hill, she assumed it was the last.

382

Before each hut a sentry stood in front of the opening, his gaze fixed on the faint glow that emanated from the rim above him. Wisps of smoke rose against the black sky. They were at the edge of the crater of Mauna Loa.

A breeze stirred the smoke and whispered its way into her prison, refreshing her with its sharp, cool touch. She unconsciously smoothed her skirt and patted her hair into place. Then, aware of the ridiculousness of her act in the presence of such danger, she settled down to assess her chances of escape.

There appeared at first to be none. Then she saw a movement of one of the mats that formed the hut nearest to hers. Galvanized into action, she crawled to the back of her prison and pushed at the back wall. It moved easily against her hand and she found herself gazing down the steep incline.

She had already begun to slip under the mat when a noise near the doorway drew her attention. She let the mat fall back into place. She would have to risk waiting. Settling in place near the doorway, she looked again at the ceremonial encampment.

Beside the guard who stood immobile before her doorway, there were many other men moving about near the edge of the crater like black ghosts against the diamond-set velvet of the sky.

Then, suddenly, the moon slipped out from behind a cloud, and at the same moment one man detatched himself from the others. Kanalio!

He was joined by Nuiaui and by a *Kahuna*, whom she recognized by his strange costume of feathers and rattles. For a moment the three men stood in silence. Then the *Kahuna* lifted his hands over his head and began to chant. The words sent a chill down Tanya's back. He was summoning the *Unihipili*, the ghost of some great ancestor of Nuiaui's, and he was praying for triumph of his two companions over the king Kamehameha!

Gradually, his chant increased in speed and rose in pitch. The *Kahuna* waved his arms over the crater, breaking the wisp of smoke into feathers. It was then Tanya realized that another figure stood behind him. A slender girl

383

dressed in flowers, her hair crowned with a wreath of the sacred 'Ohi'a'ai, traditionally known as the mother of life, since its fruit sustained mankind when all others failed to grow, stepped to the edge of the crater. Lifting her hands in silent mime of the priest, she leaped over the precipice. She fell without a sound. The wreath of flowers slipped as she vanished from sight.

Tanya shuddered. She had not believed Father Timeteo when he spoke of human sacrifice being used by the natives to further their goals and to appease their gods. But she was watching it now. What startled her most was that the girl went willingly. She wondered what the others were thinking, each in her own little hut. Was there another who, like her, felt horror and terror?

The three men at the brink of the volcano stepped forward and gazed down, and Tanya could only assume they were watching the victim's fall. Gasping, Tanya turned from the sight and retched miserably, filling the hut with the stench of vomit.

She leaned momentarily against the frame of her hut. This could not be real! It was a nightmare—a horror story brought on, once again, by Adam Czerwenki!

The *Kahuna* renewed his chant. The tall guard who had stationed himself beside the first willing victim turned and moved toward the second hut.

Tanya wiped her face and brushed the perspiration from her brow. She had counted nine huts before her own. Eight more victims would step into the lava pit—and then her time would come. She backed into the shadow. It was time for her to make her escape. Her head reeled and she felt overwhelmed by a great weakness, but she dared not wait again.

Suddenly, a man bent low in the doorway. In his hand he held a small cup made of coconut shell. She had seen the likes of it before, carved all around with sacred symbols, but she had not realized the use to which it was put. His face wrinkled up in disgust, but he showed no other recognition of her weakness. "Drink this!" The gruff voice seemed almost kind.

Tanya pulled back.

"It will help you center your thoughts on the great goddess Pele, to whom you will go. And it will wipe fear from your heart." He glanced with a frown at the splotch that marred the black surface of the lava.

The shadowy man in the doorway put the cup in a small hollow formed in the floor. "I will leave it here. Be sure to drink it before the sixth sacrifice. It will take that much time to take effect." He was gone.

There was a movement in the darkness before her. A second victim stood proudly beside the guard at the edge of the rim, and when the *Kahuna* reached the climax of his prayer, she leaped suddenly and was gone. Tanya moaned. There was little time left. With an angry glance at the cup that had been left near the door, she crawled to the loose flap at the rear of her hut.

It lifted before she reached it, and a familiar face appeared. "Tanya?" She stared at him in surprise. "Kekua!"

Kekua crawled inside, followed by the slight figure of a woman. Both held their fingers to their lips. "We must be silent." Kekua whispered. "If it is found that we are here, we will all three be killed."

CHAPTER X

Tanya met the eyes of 'Ohi'a'Lehua! "What are you doing here?" She was barely aware that the eyes that met hers were calm and quiet. "You should be back at the mission, where you are safe!"

"No." 'Ohi'a'Lehua's voice was steady. All the fear that had torn her soul seemed to be gone. "It is you who do not belong here. I have come to take your place."

Tanya shook her head. "No! Surely we can all escape the same way you came!"

Kekua touched Tanya's hand. "You must listen to 'Ohi-'a'Lehua. What she says is the truth. We overheard plans for this ceremony and sacrifice. Kanalio and Nuiaui are seeking help from Pele to destroy the encampment made for Kamehameha. They want him to die so they can rule the islands."

"But then, we must hurry and warn Kamehameha!"

"We will. But he is worshipping in his private temple, and he would not listen if we disturbed him now. It was 'Ohi'a'Lehua who persuaded me to do it this way. She will take your place." He paused. "We were afraid to wait to rescue you, for they might have sacrificed you at the beginning of their ceremony."

"But why must 'Ohi'a'Lehua stay?"

"Someone must be here, or Kanalio will know you are gone—and he will send warriors down to catch us. They will signal others in the village to stop us before we can reach the king."

'Ohi'a'Lehua pulled off the loose *muu muu* Father Timeteo provided for all his female converts. "Quickly, you must give me your dress!" Tanya did not move. The high call of the *Kahuna* told her that another victim had been sacrificed.

"Please, Senora del Norte! You must do as she tells you!"

"I have no fear of death." 'Ohi'a'Lehua began to unbutton Tanya's dress. "And I know that I must die. It is not the fault of the king that the *kapus* exist. It is only his duty to see that they are not broken. But Kamehameha is a good ruler who loves his people. He will protect us against the Russians who try to kill us with opium, and he will keep our land for our use. I cannot let him be killed by Kanalio and Nuiaui, for they will destroy us."

Tanya looked deeply into the eyes of her friend. 'Ohi'a'Lehua met her gaze without flinching. There was no indication that she had been drugged. The agony that had haunted her for so many weeks was gone.

Kekua helped 'Ohi'a'Lehua pull Tanya's dress over her head, and slipped it onto his sister's shoulders. "*Senora*, 'Ohi'a'Lehua has learned the sacred words that will turn the magic the *Kahuna* is making against Kanalio and Nuiaui. She will say the sacred words as she enters the gates of Pele's kingdom, and they will be the ones to be destroyed. Hurry! There is little time."

"You must listen to Kekua, Tanya. He speaks the truth." 'Ohi'a'Lehua pointed down the mountainside. "Go quickly. Kekua must get back to the village and tell the king. When he learns what Kanalio and Nuiaui are doing, he will destroy them."

Tanya pulled the girl into her arms. "Oh, little Flower! I cannot leave you to die!"

"You must! And you must hurry!" 'Ohi'a'Lehua settled herself before the door of the hut. "Please, go! There is little time left!"

Kekua lifted the mat and gestured for Tanya to crawl out. Tanya hesitated for one more moment, her heart aching with the pain of such a terrible parting. 'Ohi'a'Lehua sat at the doorway, her slender form hardly filling the dress she had taken to replace her *mumu*. But in the darkness the looseness did not seem to matter.

She sat proudly, her head high, and in her hand she held the cup that had been left by the guard. She brought it close to her lips and then, with a sudden movement, she poured it out onto the ground.

Kekua touched Tanya's shoulder. "Quietly. They have brought another sacrifice to the brink. They will not notice us as we go." He dropped the mat behind them and took her hand. Behind her, Tanya could hear the voice of the *Kahuna* rise in a savage climax.

CHAPTER XI

The moon had not yet left the shelter of the clouds. The men at the brink of the crater were black outlines against the star-strewn sky. The fourth sacrifice was about to occur, and the *Kahuna*'s voice reached a sudden high screech. Tanya shuddered.

"Kekua," she whispered, "I can't do this! I must go back! I can not let 'Ohi'a'Lehua take my place!"

Kekua took her hand and began to run. He moved with a sure-footed ease.

When at last they reached the shelter of the woods, Kekua paused. His voice, when he spoke, was harsh with inner pain. "You must not destroy 'Ohi'a'Lehua's sacrifice! You do not understand. It is for the great king Kamehameha, and will rescue us all from the wicked Kanalio and

Nuiaui. She spoke the truth. She would die anyway. The *Kahunas* would not let her live after she violated the *kapu*. Now she will be remembered by all as the one who saved her people."

He gazed for a moment at the distant crest, and then, deliberately, at the sky. "Look. The sun already lights the great water. Soon the night will be past and. . . ." He swallowed, his face twisted and dark. "Hurry. We must be on our way."

Once more Tanya glanced up at the volcano. It was too far away. Even if she ran back, she would be too late. She turned with Kekua toward the woods. They were not as dark as they had been moments before. Kekua was right. Daylight would soon be upon them.

A figure materialized before them, separating itself from the tall trees, massive, awesome. She gasped in fear.

Kekua said, "This is Mauleo. A follower of Kanalio." He was blocking her road to freedom!—hers, and Kekua's! The boy had risked his life to save hers. And to save the king.

Mauleo advanced. He was almost upon her when a cry caused him to turn toward the darkness behind him. As if propelled from a cannon, a figure flew into the clearing.

Tanya saw the glint of a sword. The threat presented by Mauleo had been turned from herself and Kekua. Like young king David facing Goliath, the stranger stood, his sword appearing fragile before the brute strength of his opponent. It was—no, it couldn't be! Alexius!

With a roar, Mauleo charged upon Alexius, his arms above his head. He moved aside with a litheness that belied his mass when Alexius lunged at him, and then, his big fists closed over the sharp blade. The next moment, Tanya heard a snap, and the sword was flying through the air, its blade broken in two.

"Alexius! Run! Please!"

Her scream went unheeded.

Urgently, Kekua touched her arm. "Come with me. We must go and warn Kamehameha."

"No!"

Kekua glanced once more at the unequal battle, then he vanished into the forest. She watched him go with a sinking heart. Then she turned back to the struggle. She could not stand by and watch her lover die. Somehow, she would have to help Alexius.

The only thing that was keeping her brave defender from being killed was his agility. In time, he would tire. And then. . . . She stifled a scream. Mauleo picked up a rock and hurled it at Alexius' head.

Alexius ducked, and the rock rattled down the hill, carrying a dozen others in its wake. But Mauleo was already searching for another weapon.

Tanya glanced quickly up the mountain. It was strewn with rocks. If she could warn Alexius in time, she might help him in his battle.

She stood for a moment, undecided. Then, inspired by her fear, she called loudly—in Russian. "I'm going to start a landslide. Be ready to get out of the way!"

She turned and began to struggle up the steep incline. When she was as far as she dared to go above the fighting men, she stopped behind one of the larger rocks and leaned against it with all her might. It refused to move.

With a sudden burst of energy, she pushed again at the rock. This time it broke loose from its resting place. She fell as it began to roll. For a moment she felt panic. Then she caught onto a protruding boulder that was not moved in the landslide. Pulling herself up, she screamed. "Alexius!"

The air was filled with a loud rumbling. Dust rose in a cloud below her. Frantic now, she cried out again. "Alexius!" There was no answer. Or, if there was one, she could not hear it over the noise of the tumbling rubble.

Suddenly a scream tore through the air, piercing its way into her consciousness like a dagger. She caught her breath and prayed. Was it Alexius?

Slowly, the rumbling ceased as the rocks piled up against the sturdy trees below her. For one moment, all was quiet. Then a figure stepped from the woods and began to climb.

Shaking with fright, she began to move toward it. If it was Mauleo who had survived, she had no wish to escape the death that awaited her. Her foot landed on a loose stone and she felt her feet go out from beneath her, felt a rock catch her temple. And then she felt nothing.

When she regained consciousness, she was in Alexius' arms. His lips were pressed against her bruised temple, and his voice washed over her heart like a balm. "Tanya, thank God we were in time!"

Her fingers traced his face—his dear face—and came to rest on his lips. "'Ohi'a'Lehua! She's up there!"

His arms tightened around her. "With the *padre*'s blessing. It is the only way."

Tanya let herself sink into his embrace. Maybe what he said was true. Maybe there had been no hope for her little friend.

"Please." Alexius kissed her gently. "The *padre* told me to reassure you. There was no other way. She wanted to help you. It was a sacrifice of love. Accept it, and be grateful—as I am—that you are still alive."

He kissed her again, and she felt his strength flow into her body. Then he lifted her up and began the descent. He stopped when he reached a hillock that overlooked the town of Keei, and the bay where a tall ship floated at anchor. "Look, my darling. This will be your last view of the island. You are coming home—with me."

She pressed against him, their hands entwined. "The *Elizabeth*! Did you come on it?"

"Yes. I met Captain Farnsworth in Canton, where I had gone to confer with a representative of the Emperor of China. When I learned that you were here, I sent my entourage back to Russia and took ship on the *Elizabeth*. Thank God I did! If I had not arrived when I did. . . ." His voice trailed off.

She lifted her lips to his. She was home at last. She wanted nothing more than to belong to him—to be loved by him—forever.

ABOUT THE AUTHOR

IRIS BANCROFT, daughter of Christian missionaries, was born and raised in China. On the death of her father, she and her mother came back to the United States. She has written for magazines and has published several paperback novels under the pseudonym Andrea Layton. This is her first major novel and she is at work on another. She lives with her husband in Van Nuys, California.

A Special Preview of
the opening pages of a wonderful
new novel—
the saga of a man and woman forging
an American dynasty.

FAR FROM INNOCENCE

by

Lois Wyse

author of
THE KISS

1

If you're not born beautiful, you have to start compromising early. Sophie Namath couldn't remember exactly when she learned that, but it was one of those things bred into her along with a love of gypsy music, *gulas* and *palachinkas*. Did only Hungarian girls think they had to be born beautiful? No, the Polish and Slovak girls in her class at Central High had seemed to know it, too. Evidently it wasn't such a Hungarian thing.

Sophie wrapped her coat tighter around her thin frame. Good grief, you'd think if you took eighteen of your hard-earned dollars and bought an all-wool coat at The May Company, the coat would at least keep you warm. But here it was the first week in November, and already she could feel the chill winter through the thin wool. It hadn't been like that when she was a child. The Cleveland winters were cold then, too, but somehow she'd liked the cold. Now the cold reminded her that she was still teaching, still a spinster, still unable to make the compromise all plain women had to make: take second best or stay single. Sophie sighed. She didn't want second best, but she didn't want what was available either.

Sophie's eyes darted in search of her tardy friend, Jeanette Reicher. Then she tapped her foot. Where was Jeanette? She was never on time.

"Soph." Jeanette's thin, high voice pierced the cold air.

"Where have you been?"

"Oh, pshaw, don't get so mad over nothing. I stayed late to talk to that dumb little Andy Granett. His mother's at school every day to find out why I'm not giving him gold stars."

"Gold stars? He can't even read and write."

"I know." Jeanette sighed. "I didn't know it was going to be so depressing being a teacher. I thought all the kids would be smart and love us. You know something, Soph. I thought all the kids'd be like us."

Sophie smiled. "So did I."

"Well, let's not just stand here on the corner on 105th and Euclid looking like we're waiting for boys. Let's go into Hoffman's."

Sophie pulled her coat still tighter and smiled. Suddenly she didn't feel so cold. Hoffman's. They were going into Hoffman's.

"What are you going to have, Jeanette?"

"The usual."

"Don't you ever get tired of chocolate sodas?" It was boring. Jeanette was so predictable, but then wasn't she? It was the fate of plain girls. They were dull, dull as dishwater, dull as the expected chocolate soda. Beautiful girls weren't dull. They weren't like Jeanette and Sophie. Beautiful girls ordered gorgeous things full of whipped cream. Well, who was to say you couldn't order beautiful even if you didn't look beautiful?

"What are you going to have, Soph?"

"Something gorgeous and full of whipped cream."

Jeanette smiled. It was nice not to be ordinary, but she wondered what had gotten into her friend. "Such as?" she asked, a small suspicion crossing her face.

"Such as a tin roof."

Jeanette giggled nervously. Was Sophie really daring or just pretending to be? Well, she'd see. She took Sophie's arm, and the two women walked into Hoffman's and slid into one of the tall wooden booths halfway down the shoppe. Jeanette nodded to a couple across the way.

"Who's he?" Sophie whispered loudly.

"Shhhh. I don't think he's from Central. He's probably from out-of-town."

Sophie nodded understandingly. Out-of-town usually meant the West Side. In Cleveland, East never met West, not even at Hoffman's. And Hoffman's was the center of the East Side universe, the place where every-one who ever went to Central High or Glenville High continued to meet even after graduation. It was at Hoff-man's that girls ordered ice cream and got dates and the gossip ran as thick as the chocolate fudge.

Nobody before or since made chocolate fudge like that. It was Hoffman's that introduced Cleveland to its first tin roof—a sundae glass filled with vanilla ice cream (no ice in that ice cream), chocolate fudge and peanuts.

Sophie ordered a tin roof and Jeanette the inevitable chocolate soda.

"What's got into you today, Soph?"

"I don't know. I just feel like something's about to happen."

"You just feel it? Well, what's so special about you?"

Sophie shrugged. Certainly her looks weren't special. Although she was thin, she was still too well-formed for 1926 tastes. Instead of a flat, boy chest, she was gently rounded and no amount of tight lacing could hide it all. Her dark hair was pulled back into a roll, and her skin was sallow—not fresh and pink like the girls in magazines. There was a swarthy look to her, almost Mediterranean, a look unlike that of anyone in her family. Sophie hated her looks. Somehow she didn't look Hungarian. Where was her pink skin, her auburn or blonde hair?

It was only in the last three years that Sophie had thought so much about her looks. Now that she had graduated from Central High and Normal School, she seemed to have more time to look about her. And wherever she looked, she saw women with fringed dresses and beaded bags and cloche hats, women who seemed to be having so much fun. Sophie wasn't against fun; it just seemed she didn't have any. Oh, not that she had anything to complain about. She had a fine father and mother and a roof over her head and two sisters—but she wasn't having fun.

When Jeanette and Sophie went to Normal School after Central High, both sets of parents had been so proud. These Hungarian immigrant parents could read fluently in Hungarian, but their English was labored.

Ah, but their daughters. Not only could they read English, they could teach it. They were educated. They represented an aristocracy their parents had never known. They were the first generation to become what every good daughter should be before she married—a teacher.

As a little girl, Sophie thought everyone in the world was Hungarian and lived on Buckeye Road or Woodland Avenue. Your family worked in the ladies' cloak and garment industry (an industry that Hungarians brought to Cleveland in the middle of the nineteenth century) or you were a craftsman, or you had a grocery, bakery or butcher shop. All Hungarian women were good cooks, had fine skin and took care of their Hungarian men. Or so it seemed to Sophie. She also thought her papa with his bristly mustache was easily the handsomest of men, and she loved to sit on his lap and play with his gold watch chain. Life was so simple then. It was just a few years before she was to learn that above her—far, far above her—was a world for women who were born beautiful and pink and blonde. But when she was little, Buckeye Road was her world. Her parents had been married in Budapest and came to the United States in 1898. They lived for a short while in New York where Sandor Namath found a job as an ironworker, and Fanny gave birth to their first child, a girl they named Mary. In 1900, the family moved to New Haven (Sandor had a cousin there). The following year they came to Cleveland (Fanny had two cousins there).

Papa Sandor continued his trade as an ironworker all his life, and Mama Fanny—well, Mama was a good Hungarian wife and mother. The Namaths arrived in Cleveland in advance of the largest wave of immigration, the years when the city was called "the melting pot of nationalities." Buckeye Road was like a little Budapest; there was even a restaurant called Little Budapest. It seemed to Sophie that the family was always involved in Hungarian activities either through the church or the family. Someone's relative was always coming to Cleveland to settle, and until a job or house was found, the Namaths offered a place in their home. So what if the girls slept three in a room? Didn't you have to help a Hungarian if you could? Sophie had been born in 1905 (there had been a miscarriage and a stillbirth between her and Mary). It seemed that two children would constitute the whole family (Fanny was hurt not to have produced a living son for Sandor), so the house off Buckeye seemed big enough to contain their lives. Like all those ordinary ugly frame houses off Buckeye, it wasn't big, but it was big enough to feed and sleep any immigrant who knocked at the doors. Sophie thought it was nice of her parents to take care of people they didn't know (except that they always seemed to sit around at night and ask, in Hungarian, "whatever happened to . . ."), and the immigrants would bring news of some long-forgotten friend or family member. Yet even though she admired their charity, there were times Sophie grew tired of the Hungarian-ness of it all. The accents. The rich smells of cooking. Why, oh why couldn't they be American? You know, Americans who landed on Plymouth Rock, signed the Declaration of Independence, and ate Tip Top bread. Why did they wait so long to come to the United States?

But as reluctant as Sophie was sometimes to admit her heritage, that's how proud Papa was. He would remind his two big girls (Mary and Sophie), and later the baby—still another girl that they named Ilona—that the largest Hungarian newspaper in the United States existed right in their very own city, Cleveland. *Szabadsag* meant liberty, Papa would say, his black mustache quivering with pride, and Hungarians always believed in liberty. Didn't our very own *Szabadsag* lead the drive to put a statue of George Washington in Budapest? The girls would nod and, for the hundredth time at Papa's prodding, recite the inscription on the statue: "Not a king among men but a man among kings."

Of course Sophie was not alone in her kind of upbringing. Jeanette came from the same kind of environment, and the two girls played together as children, slept at each other's homes (often because one or the other was displaced by an assortment of immigrants), went to Normal School together, were graduated and went on to teach the second and third grades at Hazeldell Elementary School, a part of the Cleveland Public School System. They loved each other, complained about one another and—like sisters—protected each other in times of danger. It seemed that lately there were many times of danger, for as teachers in the same school, they had to be careful not to appear as schoolgirl friends. They were grown-ups now, adults who knew better than to discuss their students' problems or their social life in the teachers' room at Hazeldell. All the other teachers were older women, professional spinsters who had been raised at a time when knuckles were rapped for misbehavior, and who thought the custom should be perpetuated. These women, their hair streaked with grey and knotted low on their necks, had nothing in common with thoroughly modern women like Sophie and Jeanette. The two American-born girls were indeed two generations beyond their own mothers. They had dates. They rouged their cheeks, and Jeanette had even bobbed her hair.

The real teachers' room for Jeanette and Sophie, however, was Hoffman's. There they met each day to talk over their classroom problems. And now they were seated side by side in a booth, ready at last to exchange the confidences of the day.

"How did your class do on that arithmetic test?" Jeanette asked.

"About as well as I would have. In other words, terrible."

"My class was so unruly today, and—"

Sophie pressed Jeanette's arm urgently. "They're here," she whispered loudly.

"Where?"

"Next to the candy counter, in front of the peanuts."

"Do they see us?"

Sophie released her grasp and shrugged. "No, of course not. They never see us until we pay."

Jeanette clucked. "Someday I'm going to get a boyfriend who comes right into Hoffman's, sits down beside me and pays for my soda."

"Well, it won't be Conrad Nagy or Tom Brown, and they seem to be the only ones we can attract."

"They're leaving now," Jeanette reported.

"And they'll walk up and down the block across the street so they can see us leave—"

"And then they'll walk us home," Jeanette said, finishing the sentence.

"Not even a streetcar ride," Sophie sighed.

"They work at the A & P. They don't have much money."

"And we schoolteachers do?" Sophie asked sarcastically. "Maybe you ought to get a bootlegger for a boyfriend. I hear they have plenty of money."

"Sure," Jeanette winked mischievously, "maybe I could get a little hooch on the side."

"Just let your mother hear you talk like that," Sophie reminded her.

"What does my mother know? She's from the Old Country. She thinks I'm wicked anyway, painting my face and bobbing my hair."

"It is kind of daring for Cleveland."

"Oh, Sophie, you're as dull as your own mother."

Sophie gave a small inward sob. It was true. She knew she was dull. Ordering a tin roof did not give her pink skin and blonde hair and make her flat-chested and desirable. "Oh, go finish your soda," she said petulantly.

"No," Jeanette said, pushing the glass away. "I'm sick of sodas and walking home. I want to go dancing and ride in a car and have a boyfriend who brings me flowers."

"Maybe you should have been John D. Rockefeller's daughter and lived high, wide and handsome in one of the mansions on Euclid Avenue."

"Maybe I should have because I'm sick of waiting for Tom Brown to ask me to marry him and for Conrad Nagy to ask you. Criminee, Sophie, aren't you sick of those smelly kids we teach?"

"Jeanette!" Sophie pretended shock at the outburst, but of course, she wasn't really outraged. She was just surprised that her best friend should share even her deepest, most private thoughts, the ones she would never articulate to anyone.

Jeanette made a small face at the reprimand. Oh, Sophie was such a perfect one. It was just too dumb. "You're such a stick in the mud, Sophie. If you had a chance to do something exciting, you'd probably say, 'First I have to ask my mother.'"

Now Sophie, despite her feelings, was defensive. "Well, that's true."

"Crim-i-nee."

"Let's go," Sophie said curtly. Another moment, and she might reveal her feelings, and that would be disloyal. After all, her parents did everything for her own good. Didn't they?

"How much do I owe?" Jeanette asked.

Sophie looked at the check. It was 30¢. "Ten cents. Mine was more expensive."

Jeanette pushed fifteen cents into Sophie's hand. "Oh, what's the diff? Let's split it evenly. What difference does it all make? No matter how you look at it, we've got a fifteen-cent life. Come on. Let's do something exciting. For once, let's forget about our parents and do something to remember."

"Like what?" Sophie asked. She knew that deep in her heart she wanted to keep an arm's length from any real adventure.

"Like what?" Jeanette repeated. "Like keeping quiet while I get those two dumb fellows to take us to Chiaro's."

"Chiaro's?" Her voice practically left her. "Jeanette, that's a speakeasy."

"Tsk, tsk."

"And you know that Tom and Conrad don't have any money."

"Well, let's chip in. You have to have a fellow to get you in the door, so we need them. But you know them. They're so cheap, they'd let us pay."

"That's not very ladylike."

"Oh no." Jeanette leaned on the counter in a mock faint. "You are too good to be true. How did you ever get to be my best friend?"

"By keeping you out of trouble."

"Oh come on. Just this once. Let's ask the boys to take us to Chiaro's this weekend."

"What will I tell my mother?"

"Nothing. Button your lip."

Once Conrad and Tom heard the girls would be paying, it was not difficult to convince them to go to Chiaro's on Saturday night. The boys even sprang for the streetcar ride. All the way downtown, as they rode the St. Clair streetcar, Sophie had a strange feeling in the pit of her stomach. She had lied to her mother for the first time in her life. And for the first time, she didn't like herself very much.

As the streetcar swayed and they sat on the long wicker benches inside the car, Conrad reached for her hand. She squeezed his desperately in return. Oh, why couldn't Conrad understand the language of hand squeezing? Why didn't he suggest they turn around and go home? Or why didn't he say, "Let's go see the new Al Jolson picture." Instead, he just sat there, and Sophie became more and more upset with herself and with Conrad. Why wasn't he saying anything? Suddenly she realized that he was excited about going to a famous speakeasy for the first time. And in that split second, Sophie made the first important decision of her life. She withdrew her hand and her heart. In that moment, she knew the truth about Conrad Nagy. He was a man who would always have secret longings, and she could never marry a man like that.

No, she thought, as she placed her hand fiercely on her knee. I will have dreams. I will have ideals. And I will not take a streetcar to my dreams.

"Hey, what's wrong?" Conrad asked. Sophie was no hot number, but he was only holding her hand. What right did she have to get so mad? But Sophie didn't speak. Her small dark face was screwed into deep thought. Conrad sighed. God, who could understand girls?

Sophie felt her heart pound wildly. She'd never thought any of these things before, but now they all seemed to come together. She knew the difference between good dreams and dirty thoughts, and here she was, going along with a trip to Chiaro's, everybody's dirty thought. Dirty. Filthy. No wonder she had such bad feelings in the pit of her stomach. Well, she couldn't turn back now. Or could she? She looked around slowly. The scene was repugnant to her, but no one had her lashed to the cane-covered seat. Couldn't she be responsible even at this moment for her own acts?

Conrad, now with his back turned from her, was talking to Jeanette and Tom, and before the other three could realize what Sophie was doing, she stood up, her purse clutched firmly in her hand, and rang the bell cord. The streetcar lurched to its next stop, the doors opened, and Sophie darted down the three steps and out the door.

"Hey," Jeanette called after her, "what do you think you're doing?"

Conrad was too stunned to speak, and Tom just sat with his mouth open.

Sophie didn't answer. She was scared. Scared to stay, scared to go. Oh, what a dope she was. The streetcar rolled toward downtown. She ran across the tracks and into a waiting streetcar going in the opposite direction. Breathless and still unnerved by her action, she slid into the first available seat and pursed her lips. What would Jeanette think? Maybe she shouldn't have left her like that. Sophie didn't much care about the boys.

Still, they were her friends. What had she done to them? Maybe she should've stayed. What could be so terrible about one silly little adventure?

Conrad would probably never talk to her again.

But maybe Jeanette would.

Sophie sank deeper in the seat. She tried to make herself invisible. If I don't look at anyone, she thought, no one will see me. It was a little girl trick. Papa used to hold her on his lap, and she would shut her eyes and say, "Now you can't see me." Oh, to be back on Papa's lap now and feel safe and secure.

Papa. Mama.

What would they say if they knew she were alone on a streetcar at eight o'clock on a Saturday night?

"Pardon me," said a voice next to her. "I don't mean to be fresh, but aren't you Sophie Namath?"

Oh no. To be recognized and by a boy. How shameful.

"I do not know you," she said stiffly. But she sneaked a look. He appeared to be about 21 or 22 and was square-jawed.

"I'm Mac Sloan," he said cheerfully. "I guess you wouldn't remember me, but I was two years ahead of you at Central."

Not remember Mac Sloan? He was only the basketball star of the Central team. Sophie could hear the cheer now:

> Central High
> Central low
> Central Cleveland
> O-hi-o .... Come on, Sloan.

Sophie sat taller. So. Mac Sloan knew Sophie Namath. "Oh sure I remember you," she said casually. The fear left her voice. She felt taller and even a little flat-chested. She tried to sound like her favorite movie star, Kay Francis.

"What are you doing on the streetcar all dressed up?" he asked.

Sophie thought fast. "Oh, I was going downtown with some friends, and then I decided I really wanted to go home and read a book. Ummm, uh . . . yes . . . I wanted to read a book, so I got off the streetcar and took the next one going the other way," she said quickly, hoping that she didn't sound too dopey.

"And what're you going to read?"

Should she tell him? Well, why not. She was tired of duplicity. "Poetry," she half-whispered.

Mac let out a low whistle. "Gee."

"Byron," she said, her voice trembling with the name.

"Lord Byron? Boy, he's my favorite poet," Mac said, and his face broke into the nicest smile Sophie had ever seen.

She gasped. "You're kidding."

"No. Honest. Cross my heart. I like him better than Shakespeare. Remember in tenth grade at Central when Miss Barber made us memorize, 'Eternal spirit of the chainless Mind. Brightest in dungeons, Liberty, thou art.' "

"You really did learn it," Sophie said, her admiration growing by the moment.

"But my favorite thing by Byron isn't something we had to learn."

"No?"

"Uh uh. I read this once in a book, and I memorized it. I never told anyone before."

"It's all right. You can tell me."

"Oh, I'm going to. If I told anybody else, they'd think I was off my rocker. But let me tell you, Sophie, this is how I feel. I mean—I mean—" he blushed, "I mean, it's how I feel about life. Not about a girl or anything like that."

Sophie nodded. People who read Byron didn't need explanations.

"It's just four lines. There's more but I never learned it:

> *I hate inconstancy—I loath, detest,*
> *Abhor, condemn, abjure the mortal made*
> *Of such quicksilver clay that in his breast*
> *No permanent foundation can be laid."*

Sophie's mouth fell open. Four lines had changed her world. What a night this was. At this moment she abhorred, condemned, abjured what might have been had she gone to Chiaro's.

"What's wrong?" Mac asked looking at the small, surprised face.

"Wrong? Nothing. It's just that it's so beautiful I can't believe it. My heavens, I never thought athletes liked poetry."

"Some do," Mac said modestly. "Besides, I'm not really interested in athletics."

"You're not?"

"Oh, you probably think so because when I was in school I did all that stuff."

"Uh huh, I guess that's it," Sophie said. She wished she could think of something better to say.

She could hear the clatter of streetcar wheels, and she was trying desperately to find words. Why couldn't she think of anything? The silence was becoming embarrassing. "Ummm, what do you do now?" she finally thought of asking.

"Not what I really want to do," he said quickly. "You know, it's kind of embarrassing because you're all dressed up, and here I am in work clothes. I suppose that's why you asked, but I have a job."

She hadn't even looked beyond his steady grey eyes and sandy colored hair. She hadn't seen anything ex-

cept his nice, strong face. Now she noticed. He was
wearing black pants and a white shirt with a lumber-
jacket, not exactly your proper Saturday night date
attire.

"Where do you work?"

"Allendorf's."

Sophie recognized the name. It was one of the fancy
downtown restaurants. "What do you do there, Mac?"

"Bus tables."

"What?"

"You know. Busboy. A lot of Cleveland swells eat
there, so I get to see a lot of rich people."

"I don't," she said, becoming more aware that the
world of the beautiful was also the world of the rich.

"What do you do?" Now it was his turn to ask.

"Teach school."

"Hey, you must be smart."

"Not really."

"Aw, I bet you are."

"And I bet you're a good busboy."

Mac Sloan sniffed the air. "Sure, I'm a good busboy,
but I won't be satisfied until I own the restaurant."

She looked at him and felt her heart beat wildly.
What right did he have to say such things? Sophie had
never heard a real live person talk like that. She knew
about the American dream, but until that moment she
didn't know there were people who lived in Cleveland
and rode the St. Clair streetcar who wanted to share
the American dream—and said so out loud.

"I never heard anyone talk like that," she said in
astonishment.

"I don't just want to own the restaurant," Mac went
on, warmed by her interest. "I want to own a lot of
things. I want to be as rich and famous as Mr. John D.
Rockefeller."

"Gosh." It was all she could manage to say.

"Hey, I just got paid tonight, and I got an extra quar-
ter in tips, so I've got enough money so if you get off
the streetcar with me at 105th and get a transfer, we
can go over to Hoffman's."

"That's my favorite place," she said, a smile lighting
her face and making her almost pretty in that ghostly
glow of streetcar light.

"Hey, you're a funny kid," Mac said shaking his head. "It's only Hoffman's, not Chiaro's."

"I know," Sophie said quietly. "That's why it's my favorite place."

"In that case," Mac said grandly, "I'll buy you a tin roof."

Sophie and Mac marry. Sophie is content with the simple pleasures of their life together. But Mac risks everything to attain his dream of wealth.

Read the complete Bantam Book—available November 1, 1979, wherever paperbacks are sold.